The Two Cities

THE
TWO CITIES

Norman St John-Stevas

faber and faber
LONDON · BOSTON

First published in 1984
by Faber and Faber Limited
3 Queen Square London WC1N 3AU
Filmset by Goodfellow & Egan Typesetters Cambridge
Printed in Great Britain by
The Thetford Press Thetford Norfolk

British Library Cataloguing in Publication Data

St John-Stevas, Norman
The two cities
1. Christian life
I. Title
248.4   BV4501.2

ISBN 0-571-13083-6

For my Privy Council Basics: Chris, John, Mary,
Brian, Petra, Liz, Eve and Murdo
And for Catharine who has now replaced them all

Two loves have created two cities: love of self, to the contempt of God, the earthly city; love of God, to the contempt of self, the heavenly.

St Augustine, *The City of God*

The only basis and bond of a true city is that of faith and strong concord, when the object of love is the universal good—which is, in its highest and truest character, God Himself—and men love one another with full sincerity, in Him, and the ground of their love for one another is the love of Him from whose eyes they cannot conceal the Spirit of their love.

St Augustine, in a letter about the Heavenly City

St Augustine placed the earthly and heavenly cities in stark juxtaposition. I see them rather as breathing together, a true *conspiratio*, one penetrating the other, and resting on the same base—the love of God.

Contents

10 *Contents*

PART ONE

Autobiographical Fragments

1

A Post-War Consciousness

APOLOGIA

This book is not an autobiography, nor is it a volume of memoirs. Such works are most suitably written at the end of a career not, as I continue to believe in my more euphoric moments, when it still has some way to go. However, I have now been immersed in the religious, political and artistic worlds for a period of over thirty years, and it seems an opportune moment to set out and review some of the themes with which I have been concerned.

One difficulty about writers in general is that nothing ever happens to them. They sit at their desks and write their books. The source of their ideas is not life as such but the imagination. As Bagehot put it caustically in his essay on Shakespeare: 'The reason why so few good books are written is that so few people who can write know anything.' Elsewhere in his monograph on Macaulay he declares: 'The exclusive devotion to books tires. We require to love and hate, to act and live.' Most activists, particularly under the stresses and demands of modern life, have little time to think about what they are doing, much less to write about it. Such thought as I have had has been formed in the midst of a life of affairs: I have certainly thought about basic principles, but have had ceaselessly to apply them in E. M. Forster's world 'of telegrams and anger'. I have not the equipment to be a philosopher, and if I had, I would not have had the opportunity to philosophize, but believe it possible to detect certain philosophical principles in my actions and that they have a consistency of their own.

My two loyalties, to religion in its Roman Catholic form and to politics in its conservative manifestation, remain, though they have developed and changed over the years. My Catholic faith was challenged by the crisis occasioned by the papal encyclical on birth control, *Humanae Vitae*, and my Conservatism by the advance of the doctrine of monetarism to prominence within the Conservative Party. In the light of history both seemed to me essentially exaggerations. I recall the words of Chesterton, applicable in these contexts, that the dull heresies sprawl to right and to left, the wild truth continues reeling but erect. I feel myself to be between sizes both in religion and politics. I have never been unreservedly committed to a Church or a party and am incapable of using either as a substitute for conscience. The inescapable duty is to take personal responsibility for one's own thought and actions.

This fixity and flexibility has enabled me to adapt and change in altering circumstances without feeling the need, as some have done, to abandon customary frameworks. The Church of my youth has largely vanished. I regard this as both loss and gain. The unity, the discipline associated with the Catholic Church are no longer the forces they were, but neither is the drive for the suppression of ideas nor the tyranny of those who, having been given a *sagesse*, make ruthless use of it to suppress the legitimate freedom of others. The decline of the Tridentine Latin mass has robbed the Church of an artistic form and a liturgical treasure, but the rise of the vernacular has enabled the faithful to participate in worship in a way which was not possible as long as a dead language dominated the liturgy.

Equally, politically there have been profound changes in the Conservative Party. By instinct I have always been a Tory—the maintenance of a cohesive society based on community in which the liberties of the people are protected by free institutions rooted in the character and history of a nation is both a great achievement and a continuing end of politics. My political ideal is the creation and preservation of one nation working together. In the political spectrum I stand in the extreme centre. The justification for capitalism—and it requires one—is that it is a system under which ordinary people are freer and more prosperous. Compassion and concern for others should be the hallmark of the true Tory who is well able to distinguish between the rejection of state-centred socialism and the promotion of social welfare. The Tory Party has never, save for brief periods, been a doctrinaire party; it has always been a comprehensive one based on broad principles, of which the most important is the maintenance of the unity of the nation. It is certainly no part of the Tory purpose to recreate two nations, north against south, rich against poor. Conservative Governments have sought for a century or more to weld these into one. The Tory Party is the custodian of a tradition rather than a dogma. Of all parties the Conservative Party would suffer the most from any attempt to reject its past. Post-war Conservatism is at times derided by those who talk about the 'New Conservatism',[1] yet it was a period of extraordinary achievements. Among these I would list the peaceful winding-up of empire, with all its economic, social and international consequences; the economic advance and social improvement made

[1] See Nigel Lawson, *The New Conservatism*, London, 1980.

possible by Lord Butler's period at the Treasury; the spread of home-ownership and the educational advances which followed the passing of the 1944 Education Act; and the achievement of membership of the European Community, a step of historic importance, of which the full consequences are still being worked out. It is self-evidently absurd to deny that Churchill, Baldwin, Macmillan, Butler, Chamberlain, Heath and other Tory statesmen were not really Conservatives.

Disraeli, not Mill, was the founder of the modern Tory Party. Disraeli's Toryism, with its national principles, its profound sense of the organic nature of society, its compassion for those in need—as evidenced by his almost lone championship of the Chartists—was sharply opposed to what he called the 'brutalitarians', the 'school of Manchester' (an original and intentionally uncomplimentary phrase), the Benthamites who would refashion England with their harsh logic and their pitiless economic doctrines, careless and possibly ignorant of basic human instincts and feelings.

Disraeli knew about, and therefore sympathized with, the lot of the poor: his knowledge of their actual life was superior to that of Dickens. He saw society in terms of a trust, drawing its cohesion from the observance of mutual obligation, its rulers ready to employ, where necessary, the huge engine of government to promote the wellbeing of the people. Toryism, he realized, needed to identify itself with forces and feelings making for stability, the preservation of national institutions and the enlargement of national prestige. Hence came the great Crystal Palace trilogy: the tasks of the Tory Party were to maintain our institutions, to uphold the empire of England and to elevate the condition of the people. They have been the lodestars of the true Tory ever since. Another great Disraelian phrase was: 'The Tory Party is a national party or it is nothing.' He saw it as both profoundly dangerous as well as un-Tory to set up an exclusive rather than a comprehensive party and to attempt to define one half of the people out of the nation. Disraelian Toryism was never a political system of rational propositions; rather, it was a series of images and ideals designed to move and inspire, to reinvigorate rather than to reconstruct society.

The contemporary Conservative Party has reasserted belief in individual freedom and enterprise as the mainspring of economic advance, along with Gladstonian views of prudent public finance. That does not mean that the Tory tradition is now irrelevant, that it can be discarded, that it was always misconceived, that it is somehow not a real part of Conservatism. Were that view to prevail, there would be an exodus from the Tory Party to that of the Social Democrats. I am sympathetic to social democracy, but my roots do not lie there, and I await a righting of the balance. This may not come in time for myself and my contemporaries to play a leading part in the counsels of the Party, but it will come about in the end. I sometimes think that the most accurate prophet of the immediate future of the Tory Party has been Enoch Powell. In some ways we are now living in a Powellite world.

Meanwhile, I am grateful to have been able to play a role on the political stage and, in particular, to have had the experience of being a member of a Cabinet. For this I am indebted to two people, Mr Heath and Mrs Thatcher. Mr Heath gave me my first political office when he appointed me to the Ministry of Education; in so doing he provided the occasion, however unintentionally, for my friendship with Mrs Thatcher and her later decision to invite me to join her Cabinet.

At the Department of Education my relations with Mrs Thatcher were cordial, friendly and, indeed, affectionate. I was able to discern in her the qualities which were to take her to the premiership.[2] I was impressed by her ability, her dedication to her task and her capacity for hard work. Some people's characters are cast; those of others grow. There is no doubt that Mrs Thatcher belongs to the former category. I marvelled that she had an opinion on everything that was clear, definite and concise. I used to wonder that she saw everything in black and white, since the universe I inhabited was made up of many shades of grey. Her prowess in argument was impressive, but I used sometimes to think that she might gain more support from those with whom she held discussions by occasionally losing a point.

Admiration and affection are one thing, but agreement is another.[3] I was never a right-wing Conservative, and it would have been impossible for me either to become or to present myself as that sort of Tory. My instincts were liberal and patriotic but also cosmopolitan, hers conservative and nationalist. Indeed, one of my few right-wing issues was education. I was sceptical about the advantages claimed for comprehensive education, believed in the upholding of high standards, the preservation of the grammar schools and the affording of opportunities to the bright child of modest background through the network of direct grant schools. I was happy to fight these battles with her, and in the Tameside case we won a spectacular victory, taking the issue of the maintenance of grammar schools right up through the courts to the House of Lords and winning there. My political views were more akin to those of the latter-day Mr Edward Heath, although I had never been particularly close to him. By temperament I was more at home with Tories such as Mr Harold Macmillan and Sir Alec Douglas Home.

Shortly after the lost election of February 1974, Mr Heath invited me to join his Shadow Cabinet, and I had the opportunity of laying the basis of a Conservative education policy of which much has survived to this day.

[2] I was, in fact, the first person to say that she would be Prime Minister. My political colleagues greeted the suggestion with scorn!

[3] Pius IX had in marked degree the faculty of separating his disagreements on principle from his feelings about people. He never let one interfere with the other.

Mr Heath lost the second election of October 1974, and I thought in those circumstances that it would be better for him to resign. However, he made it clear to me at a party held by *The Economist*[4] to mark the publication of the political volumes of my edition of the works of Walter Bagehot that he had no such intention. He made a brilliant speech about Bagehot's political thought and confided his intentions to me later in the evening. Despite my reservations about the wisdom of the course he was taking, I gave him my support. It was during this period that I came to know him best. He was clearly feeling isolated and alone and sought something in which he had never before been especially interested, my advice. At times we had almost daily telephone conversations. I did what I could and counselled on various tactical points, but in the end an election within the Party became inevitable. It was held on 11 February 1975.

The question of how to cast my vote was a perplexing one. On the one hand, I was bound to Mrs Thatcher by ties of friendship; on the other considerations of gratitude and loyalty linked me with Mr Heath. In the end I decided that I owed my vote to Mr Heath and so cast it. Mrs Thatcher emerged ahead on the first ballot, and at this point Mr Heath declared that he would resign the leadership.[5] I was then free to cast my vote where I wished, and had no hesitation in supporting Mrs Thatcher against the other principal candidate, Mr William Whitelaw. I made my support for Mrs Thatcher known publicly and was recruited by the campaign committee working for her election. In fact, apart from Sir Keith Joseph, I was the only member of the Shadow Cabinet to support Mrs Thatcher. Most of the others were supporting Mr Whitelaw or else standing themselves!

On the second ballot Mrs Thatcher emerged as a clear victor. She had belled the cat and had reaped the reward of her boldness. I was with her when the news was conveyed to her. She received it in an elated but controlled way.

Mrs Thatcher reappointed me to the Shadow Cabinet, holding the dual portfolio of Education and the Arts. I spent most of my time during these years working on restatements of Conservative policy and campaigning for them in different parts of the country. In the arts world in particular I was able to build up a goodwill for the Conservative Party which had not existed before. In 1977 Mrs Thatcher appointed Dr Rhodes Boyson as my assistant. I had hitherto managed reasonably satisfactorily without one. Many people regarded the joining of such disparate personalities with such opposed views on education as something of a joke. In the event it did not turn out to be a very good one. We did not work happily together

[4] On 14 October 1974.
[5] The voting figures in the first ballot were: Mrs Margaret Thatcher 130; Mr Edward Heath 119; Mr Hugh Fraser 16. Five ballot papers were spoiled. On the second ballot Mrs Thatcher won by a clear and overwhelming majority, gaining 146 votes to Mr Whitelaw's 79.

and, looking back, I regret that I did not make greater efforts if not to bridge the gap, then at least to narrow it. It was during this period that I was able to develop so much of what has subsequently become Conservative educational policy in government, namely, the stress on high standards, the extension of parental rights, the sponsoring of the assisted places scheme and the retention of such selective schools as survived. I also played my full part in the Shadow Cabinet in discussing our general economic policies and even at that stage found myself in disagreement with the direction in which they were moving. With Mr James Prior and Sir Ian Gilmour I formed a counterweight to the group gathered around Sir Keith Joseph. I believed that whatever conclusions we came to, they would not be normative, as they would have to be modified in practice when we were in government.

In the event this turned out to be a misjudgement, at least for the first years of the Government. I found myself to be a member of a Cabinet and was proud to be so, but was out of sympathy with the general thrust of the economic policy, and more so with the tone and approach, of the Government. I used to reflect that these should have been the happiest and most fulfilling days of my life, but they were not. I argued consistently, as was my right, for moderation in the proposals for cutting public expenditure and for trade union reform. I believed that we should proceed in these directions but at a slower pace. I was especially concerned about the increase in unemployment and about the various proposals that were put forward to cut social benefits. The Cabinet group of which I was a member had a significant impact on the course of economic policy, but this is not the place to write about that issue in detail.

I also defended the arts budget strongly in Cabinet with a certain success and pushed forward at an early date with the parliamentary reforms about which I felt passionately. Looking back at that period, I remain convinced that I played a role that was proper to a Cabinet Minister; that is, I expressed views strongly, but once a majority decision was reached, loyally accepted and supported it. This, however, was not the Prime Minister's view of how a Cabinet should proceed. She regarded the Cabinet very much as her own and Cabinet Ministers as her agents, rather as popes saw bishops in the days before the doctrine of collegiality emerged at the Second Vatican Council. They were there to do her bidding. Mine was the classic view of the role of the Cabinet, with the Prime Minister as *primus inter pares*. The constitutional convention in the nineteenth century was that no Cabinet Minister could be dismissed for a difference of view, only for delinquency or incompetence.[6] This seems no

[6] Thus in 1877 Lord Salisbury reassured a nervous Carnarvon that neither of them would be dismissed for their disagreement with the Prime Minister, Disraeli. The last time that had happened was in 1792, when Pitt had dismissed Thurlow.

longer to be the case—regrettably, for a moral notion lay behind the convention. Power over others has to be used with restraint and economy, otherwise it can degenerate into bullying. Mrs Thatcher, however, had expressed a very different view in a famous and enlightening interview which she gave to Kenneth Harris of the *Observer*.[7] Mr Harris asked her how she would form her Cabinet, and she replied:

> If you're going to do the things you want to do—and I'm only in politics to *do* things—you've got to have a togetherness and a unity in your Cabinet. There are two ways of making a Cabinet. One way is to have in it people who represent all the different viewpoints within the party, within the broad philosophy. The other way is to have in it only the people who want to go in the direction in which every instinct tells me we have to go. Clearly, steadily, firmly, with resolution. We've got to go in an agreed and clear direction. As Prime Minister I couldn't waste time having any internal arguments.

She proceeded to put these views into practice when she became Prime Minister.

There were thus stresses and strains between the Prime Minister and a number of Ministers, including myself. However, when I was expelled from the Cabinet one cold and wintry January day it was totally unexpected. It had never been suggested that I had not done my three jobs competently, and indeed the Prime Minister assured me that this was not her reason for asking me to yield my Cabinet place. There is no doubt that my departure was the first instalment of a process which was to continue with the removal of Sir Ian Gilmour, Lord Soames and Mr Mark Carlisle from the Cabinet in the late summer and culminated in the sacking of Mr Pym from his post as Foreign Secretary in June 1983. The Prime Minister offered me a position as Minister for the Arts but outside the Cabinet. Furthermore, the independent office of Arts and Libraries which I had set up was to be disbanded and returned to the Department of Education and Science as an integral part of that Department and subject to the Secretary of State for Education. It never occurred to me to accept this offer, but I dare say it was kindly meant. I had long argued that the arts were of sufficient importance to merit direct Cabinet representation, and I could hardly have presided over the office which I had set up and which was being so diminished in independence and status. I did not, however,

---

Two purges of the Cabinet were carried out subsequently—one by Balfour in 1903 and the other by Macmillan in 1962. Mrs Thatcher has three times reshuffled her Cabinet on ideological grounds.

[7] Published on 25 February 1979. It was in this interview too that Mrs Thatcher made a celebrated distinction: 'I'm not a *consensus* politician or a *pragmatic* politician. I'm a *conviction* politician.'

refuse the offer immediately (it seemed impolite to do so) but asked for time to consider the matter. I returned to my room in the Privy Council and sent back a message through the Prime Minister's Private Secretary that I did not wish to take up the appointment. As a Minister I did not see the Prime Minister again.

I found my expulsion from office a dispiriting, depressing and wounding one. What upset me most was that at a stroke it deprived me of my sense of purpose. I had valued office not for the stage properties, such as the red boxes, the car and the deference paid to Ministers by civil servants, although I enjoyed these, but because it gave me an opportunity to achieve things and to influence events. Because I like to make little jokes, see the funny and contradictory aspects of human activity and am burdened with a capacity for wit, people have sometimes had the impression that I am not serious in my approach. Nothing could be further from the truth. I am deeply conscious all the time of the swiftly fleeting character of life, of the need to organize one's time and efforts and to apply oneself, of the duty to use one's talents and to achieve objectives. I have not, however, wished these things to be too obvious.

In the House of Commons I had been able to push through a series of reforms of major importance, and in the arts I had managed not merely to protect a budgetary position but to improve it and to initiate a number of new projects. As Chancellor of the Duchy of Lancaster I was privileged to serve the Queen and to set in train an overhaul of the administration of the Duchy. I had a first-class private office, which was well organized originally under the control of an Assistant Secretary, Mr John Stevens, who dealt with the parliamentary side ably and humanely, and Miss Mary Giles, an outstanding, charming and experienced lady, who helped me with the arts. In addition I had an extremely good press office led by Miss Liz Hall and a fine driver, Mr Brian Wood, who had looked after me five years before, when I was a Minister in Mr Heath's Government. These losses apart, there were some painful moments, such as my having to take my seat on the back benches in the House where I had so recently been leader. I was greatly comforted by the cheer with which my entrance was greeted from all parts of the House.

I resolved that I would not be defeated or destroyed by a potentially crippling blow. My constituents at Chelmsford remained splendidly loyal in their support, as did my friends and many members of the public. I received hundreds of letters from unknown citizens expressing appreciation of what I had been able to do. As is inevitable in such circumstances, some who had courted me ceased to do so, but this was not so in the arts world, where I have been warmly welcomed ever since and treated more as a Minister in exile than as a backbencher. I have been able to support the arts in a number of ways and will continue to do so. I determined that I would not let my experiences embitter me in any way—I have seen too many people in politics destroyed by such self-indulgence, understandable though that it may be. I was also resolved not to utter a word of personal criticism of the Prime Minister and have not done so. I have remained a loyal supporter of the Government in which I at one time served, but I have used the freedom of the back benches to speak my mind on the social, economic and artistic issues of the day and to uphold the principles in which I believe.

During my period in office, work on my collected edition of Walter Bagehot had necessarily slowed down, but I have been able to take this up again, and the last two volumes of letters and bibliography will be published shortly. I also had a singular stroke of luck when in 1982 I drew second place in the ballot for Private Members' Bills and used this opportunity to introduce a Bill strengthening parliamentary control of public expenditure and making the Comptroller and Auditor General an officer of the House of Commons. I could never have done this from within the Government because the opposition to these proposals was so strong. However, from the back benches I was able to pursue this end. I recalled A. P. Herbert's words to me of years ago, when I was engaged with him in a campaign to reform the obscenity laws: 'A resolution is a whine; a Bill is a weapon'—and so it has proved to be.

In May 1983 Mrs Thatcher called a general election. My seat of Chelmsford had for a third time been radically altered. What had once been a safe Conservative county seat had been transformed into an urban redoubt. I had to accept the probability that in June I would no longer be a Member of the House of Commons. At this crisis in my fortunes, as in others, I had to rely upon the strength of my faith. This faith has never been a comfort to me in the sense of some kind of pudding in the sky but rather has provided a rock on which my feet can be firmly planted. From my Rosminian school I imbibed early a sense of the importance of Divine Providence in one's life.[8]

In the event, although prepared to accept the outcome philosophically—*Vox populi, vox Dei* has to be accepted politically whatever its theological limitations—I did not have to draw on these reserves. Despite the loss of 15,000 voters, most of them Conservative, I was returned, after a recount, with a majority of 378.

One of the great texts from which I have drawn strength is 'all things work together for good to them that love God . . .'[9] God does write straight but sometimes with crooked lines; time is not only the great healer but the great revealer as well.[10] I am perennially grateful for the gift of life and for

[8] Antonio Rosmini was a nineteenth-century idealist philosopher whose spirituality centred on a positive and dynamic sense of the providence of God and who founded a religious order that spread from Italy to England. Its principal foundation is Ratcliffe College.
[9] The Epistle of Paul the Apostle to the Romans 8:28.
[10] An abiding trust in Divine Providence is one of the great bestowals. Regret is both a futile and a destructive emotion. Everything is capable of being redeemed.

those talents which I have received; I am grateful also to have been able to be of some service to the causes in which I believe.

RELIGION

My consciousness is a post-war one. I was 10 years old when the Second World War broke out and have a clear recollection of that September day. I can still hear the noise of the sirens sounding in London and the echoes of Neville Chamberlain's sad broadcast declaring that Great Britain was now at war with Germany. Before that I have few political memories. There was no political tradition in my family on either side. We had produced diplomats, civil servants, businessmen and even the occasional bishop, but politicians had made no appearance. I remember being taken by my nurse to see King George V and Queen Mary drive through London on the occasion of their Silver Jubilee. My only other pre-war political memory was that of the abdication crisis when, despite the views of many other people, I was firmly on the side of the King against the people who would have deprived him of his throne; thus I was a legitimist from an early age. I received a conventional Roman Catholic education, but I was early aware that my religion rested on deeper foundations than that. I have always enjoyed the gift of a deep and unshakeable faith and Tertullian's phrase *anima naturaliter christiana* has long been meaningful for me. I also received early an appreciation of the importance of the contemplative life. I have never felt called to take up existence in an enclosed monastery, but have always appreciated the vocation of those who do. My ideal, however, has not been that of cloistered virtue apart from the world but rather of one world penetrated by the other. The great divide today, as I see it, is between those who have a two-world-centred view and those whose insights are confined to one.[11] Catholic and Conservative, I have moved within two frameworks, but have never doubted that in the last resort it is the individual who is king. I would no more surrender my conscience to a Church than to a political party. The Church is a part of one's conscience but is not a substitute for it. Even the effective authority of the Roman Catholic Church rests upon conscience, on the acceptance by the individual of her extraordinary claims. I agree with the position outlined by Cardinal Newman in his letter to the Duke of Norfolk, in which he gives the highest human place to conscience, describing it, in an arresting phrase, as the 'aboriginal Vicar of Christ'. He goes on to say: 'I add one

---

[11] One of the best representations of my view in art is Epstein's *Lazarus*, which is quite at home in New College's medieval chapel at Oxford. Lazarus is seen breaking out of the grave bands and returning to this life but looking back longingly to the other world which he has glimpsed.

remark. Certainly, if I am obliged to bring religion into after-dinner toasts (which indeed does not seem quite the thing), I shall drink—to the Pope, if you please—still, to conscience first and to the Pope afterwards.'[12] Yet he makes it clear that conscience is not the source of right but a witness to it, the 'internal witness of both the existence and the law of God'.

The temptation of Catholics is to distort authority into authoritarianism, and there is no doubt that the Roman Catholic Church appeals to those who want a strong line to be taken for them. This does not appeal to me. I am much in sympathy with Lord Acton's declaration: 'I find that people disagree with me either because they hold that Liberalism is not true, or that Catholicism is not true, or that both cannot be true together. If I could discover anyone who is not included in these categories, I fancy we should get on very well together.'[13]

The papacy lost its temporal power in 1870 but proceeded to replace it by a centralized spiritual power of far wider-reaching effect. From the time of Pio Nono to that of Pius XII the spiritual authority of the popes was continually increased: the Catholic Church suffered from a creeping infallibility, which was turned back only by the advent of Pope John XXIII and the Second Vatican Council.[14]

I had long felt uneasy with the authoritarianism of the Church under cover of which there was alleged to be a Catholic view on everything, and all papal utterances were subject to a deference and exegesis worthy of the Scriptures themselves. The Second Vatican Council came as a great relief: it righted the balance between authority and liberty. It reasserted the rights of the individual and promulgated the essential freedoms that are the birthright of Catholics as well as everyone else. Pope John threw open the gothic and baroque windows of the Church to let in a great gale of fresh air. Nowhere was the effect of his new approach more dramatic than on the ecumenical movement. The Pope's charity and openness provoked a response from Dr Geoffrey Fisher, the Archbishop of Canterbury, who in 1960 set out to visit the Pope in the Vatican, the first such visit since Archbishop Arundel went to Rome in 1397.[15]

[12] 15 June 1875. Of all Newman's writings, with the exception of the *Apologia*, this had the most immediate and far-reaching effect. It answered Gladstone's attack on papal infallibility.
[13] Letter to Mandell Creighton.
[14] The calling of the Second Vatican Council was announced by Pope John XXIII in January 1959, three months after his election to the chair of Peter. After more than three years of preparation, the Council was finally opened on 29 September 1962 and ended in December 1965. I was able to attend all of the sessions.
[15] I made a statement welcoming the visit: 'I hope and pray this may be the first move towards the reunion of the Anglican and Roman Catholic Churches. Pope John and the Archbishop have set all Christians an example in courage and charity. This opportunity should not be missed. Rank-and-file members of the two Churches should seize every opportunity of working more closely together' (*Guardian*, 20 November 1960). Other comments were more inhibited.

It would be difficult to think of a less likely prelate to have made that historic breakthrough than the schoolmasterly, slightly pendantic, distinctly Protestant Dr Fisher, yet it was he who had the vision to respond wholeheartedly and uncalculatingly to the opportunities opened up by Pope John. Pope John will surely be seen as the greatest pope of the century: the caretaker pope elected in the autumn of 1958 who proceeded to turn the Church upside down, the pope who, by the transcendence of his charity, his understanding and care for all human beings, his profound yet enigmatic words, is the pontiff of modern times who most resembles Christianity's founder.

I was in Rome for the meeting with Archbishop Fisher and was able to observe at first hand the consternation of the Vatican and its officials at the arrival of their historic visitor. The popular press grasped early the significance of the event, which was headlined in the *Daily Mirror* as the 'Holy Summit'. Dr Fisher was received at the Vatican with all the enthusiasm accorded to a germ in a maternity ward. The Vatican paper, *L'Osservatore Romano*, was uncertain even what to call him. Photographs of the event, which are normally freely allowed, were forbidden; the Vatican press office was almost totally obstructive. The qualities of the two participants overcame all obstacles, however. Dr Fisher remained serene, practical and very English; Pope John's warmth and love transcended any hitches in protocol. Dr Fisher's first words, as he swept into the papal study on that bright and hopeful December day, were: 'Your Holiness, we are making history.' The actual conversation between the Pope and the Archbishop was shrouded in secrecy, but at a press conference at the British Embassy later in the day Dr Fisher lifted the hem of the iron curtain and stressed the cordiality of the encounter.

I was present at the press conference and raised the question of how the two ecclesiastics had greeted each other. The Archbishop answered that they greeted each other as any two clerics would in such circumstances, 'in the ordinary friendly way' and we deduced that there had been no kissing of rings but that they had shaken hands. Dr Fisher then provided a little verbal embroidery: 'There was no preliminary build-up,' he said, 'no theatrical staging; it was nothing like visiting Hitler or Mussolini!' At these words I saw the Holy Summit going up in smoke, but the Archbishop's resourceful press officer, Colonel Hornby, jumped to his feet and uttered the words, 'Off the record, I presume, your Grace,' and off the record it has remained for many years.

The evening before the papal audience there had been evensong at All Saints, the preposterous little Victorian gothic Anglican church in the Via Babuino, and after the service I was able to greet the Archbishop, offering words of welcome and discharging a mandate which I certainly had not received: 'On behalf of English Roman Catholics I welcome you to Rome, your Grace, and I hope and pray that this may be the first move towards the reunion of the Anglican and Roman Catholic Churches.' These were prophetic words, but Dr Fisher, who had a practical turn of mind, when he had got over his astonishment replied simply: 'Thank you very much, but your hierarchy will have to catch up with you.' There had been quite a lot of 'catching up' by the time Dr Ramsey visited Rome in 1966 and was accorded all the honours of a prince of the Church. There was even a joint ecumenical service at St Paul's-outside-the-Walls, in which both Paul VI and Dr Ramsey took part. The Church of England was raised from the somewhat grudging technical status of an 'ecclesial community' to, in the words of the Pope, a 'sister Church'.

The fruits of Pope Paul's generosity were reaped when the present Pope, John Paul II, visited Canterbury in June 1982 for a service conducted by them both. The Pope gave an inspiring address. No one who witnessed it will forget the sight of the two prelates advancing up the aisle of Canterbury Cathedral to the applause and cheers of the faithful of all Churches. Canterbury provided the high point of the papal visit.

During the late 1940s and the 1950s I was engaged in a number of religious controversies. In fact, I had started my public speaking in a religious-political context at Hyde Park Corner, where I used to be a regular attender at the Catholic Evidence Guild, supported by my Aunt Beryl.[16] On one occasion, when I was 12, I drifted over to heckle a communist speaker and needled him with so much success that he unwisely invited me, 'if I knew so much', to come up and take his place on the platform. Naturally, I at once accepted, and when the wretched man demurred, the fair-minded British crowd insisted that he keep his word. I mounted the platform and held forth on the rights of the Polish people and the merits of Our Lady until an irate superior communist turned up and put an end to my first public oration.

Later I became a regular speaker at the Guild, which at that time was at the height of its influence. It was led by a brilliant pair, Frank Sheed and his wife Maisy Ward. I was 'licensed' to speak on a number of subjects, but my star turn was the Four Marks of the Church. Father Vincent McNabb, the great and eccentric Dominican, was active at the time, and a gentleman in the crowd, Mr Siderman, a Jewish believer, was one of his regular hecklers. Later he wrote a book about Father McNabb entitled *A Saint at Hyde Park*. Mr Siderman conferred his heckles only on the great, and it was a red-letter day when he condescended to interrupt me.

---

[16] Beryl de Vere Gibson. She was an intriguing personality. She worked for the Ambulance Service during the Second World War, then for the censorship, and finally became a spy (for Britain). In her youth she had been a concert pianist and a model. She retained her striking looks into old age. She moved from the Anglican to the Roman Catholic Church and used to change the colour of her raiment in accordance with the liturgy. On Holy Saturdays at Westminster Cathedral she would throw off a purple cloak at the moment of transition from Holy Week to Easter and reveal herself attired in dazzling white. She died in 1979.

At Cambridge I championed a number of Catholic causes, including the right of Catholic bishops to use their titles, which they are forbidden to do by the Ecclesiastical Titles Act of 1871. In 1949 I was actually expelled from the Union by the left-wing president for refusing to withdraw a motion condemning the 'trial' of Cardinal Mindszenty. A judicial committee met for the first time this century to censure the president, and although the motion was defeated, I felt vindicated, since later in the term I was elected secretary of the Union and subsequently became president.

In January 1950 I took part in a debate on birth control which I had organized at the Union. The motion read: 'This house would welcome the wider application of birth control as being in the best interests of morality and social welfare.' It was supported by Mr Norman Haire, a well-known 'sexologist' and opposed by Dr George Andrew Beck, then Coadjutor Bishop of Brentwood, later Archbishop of Liverpool. I vigorously opposed the motion.[17] My peroration was unqualified and caused me some wry amusement when I re-read it recently:

> Let us, sir, tonight reject this motion. Let us read the lessons of history right. The mighty empire of Greece was conquered because of the practice of birth control and the consequent declining of population. The Emperor Augustus faced the same problem, and the penalty for his failure to solve it was the fall of the far-flung Roman Empire. The information available to us all in the reports of the Royal Commission on Population convey as clearly as did any writing on ancient palace wall a solemn warning. It says: 'Populate or perish. Increase and multiply, or vanish forever into the dust of the civilizations of the past.'[18]

In subsequent years I became an established Catholic apologist defending Church doctrine and practices at public meetings, as well as on the wireless and eventually on television. I took a prominent part in debates on euthanasia, abortion and capital punishment; my position was reasonably consistent, since I opposed all three.

As to birth control, I had no difficulty in accepting the Roman Catholic position, nor the arguments put forward to support it, until some doubts began to assail me in 1958, when I was working on my doctoral thesis at Yale on the subject of law and morals. In the course of my researches into birth control and its treatment by the law, I studied various contributions which had been made on the religious aspects of birth control by Roman

[17] It was in fact carried, with 432 votes for and 260 against.
[18] A year or so later I debated the subject again at the London University Union with Dr Marie Stopes, the birth-control pioneer, using many of the same arguments. At the end of my speech Dr Stopes leaned over the table and hissed at me: 'Very clever but very meretricious, like all Roman Catholics.' We were, however, reconciled after the debate at a dinner at the defunct (alas) Frascatis, and I toasted her health in champagne, drunk out of her slipper!

Catholic writers in theological journals and found them unconvincing. I contrasted their slavish following of authority with the treatment of the issue by Anglican theologians and Protestant thinkers such as Reinhold Niebuhr. I was particularly struck by an Anglican publication, *The Family in Contemporary Society*,[19] in which the issues were honestly faced and the contributors expressed varying degrees of approval for the employment of contraception by Christians. I found their line of argument persuasive and attractive but was not entirely convinced. Perhaps I did not allow myself to be and contented myself with presenting their arguments with the minimum of comment. I did, however, conclude that in view of the general acceptance of contraception in England and the United States, legal sanctions against the distribution of contraceptives and the dissemination of birth-control information were no longer appropriate. This view was put forward in my pamphlet, *Birth Control and Public Policy*, published in the United States in 1960, which attracted widespread attention at the time.[20]

My intellectual position in the early 1960s was, then, that I was attracted to the Anglican position on birth control; I found its theological reasoning more convincing than that of the Catholic natural lawyers, but I was not prepared to make a change. Freedom of discussion and thought was still severely circumscribed within the Roman Catholic Church, and the emotional feeling against contraception was strong. I shared this revulsion from the idea of contraception and indeed still feel it to a certain extent. I have always felt uneasy about the simplistic viewpoint of the anti-fertility crusaders.

In the early 1960s tremors about birth control began to be felt in the Roman Catholic theological world. Shortly afterwards, thanks to the calling of the Second Vatican Council, discussion on this and other matters became much freer within the Catholic Church, and the traditional position was under open attack. I became convinced that a revision of the traditional Catholic teaching was inevitable and that it was only a matter of time before this came about. In July 1967 I expressed these views publicly for the first time to a conference on population policies at the Catholic University of Georgetown in Washington and suggested that the normative Catholic position in the future would be to leave the matter principally to the individual consciences of Catholics. I could not know what form the revision would take but felt that it would either be a new position all together, legitimating the use of contraceptives in certain circumstances, or else the presentation of new arguments to justify the ban. What I did not anticipate was a flat restatement of the old position

[19] The report of a group convened by the Church of England Moral Welfare Council, SPCK, London, 1958.

[20] President Kennedy used this pamphlet to counter objections that a Roman Catholic was 'unfit' to be President of the United States.

with virtually no modification of either practice or theory. Yet this is precisely what came about with the issue of the encyclical *Humanae Vitae*.

The encyclical was published on 29 July 1968. Rumours had been circulating for some days that a Vatican statement was imminent, but these had proved false on so many previous occasions that not everyone took them seriously. On this occasion they proved well founded. On the morning of publication, before accounts of the contents had appeared in the newspapers, I had spoken to the then apostolic delegate, Archbishop Cardinale,[21] who sent me, by car, a copy of the encyclical. I read it with incredulity and dismay. I was requested to appear on *Panorama* that evening with the Bishop of Leeds, Lady Antonia Fraser and various other Catholics, and passed the day resolving what I should say.

As time went on, I became convinced that the time had come to speak out quite openly on the whole issue. For me this was especially difficult, as for over twenty years I had been defending Catholic attitudes, putting the most favourable arguments for papal positions, and consistently defended the utterances of the Pope. Nevertheless, I felt I had come to a turning-point and would be failing in my duty as a churchman and a legislator if I failed to make my views known. The situation was the more agonizing because of the personal friendship I enjoyed with the Pope and the high esteem in which I held him. During the programme I made it clear that I rejected the encyclical and its arguments. While the broadcast was a traumatic experience for me, I found that my religious faith, far from being destroyed, was strengthened; my belief in the Catholic Church never wavered, and I remained convinced of the validity and importance of the Roman primacy.

Others, as I know, have been less fortunate, and for them *Humanae Vitae* marked a parting of the ways, leading them to the abandonment of the Roman Church. *Humanae Vitae* precipitated for the Church as grave a crisis as any she had faced since the Reformation. Birth control is in itself a highly important and emotive issue. Paul VI, by forthrightly rejecting any artificial means of birth control as contrary to the law of God, and by using his ecclesiastical prerogatives to do so, linked it with another equally explosive issue, which had already been half-detonated by the Vatican Council: the place of papal authority in the contemporary Church. *Humanae Vitae* highlighted what was already an issue within the Church and concentrated Catholic and world attention on it. What might previously have been thought of as an academic dispute among theologians was suddenly transformed into a dispute of immense practical importance, affecting millions of people in their daily lives. The encyclical was an attempt both to find a solution to a dilemma and to stem the undermining of papal authority, reasserting it in the old style. It failed

[21] Later apostolic nuncio in Brussels; his untimely death in 1983 came just as he was to be nominated to the cardinalatial see of Florence.

on both counts. Since its issue the debate on birth control has continued, and the meaning, extent and limits of papal authority have been scrutinized by Catholics as never before. A document intended to restore a position fomented a revolution.

Interest in the encyclical was intense. It became the subject of comment and correspondence in the daily papers, especially *The Times*, the *Guardian* and the *Daily Telegraph*, as well as in the weeklies such as *The Economist*, and the *New Statesman*. These papers were virtually unanimous in their rejection of the encyclical. *The Economist* described it as a 'tragedy for the world and a disaster for the Roman Catholic Church'. *The Times* received letters about the encyclical at the rate of 1,000 a week; at times so great was the flood of correspondence that the entire leader page, apart from the editorial articles, was given over to the expression of various points of view.[22]

Many members of the Roman Catholic laity and some of the clergy protested against the encyclical, and a number of the priests were suspended from their functions. This action by certain bishops convinced me that something further needed to be done to hold the position. The laity protest had been spontaneous and to a certain degree effective, but if priests were not able to speak their minds, it was clear that the battle would be lost. Accordingly, in company with a number of sympathizers, I launched the Freedom of Conscience Fund on 3 September 1968 in order to provide support for those priests who were suffering because of the stand they had taken. The problem was a very real one, since Catholic priests in England rarely have private means or large savings. I also felt that the existence of such a fund would discourage those bishops who were inclined to take a hard line from proceeding to extreme courses. The trustees of the Fund, apart from myself, were Lady Asquith, Dr Anthony Boyle, and Mr Anthony Spencer.[23]

The Freedom of Conscience Fund played a major part in securing a moderate attitude on the part of the English Catholic bishops towards dissident priests. Cardinal Heenan in particular did not want a show-down with priests in his diocese and adopted a policy of peaceful coexistence, making it plain that he was not seeking a confrontation with dissidents. A number of priests abandoned their orders, and others subsided into silence, but in the end the argument was won by the critics of the encyclical. In practice, today in the Roman Catholic Church in

[22] One congratulatory letter among the hundreds I received caused me mixed feelings: 'Enoch has saved us from domination by the blacks and you have saved us from subjugation by something worse than communism—Catholicism.'
[23] Lady Asquith, although over 80 and with no particular sympathy for Catholicism, immediately agreed to be a trustee of the Fund and entered into its activities with the greatest enthusiasm and skill. She proved to be the most prescient of our trustees and never missed a meeting until shortly before her death. Lord Longford, although he was approached, declined to be a trustee.

England, birth control is a matter left to be decided by the consciences of the faithful. The Freedom of Conscience Fund developed into a society for helping priests and nuns in difficulties with their ministry and was renamed New Bearings. Although it had originally begun in circumstances which rendered it suspect to the hierarchy, it is now a recognized body within the Church and receives an official grant from the bishops.

In singling out contraception for attack, the Vatican, I was convinced, had chosen the wrong target. An anti-contraception line was impossible to hold, and Vatican influence would have been better used if it had been directed against abortion. As it was, by equating birth control and abortion the papacy had weakened the case against the latter. In 1966 Mr David Steel introduced a Bill into the House of Commons to legalize abortion. It was read a second time on 22 July, and only a handful of members voted against it.[24] As I passed through the 'no' lobby, Mr Enoch Powell turned to me in surprise, with the query 'Where are the Romans?' Later in the year the 'Romans', joined by a number of others, had appeared on the scene, and it fell to me to organize the campaign against the Abortion Bill both in the House of Commons and outside it. The Bill went into Committee in February and was fought fiercely all the way.

Meanwhile outside the House of Commons a national petition was organized against the Bill that attracted over half a million signatures; we presented it to Mr Wilson at No. 10 Downing Street in May. The Bill would undoubtedly have failed on the report stage but for the fact that the Government granted it two extra days and allowed the time rule to be suspended so that it could run all through the night. The report stage is always the point at which Private Members' Bills are most vulnerable because in normal cases only one day and a few hours of debate are available. Members opposed to a Bill can put down amendments in sufficient numbers to ensure that no controversial Bill sponsored by a private Member has any but the slimmest of chances of reaching the statute book. After two all-night sittings the Abortion Bill eventually became law. The voting was very different on the third reading from the second; on 14 July 1967 167 Members voted for the Bill and 83 against. My opposition to the Bill had been based on a number of grounds, but in particular on the fact that I believed that whatever safeguards were written into the Bill, it would eventually lead to abortion on demand and a whole series of legalized rackets would be able to flourish under its protection. These fears have, unhappily, been proved wholly justified.

Other moral legal controversies in which I became involved were those over capital punishment and euthanasia. I was able to vote for the abolition of capital punishment in 1965, a position which I have

[24] The actual voting figures were 223 ayes to 29 noes. When the third reading took place on 13 July 1967 the voting was 167 ayes and 83 noes.

consistently maintained since, and in 1970 I opposed a Bill introduced by Dr Gray to legalize euthanasia, which was rejected by the House of Commons without a division.[25]

POLITICS

My first experience of politics was at school in 1945, when I fought a mock election as a Conservative and was elected. Later I joined the Young Conservatives and was active in local politics in Kensington, where I lived. At this period I was interested in the concept of human rights and in the United Nations declaration on the subject. In 1947, before going up to Cambridge, I founded a society called the Defenders of Human Rights. Our purpose was to provide a philosophical basis for the rejection of totalitarianism and to create support in Britain for the concept of human rights. I wrote to Mrs Roosevelt, who kindly agreed to become a patron, along with the Duchess of Atholl and a number of Conservative and Labour MPs. At one stage I had taken the Albert Hall for a rally in defence of human rights, but this proved too ambitious an undertaking, and in fact our opening rally took place at Kensington Town Hall on 15 December 1947, with speakers who included Christopher Hollis and Dorothy Crisp, then Chairman of the Housewives League.

In May we held a lively meeting to discuss the National Health Service, at which Dr Letitia Fairfield and Dr Hyacinth Morgan, MP, spoke and clashed. Dr Fairfield appeared to be under the impression that we were an extreme right-wing organization, and not even the participation of Dr Morgan, a Labour MP, could convince her otherwise. I remember the meeting chiefly because of a delightful remark of Dr Morgan, who when he was hissed by the audience, riposted: 'There is always hissing when the waters of heaven fall upon the fires of hell.' In the autumn of 1948 we held a further rally at Caxton Hall, which was addressed, among others, by Father Martin D'Arcy, the Jesuit.[26] He warned: 'Everyone is exhausted after a hideous war—inclined to take things easy and not to notice the changes that are taking place. But we may wake up from our inertia one

[25] The second reading of the Bill to abolish capital punishment was carried on 21 December 1964 by 355 votes to 170. The third reading, on 13 July 1965, was carried by 200 votes to 98. In our election manifesto of 1979 we promised (unwisely, I thought) to have a further vote on the issue. I wanted to get it out of the way as quickly as possible and, as Leader of the House, was able to provide an opportunity for a vote on 19 July 1979. A motion to reintroduce it was defeated by 362 votes to 243. I voted with the abolitionists. The Home Secretary voted the same way, but the Prime Minister voted in support. On 13 July 1983 the House of Commons, despite its overwhelming Conservative majority, once again rejected any form of capital punishment. I voted against its restoration in all the divisions.

[26] A number of rhymes were in circulation about this famous priest, including 'D'Arcy, D'Arcy—Very Classy' and 'Objets D'Arcy', which he had collected at Campion Hall, Oxford.

day to find ourselves in chains.' My cousin, Lady Evelyn Chetwynd, was President of the Society and gave unstintingly of her support, both in time and in money. However, it was difficult to keep it going, and it gradually faded away.

I came to the conclusion, that it was not of much utility to launch small new organizations; rather, one should work to influence more established bodies from within. Accordingly, I concentrated my attention and energies on the Conservative Party, of which I became an active member at Cambridge. There I became Chairman of the University Conservative Association and also, as I have already mentioned, President of the Union, so that I had ample opportunity to put my views forward. In 1949 I made my first speech at a Conservative Party Conference at the Empress Hall, calling upon Mr Butler to modify the workings of the welfare state so that the rights of the individual were better respected. In the autumn of the previous year I had paid a visit to Swinton, known as the 'Conservative College of the North', where I tried my hand, along with a number of fellow undergraduates, at drawing up a report of Conservative principles. This report (which is reproduced in Part Four), with its stress on the importance of moral values, of tradition, of the necessity to maintain our institutions and to uphold the rule of law, still expresses my mind on the basis of conservatism. Over thirty years later I find that I can subscribe fully to its conclusions. At this time I also began to write. The first article I published appeared in the *Westminster Cathedral Chronicle* in October 1947. Its subject was a visit I had paid to the Abbey of Monte Cassino. The fee I received was one guinea. No money I have earned through journalism since has given me the pleasure and pride of that first modest gain.

In the spring of 1951, at the age of 21, I was adopted as Conservative candidate for Dagenham. I had earlier secured inclusion in the Central Office candidates' list and had asked for my name to be put forward for a difficult seat. Central Office sent my name into Dagenham and, rather to my surprise, the locals adopted me. The practice of young candidates fighting a 'hopeless' seat is a good one. The 'hopeless' gain young, energetic and idealistic champions, and the champions earn valuable experience. They can make mistakes which are both unobserved and marginal in their impact. I made full use of the correspondence columns of the *Dagenham Post*, which provided a convenient forum to expound my views.

My opponent was Mr John Parker, former Secretary of the Fabian Society, until 1983 Member for Dagenham who became Father of the House of Commons. One of the issues which interested me even at this early stage was religious education, and I made its maintenance and improvement a central plank in my platform. As a large number of voters in Dagenham were of Irish origin, this alarmed Mr Parker and his supporters, who felt that I might be undermining his position. The *Catholic Herald* gave me full coverage and Mr Andrew Boyle wrote a flattering and supportive piece headed 'Daniel in the Dagenham Den'.

I took to holding meetings outside the factory gates, where I at first received a rough reception, being told to 'Go back to Bond Street where you belong.' However, I persisted, and at the end, although I did not receive many votes from the audience, they did give me a cheer. My most enthusiastic supporters were a convent of nuns. One doubting sister who had once thought of voting something other than Conservative, and was hence considered a 'Red', was introduced to me and converted. She became most enthusiastic and announced, 'You have a tough fight here. But faith will move mountains.' The Reverend Mother commented, 'Sister, it may move mountains but it will not move Dagenham.' I understood then why she was Reverend Mother. Mr Parker, however, need not have worried, since he was returned at the election in October with a majority of over 30,000, but I had the satisfaction of cutting this plurality from its previous high point and gained over 14,000 votes myself.

The post-war Britain in which I was spreading my wings was both drab and dismal. The country was exhausted by the efforts of years of war. Shortages of all kinds remained, and food was still rationed. London was a capital unbowed but very definitely battered. Greyness, drabness, shabbiness—those are the subfusc and achromatic tones in which I see the late 1940s shrouded. In a run-down, exhausted country people really did look down-at-heel, frumpish and dowdy; only the royals still glittered. I remember standing on a balcony in the Mall, thanks to a ticket obligingly provided by my aunt in the Foreign Office, on a cold November day in 1947 and watching Princess Elizabeth and Prince Philip drive past in the glass coach from their nuptials at Westminster Abbey. I can still recall my sense of delight at the brilliance of that colourful procession against the physical and spiritual greyness of London.

There were other shafts of light amidst the gloom. I recall my pleasure at going to Syon House for the coming-out ball of a young and beautiful débutante, Lady Mary Baillie-Hamilton. I had never before been to such a grand and stylish function. It was attended by the King and Queen and the two princesses, four dukes and a cluster of ambassadors. The Champagne flowed and the bands played—inside Mr Tommy Kinsman, outside a gypsy quartet.

It was part of a gallant and vain attempt to return to 'normalcy'—and why not? Had it not been just this that had been achieved in the year of 1918? People forget that it was the Second World War, not the First, that destroyed London Society and Victorian country-house life. There were more people in domestic service in 1939 than in 1914. In any event, the attempt to revive the glories of the London season, after a brave effort, petered out. The combination of high taxation and lack of self-confidence proved fatal. 'Normalcy' never did return.

What did happen was something novel, unprecedented and much more exciting. The days of domination by the chinless wonders were over; it was someone else's turn. From the wastes of south and north London and the suburbs of the great cities a long-suppressed tribe emerged, made up of the young, of the working and lower-middle classes. By the end of the 1950s and the beginning of the 1960s they were carrying all before them. Fuelled by an affluence their parents had never known—the income of the young increased at a rate 50 per cent higher than that of their parents during this period—they not only broke through the surface: they set the tone. The middle and upper classes imitated them, their clothes, their music and even their accents. The revenge of the working classes, like the defence of sex, would make a fine subject for an Academy painting.

Five million teenagers with money to spare proved an irresistible horde. Society simply capitulated. The way forward, as always, was fore-shadowed by the arts: John Osborne carried them onwards and upwards with *Look Back in Anger* in 1956 and was followed by Harold Pinter and John Mortimer.

The revolution was heralded by the rash of espresso coffee bars that very soon covered the country. Where had the young gone before? I narrowly escaped being drawn into the vortex, since I was sharing a flat with Michael McCreery,[27] a friend of Mary Quant and Alexander Plunkett Green, whose head was full of the ideas of the future—not only coffee bars, but also supermarkets, launderettes and paperbacks. Alas, I missed my opportunity, sticking to the respectable, bourgeois occupations of law and journalism.

The more I reflect upon it, the more I conclude that the developments in the 1950s and 1960s constituted the real post-war watershed. Everything changed: clothes, hair and cooking. Pop music drove out Ivor Novello. Noël Coward was replaced by such stars as Cliff Richard and Helen Shapiro. Nineteen-fifty-six was the year of the rock 'n' roll, riots, and in 1957 even I managed to get to New York's Peppermint Lounge. The changes were not superficial but deep and complex. Young people looked

---

[27] Michael McCreery had an extraordinary and tragic career. We had been undergraduates together at Christ Church and decided to share a flat when we came to London. We found it in Harley Street. Michael was the son of General McCreery, who had commanded the Eighth Army after Field Marshal Montgomery. He was recruited into MI5 but developed left-wing tendencies and resigned. At one time the flat in Harley Street was filled with royals, but subsequently it was mainly blacks! Michael, who was an idealist, joined the Labour Party; finding it too bourgeois, he became a Communist. In the great Sino-Soviet split he was expelled from the British Communist Party. In 1965 he died prematurely of cancer in New Zealand, where he had gone to seek a cure. He was strikingly handsome and had great charm, a beautiful smile and a violent temper. *Requiescat in pace.*

no longer to their parents for standards but to their own peer groups. They had yet to learn that they had exchanged one tyranny for another, one that would be even more demanding. Yet as compensation they had Tommy Steele and, later, the incomparable Beatles, and I reflected on the resources of the nation which could produce brightness and vitality out of the decaying slums and dark cellars of Liverpool.

In the wake of the economic and social revolutions came permissiveness. Young people were liberated from their parents not only economically but also morally, just at the time when the older generation was losing confidence in its own standards and its ability to impose its views. The permissive young speedily established a new moral landscape. The inhibitions and taboos which had gripped the majority of the King's and Queen's subjects at the time of their daughter's marriage were swept away.

One of the breakthroughs came with the movement to reform the obscenity laws which followed a campaign in 1954 against 'dirty books', one of those swirls of trouble that have marked the literary history of England.[28] But this time the authors hit back and, under the leadership of A. P. Herbert in the country and Mr Roy Jenkins in Parliament, actually won the day. I was a don at the time, working on a book on the censorship laws and the relationship between law and literature, and was recruited as legal adviser to A. P. H.'s high-powered and thoroughly respectable committee. We presented a report and a draft Bill to the then Home Secretary, Mr Gwilym Lloyd George. Mr Lloyd George was cordial but took no action, and it was left to Mr Roy Jenkins to introduce our Bill under the Ten Minute Rule. Leave was granted without a dissentient voice. So the Bill was formally 'read a first time' and 'ordered to be printed'. In his preface to my first book, *Obscenity and the Law*, which was published in 1956, A. P. Herbert kindly contributed an introduction in which he wrote: 'Mr St John-Stevas is entitled to regard the Bill as his first publication. I hope that his second will bring him greater rewards. . . . Here is a ready weapon for the law reformer. On behalf of all those who love good art and literature, good sense, good law, I salute and wish him well.' This was the Bill which provided the basis for another measure, which eventually passed into law in 1959 as the Obscene Publications Act. This Act provided a new defence in an obscenity prosecution of publication: for the public good as 'being in the interests of art or literature or other objects of general concern'. It also, for the first time, allowed expert witnesses to be called in a book's defence. Although criticized, the Act is still on the statute book.

In the following year Sir Allen Lane published D. H. Lawrence's *Lady*

[28] I recall Macaulay's words in his essay on Byron: 'We know of no spectacle so ridiculous as the British public in one of its periodical fits of morality.' *Vide* the Cecil Parkinson affair in 1983.

Chatterley's Lover in paperback, and Penguin Books found themselves in the dock. The Old Bailey became the focus of literary London; not to have given evidence at the trial was to qualify as literary failure of the year. E. M. Forster, the Bishop of Woolwich, Ann Scott James and myself, among others, spouted from the witness box. I pronounced that 'Every priest should read this book' and was rewarded by being denounced by Monsignor Gordon Wheeler from the pulpit of Westminster Cathedral. Mr Griffith Jones for the prosecution earned both fame and ridicule by a rhetorical question to the jury: he asked them whether they would let their servants read the book. In the end *Lady Chatterley* was liberated and so was everybody else. No doubt there were losses as well as gains, but I have never doubted that the latter outweighed the former.

In 1967 I served on the Select Committee which considered the Lord Chamberlain's jurisdiction over the theatre, and we recommended that it should be done away with. In February 1968 theatre censorship, which had become as ridiculous as it was sinister, was finally abolished. I was also a sponsor of the Homosexual Reform Bill which sought to implement the recommendations of the Wolfenden Committee. This reached the statute book in July 1967. The divorce laws were also reformed during this period. These changes may be considered plusses. In the other scale I would put the Abortion Act of 1967, which was meant to authorize abortion for serious reasons but has ended up by delivering abortion on demand.

The most radical change that has come over our society in the years since the end of the war has been the transformation of Britain from a racially homogeneous to a multi-racial society. London, of course, like any capital city worthy of the name, has always been cosmopolitan, but in 1945, apart from London and a few big seaports, black and brown faces were rarities. Things are different today. Commonwealth immigration reached a high point in the 1950s, when Britain was a prosperous economic magnet, and it was only gradually that voices were raised in warning of trouble ahead. The loudest was not that of Mr Enoch Powell, who was silent at this period, but that of a backbench Tory MP, Sir Cyril Osborne.

In 1962 the drawbridge was raised against the bitter opposition of the Labour Party, led by Mr Hugh Gaitskell, but it is now generally accepted that this was a necessary measure. I chose immigration as the subject of my maiden speech, which I made in the House of Commons on 17 November 1964.[29] One principle, which I stressed should remain sacrosanct, was that whatever controls are imposed at the ports, a

---

[29] I had been selected as parliamentary candidate for Chelmsford in 1962, but because of the hostility towards the Government at that time no by-election was held, and I had to wait until the general election of October 1964 to get into Parliament. At my selection meeting the final question was whether I thought it would be a disadvantage in Chelmsford to be a Roman

commonwealth citizen once admitted to the country enjoys equal rights with every other citizen. Any proposal to create a second-class citizenship or deprive immigrants of the full protection of the courts, especially in matters such as deporting, should be vigorously resisted. And if the ordinary rights of citizenship cannot be guaranteed to immigrants by normal social processes then we should be prepared to see the legislature intervene to ensure that one of the things that makes life in this country most worthwhile, namely equality before the law, is in fact achieved.[30]

My principles on immigration have remained constant. I believe that there is a necessity for strict control of entry to this country but that any law should be compassionately administered to take account of individual cases. Further, it is essential that anyone settled here should have full equality of treatment before the law and should enjoy equality of opportunity. In 1965 I joined an all-party group, with Mr Roy Hattersley and Mr Jeremy Thorpe, to promote these ends, and it was for this reason that I was among the twenty-four Tories who on 24 April 1968 refused to vote against the Race Relations Bill. In this I was joined by a number of colleagues, including Sir Edward Boyle. Again in February 1968 I was among a handful of Tories who voted against Mr Callaghan's measure to deprive East African Asians of their British passports.

The coming of television has been another major change that has mutated the British lifestyle since the end of the war. At that time only a tiny minority possessed the dread box. Today Aldous Huxley's vision in *Brave New World* of 'a television box at the foot of every bed' has become reality. In 1947 the BBC had the television ball at its feet, but it fumbled the chance, gave sound broadcasting too high a priority and opened the way for commercial television. In spite of the opposition of the Archbishop of Canterbury, the Labour Party and the then Mr Quintin Hogg, Mr Norman Collins carried the day and the first independent transmission took place in 1955.

I appeared early on the television scene, since I participated in the first telecast of the Cambridge Union. This, in fact, took place not in

---

Catholic. I gave a Bellocian reply and declared that if the people of Chelmsford were the sort of people who would discriminate against me because of my religious views, sincerely held, then they were not the sort of people whom I would want to represent. A few minutes later I was selected. My predecessor, Sir Hubert Ashton, who was married to Hugh Gaitskell's sister, Bunty, had run into some 'flak' at the time of Suez. At a meeting someone had referred to Gaitskell as a 'traitor', and quite rightly Lady Ashton had swept off the platform, taking Hubert with her. She declared, 'No one is going to call my brother by such a name in my presence.'

[30] I received a number of congratulatory notes from both sides of the House, including letters from Mr Roy Jenkins and Mr Aubrey Jones, but the one that I appreciated most was from Mr Ian Macleod, which was typically generous: 'It was a brave speech to make and it came off. More than that: it actually turned and saved the debate. Few men achieve that in twenty years of membership.'

Cambridge but at Alexandra Palace, in London, in 1950. The furniture from the Union, including the president's chair in which I sat, was transported to its new site and later sent safely back to Cambridge. Since then I have been a fairly constant appearer on television, starting with Donald Baverstock's *Tonight* and continuing through a wide variety of programmes, including *That Was the Week That Was, Panorama* and others.

Cassandras such as Milton Shulman believe that television has been a trivializing influence: my own judgement and experience indicate quite the opposite. The British people have never before been so well informed about current international and domestic political affairs, as any parliamentary candidate can testify. The national danger is not too broad but too narrow a vision; television has widened people's horizons and enlarged their grasp of a range of possibilities.

One major feature of the present political scene which was not evidently present at the end of the war is the Irish problem. Of course, the injustices of the Stormont regime were there, but they were not part of British political awareness. The volcano was quiescent, but it was dormant, not extinct. What the Catholic population had to put up with from Protestant extremists in Northern Ireland was revealed to the British public for the first time during a televised debate I had with the Reverend Ian Paisley at the Oxford Union in 1967. In the course of his peroration Dr Paisley held up an unconsecrated host, thundering, 'Roman Catholics believe that this becomes the body, blood and bones of Christ' and threw it on the floor. I told him he had insulted not only the Roman Catholics but every religious-minded person in Britain. The motion declared that the Roman Catholic Church had no place in the twentieth century, and it was massively defeated. It was the Reverend Ian Paisley who was branded as the dinosaur.

In the 1960s the shortcomings of the regime in Northern Ireland ceased to be obscured and were clearly revealed. Peaceful evolution remained a possibility, but Lord O'Neil and, later, Mr Brian Faulkner both failed to command enough support to occupy the middle ground.

In 1973 Mr Heath, then Prime Minister, sent me to Northern Ireland to report on the conditions in Long Kesh, the camp in which many Catholics were imprisoned under the internment regulations. My visit illuminated for me the nature of the problem. Behind the barbed wire, dirty, smelly and dangerous, were representatives of the indigenous population, while up the road at Stormont, beneath the proconsular figures of Carson and Craigavon, preserved in marble, were representatives of an immigrant race with different assumptions, different accents and a totally different sense of loyalties and priorities. This I saw as the root of what even then looked like an insoluble problem: two races with different political values, different social expectations and different religions, struggling for the occupation of the same territory. The Catholics were the inferiors, the hewers of wood and the drawers of water for their Protestant masters. Religious differences exacerbated and advertised the conflict but did not lie at its root.[31]

I reported to Mr Heath on my return and over the abolition of Stormont counselled caution. However, Mr Heath failed to secure co-operation from Mr Faulkner and decided to do away with Stormont. From the mainland point of view, its abolition now looks like a mistake, since it removed at a stroke both a buffer and a forum through which con-stitutional progress might have been made. At the same time it was clearly impossible for Mr Heath to surrender control of the security forces to the old Stormont. Britain today is conscious of the Irish problem in a manner quite unimaginable in the 1940s but with a despairing pessimism equally unforeseeable.[32]

British domestic politics and its assumptions have altered radically from those of the post-war years, but the one thing that has not changed is the endemic economic crisis. Thirty years on it still threatens to engulf us, and we seem as far away from resolving it as ever. What seems now to have vanished is the consensus established by the wartime Coalition Government of Mr Winston Churchill, based on the fostering of economic growth and the maintenance of full employment. I remember that when I was campaigning at Dagenham the albatross round the Conservative Party's neck was its pre-war record of unemployment. It was as though, in Newman's phrase, the people bore a stain upon their imagination when they looked at the Conservative Party and could see only the horrors and the hunger of the 1930s. Unemployment today, surprisingly enough, does not seem to be having a similar effect, but it may well be a time bomb which will detonate at a later date. The Attlee Government of 1945 resolutely refused to return to the deflationary policies of the 1930s, and so did its Tory successors. It was over the present Government's policy towards unemployment that I found myself most in conflict within the Cabinet. My view was and is that it is a primary duty of any Govern-ment to take measures to relieve immediately the appalling blight of

[31] Years later in 1980 Pope John Paul II surprised me by telling me that he saw the Northern Ireland conflict as a racial, not a religious, problem.
[32] I had given up hope of any solution to the Irish problem, but when John Paul II visited Ireland in 1979 I watched on television his address at Drogheda, where he made a dramatic appeal for peace: 'On my knees I beg you to turn away from the paths of violence and to return to the ways of peace.' I was then a member of the Cabinet, so I sat down and wrote to Mrs Thatcher, the Prime Minister, expressing my view that the Pope's visit had dramatically altered the situation in Ireland and that there was a chance not of changing the IRA but of separating those members of the Catholic population who supported the terrorists from the others. The Prime Minister seemed to have reached similar conclusions, as the result was a new initiative taken by the then Northern Ireland Secretary of State, Mr Humphrey Atkins; nevertheless, like so many others it came to nothing. Mr Prior's 'Assembly' has, however, now been set up.

unemployment. Since leaving office I have spoken on this theme in the House of Commons on a number of occasions.[33]

These profound changes have been taking place over the past three decades against a background of continual adaptation to Britain's changed position in the world. When Princess Elizabeth drove down the Mall in 1947 one quarter of the world's surface was still coloured red on the globe: today only a few isolated scarlet dots remain. The peaceful transformation from Empire to Commonwealth has been one of the major post-war achievements, with only one failure—the ill-judged Suez adventure.

Suez aroused passions and visions not experienced here since Munich; it split friends, families and parties. Although I was not in Parliament at that time, I felt deeply emotionally involved. I was against going in and against coming out and ended up by being anti-Eden, anti-Nasser and anti-American. A curious memory is that of a dinner party given by Lady Asquith in honour of Sir Edward Boyle's resignation from the Government, which was somewhat marred by his being back in office by the time the celebration was due to be held. This was widely welcomed and of some significance. The country had realized its mistake and was determined to forget about the whole wretched business.

This was the mood which Mr Harold Macmillan so brilliantly orchestrated and which was an essential prerequisite for a Tory recovery. I recall my anxiety as to what I should say about my attitude to Suez to a Conservative selection committee in a constituency where I was seeking nomination only a few months after the débâcle. I need not have worried, since the issue was never raised. Such intuitive wisdom is possible only in a nation with a long history, whose intrinsic self-confidence remains unimpaired.

Britain lost an empire with good grace but the second part of Mr Dean Acheson's apophthegm of finding a role proved more intractable. I had long been a supporter of the movement for European unity on cultural and historic grounds; I also believed it to be essential for our economic prosperity in the future. I joined the European Movement in 1947, but I had to wait a quarter of a century to see Britain take her rightful place in the European Community. The great post-war failure of British foreign policy was missing the European opportunity, first in 1951 with the refusal to join the Coal and Steel Community and again in 1957 when we turned down the chance to sign the Treaty of Rome. Later the matter was out of our hands, and we suffered the humiliation of the Gaullist rejection and veto. At least it was not then our fault.

[33] See, for example, House of Commons debates of 16 March, 24 June and 8 December 1981, *passim*.

Mr Heath's lasting triumph, and the achievement which will ensure his place in history, was to take us into the European Community in 1973. I was charged with the duty to help Mr Humphrey Atkins, then Conservative Chief Whip, to ensure a Conservative majority in the lobby. I worked on this task for many months, and it came to a successful conclusion.[34] The motion favouring British entry was debated at the Conservative Party Conference held in Brighton, 13–16 October. The 13th proved to be Mr Heath's lucky day: British entry was approved by 2,474 votes to 324. I spoke in the debate, and in response to fears that had been expressed about the future of the monarchy declared that the only effect our entry into Europe would have on the Queen was that she would become 'Empress of Europe'.[35]

In Parliament the crucial vote came on 28 October. The debate in Parliament had been going on for months. It had had its lighter moments, one of which was provided by Rear-Admiral Morgan Giles at a meeting of the 1922 Committee in May, when he steadied the party with a slogan that became famous: 'Pro bono publico no bloody panico'. When the vote was taken, with the whips off, 356 Members voted for entry and 244 against, a majority of 112. Forty-one Tories voted against or abstained. I did not get the result wholly right in my forecast but came within two votes of the correct figures. By the time of the second reading debate on the European Communities Bill party differences had asserted themselves once again, and it passed the Commons on 17 February 1972 with a majority of only eight votes, 309 for and 301 against.

The night before the final vote the Bow Group held its annual dinner, with Mr Norman Lamont in the chair.[36] Mr Heath was the principal speaker and was hard put to conceal his nervousness. The following night the die was cast successfully: history will not easily be reversed.

The Britain of 1983 is light years away from that of 1945. Yet we remain an extraordinary cohesive nation. Ideologies rise and fall, but the nation abides. One of the institutions that has contributed most to this end is the monarchy. The Queen's sense of dedication and service has done more

---

[34] For an account of these and other activities see Uwe Kitzinger, *Diplomacy and Persuasion*, London, 1973.

[35] This made 'Sayings of the Week' in the *New York Times* the following day.

[36] *Mutatis mutandis*, I thought of it as the twentieth-century equivalent of the Duchess of Richmond's ball before the Battle of Waterloo but rather less enjoyable.

In January 1973 a series of celebrations were held by the Government to mark British entry. One was a banquet at Hampton Court Palace, held in sub-zero temperatures. I understood why Cardinal Wolsey had given the building to Henry VIII! Another was a gala performance at Covent Garden. I came out with the Archbishop of Canterbury, Dr Ramsey, who was very upset by the cries of 'Traitors' that greeted us from anti EEC demonstrators. Various Ministers were asked to host musical events and dinner parties. I gave one for the Luxembourg Ambassador and was fortunate to be able to sponsor a concert of early English music at Lincoln's Inn, with David Munrow leading the group. He had a rare musical talent; sadly, he committed suicide while still young.

than anything else to ensure that Britain has remained buoyant on the high seas of change. As we move into the final decades of the twentieth century, we do so against what the Albermarle Report called the 'massive and belittling backdrop' of nuclear weapons. In 1945 we were not a nuclear power; by 1952, with the explosion of the first British atomic bomb, we had achieved that perilous status and have maintained it ever since. For thirty years a general war has been kept at bay by the balance of nuclear terror, and the instinct of self-preservation has proved a surer foundation for peace than the idealism of the League of Nations or of UNO. Whether this will continue or will disintegrate under the impact of the proliferation of nuclear weapons remains the unanswered and supreme challenge of our time.

2

A Parliamentary Life

During my twenty years in Parliament I have always taken an interest in economic and financial issues, although I have no special expertise in these fields. My contributions in Cabinet on economics were clearly not welcome and were a principal cause of my being requested to resign.[1] I do not, however, regret the course I took. It seemed to me then, and does now, that I would be depriving myself of any *raison d'être* for Cabinet membership if I did not make a contribution to the central political issues of the day. Cabinet Ministers who sometimes declared that they had nothing to say, as they had 'no departmental interest', caused me to shudder.

My approach to both economic and financial problems was never wholly statistical. I felt, whatever the figures might say, that problems could be satisfactorily resolved only in relation to the real world and to the needs of the people concerned. I was thus unreceptive to monetarist doctrine, which seemed to be not only incapable of demonstration but also to arouse as much disagreement as agreement among its proponents. Furthermore, the belief that human beings are guided purely by motives of self-enrichment and that their problems can be resolved by self-help struck me as pitifully inadequate to delineate the human situation, with its tragic and cosmic overtones. Samuel Smiles does not begin to have the answer.

Leaving aside these metaphysical considerations, the monetarist approach seemed to me equally inadequate to an old society such as Britain's, with all its variations and complexities. The practical effect of seeking to apply such doctrines was inevitably to divide the country rather than to unite it, and this never held any appeal for me. Fraternity may be the Cinderella of the famous trilogy, but in practice it is of equal importance. I could not share either the *sangfroid* which was displayed by

---

[1] So, I think, was my lecture to the Bow Group at the Conservative Party Conference at Brighton in October 1980, 'The Moral Basis of Conservatism', intended as a counterweight to monetarism.

some, much less the callousness which was displayed by others, to unemployment figures, which were continually mounting and which eventually exceeded 3 million. I was particularly concerned about the fate of the increasing number of long-term unemployed and about unemployment among young people. As I said in the Budget debate of 16 March 1981, in the first parliamentary speech I made after I left the Cabinet.

> Inflation is a moral as well as an economic evil. It undermines confidence in our financial institutions and, ultimately, our political institutions. But unemployment is a moral evil, too. The loss of a job involves personal humiliation, a loss of dignity and a feeling of diminishment as a human being. It leads to strains and tensions in the family; it can cause want, and leads on to other social evils such as vandalism, delinquency and crime. One cannot dispose of the problem by the simple statement that if we conquer inflation, we shall solve our employment problem. If we conquer inflation, it will be easier to deal with unemployment, but much more will have to be done in that regard.
>
> It is not acceptable morally, nor is it even sensible economically, to speak as though we can pursue one economic aim to the exclusion of all human and social values. Man is a moral being first and an economic animal second. Of all parties, I believe that the Tory Party should be the first to recognize that. I believe we do recognize it, but we do not always speak as though we do. Not the least of the responsibilities that rest upon our economic Ministers is to demonstrate that we have the means to reduce unemployment and also fashion a discourse to demonstrate that truth both to this House and to the country.[2]

I returned to the theme in June of that year:

> The opportunity to work, to contribute by the fruits of one's labour to the support of oneself and one's family, to seek to enrich the community by the exercise of one's God-given talents, is essential to the dignity of every human being. Every man and woman who is denied that opportunity is diminished and devalued. Today we know that 2,600,000 of our fellow citizens, through no fault or responsibility of their own, through circumstances which they cannot influence nor

---

[2] Hansard, 16 March 1981, vol. 1, col. 35. In the same speech I stated: 'Many of us are uneasy about the wisdom of seeming to base a whole economic strategy on a single set of monetary aggregates of dubious reliability. Of course, control of the money supply is one of the weapons at a Government's disposal to promote a prosperous economy. It is one, but there are others, such as the promotion of investment and the moderation of wage claims.' On 8 December 1981 I again stressed the importance of communication, saying: 'It would not be a disaster if the gift of tongues suddenly descended on the whole Treasury team' (vol. 14, col. 782).

control, are unable to obtain work, some for long periods and some semi-permanently. That knowledge should stir the conscience of the nation, if we are to be worthy to be called a nation.

The House is representative of the nation, as my right honourable friend the Secretary of State said. We speak here through the voice of party; that is true. That is our system with its attendant good and evil. But there are occasions when the House of Commons has to transcend party politics, to transcend party ties, when the challenge is so grave that we have to speak on behalf of the community and the nation which we as a body represent. I believe that this debate is one of those occasions.

My point of departure this afternoon is the recognition that the Government—any Government—has the duty to help create the conditions in which people have the opportunity to work. Of course, there should be a fair day's work for a fair day's pay, but there must be an occasion to earn the pay—actually to have the chance to work. The situation is now so grave that the reduction of unemployment must be given a higher priority in the Government's thinking over the whole economic sphere. The determining criterion in any further reductions in Government expenditure must be whether they hinder or help to reduce the jobless total.

Ministers must concentrate their minds on both short-term and long-term measures that provide more jobs. The whole discourse of the Government must adapt itself to that set of priorities. The time has come to concentrate on the second part of the Government strategy— the invigoration and renewal of British industry, whether that industry be on the manufacturing or the service side.

May I take, first, the long-term problem, to which all the resources of the Government should be devoted? It is how best we can make the transition to a society that is bound to be based more on service industries and less on manufacturing industries. It is a repetition in another form of the nineteenth-century problem, when we had to move from an economy based on agriculture to one based on industry—and the problem faces all the older industrial countries of the world. We should also in the long term be considering whether it is desirable to have planned early retirement, and how we can move towards greater equality between men and women in that regard.[3]

I concluded by saying:

It is the duty of every member of the Government and the House to recognize unemployment for what it is—a moral evil of the first order. We must be determined to remedy it in so far as it is within our power so

[3] Hansard, 24 June 1981, vol. 7, cols. 267–8.

to do. If it is left unchecked, it will destroy not only the traditions of civility that are so important to public life, but our cohesion as one nation, and ultimately it will undermine our free institutions themselves.

It is no part of Government policy, nor should it be, to write off any part of this country, or to bypass any part of it through callousness or electoral calculation. It is to that vision of a society based on shared interest and community that we must respond, and we should do so sensitively, intelligently and determinedly.[4]

The three subjects, all subsidiary but nevertheless of crucial importance, to which I have endeavoured to make a special contribution during my parliamentary years have been education, the reform of Parliament and the arts. I was appointed Under-Secretary of State for Education by Mr Heath in November 1972 and will always remember the courtesy of the Secretary of State, Mrs Thatcher, who met me at the door of the Ministry when I arrived (fortunately on time) as a fledgling and a rather nervous Minister. I was put in charge of higher education, but in effect, whatever the delineations, policy is determined by the two great powers in the ministerial world, the Secretary of State and the Permanent Secretary. A junior Minister is able to influence events only at the margin. In reality he is waiting for some more senior position and is serving a form of apprenticeship. A junior Minister has no weight to throw around, and if he attempts to do so the only certain result is that he will throw himself out of the window. Junior Ministers are treated by the Civil Service rather as bishops are in Rome. They are two a penny, and the only politicians to whom civil servants pay attention are Secretaries of State and members of the Cabinet, who constitute the cardinals of the British political system.

EDUCATION

I arrived at the Department of Education during a period of student trouble and violence. While I was always sympathetic to the legitimate demands of students and their struggle to survive on inadequate grants, I was strongly opposed to attempts to deny freedom of speech to others. Thus while I did my best to improve the financial situation of students, and with some success, giving priority to the reduction of the parental contribution, I was firm in my condemnation of violent demonstrations that impinged on the rights of others.

Almost my first public engagement was to designate the North London Polytechnic at the Festival Hall on 30 November 1972. I was greeted by a howling crowd of students who were conducting a vendetta against their

[4] Ibid., cols. 271–2.

principal, Mr Terence Miller, and who regarded my visit as a heaven-sent opportunity to mount a demonstration against him. I went through my speech from beginning to end, but no one heard a word, save for one phrase which I managed to get over during a lull in the general hubbub. Her Majesty the Queen had recently been demonstrated against at Stirling University, and I was able to pronounce the audible words: 'What's good enough for the Queen is good enough for me', but the only effect this seemed to have on the students was to inspire them to shout more loudly. They then left the hall, descended on a room where our tea had been laid out and scoffed the lot! When the VIPs arrived shortly afterwards there was not a lettuce leaf in sight. The *Daily Express*, in a splendid misprint, described the occasion as a 'ceremony of denigration'.[5]

More serious was the violence shown to Professor Eysenck by students at the London School of Economics in May. Where they came from was never wholly made clear, but Lord Robbins and others denied vigorously that they had anything to do with the LSE itself. To the annoyance of my civil servants, I made a sharp condemnation of the incident, but I was backed by the Secretary of State, Mrs Thatcher. Professor Eysenck was not only prevented from speaking but was also pushed, punched and pummelled; he had his hair pulled, his nose cut and his glasses broken. I suggested that those responsible should be charged with criminal assault.

Although they were not my direct ministerial concern, I also championed the cause of the independent and direct grant schools. In September 1973 Mr Roy Hattersley, at the Conference of Preparatory Schools at Cambridge, had attacked the independent sector and had declared that the Labour Party would make the provision of such education a criminal offence. I seized the opportunity provided by my own address to the Headmasters' Conference, also in Cambridge, on 26 September, to reply. I urged the assembled headmasters to put their case in the public forum so that it did not go by default. The time for lying low had passed. I concluded my speech by saying:

> Sentence of death has been passed: only execution remains. This is not the moment for doing good deeds by stealth. If your position is buttressed by the minds and hearts of the people, it will be secure. In Britain public opinion is still sovereign, and no party, no group, no individual, however temporarily powerful or permanently arrogant, can hold out against its sway, so look to that sure moat. As to the Government, I give you this pledge: you will not get privilege from us, but you will get a fair deal. We will not countenance your being harried as if you were malefactors, and we reject as hateful the rigging of the law against those who have made so sustained and notable a contribution to both the private and public weal. We will ensure, as far

[5] 1 December 1972.

as it lies within our power, that you continue to make your contribution to society's good under the equal protection of our laws.

Later in the year, at the Merchant Taylors School in Liverpool, I took the opportunity of making a defence of the direct grant schools.[6] The principal point I made was that they constituted a bridge between the two educational sectors.

In the building up and multiplying of such bridges lies the best hope for an harmonious educational future. How much better it will be for our children if the two sectors of the educational system can move closer to each other and work together in mutual respect and fruitful co-operation rather than be driven apart by fanatical, intolerant and ill-thought-out policies designed to produce the very divisiveness of which the private sector is so unjustly accused. We cannot afford a cold war in education. Seen in the perspective of the future, the direct grant schools, far from being hyphenated hybrids surviving from a dead past, are pioneer and relevant institutions fitted to make a unique contribution to the resolution of the tensions within our educational system.[7]

After the Conservative electoral defeat of February 1974 I was appointed by Mr Heath to be Opposition arts spokesman and, in June of that year, I was appointed to the Shadow Cabinet as Opposition spokesman on education. I retained the arts portfolio. It was clear that an election would not be long delayed, and I entered on an intense period of activity, restating Conservative education policy in a series of speeches. I travelled from one end of the country to the other stressing the issues of parental rights, freedom and high standards, as well as the need for variety and choice of school. At Stockport in 1974 I launched the Parents' Charter, most of the provisions of which were to be implemented by the Conservative Government in 1979.[8]

Despite the efforts of Mr Heath and his supporters, the tide was flowing too strongly against the Tory Party to be turned back, and in the October election of 1974 Labour was returned with an increased majority.

During the years between the elections of 1974 and 1979 education

---

[6] 1 November 1973.

[7] I also pledged the Government to their support: 'You have the unqualified goodwill of the Secretary of State, and we are all grateful to you for the work you are doing. Your schools are under threat: you are in the front line of fire, which is both dangerous and exhilarating. I give you this pledge on behalf of the Government. We will continue to cherish, guard and back you so that you may continue in the future, as you have done in the past, to make a contribution to the education of the nation, both notable and profound.' This pledge was in fact speedily redeemed, since that day the capitation grant per pupil at direct grant schools went up to £79, which gave an overall increase to the direct grant schools' revenue of £800,000.

[8] In the Education Act of 1980.

became a major political issue centring on the question of standards and freedom. The party conflict grew sharper, but I had no desire to see education become a political football. On two occasions I offered a concordat to the Labour Party on the subject, first to Mr Mulley in June 1975 and later to Mrs Shirley Williams, when she had become Secretary of State for Education, but to no effect. My suggestion to Mr Mulley was that he should call off the campaign against the direct grant schools in return for a Tory pledge not to expand them further. This received a dusty answer. The campaign in the country and the lobby of Parliament went on. Five thousand parents turned up at Westminster in June 1975 in support of the schools. We also received some welcome encouragement from the then Archbishop of Liverpool, Dr G. A. Beck, who was concerned about the future of Catholic education in the city should the direct grant schools be done away with. Despite all our efforts, the Government was intent on bringing the direct grant schools system to an end, and late at night on 27 October 1975, after a debate lasting only three-quarters of an hour, our 'prayer' for their continuance was defeated and the system was abolished. Their status rested on an order in council, and they could therefore be done away with after only the shortest of debates. I obtained from the Shadow Cabinet a pledge that they would be restored on a statutory basis. This was the highest degree of protection they could receive, since the doctrine of the supremacy of Parliament precludes any entrenched measures.

We conducted a parallel fight to save the remaining grammar schools. I championed excellent schools such as Emanuel School, Wandsworth, and St Marylebone Grammar School, but the juggernaut pressed on. Support of the grammar schools was a uniting issue within the Conservative Party, since both left and right were in favour of their continuance. In February 1976 a Bill was introduced to do away with grammar schools and to impose comprehensive systems on the whole country. I organized a petition against this measure, and in May 1976 it was presented at the House of Commons bearing half a million signatures. We supported Kingston and Berkshire and other Education Authorities who were working to retain their schools. Essex, my own county, were keen to retain the grammar schools in Chelmsford, and we worked on their behalf. In the Commons a war of attrition was carried out against the Education Bill, and we did all we could to delay its passage. The committee stage was long and protracted, as was the report stage, during which at times the Government majority dropped to three, but on 21 July, with the aid of the guillotine, it received its third reading. These tactics were not totally fruitless; they provided an opportunity for councils to delay their plans for going comprehensive, so that when the Act was repealed on the return of a Conservative Government in 1979 there was still a number of grammar schools left to save, although by this time they were in a small minority.

Before the Education Bill had passed through the Commons the Tameside Council provided a high drama. Tameside, despite its name, lies near Manchester, and the local council wished to keep its selective schools as well as the 11-plus examination. In May 1976 I persuaded the councillors to drop the 11-plus, since it was widely unpopular and unnecessary, but I backed them in their struggle to keep their selective schools. The advice I gave, which they followed, was to employ some other means of selection. These tactics infuriated the Education Secretary, Mr Mulley, and in June of 1976 he used his powers under Section 68 of the Education Act of 1944 to order them to go comprehensive. The Tameside councillors, led by Colin Grantham, turned out to be a robust body of men who were not going to be bullied. After a private conference with me in London, they decided to resist. I was able to obtain for them the legal services of Mr Leon Brittan, who generously gave them free of charge, and the ruling of Mr Mulley was challenged.[9] However, on 12 July Mr Mulley's action was upheld by the High Court, as had generally been expected. Challenges of the Secretary of State's sweeping powers under the Education Act had been few and far between. We held a further council of war, and the courageous councillors decided that they would go to the Court of Appeal. Faced with a threat of being saddled with the costs of the action, they determined to go ahead. I assured them that we would raise as much as we could by a public subscription, but they were undoubtedly at risk.

The case was heard by the Court of Appeal on 26 July, and Lord Denning with two other judges ruled in favour of the Council. The Court held that the Education Secretary had acted unlawfully and that the Council was entitled to use a method of selection which it reasonably and honestly believed would be effective. Mr Mulley had contended that the selection procedure was a sham and would not achieve its intention. Despite strong advice to the contrary, the Education Secretary resolved to appeal to the Lords. The Tameside case was presented by Mr Tony Loyd, QC (now Mr Justice Loyd), supported by Mr Leon Brittan. Because of the need for a swift decision before the school year opened, the Lords took the almost unprecedented step of sitting on a Saturday, the first time this had happened in 200 years. The case was heard on 1 August, and five law lords were unanimous in upholding the Tameside contention. The Shadow Cabinet was meeting that day at Conservative Central Office for a general policy review when I arrived with the news. Mrs Thatcher was presiding. I passed her a note so that she was able to interrupt the proceedings and announce the result. The assembled shadows burst into applause, and a telegram of congratulations was despatched to Tameside. I was both overjoyed and, to tell the truth, somewhat surprised at the result. I had

[9] Mr Brittan not only gave excellent legal advice but also raised the morale of the councillors at a critical moment.

not rated our chances higher than evens, but, as usual, boldness paid off. I too sent a message to Tameside, stating: 'A further blow has been struck in the fight for parental influence and choice in education, for the independence of the local authorities and for the liberty of the subject. Never again will an education Minister be able to behave with dictatorial arrogance to parents and councillors.' The *Daily Mirror* of 3 August put the matter more succinctly in its banner headline 'Blackboard Bungle'. Shortly after the Tameside case was decided the Education Act passed into law, and eight dissident councils were then lawfully requested to submit plans for comprehensive schooling. I was able to pledge that as soon as a Conservative Government was returned a Bill would be introduced to repeal the Education Act. This pledge was among the first to be fulfilled in the new Parliament of May 1979.

Education continued to occupy a prominent place in public affairs. In October 1976 the Prime Minister, Mr Callaghan, launched a campaign for raising educational standards. We had been in the course of preparing our own campaign, but we were not quick enough off the mark and were pipped at the post by Mr Callaghan's initiative. In January 1977, however, I was able to launch a campaign for higher standards in education. The campaign started in London, and the first of our regional conferences was held shortly afterwards. Another activity of this period was the creation of the assisted places scheme. This concentrated government help on the individual pupils at independent schools rather than on the schools themselves. The plan was that 200 schools should participate in the scheme and that they would be distributed evenly throughout the country. One of the requirements we laid down for taking part in the scheme was that at least a quarter of the pupils should come from the maintained educational system. A means test was built in so that help could be given to those who needed it most.

I had realized that, important and exhilarating as these campaigns were, there was a danger that the party would be identified too closely with minority interests. Accordingly, we launched another campaign to improve comprehensive schools at the Party Conference of 1977. I concentrated my criticism on the proliferation of monster schools and the indiscriminate use of mixed-ability teaching. It was during this period too that I resisted, on behalf of the party, the abolition of the dual system of General Certificate of Education (GCE) and Certificate of Secondary Education (CSE) examinations, since I feared that an ill-prepared examination system would lower standards. The vital feature, which was eventually retained in the reformed system, was the maintenance of the separate GCE boards.

Religious education was another major concern, and in February 1978 the Human Rights Society held a conference on the subject at the Caxton Hall in London. The advantage of the conference's being held under these auspices was that it did not have a party political flavour.[10]

All shades of opinion were represented, from Roman Catholicism to agnosticism. Two general sessions were held, and between them the Conference divided into various study groups. The final session was addressed by the Archbishop of Canterbury, Dr Donald Coggan, the Archbishop of Westminster, Cardinal Hume, and the Moderator of the Free Church Council, the Reverend Morgan Williams, but undoubtedly the star of the show was the Chief Rabbi, Dr Immanuel Jacobovits, who made an impassioned plea for the continuation of religious and ethical education in schools.[11]

REFORMING PARLIAMENT

My interest in Parliament and its workings was first aroused when I was an undergraduate at Cambridge, where constitutional law was included in my studies. But it is to Bagehot that I am principally indebted for giving me an insight into the psychological realities that form the basis of the English parliamentary system. I first heard of Bagehot through a debate about the reform of Parliament that I conducted at Cambridge with Mr Douglas Hurd—who quoted him against me. This interest was reinforced by the continual references I found to Bagehot not only in books dealing directly with the nineteenth century but also in weekly periodicals and even in daily newspapers. Who was this man who enjoyed such an immortality of quotation ninety years after his death? A final impetus which drove me to consult his works in the British Museum Library was G. M. Young's essay, 'The Greatest Victorian',[12] in which, having considered the claims of George Eliot, Tennyson, Matthew Arnold, Darwin and Ruskin to the title, he rejects them all in favour of Bagehot.

> We are looking for a man who was in and of his age and who could have been of no other; a man with sympathy to share, and genius to judge, its sentiments and movements; a man not too illustrious or too consummate to be companionable, but one, nevertheless, whose ideas took root and are still bearing, whose influence, passing from one fit mind to another, could transmit and still impart, the most precious element in Victorian civilization, its robust and masculine sanity. Such a man there was: and I award the place to Walter Bagehot.

My researches led me to the discovery that little had been written about him and that, apart from the biography of his sister-in-law, Mrs Russell

[10] I was chairman of the Human Rights Trust, which helped to finance the conference.
[11] Messages of support were received from the Prime Minister and the Leader of the Opposition.
[12] By this he meant *Victorianum maxime* and not *Victorianum maximorum*.

Barrington, published in 1915, and another by Professor Irvine, an academic at Stanford University, in the 1930s, no biography of him existed. Accordingly, I decided to make him the subject of my second book *Walter Bagehot: A Study of His Life and Thought*, which I combined with the text of *The English Constitution* and a selection from his political writings. The book was commissioned by Douglas Jerrold, then a leading luminary in the publishing world, in 1957, and it was published by Eyre and Spottiswoode early in 1959. It caught the attention of Geoffrey Crowther, and in April 1959, when I was studying and lecturing at New Haven, he summoned me to the Yale Club in New York for luncheon. There he unveiled a plan which was to have a profound effect on my future. He told me of his long-cherished project to publish a complete edition of Bagehot's works and invited me to undertake it. I agreed, subject to the proviso that I should also be able to write for *The Economist*. So for twenty-five years Bagehot has been my intimate, if intermittent, companion. Through all the vagaries of journalistic and political life I have continued this work, and it will shortly be brought to a conclusion with the publication of the last two volumes of the thirteen-volume edition.

Bagehot had a profound understanding of the nature of parliamentary government and acute psychological insights into the character of those who participated in it. Parliamentary government was effective because its principal instrument, the House of Commons, had a strong corporate character:

> The House of Commons [he wrote] is able to accomplish much because it is not a meeting of strangers, but of persons who know one another, who are bound by implied ties and by tacit agreements to one another, who have certain leaders whom they all, more or less, choose to follow—and can, therefore, calculate on one another and rely on one another.[13]

He appreciated the collective wisdom of the Commons:

> The House of Commons, according to the saying, is wiser than any one in it. There is an elective affinity for solid sense in a practical assembly of educated Englishmen which always operates, and which rarely errs.[14]

He hit off in a single phrase the essence of existence in the House of Commons—'A life of distracting routine'.[15]

Bagehot marvelled at the curiosity of Parliament and found a psychological solution to the puzzle of Question Time.

[13] 'The Necessary Consequences of Government by a Minority', *The Economist*, 9 May 1868.
[14] 'Sir George Cornewall Lewis', *The Works of Walter Bagehot*, ed. N. St John-Stevas, vol. 3, London, 1968, p. 396.
[15] *The English Constitution, Works*, vol. 5, London, 1974, pp. 274–5.

As soon as bore A ends, bore B begins. Some enquire from genuine love of knowledge, or from a real wish to improve what they ask about; others to see their name in the papers; others to show a watchful constituency that they are alert; others to get on and to get a place in the Government; others from an accummulation of little motives they could not themselves analyse, or because it is their habit to ask things.[16]

Anyone writing today about Parliament would not have to add or subtract a word from this analysis. Depth of comprehension, combined with a brilliant surface style, have proved efficacious preservatives. Many have written more learnedly on British politics since Bagehot, but no one has matched his insights and powers of expression. And certainly no one else has succeeded in making the English constitution amusing!

Great as Parliament is, Bagehot recognized that it is far from perfect. It could in fact, he thought, be capricious in its choices, and the remedy for this, party organization, constituted another evil. He saw Parliament as always capable of improvement.

There is no reason [he wrote] why we should not make our law, policy and administration work like a scientific machine, precise in detail as well as effective in broad results—why it should, like a bad old watch, be right only as to the hours, and not, like a good watch of the nineteenth century, be correct also for minutes and seconds.[17]

From Bagehot I derived my appreciation of the importance of institutions in British political life. At the same time I recognized with him the need for change and improvement. When I was appointed Shadow Leader of the House by Mrs Thatcher on 15 November 1978, I had the opportunity to put these principles into practice.

From the first, I was a reformer. The way had been prepared by my predecessor, Mr Francis Pym, who was of a like mind. I regarded it as a major task to secure the implementation of the report of the Procedure Committee of 1976, which had been published the previous year and which had recommended the setting up of a new select committee system

---

[16] Ibid., p. 320.

[17] 'The Provisional Government. Its Advantages and Disadvantages', *The Economist*, 25 March 1865. Cf. the following passage in 'The New Ministry', *The Economist*, 28 October 1865: 'Most English institutions were not made but have grown; they are the aggregate result of the labour of many generations, each of which looked mainly to its own benefit, and none of which thought much of what was to come after. They are an historical accumulation of temporary expedients; they work fairly well because they were commonly made with judgement; the continuity of our history for the most part makes them still advantageous; still they mostly present matter for improvement. Anything that began in one era of politics and has lasted into another—in many respects much different and in other respects wholly opposite—must need many changes and many alterations—much to be added here, much to be diminished there. In politics we are wisely wearing our fathers' shoes; our feet are like theirs, and we step tolerably well; still they are not like a made pair; the fit cannot be and is not perfect.'

to check the executive, and shadow government departments. There was widespread support in the House for this reform but, curiously enough, the Leader of the House, Mr Michael Foot, was strongly opposed to the committee system. He felt that it would detract from the importance of the chamber, of which he took a romantic rather than a realistic view. In the new year, 1979, I managed to secure a two-day debate on the procedure report, which took place on 19 and 20 February. It was clear that Mr Foot remained hostile to reform, but such was the feeling in the House that on the second day of the debate he requested permission to make a second speech and in effect accepted that the House should have an opportunity of coming to a decision on the matter. This was a notable advance. A further one was achieved when I secured the insertion into the Conservative election manifesto of an expression of sympathy for the setting up of select committees[18] and, more important, a pledge that the House would have an early opportunity of coming to a decision on the principal recommendations of the report. I was aware of the importance of this undertaking. There was clearly a majority for reform of the House, but the difficulty lay in securing an opportunity for that majority to make itself felt and for a decision to be taken.

Two things are needed for a reform of the House of Commons—a reforming mood in the House and a reforming Leader. The mood was undoubtedly there but, as I have indicated, Mr Michael Foot was the reverse of a reformer. When the election was fought and won, and I was appointed Leader of the House by Mrs Thatcher, the two necessary parts of the equation were in place. I realized that I would have to act swiftly. On 15 May the Queen's Speech included a pledge that the Commons be able to debate its own reform. The Prime Minister did not give a high priority to institutional reform and, as a natural executive, looked askance at any proposals for strengthening parliamentary power. I knew too that Ministers, as they grew established in their departments, would take a similar view. It was therefore essential to get my proposals before the Cabinet at the earliest possible moment. In this I was helped by the Civil Service, which had prepared a series of measures based on the recommendations of the Procedure Committee report, which I found waiting on my desk the day on which I took office. Much work had to be done on these, but the foundations had been laid. I never found the Civil Service to be unduly obstructive. Provided a Minister is clear about what he wants, full co-operation will be forthcoming; on the other hand, a Minister whose mind is vacant or whose will is unsure finds himself taken over by the machine. Nature abhors a vacuum, and so does the Civil Service. Government has to be carried on, and if a Minister is not prepared to do it, then civil servants will come forward to do it for him.

[18] An expression of sympathy was also given for the other reforms recommended by the Procedure Committee, including those concerning the Comptroller and Auditor General.

We pressed ahead then with preparations for the Cabinet paper, and shortly before the crucial decision was to be taken I secured some powerful supporters in the Cabinet. The Chief Whip, Mr Michael Jopling, was a reformer at least as far as the setting up of the select committee system was concerned. I went privately to see the Home Secretary, Mr William Whitelaw, and the Lord Chancellor, Lord Hailsham; both pledged their support, the price of the Lord Chancellor's acquiescence being an agreement to leave his department out of the supervisory system. I did not approve of this in principle but felt it was a price worth paying to get the bulk of the reform measures through. On 14 June the proposals to set up a new system of fourteen select committees was approved by the Cabinet, and the motions were taken in the House of Commons shortly afterwards.[19] On 25 June they were debated, and the discussion which started at 3.30 in the afternoon did not conclude until one o'clock the following morning. I opened the debate with these words:

> Today is, I believe, a crucial day in the life of the House of Commons. After years of discussion and debate, we are embarking upon a series of changes that could constitute the most important parliamentary reforms of the century. Parliament may not, for the moment, stand at the zenith of public esteem. There are tides of fashion that rise and fall as there are tides of opinion that move. We should not be too concerned about that. One truth abides and that is that parliamentary government has been one of the great contributions of the British nation to the world's civilization, and we should do well to remember that. Great nations fail only when they cease to comprehend the institutions that they themselves have created.
>
> That is not to say that I believe that Parliament is impeccable. The greatness of Parliament and the reason why it has survived for seven hundred years is that it has always been ready to reform itself. It has found the will to put matters right when they have gone wrong and to review itself when it has discerned the sign of the times. . . .
>
> It has been increasingly felt that the twentieth-century Parliament is not effectively supervising the executive and that while the power and effectiveness of Whitehall has grown, that of Westminster has diminished.
>
> The proposals that the Government are placing before the House are intended to redress the balance of power to enable the House of Commons to do more effectively the job it has been elected to do. In doing this the Government are redeeming a pledge in their election manifesto, which was repeated in the gracious speech, that the House

---

[19] A fifteenth committee was added later, to deal with the work of the Parliamentary Commissioner.

should have an early opportunity to amend their procedures, particularly as they relate to the scrutiny of government.[20]

I concluded by declaring:

I believe that this Chamber is one of the **great** political inventions of our history. It remains, and will remain the means by which the mind of the nation is focused on the great issues of the day. It will remain the channel through which the expressive power of Parliament is exercised. But the scrutinizing function of Parliament is now too detailed to be discharged effectively by this Chamber alone. To pretend otherwise is not to exalt parliamentary government, as some honourable members imagine. It is simply to degrade it. It is to turn what is a legitimate object of respect and reverence into some kind of irrational idol.

We believe that the motions on the order paper provide the coherent and systematic structure of select committees that the Procedure Committee considered, and that the Government agree, to be a necessary preliminary to the more effective scrutiny of government and the wider involvement that honourable Members on both sides of the House have sought for many years. It will provide the opportunity for closer examination of departmental policy and of the way in which Ministers are discharging their duties. It will increase parliamentary understanding of the pressures and constraints under which Ministers and their departments have to work. It will bring about a closer relationship with Ministers themselves. It will also be an important contribution to greater openness in government, of a kind that is in accord with our parliamentary arrangements and our constitutional traditions. It is in that spirit that I commend these proposals to the House.[21]

All went well and the select committee system was set up with the overwhelming approval of the House. Thus within six weeks of the meeting of the new Parliament this major reform had been accomplished. As the weeks and months passed, so my ministerial colleagues' criticisms of the committees grew and there were continual problems to be ironed out, but I concluded that the louder the criticism from the departments, the more competently the committees must be doing the job for which they were set up.

In the contemporary House of Commons there are not enough ministerial jobs to go around. In other words, there are more Members capable of exercising ministerial functions than there are Ministries. I saw the select committee system as offering an alternative career structure for

[20] Hansard, 25 June 1979, vol. 969, col. 36.
[21] Ibid., cols. 48–9.

Members. Contrary to vulgar belief, Members of Parliament are not intent on feathering their own nests or in promoting selfish interests. They desire to do a useful job of work, and the select committee system provided them with a new opportunity. As an essential part of the reform I wished to see Members' salaries raised to a level which, while not providing a major financial inducement to enter the House of Commons, would nevertheless allow those Members who wished to devote themselves full-time to their political duties to do so. Since if it were to work satisfactorily the select committee system would require a considerable number of Members to spend many hours on committee work, the raising of salary levels was an intrinsic part of the reform.

The previous Government had long neglected the issue, and Members' salaries had fallen far behind during a period of rising inflation. Lord Boyle's committee had recommended substantial increases, but I met strong opposition within the Cabinet to the implementation of these recommendations. In the event, after a sharp struggle, I did succeed in getting MPs' salaries nearly doubled, from £6,890 a year to £12,000 a year, and secretarial allowances were similarly increased. The Prime Minister and the Cabinet insisted, against my advice, on the increases being spread over two years and paid in three instalments. I realized that politically this was a mistake. Raising Members' salaries is always unpopular, and doing it in three stages would merely ensure that there would be three parliamentary and public rows instead of one. On 21 June the pay proposals went before the House of Commons and caused such an explosion of fury from Members, because of the staging of the increases, that the proposals had to be drastically modified. Members thus got a higher percentage of the increase at an earlier date. During this period I was able to introduce a research assistants' allowance for Members, to write off the House of Commons catering deficit of £3 million and to put the finances on such a basis that they were capable of showing a profit, as well as introducing a scheme of insurance for injuries received by Members either at the Palace of Westminster or on parliamentary business. I was also able to get a committee appointed to look into the whole question of index-linking for Members' salaries. In practice this came to nothing but an annual review of salaries was instituted. During my period of office severance pay was provided for Members for the first time, and payment was authorized to be made to Members' secretaries after the death of a Member. Formerly payment had been stopped from the day of the Member's death, and this had caused unnecessary stress. Other changes I was able to introduce were pensions for Members' secretaries who had hitherto been without them and a measure enabling Members to buy additional years for pension purposes. Free travel on parliamentary business within the United Kingdom was also provided for the first time. We were also able to increase the grant to the Opposition parliamentary parties by 25 per cent on 12 November 1980. For these various efforts I was paid a bizarre tribute by a Labour Member, who labelled me as the best shop steward Members of Parliament had ever had.

My second tranche of procedural changes, which went through the House on 30 October 1979, caused little trouble. The conservative nature of the House of Commons however, was well illustrated by its refusal to abolish the practice of wearing a top hat when raising a point of order in a division. Indeed, the House went further than that and insisted that two top hats should be made available.

From this time onwards, however, my path as a reformer grew stonier. Both the Prime Minister and individual Ministers had had enough of my select committees and looked with hostility or cynicism on proposals to introduce a new Public Bill procedure.[22] The Chief Whip too had exhausted his reforming zeal, and I experienced great difficulty in getting the Cabinet to agree to any further changes. However, I was helped by an early-day motion tabled by nearly 200 backbenchers, led by Mr Kenneth Baker, demanding that the new Public Bill procedure should be brought into operation. I was also strongly supported by Mr Edward Du Cann, Chairman of the 1922 Committee, who throughout the struggles was a doughty champion of backbench rights. The proposals just squeaked through the Cabinet, and on 30 October 1980 were approved by the House. As part of the package I had secured agreement from the Cabinet that a new procedure committee should be set up to consider the way in which the House of Commons grants taxation and to suggest improvements. Further than this I was unable to go.

The Government was hostile to the recommendations of the procedure committee that the powers of the Comptroller and Auditor General should be extended, and that he should take the nationalized industries into his purview.[23] I was removed from the Cabinet before I could take any further steps to implement this reform. Then, by an odd irony, I found myself in a position to introduce a measure which, had I remained in the Cabinet, I would have been unable to propose. I drew second place in the ballot for Private Members' Bills in November 1982. On the suggestion of Mr Edward Du Cann, I decided to introduce a Bill to implement the recommendations of the procedure committee on the Comptroller and Auditor General. As I remarked at the time to the then Leader of the House, Mr John Biffen, it was as though one had been expelled from the Ark and then, like a dove, had returned with a Bill in one's beak. He accepted the analogy but added, 'It is hardly an olive branch.' After various vicissitudes, changes and modifications, the Bill received its third

[22] For an account of this procedure, see p. 107.
[23] For a more detailed account of this matter, see p. 108–11.

reading in the House of Commons on Wednesday, 11 May 1982. It then passed to the Lords, where it was sponsored by Lord Boyd Carpenter and finally reached the statute book on Friday, 13 May.[24]

A further irony occurred after the general election of 1983. I was able to achieve the second reform which I had been stopped from making when I was Leader of the House—the indexing of Members' salaries. The Government, having learned nothing from past experience, had resolved not to implement the independent review body's recommendations on Members' pay and allowances in full.[25] Instead of the 30 per cent increase in salary suggested, the Government wished to confine it to 4 per cent, which, with the additional contributions to Members' pensions, would have meant a rise of only 1 per cent. Not unreasonably, the Commons was outraged. Mr Edward Du Cann then worked out a compromise, acceptable to the Government, by which Members' salaries would increase over the lifetime of the Parliament in five equal instalments. After this they were to be linked to the grade in the Civil Service paid £18,500 on 1 January 1987. As I pointed out to Mr Du Cann, his suggestion was fatally flawed, for when the link became operative on 1 January 1988 Members would once again have fallen behind, given even a minimum rate of inflation over four and a half years. Accordingly, jointly with Sir Hugh Fraser, the most senior backbencher on the Government side of the House, I put down an amendment of a simple but crucial character. It substituted as the date from which the linkage would be calculated 13 June 1983 for 1 January 1987. The link would still not become operative until 1 January 1988. The Government whips advised that our amendment would be defeated, but in the event it was carried by 226 votes to 218. Thus by eight votes a long overdue reform came about, and in future the House of Commons will be spared the embarrassing need to vote itself increased salaries after highly publicized major debate. The linkage resolution will have to be renewed in each Parliament, but that should prove a minor matter.

The position of Leader of the House is a unique one. It carries a place in the Cabinet and brings both prestige and influence, but, unlike other great offices of state, the Leader has no back-up Ministry. My own staff, although devoted, constituted a mere handful, and I had to draw on the Cabinet Office for supplementary help. Leaders of the House have no executive power. Many have found this frustrating and have bemoaned the fact that they have not had a Ministry of their own. Fortunately, I was spared the need for such pining through my possession of a mini-Ministry, the Office of Arts and Libraries.

Leading the House of Commons is a difficult task, which requires an

---

[24] For a more detailed account of the Bill and its fate, see p. 108–11.
[25] The Plowden Committee Report on Parliamentary Pay and Allowances, May 1983.

unusual combination of qualities. In one sense the Leader is in the midst of the parliamentary dog-fight more than any other Minister, but in another he is removed from it altogether. The key to the successful discharge of the duties of the office lie in the title 'Leader of the House'. The Leader is charged with the duty to get the government legislative programme through Parliament, but he represents in the last resort not the Government but the whole House and no particular part of it. His duty is to represent the view of the House in the Cabinet, whereas the responsibility for assessing party opinion rests with the Chief Whip.

It is a testing and often difficult position. The Leader of the House is caught between a number of powerful forces. Most Prime Ministers take a keen interest in parliamentary proceedings, and the present Prime Minister is no exception. This can cause complications. Ministers can be difficult and devious. Their primary aim is to get their own Bills through, irrespective of the effect this may have on the Government's legislative programme as a whole. On occasions I found they were prepared, in pursuit of their own aims, to go behind the back of the Leader and to press their case directly with the Prime Minister. Such activities cause trouble, and I certainly suffered from it. I believe that the only way in which the system can work satisfactorily is for the Prime Minister habitually to back the judgement of the Leader of the House except in the most unusual circumstances.

Another problem that the Leader of the House has to cope with is the tendency of the Cabinet to become remote from Parliament. Members of Parliament are sometimes regarded by Cabinet Ministers as pestilential obstructors. There is also a tendency for those in office to regard those who are not as a somewhat inferior breed. At one point I grew so exasperated by these attitudes that I shocked my Cabinet colleagues with an outburst. 'What,' I asked rhetorically, 'are all of us anyhow but a set of jumped-up Members of Parliament? We all came from the backbenches and in due course, no doubt, we will have to go back to them and be glad to do so.' The Prime Minister and the Cabinet are executives, but they tend to forget that they are executives with a difference who move and breathe and have their being in the hot-house atmosphere of the House of Commons.

The Leader of the House often has to carry the can for his colleagues. When something goes wrong, the one Minister whom Members can get at straight away is the Leader. On occasions he has to take the abuse for decisions of which he does not approve. Well, that is politics. The oddest situation I was to find myself in was over the clash that occurred between the Archbishop of Canterbury's enthronement at Canterbury Cathedral and the opening of the Chancellor's annual Budget, which were both fixed for the same day, 25 March 1980. I was the only member of the Cabinet to protest about this and to point out that it would create a politically untenable position. The piquancy of the situation was increased by the fact that I was not a member of the Church of England but a Roman Catholic. My objections, however, were brushed aside, and I was obliged to announce the Budget date to a House whose immediate reaction was hostile. I was blamed for a decision against which I had been the only person to protest! The Cabinet then had to give way. The Budget was shifted to 26 March and the majority of the Cabinet, led by the Prime Minister and including myself, attended the ceremony at Canterbury Cathedral. The Archbishop, Dr Runcie, preached a notably 'wet' sermon, which struck at the heart of many of the Government's assumptions, but the Prime Minister sat through it stoically and unflinchingly, registering no emotion.

In practice no Leader can get his legislative programme through without the acquiescence of the House. The House of Commons works by consent, and agreement between the usual channels—namely, the offices of the Chief Whips of the Government and the Opposition—is essential if the machine is to work. When consent and consensus in the House of Commons break down, as they did over the question of Ireland in the years before the outbreak of the First World War, the system seizes up and anarchy threatens. I was particularly aware of this, not only on constitutional grounds but also on the practical one that I had to pilot through the House the heaviest and most overloaded legislative programme since the war. An inexperienced Cabinet legislative committee, which included myself, although unusually I did not preside over it, had allowed this to happen and some Ministers were notoriously late in bringing their Bills forward. However, all went well, and at the conclusion of the first marathon parliamentary session in August 1980, the Prime Minister paid a generous tribute to myself and the Chief Whip for our efforts.

It was the legislative programme that most concerned the Prime Minister, but what I cared for was the reform of the procedures of the House and the rendering of the Commons into a more effective instrument to check and control the executive. I was always aware that when the economic questions that bulk so large in contemporary consciousness have been forgotten and the passions which they aroused have been consigned to the bound volumes of Hansard—than which there can be no greater oblivion—the reforms I was able to introduce would remain alive, effective and influential.

The Speaker, Mr George Thomas, made the same point, together with a too flattering reference to myself, in his Hansard Society lecture, 'The Changing Face of the Parliamentary Democracy', transmitted on BBC Television on Monday, 17 May 1982.

The setting up of these select committees [declared the Speaker] has proved to be a giant step forward in bringing back to the Commons a power and authority that it had lost. These reforms were rightly hailed in the debate that initiated them as a step that would alter the relations between the executive and the House of Commons and go a fair way towards redressing the balance of power. The Leader of the House at the time was Mr Norman St John-Stevas who, in my judgement, will rank as one of the greatest parliamentary reformers in this century because he fought to bring power back to the Commons through these select committees.

THE ARTS

Arts Minister and Ministry

The post of Arts Minister is not the most important in the British Government. Perhaps that is why I have established a record as the only person to have held it twice—first under Mr Heath for a brief period from December 1973 to February 1974 and again under Mrs Thatcher from 1979 to 1981. In fact, my political connection with the arts had begun earlier. When I joined the Government in 1972 I was *de facto* spokesman for the arts in the Commons, since the Arts Minister, Lord Eccles, was in the Lords. My maiden ministerial speech was made on a Bill increasing the amount of money available to the National Theatre. The total expenditure on the Theatre authorized by the Bill was £5,700,000, an increase of just under £2 million on the previously authorized figure of £3,750,000. This was money from central government. The Greater London Council (GLC) provided the site and also gave the Theatre generous financial support.[26]

From 1974 to 1979 I was Opposition spokesman on the arts. Thus I have devoted nearly a decade to the consideration and working out of their official role. The Arts Minister may not have the most central role in Government, but he certainly has the most enjoyable one. When I first became Arts Minister I used to reflect on my good fortune in being paid to do in government time what I had previously had to struggle to do in my own. At the same time I came to the conclusion after my two periods of office that intrinsically there is not enough to do for a Minister in the job itself unless he is prepared to play a creative role. I spent a considerable

---

[26] I concluded my speech by saying: 'I suppose that in a sense this is a minor Bill. It is a little byway, whereas the main road of politics is filled with the clash of armies over prices and income and inflation. It is true that those are important issues. I think, however, that future generations may well not even discuss some of the issues which to us as contemporaries seem so important. Perhaps they will be more affected by our modest little Bill and modest conclave this evening, and the building that will arise out of it as a permanent embellishment on the London scene, than anything that is likely to emerge from the world of telegrams and anger which dominate our discussions so often and to which we this evening are a mere modest footnote.' Hansard, 9 November 1972, vol. 845, col. 1343.

amount of my time thinking up new initiatives for the arts and my office of Arts and Libraries.

The difficulty facing any arts Minister is not so much a political as a cultural one. The arts are not taken seriously by the majority in Britain. They are considered either frivolous, or irrelevant, or corrupting, or in some way effeminate, and sometimes they are looked on as if they were all of these at the same time. I recall the words of Robert Hitchins in his novel *The Green Carnation*: 'They dislike poetry and are good at cricket. That is what the English consider virtue in boys.'[27]

Things are different in France, still the home of the most civilized (if the most maddening) people in the world. I often reflect on how much that is good in British culture derives from France in general and from the Norman conquest in particular. From the artistic point of view, British life looks remarkably like a Shakespearian play with a Norman main theme and an Anglo-Saxon sub-plot. In France, whatever the nomenclature, the Arts Ministry remains one of the most prestigious and important in the Government. The exact opposite is true in Britain. A Ministry of the Arts does not exist, though one had a brief life as the independent office of Arts and Libraries from 1979 to 1981, with its own staff and, most important of all, its own accounting officer and was represented directly in the Cabinet. With my resignation it became once again an appendage of the Department of Education and Science, a poor relation without independent means or life of its own, and after the 1983 election was placed in a similar position in the Privy Council, where it is linked with the junior Minister responsible for the Civil Service.

When I became Minister for the Arts for the first time on 2 December 1973 the arts had their own building in Belgrave Square. This was thanks to the foresight of Lord Eccles, who had acquired the building when he was appointed to the post by Mr Heath and had reigned there in an independent and vice-regal manner as Arts Minister, a position he combined with the prestigious but sinecure office of Paymaster General. There was no Arts Ministry; Lord Eccles was, in fact, an intrinsic part of the DES, with no separate Permanent Secretary or accounting officer. Yet geography is more important than history. A separate building and the considerable distance between Belgrave Square and Waterloo Road conferred a *de facto* independence on the whole operation. This was not to the liking of the civil servants in the DES. When I was appointed Minister by Mr Heath a determined effort was made by the then Permanent Secretary to move me and my staff back into the DES building. I resisted this strongly and so, to his credit, did my successor, Mr Hugh Jenkins.

---

[27] The book was originally published anonymously by William Heinemann in 1894 and reprinted in the same year with the author's name attached. After the trial of Oscar Wilde it was withdrawn and republished in 1949 by the Unicorn Press. It is an amusing skit on the friendship between Oscar Wilde and Lord Alfred Douglas.

Alas, Lord Donaldson, Mr Callaghan's nominee as Arts Minister, gave in to the pressure and went back into the DES, where the office languished.

When I was appointed Chancellor of the Duchy of Lancaster and Minister for the Arts by Mrs Thatcher, the first question I asked her was whether they would be attached to me or the DES. 'You, Norman,' she replied. 'Take them with you', and I did. The independence was still not to the liking of the DES, and a sharp struggle ensued over the status of the new office for Arts and Libraries. I was offered a Deputy Secretary whom I would have to share with the science component of the DES. He would have been head of both branches. I resisted this plan vigorously. I felt it essential that we should have a head of the office who would not be part of the DES and who would devote his whole time to the arts. Sir Ian Bancroft, then head of the Civil Service, was adamant that the office would not justify a separate Deputy Secretary, so I trumped his ace by saying I would, in fact, accept an Under-Secretary as head of the office, provided this was his exclusive function. Thus I got a Civil Service head of my own.

I built up my staff swiftly, the first appointment I made being that of Mary Giles as the head of my private office for the arts.[28] She had worked for me in my first incarnation and had served other Ministers devotedly and well. Her name was respected throughout the arts world. At the time that I assumed the arts portfolio civil servants were being subjected to a campaign against them promoted by the *Daily Telegraph*, but her appointment reassured the critics. I also got my old chauffeur Brian Wood, back again. A Minister's chauffeur is a person of much greater importance than the title indicates. A Minister spends a great deal of time with his driver who, in our case at any rate, was treated as an intrinsic part of the private office. There was some resistance to his appointment too, since it was pointed out to me that I was a Cabinet Minister and that Mr Wood was still a fairly junior driver. This gave me my opening, and I asked the rhetorical question: what is the point of being a Cabinet Minister if you cannot have your own driver? Furthermore, I threatened, if I could not have Brian Wood, I would have no one and would walk to my office every morning with my boxes. The horrific spectacle of Cabinet papers being scattered across St James's Park was sufficient to clinch the deal, and Brian returned. I was also extremely fortunate in being able to appoint Chris Patten as my Parliamentary Private Secretary. There was resistance here too, because Mr Patten had just been elected to Parliament, and it was the policy of the Prime Minister that new Members should not be appointed to such positions. I therefore waited until the end of October, when it could no longer be said that Chris was inexperienced, and he was then appointed. He proved a first-class assistant. Of the whole of the 1979

---

[28] The private office was both loyal and efficient. They gave me a splendid dinner at the Garrick after my demise. I miss them all very much.

intake of members, he is the most outstanding, combining a lucid intelligence with an extraordinary capacity for getting on with people. Furthermore, his intelligence is matched only by his integrity. Despite these outstanding gifts, he has—like the late John Mackintosh, the outstanding Labour MP of *his* generation—not found great favour with his party establishment. However, after the general election of 1983 he was appointed Under-Secretary in the Northern Ireland Office, and I am sure that this will mark the beginning of a distinguished political career.

So far, I thought to myself, so good. But the next stage of the struggle had a less satisfactory resolution. I wished to get back some independent premises of my own, and I combed Whitehall and elsewhere to find somewhere suitable. My efforts failed, since new premises were ruled out on grounds of expense. Mindful, however, of Lord Eccles's experience, I did not give up the idea but hoped at a later date to be able to realize it. The fledgling Arts Ministry would be established on a temporary basis, but I calculated that after five years it would have become an accepted part of the political and Whitehall scene. Alas, these expectations were not to be fulfilled.

I have come to the conclusion that if the arts are to have the recognized place in our society, which they deserve, a full Ministry of the Arts is essential. The present situation derives from a typical Wilsonian compromise. The title of 'Minister for the Arts' exists, but there is no actual Ministry. The shadow has been obtained but the substance remains elusive. The subjects for which the Arts Minister is responsible at the moment are not sufficient to justify a seat in the Cabinet, yet that too is essential if the arts interests are to bring their influence to bear directly and effectively upon government. I therefore welcome the suggestion put forward by the House of Commons Education Science and Arts Committee in their report of October 1982 that a new Ministry should be set up with responsibility for the arts, libraries, films and broadcasting, Britain's heritage and tourism.[29]

My Hundred Days as Arts Minister

When I was appointed Minister for the Arts by Mr Heath on 30 November 1973, it came as a pleasant surprise. A few weeks earlier I had had a clash with No. 10 over my appearing on a television programme to debate the future of the monarchy with Mr Willie Hamilton. No. 10's press office had advised against my taking part, but I had been determined to defend the Queen and had appeared. I was sent a sharp rebuke in my box that weekend by Mr Heath's Private Secretary. A little later I met the Prime Minister in the lobby and said to him, 'I hope all that disagreement about

[29] See report: *Public and Private Funding of the Arts*, 18 October 1982, pp. 49–1.

the monarchy programme is water under the bridge.' Mr Heath gave a typically astringent reply: 'No, not water under the bridge, promotion down the drain.' I found this a dispiriting remark, but Mr Heath's bark is invariably worse than his bite, and he did in fact promote me shortly afterwards. Another surprise was his words to me in the drawing-room of No. 10, when he offered me the position saying, 'You are a communicator. We have got a good arts policy but we have not got the credit for it. I want you to get it for us.' This was a broad brief but one I felt I could discharge. Mr Heath was probably, of all our Prime Ministers, the one most interested in the arts. I think he regarded them as an important counter-point of relief to his political duties. Accordingly, during my tenure of office I kept him fully in touch with what was going on.

Lord Eccles was a far-sighted Minister for the Arts. His ideas were always interesting and stimulating and often right. He had, however, aroused considerable hostility in an arts world always ready to take offence and full of *amour propre* or rather *amour impropre*. In addition, the long-running dispute over museum charges had soured his relationships with many. The proposal to introduce museum charges had been included in the Conservative manifesto of 1970. Three years later they still had not been introduced, and this task fell upon me as one of my first duties. Theoretically the arguments for museum charges had some appeal. It was, after all, common continental practice, and I took Lord Eccles's point that people tend to value only what they pay for. However, the opposition to the scheme had been so great and it would have raised so little money (a mere £1 million) that I had come to the conclusion that the game really was not worth the candle. As soon as I was appointed I resolved that I would get rid of this venomous reservoir which was poisoning relations between the Government and the arts world.

My difficulty was that I could not wholly repudiate the policy of my predecessor, but had that not been offensive to him, I would have been quite happy to do so. A revolution was not possible, but a reformation was. I at once tackled the Treasury, which, as usual, was not anxious to surrender a penny, but we eventually came to an agreement. First, the museums were to be allowed to keep the proceeds of the charges and to devote them to acquisitions if they so wished. There would be no corresponding reduction in the arts grant. Second, it was agreed that they should have a free day on which the public would be admitted without paying. Third, I was able to tell the trustees that old-age pensioners would be allowed in free of charge as well as organized parties of schoolchildren and students. I was also anxious to get free entry for the disabled, but for some recondite reason the Treasury was strongly opposed to this further concession. On the day before I was to announce the new arrangements I set off to see the Chief Secretary to the Treasury, Mr Patrick Jenkin, in order to try to persuade him to change his mind. However, I had forgotten the state visit of the Prime Minister of the Congo on that day, and the streets between Belgrave Square and Whitehall were so choked with traffic that I had to turn back. I did what I could on the telephone, but my blandishments were to no avail. However, I told the museum and gallery directors that if they put on their notice boards in the smallest print that the disabled could come in for nothing, I was notoriously short-sighted and would be unable, in all probability, to decipher the message.

Remembering the Prime Minister's exhortation to put our case over to the public, I told my advisers in the arts office that I intended to hold a press conference. This caused consternation. I was informed, to my surprise, that the Office of Arts and Libraries had never contaminated itself by such activity. Indeed, the atmosphere in Belgrave Square when I arrived was rather like that of a fortress under a state of siege. Occasionally a journalist would get through the defences, but that was like an arrow coming over the battlements. On my first day one rang up. I was informed of this by my press officer. 'Put him on to me at once,' I cried. 'Put him on to you, Minister?' came the horrified response. 'Yes,' I said, 'and do it quickly before he rings off.' The press conference was reluctantly agreed to. Gloomily it was forecast that it would do us no good and that we would be pilloried once again. I countered this by saying that we would lose nothing by trying. If it was a success, we would have gained something, and if the reverse, we would know not to put one on again. Foiled by this argument, the resisting civil servants fell back on a refusal to issue any press release which the journalists could carry away with them. I knew from my own experience in the press gallery that journalists like to have something to refer to. On the morning of the press conference I found that nothing had been prepared; after a major row, pen was finally put to paper. On 11 December 1973 history was made, and the Arts Office held its first press conference, which was a triumphant success. We got extensive and favourable coverage for the changes the following day.

As soon as the museum charges issue was out of the way, I turned to another thorny problem which had been causing friction, this time between the Arts Office and authors, namely public lending right (PLR). I had been interested in the subject since the campaign was first started many years ago by my friend, A. P. Herbert. Lord Eccles, backed by his civil servants, was adamantly opposed to a lending right but was prepared to concede a purchase right, by which libraries would pay an extra royalty to authors for any books they acquired. This would have been a once-and-for-all payment. The Society of Authors was willing to go along with this, if unenthusiastically, but it was ferociously opposed by the Writers Action Group led by Miss Brigid Brophy and Miss Maureen Duffy. To the chagrin of my civil servants, I resolved to call in another of their *bêtes noires*, Lord Goodman, to help promote concord. I felt that he had just the catalytic qualities needed to bring about an agreement, and I was proved right.

Meeting after meeting took place between the authors' representatives, Lord Goodman and myself. To begin with they were frigid, but the atmosphere gradually improved. Miss Brophy's visage was particularly stony; no flicker of emotion passed over her dedicated features save a faint sign of pleasure when sandwiches were brought in. Noticing this, I pressed the bell and ensured a continuous flow of these ameliorating objects. Agreement was finally reached but not without difficulty. I was able to propose that a Bill should be introduced containing two propositions, one for a purchase right as the preferred solution and, in second place, a lending right. This did not appeal to Mesdames Brophy and Duffy, but Lord Goodman saved the day by suggesting that these alternatives should be put on an equal basis. I agreed to this, and so a concordat was reached. Lord Goodman later wrote me a charming letter: 'In this matter you have achieved in the course of a few weeks more than your predecessors achieved in a decade. My warmest congratulations and thanks.' On 29 January I gained grudging and provisional Treasury approval, and on 1 February the matter went before the Home Affairs Committee of the Cabinet. Throughout I was strongly supported by my Secretary of State, Mrs Thatcher. The Treasury, however, was still being difficult, but Margaret effectively disposed of their representative, the Financial Secretary, Terence Higgins, before the discussions had even commenced. Mr Higgins is of somewhat forbidding visage and, seeing him hovering outside the door, she gave him one of her looks and said: 'Terence, why do you *always* look so miserable?' The unfortunate Mr Higgins never fully recovered from this observation, and the authors were the beneficiaries. The Cabinet approved my proposals for the Bill, including a vital provision that the right should be financed from central government sources. If the money had come from local government, local library authorities would simply have reduced their purchase of books and authors would have been no better off. So PLR was through, but the day after the final agreement had been reached, Thursday 7 February, the general election was announced. The project went into limbo.

I recall clearly those last hectic days of Mr Heath's Government. Just before the election decision was taken, the American Ambassador and his wife, Walter and Lee Annenberg, gave a dinner party for the Prime Minister at Winfield House, at which I was present. Initially, along with Mrs Thatcher, I had been opposed to an early election, but we had come around to accepting its inevitability. At the Annenbergs' dinner I mentioned to Lord Carrington that I had changed my mind, and he urged me to inform Mr Heath. Lord Carrington had been in the van of those wanting an early election. The Home Secretary, Mr Whitelaw, was also present at the dinner, and I put to him a question which was never satisfactorily answered: what difference will it make if we do have a general election? After all, we already have a viable working majority. Mr

Whitelaw replied: 'We'll be in a different ball game.' And so we were—or, rather, we were out of the ball game altogether. Parliament was sitting the day after the general election was announced, and I went into the House on parliamentary business. So swiftly had events moved that by the time I got there in the early afternoon dissolution had already taken place. I passed the Prime Minister in New Palace Yard, and with disturbing intensity the thought came into my mind, *You will never see him as Prime Minister again*. Hardly had I expelled this dismal intruder when Brutus' words to Cassius came clattering in on its heels:

> There is a tide in the affairs of men,
> Which, taken at the flood, leads on to fortune;
> Omitted, all the voyage of their life
> Is bound in shallows and in miseries.

Meanwhile the public lending right saga was not yet over. The election manifesto was being hastily drafted and redrafted, and I was determined to get a commitment to PLR included. Thanks to the good offices of Mr Nigel Lawson, who was charged with drawing up the manifesto, authority was obtained to insert it. On Saturday, 9 February, I received a telephone call from an apologetic Mr Lawson, who told me that the manifesto had been typed quickly, so quickly in fact that the typist had left out the passage on PLR. Apparently it had been added at the bottom of the relevant page and she had simply overlooked it. The manifesto had gone to the printer and it was too late to do anything about it. I was temporarily dismayed, but in a crisis it is no good repining. The important thing is to find a means of extrication. On the Sunday, therefore, I took round a note to Mr Heath at No. 10 Downing Street explaining what had happened and asking him to insert a pledge about PLR into his first election speech on the following day. He agreed and was as good as his word.

During my period of office I was determined to do what I could to show that the arts were not in an ivory tower but of concern to society as a whole. I supported Joan Littlewood strongly in her dramatic efforts at the Theatre Royal in Stratford and attempted to get her a grant from the Department of the Environment. At the end of January, I paid a visit to the Theatre and was impressed by what I saw. The Theatre was a bastion of community in an area which had been devastated by slum clearance and the erection of tower blocks. With the same aim in mind, earlier that month, to the surprise of my officials, I had accepted an invitation to present a gold disc to Emerson, Lake and Palmer, the first time an Arts Minister had taken part in a rock function. At this time I also met Liberace on a television programme and, reflecting on how much he had done to popularize good music, I invited him to call at the Office of Arts and Libraries at Belgrave Square. It was the same impulse to relate the arts to as many people as possible that led me to agree to sponsor a party for a group of pop stars at the House of Commons in 1980 to celebrate their achievements in selling their discs. Quite apart from their contribution to music, they had also benefited the country economically. Some doubts were expressed as to how they would conduct themselves, but in fact they behaved impeccably and departed quietly when the party ended at 10.00 p.m. None of them had ever been in the House of Commons before, and they were delighted to have been asked.[30] I also gave a modest party in the same year, at the Privy Council, for Woody Herman, Muddy Waters and a number of other jazz musicians. They enjoyed the party and it was wholly decorous, but I can still see the look of surprise on the face of the Privy Council doorman as they marched up the stairs.

Polling for the election took place on Thursday, 28 February 1974, and by the following day it was clear that although we had emerged as the largest party, we lacked an overall majority. I was strongly in favour of a coalition with the Liberals to keep the Labour Party out, and I still believe that if the project had been pursued with a sense of urgency, it could have been carried through. It was rumoured in the press that I had been the intermediary between Mr Heath and Mr Thorpe. They met finally on Sunday, 3 March, but the meeting was neither constructive nor cordial, and by the following day the negotiations had broken down altogether. Monday, 4 March, was a dreadful day, with Mr Heath still at No. 10 and Downing Street filled with rent-a-crowd demonstrators crying, 'Heath Out!' As Mr Heath left for the Palace he turned and said with dignity, 'You don't have to shout.' There was one brave lady, whom I greatly admired, who was conducting a counter-demonstration and shouting in a lone but loud voice, 'Heath In!' The Prime Minister tendered his resignation to the Queen, and the Conservative Government of 1970 was at an end.

Earlier in the day I had left Belgrave Square to attend the birthday party of Sylva Stewart Watson at the Haymarket Theatre, of which she was licensee. As we came out of the door, a parcel was delivered. I guessed

---

[30] Unfortunately, a rumour started that either I had sat in the Speaker's Chair or had placed Elton John in it. This was a complete fabrication, but it was reported in some of the popular press. I issued a denial but the canard reappears from time to time.

Important misstatements of fact should be corrected because they pass into the files of press cuttings and can pursue one ever afterwards. Years ago, in the early 1960s when I was looking for a seat, an article about me appeared in *Town* magazine, then owned by Mr Michael Heseltine, which stated: 'After various disappointments with Conservative Central Office, he was under instructions to join the Labour Party but was found even by Mr Roy Jenkins to be insufficiently working-class.' This had its amusing side, but it was potentially damaging to me, since I was at that time seeking nomination for a Conservative constituency. I insisted on the publication of an apology and a retraction. Two years after this I was adopted at Chelmsford as prospective Conservative candidate. At a later date, discussing the matter of press corrections with my agent, Mr Harry Liddell, I recounted the story of my clash with *Town*. He then told me that on the day of my adoption meeting, as we were making our way to the platform, somebody in the audience had pressed a copy of that cutting from *Town* into his hand. I asked him what he did with it. He said he threw it in the wastepaper basket. With a less sagacious or a less trusting agent I might have been in trouble.

intuitively what it contained. I stood on the doorstep, tore off the wrapping paper, and revealed the brass plate which I had ordered for the front door, which bore upon it the legend 'Minister for the Arts'. During the party news came of Mr Heath's resignation, and I did not return to Belgrave Square again. The following day a somewhat grisly gathering brought this distressing period to an end. Lady Hartwell had arranged a dinner party for Mr Heath before the election, to which she had kindly invited me. 'We will hold it', she said, 'in any event'—but of course she had never expected the event that did in fact occur. It was more like a wake than a celebration; everyone was depressed but trying not to show it. Mr Heath rose to leave early, and I gave full marks to Lady Hartwell for her farewell remark. She said, 'You are quite right to go home early, Ted, because you must be very tired, although you don't look it.' In fact, he looked exhausted. I could think of nothing to say. I tried to shake him by the hand, but he would not have this. 'Members of Parliament don't shake hands,' he said, sadly and correctly, and was gone.

Two other incidents from this period remain in my mind. On Wednesday, 6 March, I took leave of the Queen. I did not have my usual driver, and when I came out from the Palace both the driver and car were gone. *Sic transit gloria mundi.*[31] The other incident concerns Mr Enoch Powell, with whom I appeared on *Any Questions* that Friday, at Newport. We were discussing the election, and when I remarked that he had not fought the election himself he exploded, saying, 'Fought it? I *won* it.' He added that it was still his ambition to lead the Tory Party. I replied, 'I see that there are worse things than losing an election.'

The Arts in Opposition

So it was back to the wilderness again and without political office of any kind. I was not even shadow spokesman on the Arts, a post which I would have liked, but which even in my most sanguine moments I could not regard as one of crucial political significance. On 3 May 1974 I was offered this position by Mr Heath and accepted it with the proviso that I would be free to speak on other subjects. This was agreed, and I held the post for the next five years. I used them to do two things: first, to formulate and restate Conservative policy on the arts; second, to build on the goodwill I had been able to create in office and to establish a close connection between the Conservative Party and the arts world, which had not existed in the past.

---

[31] Nothing is so ex as an ex-Minister, and one's trappings are soon stripped away. I recall Harold Macmillan's story that when he was lying in bed in hospital after his resignation as Prime Minister in 1963, he was awoken from slumber by the sound of a gentleman taking away his red scrambler telephone. The custom of ejecting Prime Ministers from No. 10 on the day of their resignation seems, fortunately, to have been discontinued. It originally had a moral but had degenerated into an undignified circus.

With this in mind we held a series of discussions, meetings, parties and luncheons at my house in Montpelier Square, all of which were well received.

Some highlights of those years still stand out. At a dinner of the Performing Rights Society on 16 May 1974, I was able to lay once and for all the ghost of the old museum charges controversy by making it plain that a future Conservative Government would not reintroduce the charges, which in the mean time had been wholly abolished by Labour. I was also able to keep party support for my beloved public lending right in spite of the efforts of a vociferous minority to secure its abandonment. In November 1976 the Labour Government's Bill to set up a public lending right passed its final stages in the Commons, and I made an attempt to get reference books included. Contributors to reference books were discriminated against by being ignored in the Bill. I realized that there were technical difficulties in the way of rewarding them, but I felt it was a case of simple justice. Unlike writers of fiction, they lacked any organized lobby agitating on their behalf, and the proposal came to nothing.

Two conferences in this period of opposition were of major importance for our arts policy. The first was that of the Historic Houses Association, which took place at the Festival Hall on 29 November 1978. I had been working on our heritage policy for nearly two years in co-operation with Mr Michael Heseltine and with the support of Mrs Thatcher. Preserving our heritage was a matter on which she felt strongly. At the Historic Houses meeting I was able to set out a new Conservative policy which met virtually all the requests of the heritage world. I stressed the intention of the future Government to reduce income tax, which would be of considerable help to the owners of smaller historic buildings such as manor houses, rectories and terraced houses in towns. I promised that special 'listed building allowances' would be built into the tax system to enable the owners to spend money on approved works. For the great houses more drastic action was needed. Owners, I pledged, would be able to designate capital assets, such as estates, to produce income to support their house and its contents, and these assets would be exempt from capital taxes. I suggested that the Historic Buildings Council could police the system and that if it were being abused to the owners' benefit, tax penalties could be imposed. A further measure on which I promised action was that, subject to safeguards, losses on the professional opening of houses should be allowed by statute to be set off, for tax purposes, against the heritage owners' other income. Art objects and pictures surrendered in lieu of tax should be allowed to stay in houses with which they had special connections. Finally, I dealt with the question of the setting up of a National Heritage Fund and announced that such a fund would be set up by a Conservative Government. It would act as a contingency fund to assist, with grants or loans, non-profit-making organizations seeking to preserve exceptional examples of the national heritage, such as buildings, landscapes or works of art and would itself have powers to make acquisitions. These proposals were well received, and they have formed the basis of the Conservatives' heritage policy when in government.

The other significant conference was that held on the arts at St John's, Smith Square, on 19 July 1978. I organized this on behalf of the Conservative Party, and it was attended by over three hundred men and women active in the arts world, probably the most representative conference on the arts in Britain ever to have been held. Mrs Thatcher attended and gave words of encouragement. The conference split up in the afternoon into five seminars. These came forward with a number of constructive suggestions, which we used in our policy statement. At the opening of the conference I sketched out our views on the relationship between politics and the arts:

> Political parties do not give the future of the arts a prominent place in their programmes. I do not want the arts to be a party political issue— nothing could be worse—but I do want them to be a political issue in the sense that at the coming election people all over the country will have the opportunity of insisting that the arts should have a higher priority in social and political programmes than they have had in the past, and put the political parties on their mettle as to what they will do to promote the arts. We look to politicians not to dominate and control the arts but to create a stable framework within which public and private patronage can flourish.

Meanwhile our work on restating Conservative arts policy had continued. On 25 November 1977 I gave the Richmond Lecture at Downing College, Cambridge, entitled: 'The Arts, the Brightest Jewel in our Crown'. While this was not an official party policy statement, it helped to create a political climate favourable to the arts.[32] In 1977 too I appointed nine study groups to look at various aspects of the arts. Their report was published in September 1978: *The Arts: the Way Forward*. We advanced the case for the arts having a direct voice in the Cabinet and a series of policy proposals, many of which were implemented when we took office the following year.

Arts Minister Again

My mother used to say to me that I would always have a second chance in life, and I thought of her words on that bright May morning, 5 May 1979,

[32] The lecture was fully reported: see *The Times*, Saturday, 26 November 1977. The Richmond Lecture became famous when it was given by C. P. Snow, who outlined his views on the two cultures in Britain.

when Mrs Thatcher appointed me Arts Minister once again. It was generous and thoughtful of her to do so, since it was not necessary, but she knew of my devotion to the arts. Having appointed me Leader of the House of Commons and Chancellor of the Duchy of Lancaster, she said: 'And, of course, Norman you will want to have the arts.' I did indeed, but they could have turned out to be a poisoned chalice. The problem immediately facing me was that great expectations had been aroused by my activities in Opposition. On Tuesday, 15 May, of that year I spoke at the Royal Academy Banquet on behalf of the Government, replying to the toast proposed to the arts. I took the opportunity to outline the principles of the policy I intended to follow.

> The Minister for the Arts [I said] has three functions. First, he must see that the arts are adequately financed from both public and private sources. There is no doubt, then, that public patronage and support for the arts is here to stay, and it is the view of the Government that there is room for increased private support. The second task of the Arts Minister is to see that the voice of the arts is heard at the highest level of the Government. I am particularly happy that for the first time the arts are represented in the Cabinet, the pre-eminent policy-making body of our parliamentary constitution. No longer will the arts have to be heard second-hand. I can promise you not that the interests of the arts will always prevail, but that at least they will always be taken into account. The third thing that I want to assure you of, and through you, the wider arts world, is that the door of the Arts Minister's office will be open to all who have a legitimate or reasonable interest to pass through it.

I stressed that a static role for the arts was not enough and that there had to be missionary endeavour as well.

> May tonight mark the opening of a new era of co-operation between government and the arts and the drawing together of all those in society who care for the preservation and creation of beauty and the advancement of the things of the spirit.[33]

Despite our election pledges there were ideologists both inside and outside the Government who wished to get rid of public support for the arts altogether, but they received no support from the Prime Minister, and I had little difficulty in beating them off. Resisting the onslaught of those who wished to reduce public expenditure on the arts proved more tricky than repelling those who wanted its abolition. I realized that the principal

---

[33] Prince Charles and Cardinal Hume both spoke on this occasion. After a moving speech about the spiritual importance of the arts the Cardinal delivered a delightful *bon mot*. He said, 'I think I may say that you have before you the three most eligible bachelors in Britain.' There was a burst of applause and laughter, which was redoubled when he went on to say, 'Ladies, may I ask you to address your letters to the other two?'

point for the existence of an Arts Minister was to get the money, and if he failed in this, nothing could be achieved. I was also aware of the political importance of the arts world and of its easy access to the media. I feared that a mood of bitterness and disillusionment might be created once again. In Cabinet I made it clear that I accepted the aim of Government policy, which was to roll back the frontiers of the state and remove it from spheres in which it was inappropriate. But I maintained that this did not apply to the vast majority of arts expenditure. Such institutions as national museums, national libraries, opera houses and the National Theatre could continue only with state support. In this argument I had the Tory tradition on my side, since while Conservatives have traditionally resisted the unnecessary dogmatic extension of state power, they have equally clearly accepted a positive role for the state in promoting the social welfare of the people. Conservatives have rarely argued for the complete removal of the state from economic and social life and for the support of unbridled capitalism.

My second line of argument was a severely practical one. The sums involved in the arts budget were so small in relation to the total of public expenditure that even the elimination of the entire budget would be only a drop in the ocean, and a scaling-down would not be noticed at all except by those in the arts world, who would be alienated and infuriated. On the other hand, by giving the arts exemption we would banish at a stroke the myth that the Conservative Party was a philistine party. Moreover, such a step would bring great prestige to the Prime Minister and the Government. As both Machiavelli and Lord Eccles knew well, power is not of much consequence without glory. I was able to deploy in my support a more down-to-earth instrument in the form of a letter which Mrs Thatcher had written, as Leader of the Opposition, to Lord Gibson, then Chairman of the Arts Council, on 14 July 1976. Lord Gibson had requested reassurance about the arts budget in the future; Mrs Thatcher had replied that because of the uncertain economic situation it was difficult to make advance commitments about specific levels of expenditure for the arts, but she had added:

> I can say, however, that I don't believe in the present economic situation it will make sense for any Government to look for candle-end economies which will yield a very small saving, whilst causing upset out of all proportion to the economies achieved. Public expenditure savings directed at the arts would come into this category and would not make any significant reduction in our borrowing requirement.

I was then well within my rights in using this argument. However, I could also be quite unscrupulous on behalf of the arts and could behave in a way which I would certainly not have done for personal advancement. After I was injured in a car crash on the M1 on 22 August 1980, when I was driven through the barrier and on to the north-bound carriageway, I limped into the Prime Minister's office to show that I was still alive and to raise three points which I wanted to be resolved in favour of the arts. I carried two, but by the time we got to the third the Prime Minister's sympathy had evaporated, and I and my argument were dismissed from the presence.

All Ministers for the Arts work closely with the Arts Council. During my tenure of office Mr Kenneth Robinson[34] was the Chairman. While he protected the independence of his position, I found him both sympathetic and reasonable, as well as a doughty champion of the arts. Between Mr Roy Shaw, the Secretary General, and myself there appeared to be a temperamental incompatibility. The constitutional theory is that it is for the Arts Council to decide how any money is spent, but unless an Arts Minister is an artistic eunuch he will have some opinions about how the money he has struggled to obtain is dispensed, and these will be made known in private. On 30 May 1979 I paid my first visit to the Arts Council and was somewhat thrown off-balance when, just before entering the room to address the entire staff, I received the message that my budget had been cut unilaterally. I had received no previous communication on this matter and had not been consulted; matters had been arranged through the Department of Education and the Secretary of State for Education, Mr Mark Carlisle. Apparently, the Treasury had not caught up with the fact that the arts were now an independent entity. This added annoyance to my distress, but it did give me a moral advantage. I protested strongly about this manner of proceeding and received an apology. It had been suggested that the arts budget should be reduced by £5 million, but I resisted this and the cut, in fact, came down to £2.6 million. This represented a 2 per cent cut-back, and the Arts Council had to bear a cut of £1 million. These were announced on 15 June. In fact, there never was a cut in anybody's art budget; there was no clawback of money for beneficiaries and no reductions. The Arts Council simply carried the sum of £1 million forward to add to its deficit. Nevertheless, Arts Council clients reacted with fury.

The system for reducing public expenditure operated in the following way. The Chancellor came before the Cabinet with a global figure and a number of suggested reductions in the budgets of the various departments. These, it soon became clear, could not be discussed in detail in Cabinet, and if there were disagreements, bilateral conversations were held with the Minister concerned and with the Treasury. I thus deployed my arguments twice over but with regard to the Treasury was in a position of weakness, since for the first time it knew it could rely on the firm backing of the Prime Minister. Her predecessors were more open to

[34] Later Sir Kenneth. I would have liked to have seen him rewarded with a peerage, but he had to be content with a knighthood after he left office.

political arguments and in practice had not proved such reliable allies. I was excellently briefed by my civil servants, and I adopted the strategy of arguing over every penny. No sum was too small to be contested.

On the whole, the results achieved were not too bad. Thus in March 1980 I was able to announce a total arts grant of £163.2 million, which represented an 18.1 per cent increase over the grant of the previous year. I allotted £70 million to the Arts Council, and it, therefore, secured an increase of 20 per cent. The grant I obtained for 1981/2 was also satisfactory—indeed, it was better than the previous year. It also helped to be able to announce it earlier, which I did on 8 December 1980. On this occasion the Arts Council grant went up to £80 million, an increase of over 14 per cent, representing an increase of 2 per cent in real terms, the first such increase for a number of years. I was able to make a grant of £1.4 million to the Crafts Council, which I was most anxious to encourage. This enabled it to acquire a new gallery as an extension to its premises in Waterloo Place. The British Film Institute came off well, with £6.4 million.

By agreement, I was able to earmark special capital grants of £1 million to the Royal Opera House, Covent Garden, and £0.5 million to the English National Opera. Despite these big increases, on 20 December 1980 the Arts Council announced cuts of £1.2 million to certain beneficiaries, and in all forty-one groups lost their grants altogether. These included the Old Vic and the National Youth Theatre. It is within the rights of the Arts Council to cut out beneficiaries even if the Council has received an increased sum of money, but in that event they must bear the responsibility. Apparently, this action had been taken in anticipation of a reduced grant from the Government, but in effect it was increased. Far from acknowledging the record grant, the Secretary General of the Arts Council, Mr Roy Shaw attempted to put the blame on the Government for the reductions. I rebutted this charge vigorously, as I was entitled to do, since I had never been consulted about the cuts. Indeed, the first I heard of them was when I took my godchildren to *Toad of Toad Hall* at the Old Vic on 19 December, only to be greeted by a prostrated management, which had just learnt that their grant was to be abolished. I felt this keenly, as I had long been a supporter of the Old Vic.[35] I was also incensed by the cutting out of the grant to the National Youth Theatre on the grounds that the Arts Council was not concerned with arts education. I read the charter differently. The National Youth Orchestra also lost its grant, and since I was a patron of the Orchestra and had been responsible for a special grant for brass band instruments which was made in 1973, I was not particularly pleased by this either. The manner of announcing the cuts, smuggling them out just before Christmas—doubtless in the hope that this would

[35] Ironically enough, I had made a reference to the theatre in my maiden ministerial speech of 9 December 1972, saying: 'The Government will show sympathetic, intelligent and informed interest in the future of that great theatre.'

lessen their impact—was also ill-judged. After I left office I was able to comment publicly on these events, and I am glad to say that they have not been repeated.[36] My only other major point of disagreement with the Arts Council was over its decision not to aid the D'Oyly Carte Company. I was a strong supporter of Gilbert and Sullivan, as their work constituted one of the few forms of folk art in Britain. The Arts Council itself appointed a committee to look into the situation, and in 1980 a report was issued criticizing the D'Oyly Carte but recommending an experimental grant of between £50,000 and £100,000 a year, which should be devoted to improving standards. The grant would be reassessed after a year's experiment. This seemed to be fair enough, since it was unreasonable to ask the D'Oyly Carte Company to raise standards when a principal reason for its being unable to do so was shortage of funds. However, the Arts Council rejected the report, and no grant was made.

I was able to put this right after I left office, thanks to the generosity and initiative of Lord Forte. He launched an appeal for a Gilbert and Sullivan Foundation in order to keep the tradition alive and contributed generously to its funds. Dame Vera Lynn accepted the position of chairman of the appeal and I served on the council. The first fruits of our efforts were seen in an excellent production of *The Mikado*, which was staged at the Sadler's Wells Theatre in the winter of 1982.[37] This production, together with the wholly commercial production of *The Pirates of Penzance* at the Theatre Royal, Drury Lane, showed that there was sufficient vitality in the Gilbert and Sullivan partnership to carry it into the remainder of this century and probably into the twenty-first.

Private Sponsorship of the Arts

The arts world had long campaigned for relief for the arts from VAT, and I would certainly have been glad to see it either reduced or abolished altogether. The Treasury, however, fearful of opening the way for a flood of claims for exemptions, has traditionally been adamant in its refusal to make any concessions. The nearest the arts came to securing relief was at the time of Mr Healey's Budget of 1978, when he seriously considered the matter and certainly personally would have liked to sanction relief, but he allowed himself to be swayed by his advisers and nothing happened. After the 1979 election I sounded out the Treasury once again; it became

---

[36] See *Sunday Times*, 8 March 1981, 'How not to Axe the Arts'. I suggested that the rules of natural justice required that bodies about to have their grants cut should have the opportunity to argue their case. Adverse decisions after this should be communicated in good time, and a right of appeal should be given to the Council as a whole. Reasons should be given for decisions taken.

[37] I found that my name had been included on the Lord High Executioner's list. *The Times* commented that this was a case of biting the hand that fed it, but I was delighted to be included!

clear that the opposition was as strong as ever. I had therefore to advise Mr Charles Wintour, then editor of the *Evening Standard* and a staunch supporter of the arts, that a campaign which the paper was contemplating would be unlikely to succeed. Newspapers do not like backing lost causes, and so the idea was abandoned. Another idea I floated within the Government was the idea of a national lottery for the arts, but there was opposition to that as well, particularly from the Lord Chancellor, and it was felt that there would be too many competing claims on the lottery proceeds.

I realized the importance of going with the grain of Government policy rather than against it. Pushing at a door which was at least half-open was likely to prove more profitable than hammering on the bars of a portcullis. I therefore concentrated my efforts on promoting private sponsorship of the arts in accordance with the Government philosophy of encouraging the private sector. The arts would gain from an expansion of private sponsorship by having not only more money but more freedom as well. Paradoxically enough, the more masters one has, the freer one is. The one-to-one relationship is in practice the most restrictive. I stressed from the beginning the principle that private sponsorship should be regarded as a supplement to state support of the arts and not as a replacement. This principle is now established and has been supported by my successor, Mr Paul Channon. I trust that Lord Gowrie will do the same.

My first step was to secure some further tax incentive for private sponsorship. In fact, money spent on the arts by firms was and is fully allowable for tax purposes, provided that it can be related to advertising or some other commercial venture. Here the problem was to draw the opportunities to the attention of firms and to establish links between potential sponsors and arts projects. Originally the tax system had enabled substantial sums to be raised from wealthy individuals for the support of the arts. Until the 1946 Budget they were able to set off donations to the arts against their income tax without limit as to level, provided that they convenanted support for seven years. As Lord Drogheda has pointed out, since the tax on the top slice of a rich person's income was levied at a rate of 97.5 per cent, the true cost to donors in the highest tax bracket of an annual donation of, for example, £1,000 was no more than £25.[38] Unfortunately, this arrangement was altered by Dr Dalton in his 1946 Budget, which provided that deductions could be made only against the standard rate of tax and not against surtax and the higher rates of taxation.[39] The Office of Arts and Libraries submitted a memorandum to the Chancellor, Sir Geoffrey Howe, urging him to return to this practice, and a modest but important start was made in his second

[38] See Lord Drogheda, *Double Harness*, London, 1978, p. 226.
[39] Had this alteration not been made, sponsorship of the arts in Britain might well have developed along the lines of the American model.

Budget of March 1980, when income tax relief was given to those contributing to the arts or to other charities against the higher rates of tax, subject to a ceiling of £3,000 a year. The potential for growth in this field is shown by the American experience. In the United States from 1955 to 1965 the level of support from private sources for the arts came to $200 million annually. Between 1965 and 1980 this figure increased spectacularly to $2.27 billion. Of course, in America private funding of the arts is primary and state support secondary. The situation is reversed in Britain, but nevertheless much more can and should be done in the private field.

From the beginning I was encouraged by the response to my efforts to gain private sponsorship. One splendid example of private support came in March 1980, when the Gulf Oil Corporation gave £250,000 to the British National Orchestra. In April of that year I was able to obtain a government grant for the Association for Business Sponsorship of the Arts (ABSA), the organization which, under its able director, Mr Luke Rittner, now Secretary General of the Arts Council, was devoting itself to raising sponsorship for arts projects from business. We also gave a grant to the Theatres Trust, which primes the pump for new commercial productions. A third recipient of a modest sum from our office was the Society of West End Theatre Managers, and this helped with the ticket booth in Leicester Square, where theatregoers can obtain tickets at half-price on the day of performances.[40] This had a highly beneficial effect on theatre attendances because, once people had set their minds on an evening or afternoon out at the theatre, they were prepared to buy tickets for another show if they could not obtain them for their first choice. Dame Anna Neagle told me that it had filled up the matinée performances of *My Fair Lady* at the Adelphi, in which she was starring.

In June 1980 I set up a formal committee of honour to preside over a campaign for increasing business sponsorship of the arts. Members included Lady Hartwell, Lord Goodman, Sir Charles Forte, Lady Spencer and Clive Jenkins. We launched a campaign with the publication of an informative booklet, *The Arts are Your Business*. Meetings of the committee were held each month and were well attended. This was partly because of interest in the subject and partly because of a series of spectacular duels between Lady Spencer and Lady Hartwell, which provided stimulus for the other members. These were of an electrifying, pyrotechnical character, and members looked forward eagerly to the next round of a battle which turned out in the end to be drawn.[41] Lectures, conferences and receptions were held in support of the campaign. One of the most

---

[40] I opened this on 4 December 1980 by buying the first ticket, for the Apollo Theatre.

[41] Lady Hartwell was a staunch supporter of the British Museum. In 1980 I was able to secure her appointment as Trustee, a post which she held with great distinction until her untimely death on 7 January 1982. She and Mrs Ian Fleming, alas also dead, were the last of the great London hostesses.

splendid of these was kindly given by the Speaker, Mr George Thomas, in his state rooms at Westminster in July 1980. Mr Thomas was an outstanding Speaker of the House of Commons, with a ready wit which endeared him not only to Members but to the public in general as well.[42]

All these activities served to increase interest in business sponsorship. In July 1981 the Philharmonia Orchestra received one of the largest donations ever made when Du Maurier agreed to provide £600,000 for the orchestra over two years. Tobacco companies have become major patrons of the arts, since they are constrained in their advertising and are on the lookout for suitable outlets. The Department of Health was concerned about my activities in this field, but I countered its objections by saying that if it was prepared to compensate the arts for any revenue loss out of its own budget, we would be happy to discourage the tobacco companies from sponsoring artistic works. I heard no more about the matter. Oil companies have been also a source of generous sponsorship for the arts. For them it is especially beneficial to be seen to be socially responsible.

I took a keen interest in the promotion of orchestral music and as often as possible attended performances by two of our outstanding orchestras, the Philharmonia and the Royal Philharmonic. London is today the musical capital of the world. A greater concentration of musical creativity and expertise is found in Britain now than in any previous period of our history. Yet there are difficult problems that have not so far been successfully tackled. Can London support four major orchestras, for example? The audiences exist for them but the finance does not, and public financial support tends to be spread rather thin. The orchestras face not only financial problems but also a shortage of rehearsal accommodation. Touring possibilities within Britain are restricted. The system by which players contract individually to play in a given orchestra may suit the performers, but does not always lead to the highest standard of performance. An inquiry into the whole question of orchestral playing, finance and management would be welcome.

One institution in which I took a particular interest as Minister was the Royal Opera House. It is extraordinary that this theatre, which suffered the indignity of being turned into a dance hall during the Second World

---

[42] I recall one occasion when a Member, on being challenged about the veracity of his facts, said indignantly, 'It's in the newspapers.' Mr Thomas replied, 'So's my horoscope.' Speaker King also had a pretty wit. Once when I raised the question of a commemorative plaque to Thomas More in Westminster Hall I pointed out to him that More was the only one of his predecessors to have been both canonized and beheaded, adding, 'In one of which precedents I hope, Mr Speaker, you will follow him.' Speaker King rose to his feet at once and said, 'I hope I have guessed the right one.' The gift of wit and humour in a Speaker is invaluable for defusing potentially explosive situations in the House of Commons. (The plaque to Thomas More was placed in Westminster Hall and unveiled at an ecumenical ceremony in which the Speaker, the Lord Chancellor, Cardinal Heenan, the Archbishop of Canterbury and the Moderator of the Free Church Federal Council took part.)

War, should have become one of the most celebrated opera houses in the world.[43] Certainly, Covent Garden has great beauty. Visually and architecturally, it is superior to such houses as La Scala in Milan, the Opera Haus in Vienna and, without doubt, the hideous new Metropolitan in New York. Yet the red plush and gilt, dazzling as they are, had long hidden appalling conditions backstage. Accordingly, the administrators of Covent Garden had launched a major capital appeal for a new building which would for the first time provide adequate rehearsal and dressing-rooms. I was able to assist them in acquiring the freehold of the site and also in raising money for their appeal. The Labour Government had promised to donate £1 million, and we honoured the promise. However, despite all the efforts of its sponsors the appeal was in danger of running into the doldrums, and Sir Claus Moser and Lord Drogheda approached me with a request for help. In May 1980 I had a meeting with the Prime Minister and the Chief Secretary to the Treasury and put the case for a further grant. I could see that the Prime Minister was receptive to the argument but was also concerned about any increase in public expenditure. The conversation started at noon; we are still talking at two o'clock. I had a luncheon engagement, but I was unable to break off the discussions or even to send a message, and I am afraid my host had to eat alone. As the conversation went on, I gradually recognized certain landmarks as they came round as if on a carousel. But it proved worthwhile, and at the end I had the £1 million which I had asked for. I presented the cheque at Covent Garden on 4 June 1980. It was a brilliant day, full of sunshine, and handing over such a splendid cheque for such a good cause made it one of the happiest of my life.

On 24 June 1980 the Prime Minister also kindly gave a reception at No. 10 in aid of the Covent Garden Appeal Fund. A number of potential donors had been invited, and I asked the Prime Minister to address the gathering. The guests were distributed in the two drawing-rooms which stand at right-angles to each other on the first floor of No. 10. The assembled company was fascinated to see the Prime Minister place a chair between the two rooms, kick off her shoes and stand on the chair to give an impromptu speech. She made a dramatic appeal for the Opera House, prefacing her remarks with the startling announcement: 'I am the rebel head of an establishment Government.' Whether because of this endearing remark or because of her speech, £400,000 was subscribed for the Opera House that evening. Another event came later in the year when an auction was held at Covent Garden for the Fund. The Prince of Wales generously donated his cello.

The most spectacular example of private sponsorship during this period

---

[43] Particularly in view of the paucity of the Arts Council grant. In 1981 the Royal Opera House was granted £8.5 million. In 1980, on the other hand, the Berlin Opera House was granted £13 million, Hamburg £11.3 million and Munich nearly £12 million.

was the offer made by Mrs Duffield, the daughter of the late Charles Clore, to provide for a Turner gallery. Turner, who died in 1851, left his collection of paintings, drawings and sketches to the nation, expressing the wish that they should all be seen under one roof. As the collection includes 300 oil paintings and 19,000 water-colours and drawings, this has presented certain difficulties. Since then the collection has been divided between the National Gallery, the Tate Gallery and the British Museum. The Turner Society had long been active in agitating that the terms of the bequest should be honoured. Early on they had approached me with the suggestion that the paintings should hang in the fine rooms at Somerset House. But after an inspection with this in mind I came to the conclusion that Somerset House was not a suitable setting. Indeed, as a result of the transfer of the Antiques Fair there in the summer of 1980, owing to a dispute at the Grosvenor House Hotel, I became convinced that what was needed was a joint exhibition of furniture and paintings. My plan was for the Courtauld collection of paintings and the Seilern collection to be exhibited there, together with a selection of furniture from the Victoria and Albert Museum. On 12 April 1983 the *Daily Telegraph* reported that this plan was about to be agreed.

On the evening of 7 December 1979 Mrs Duffield, accompanied by Lord Bullock, the Chairman of the Tate Gallery, and a bevy of officials came into my room at the House of Commons to tell me that Mrs Duffield wanted to give at least £5 million for a Turner Gallery in memory of her father. My breath was taken away by this splendid offer, which at a stroke would solve the pestilential problem with which the Turner Society had plagued me since I took office. One difficulty was that Mrs Duffield was not willing for any part of the bequest to be devoted to the running of the gallery. Since I required authorization from the Treasury that we could underwrite these costs, I was unable to accept the offer straight away, as instinctively I wanted. I was in the position of someone winning a goldfish in a raffle, when what at first sight appears an uncovenanted benefit very soon turns into a liability. It was unthinkable to me that this chance should slip through our fingers, and I did all I could to make sure that this munificent donation should be gratefully accepted. Negotiations went so well that at the end Mrs Duffield said to me, 'You have been so helpful over this matter that I think we can give you an extra £1 million.' *O si sic omnes.* James Stirling was engaged to design the gallery, and we agreed that it should be called the Clore Gallery, although it would be an integral part of the Tate. I was able to announce the acceptance of the project by the Government in May 1980, and the foundation plaque was unveiled by Queen Elizabeth the Queen Mother on 19 April 1983. The Gallery is due to open in the summer of 1985.

During this period I conceived a number of other ideas, which unfortunately have not come to fruition. In 1980 the clearing banks announced record profits, and this aroused certain jealousy and hostility. It occurred to me that much of this rancour could be countered if the banks were seen to be strongly in support of the arts. What I had in mind was that they should make a joint capital endowment of £50 million or more to set up a Clearing Banks Foundation for the arts. The capital would not be touched, but the income would be devoted to supporting arts projects. The banks as a whole would benefit and their status as the premier institutions of a capitalist society consolidated. The arts would gain because they would have access to a new and permanent source of finance. Accordingly, in July 1980 I made a tour of all the banks to see their chief executives and ended up with a visit to the Bank of England, where I was warmly received by the Governor. The other bankers were equally cordial; the most forthcoming was the Chairman of Barclays Bank, Sir Anthony Tuke. However, when it came down to the question of jointly contributing the cash, the Council of Clearing Banks became less winning and turned my project down. The difficulty was that each bank wished to continue its own particular line of support for the arts. Thus the National Westminster wanted to support the arts in the context of its community support programme; the Midland Bank was keen to reap the publicity rewards of its efforts; Lloyd's Bank preferred to concentrate its help on young people; and Barclays Bank wished to continue its support of the ballet and the D'Oyly Carte Company. I had also thought that the foundation might be a useful weapon in the banks' hands for fending off the Treasury, which was considering imposing an excess profits tax on the banks. The Treasury realized this too, and alarm was expressed at my initiative. However, it need not have worried, since the banks had not established sufficient consensus among themselves to allow the scheme to go forward, and the tax was duly imposed in 1981.

The second project in which I interested myself was connected with the Getty Museum in California. The Museum had come into £4,000 million from Paul Getty, a bequest requiring the Museum to spend the majority of the interest each year. Alarm spread throughout the arts world about the effect that a vigorous purchasing policy might have on the prices of paintings and antiques. In August 1980 I visited Los Angeles to see the Museum for myself, and after conversations with the Director I proposed that the Museum should establish an out-station at the Victoria and Albert Museum in London.[44] The Getty collection could acquire works of art, thus fulfilling the purchasing requirements of the trust. These could be kept and exhibited in London and would not therefore require export licences. Links could be established in the work of both institutions for the conservation and restoration of art objects. Repercussions of this idea

---

[44] I find the Museum both fascinating and beautiful, a folly in the form of a Roman villa, quite at home among the other Californian fantasies. Others have not been so approving.

have continued to the present day, the latest being that of establishing the out-station in Spencer House now that it is no longer to be taken over by the National Trust, but nothing has yet been done.

A final idea, which I still believe to be an excellent one, was to set up new arts awards along the lines of the Duke of Edinburgh's Awards for Industry except that they would be styled the 'Prince of Wales Awards for the Arts'. The awards would be given annually to the company or firm which produced the most imaginative and productive private scheme for arts support. Such schemes would, in practice, raise millions of pounds for the arts, and the Prince of Wales would be the right person to sponsor it. A number of members of the Royal Family take an active interest in the arts, including Queen Elizabeth the Queen Mother, Princess Margaret and Princess Michael of Kent, but the Prince of Wales is regarded by the arts world as their special patron. The suggestion was sympathetically received at Buckingham Palace, but I left office before it could be pursued, and nothing further seems to have come of it.

Private sponsorship of the arts has a bright future, but it does need vigorous promotion. Hard figures are difficult to come by, but we probably increased private sponsorship of the arts from about £3.5 million to £7 million by our campaign. By 1983 it had reached more than £12.5 million.[45] There is much future potential which could be imaginatively and effectively exploited.

Keeping Everything Going

To be Arts Minister at a time of financial stringency and an active policy of reducing public expenditure is not particularly good timing. The course I decided upon was not to lose anything but to keep everything going, even if it had to be on a reduced scale. As to new projects, I followed a similar policy of getting them off the ground and into orbit even if the blast-off had to be modest.

An early concern was to implement PLR. The Treasury would still have welcomed its killing off, but this time the *status quo* favoured me, as the Bill was, in fact, on the statute book. The point at issue was not whether, but when and how much. On 27 October 1979 I was able to allot £2 million for PLR, and on 22 February 1980 the scheme was brought into being by statutory instrument. We succeeded in reducing administrative running costs by over 50 per cent. Authors will draw a minimum of £5 a year from the fund, and a maximum of £5,000, in order to prevent any single author from scooping the pool. The first payments will be made in 1984.

The other major project which I was determined not to lose was that of the British Library. In the early 1970s I had been captivated by David

[45] See the *Daily Telegraph*, 1 June 1983.

Eccles's grand scheme for a new building in Bloomsbury which would have formed a part of a general cultural complex. But this had been dropped as a result of a lobby jointly conducted by an unholy alliance of those who wanted to make economies and those who wanted to preserve the existing run-down environment. A more modest scheme was therefore put forward for the Library to go up on a site next to St Pancras Station. Now this too was threatened. In December 1979 a campaign led by Professor Hugh Thomas and supported by authors such as Lady Antonia Fraser was launched in order to preserve the old Reading-Room. Much of this appeal was sentimental, but I was not unsympathetic to its approach. I therefore made arrangements with the British Museum authorities that when the Reading-Room became part of a new concourse, books would continue to be displayed on its shelves. The campaigners' suggestion that there should be an underground railway link between St Pancras and Bloomsbury was simply not feasible. The Treasury was adamant that all the money could not be paid over in one sum, and I therefore negotiated a scheme by which £72 million was to be made available for the Library, spread over twelve years. In December 1980 the Prime Minister announced that the building would go ahead— appropriately enough, on the occasion of the unveiling of a bust of Lord Eccles, a former Chairman of the Library Board. I exhorted the Library authorities to start the building as soon as possible, realizing that once the bricks began to be laid the project was unlikely to be set back again. The Prince of Wales laid the foundation stone on 7 December 1982.[46]

Other projects which were able to go ahead were the Photographic Museum at Bradford, the Craft Gallery in Waterloo Place, the Henry Cole Building at the Victoria and Albert and the reorganization of the Egyptian Sculpture Gallery at the British Museum. I took a keen interest in the Royal School of Needlework and suggested it should be given a grant of £25,000 to help it in its unique and valuable work. Unfortunately, this was not supported by the Office of Arts and Libraries after I had resigned, so the School never obtained the grant. I was also determined that the Theatre Museum should be saved.

A national theatre museum had been mooted since the beginning of the century. In 1924 a leap forward was made when Gabriel Enthoven left a major collection of playbills, letters and photographs to the nation. Lawrence Irving, grandson of the incomparable Henry, followed this up and presented the entire Irving archive to the projected museum. Further splendid gifts and bequests followed, and others were only waiting for a worthy home for their collections to be presented. For the time being the material found a home in Leyton House in Kensington, but this proved

---

[46] By a rather mean oversight, I was not invited to the ceremony. The Tate behaved better in relation to their plaque for the Turner Gallery!

inadequate. The museum was then to be transferred to Somerset House and administered by the staff of the Victoria and Albert Museum, but storage space was too restricted. When the market moved out of Covent Garden a reasonable substitute was found in the basement of the old flower market. I supported this expedient when I was Minister for the Arts for the first time under Mr Heath, but unfortunately the Labour Government's spending cuts of 1975 caused a further postponement, and when I took office again in 1979 nothing had been started. By 1980 I was able to give the project the green light but resigned my office before the contracts could be signed. Then came a further setback, a report published as part of a general scrutiny of the departmental museums. Sir Derek Rayner, the Prime Minister's economic guru, recommended that the whole enterprise be abandoned. I mounted a campaign to save it, and with the aid of Mr Alexander Schouvaloff, Director of the Theatre Museum and the *Evening Standard*, the museum was saved, or so I thought.

On 7 July 1983 the lease for the museum, the site of which was owned by the GLC, was due to be signed and the first instalment of £900,000 worth of building work started. That day the new Chancellor of the Exchequer, Mr Nigel Lawson, had announced another series of government expenditure cuts, and to my horror and dismay, Lord Gowrie, the new Arts Minister, at two hours' notice refused to sign the lease and consigned the whole project to limbo. Swift action was necessary. I immediately got in touch with Mr Schouvaloff, the arts spokesmen of the other parties and leading stage luminaries such as Sir John Gielgud, Sir Ralph Richardson and Dame Peggy Ashcroft. A high-powered delegation was put together, including Mr Donald Sinden, Mr Patrick Cormack, the Countess of Harewood, Mr Andrew Faulds, Mr Hugh Leggat and myself, which was received by Lord Gowrie on 13 July. That day *The Times* published a letter from me setting out the history of the unhappy matter, stressing the breach of faith that had taken place, especially with those who had left or donated their collections on condition that they were displayed in an independent museum. What difference, I asked, could a cut of £1 million make in a public expenditure total running at about £120,000 million a year? The delegation was courteous but firm: I have never known one put on a better show of determination and fury. Lord Gowrie was clearly shaken. The London *Standard* once again took up our case, and we received sympathetic support even in the *Daily Telegraph*. As a result there was another about-face, and after questions raised by me in the Commons on Monday, 18 July, and further campaigning in the press and through the media, the Arts Minister announced on 30 July that the museum was to go ahead after all. The GLC generously offered to modify the terms of the lease; an anonymous donor came forward with a grant of £250,000; and the Minister undertook to sign the lease without further delay.[47] So

[47] See *Daily Telegraph*, 1 August 1983.

the Theatre Museum has been saved once again or so we hope. *Videbimus.*

The National Heritage

I shared responsibility for protecting the national heritage with Mr Michael Heseltine, then Secretary of State for the Environment, whom I always found sympathetic and helpful in the battle against the philistines. It was agreed that I should take the lead over the national heritage fund, and my position as Leader of the House helped to obtain legislative priority for the Bill. It came before the House of Commons on 3 December 1979 and was agreed to without a division. The Bill set up the fund with an initial endowment of £15.5 million. Independent trustees were to be appointed jointly by myself and the Secretary of State for the Environment but would be subject to the Prime Minister's approval. The fund was to be topped up annually with subsidies of £5.5 million each year. This was a modest sum, but the important thing was to get the project on to the statute book. I was convinced that extra money would become available for the fund once it had been started, and my hopes have been fulfilled. As I said in the debate: 'Great oaks from little acorns grow. I believe that in the future the branches of this tree will spread over the heritage ever more widely, protecting it from the economic storms and changes which make it especially vulnerable.' The Act passed into law when it received the royal assent on 21 March 1980.

When the Bill went to the House of Lords it was amended so that the Prime Minister made the appointments personally. In fact, her influence was already decisive, but I did not welcome the initiative passing to the officials at No. 10, who would not be as familiar with the situation as myself and Mr Heseltine and who would be open to lobbying of one kind or another. Intense speculation raged in the press about who would be appointed chairman. Names like those of Lord Charteris and Lady Spencer were bandied around. Lady Spencer was strongly opposed, but Lord Charteris's appointment was more favourably assessed in the arts world. On Thursday, 6 March, I dashed from the Cabinet to St Martin-in-the-Fields for the memorial service for Cecil Beaton and, diving into a pew, found myself next to Lord Charteris. I told him I had read in the papers that he was going to be appointed chairman of the Heritage Fund. 'Nobody has asked me,' he replied. 'Well,' I said, 'come round to the Office of Arts and Libraries next week and I will see what I can do.' The Prime Minister approved the suggestion. Lord Charteris was appointed and has been an outstandingly successful chairman.[48] I would have liked Lady Spencer to have been made a trustee and she would have been an excellent one, but the opposition proved too strong. Lady Spencer is a

[48] Another outstanding appointment I was able to make was that of Caryl Brahms to the Board of the National Theatre. She served devotedly until her death in 1982.

woman of outstanding ability, drive and energy, but unfortunately she arouses jealousy among smaller and less talented fry. This is a sad reflection on the meaner side of human nature.

I was also anxious to redeem the pledges which I had made to the Historic Houses Association at its meeting shortly before the election and sent an early memorandum in May 1979 to Michael Heseltine urging the implementation of these reforms, including the setting up of funds for the upkeep of houses and gardens that would be free of tax but subject to the perpetuities rule. These and other provisions favourable to the Historic Houses Association were contained in the Budgets of 1979 and 1980.[49] Other heritage matters with which I became involved in during this period were the effort to save Keddleston Hall and its contents for the nation and the protection of Luton Hoo. In the arts sphere I was able to extend government indemnity for the insurance of works of art to include items lent from private collections as well as from public ones. This was a major help in staging exhibitions which would otherwise have been impossible to put on because of soaring insurance costs. In November 1980 I was also able to help the National Gallery acquire Albrecht Altdorfer's *Christ Taking Leave of His Mother*, for which it paid £5 million.

The Arts Minister is also responsible for a number of archives, including the Duke of Wellington's papers. It fell to me to decide where they should be allotted. The Historical Manuscripts Commission recommended that they should go to the British Library, but I had received urgent representations from Southampton University that they should go there. Hampshire was the Duke's own county, and the family has connections with the University.[50] Accordingly, after consultations with Lord Denning, the Chairman of the Commission, I decided to overrule the Commission. This had never happened before, and my decision was ill-received by some of its members. On the other hand, I was determined that provincial universities should have the opportunity to develop their own specialities, and I saw scope for Southampton, at which I had taught many years before, to become a centre for Wellington studies. Stringent security conditions were laid down by the Commission; the University managed to meet these; and the repository for the papers was opened in 1983.

Exporting Works of Art

One of the Arts Minister's duties is to approve applications for exporting works of art. He has some limited powers in this sphere. He can, for example, impose a ban on export in order to give time for another

---

[49] See Capital Gains Tax Act (1979) and Finance Act (1980). Cf. Finance Act 1976.
[50] The Seventh Duke was Chancellor of the University.

purchaser to come forward or to enable a national institution to raise the necessary money. In theory the ban may be permanent, but in practice it can be only temporary. The rules governing this matter had become out of date, and at the end of 1979 I initiated a review.

Early on I was faced with a difficult problem. The Royal Academy had applied for a temporary export licence to allow their most precious possession, Michelangelo's *Tondo*, to be exhibited in the Soviet Union. The relevant advisory committee had counselled against its being granted, and I found this recommendation on my desk when I arrived in the Privy Council just after the election had taken place. I was not unsympathetic to the Academy's case but felt it was difficult to overrule the Advisory Committee so early in my period of office. Furthermore, the dispatch of art objects around the world has its disadvantages as well as advantages: the risk of damage is always there. I could see that I would become vulnerable if I overruled the Committee and then damage of some kind was sustained. Just as there are arguments for popes to stay in Rome and to let the world come to them, so there is a case for allowing art objects to remain *in situ* and letting art lovers come to them on pilgrimage.

My policy in relation to permanent export was to let nothing go and to try to save art objects for the heritage if at all possible. If there were exceptional and persuasive reasons for exporting, I was prepared to support the granting of a licence. Thus in June 1980 I was able to save Louis XVI's magnificent service of porcelain, which he had presented to the Duke of Wellington and which the French Government was anxious to acquire. In the end it was retained for the Victoria and Albert Museum, where it can be seen today. On the other hand, I was prepared to let an early copy of Magna Carta go to the United States, since there are a number of these documents in Britain and constitutionally Magna Carta is as important to the United States as it is to ourselves.

Perhaps the most difficult problem I had to deal with was that of the projected export of the Leonardo Codex in 1980. The thirty-six-page work, known as the Codex Leicester, had been in the possession of the Coke family for many years. Its subject 'of the nature, weight and movement of water', is not at first sight compelling, but the work was in fact of fundamental importance to the artist when he created the landscape in the *Mona Lisa*. In any case, I felt that anything connected with the greatest artist the world has so far seen was of such value that it should be retained in Britain. The manuscript was written, from right to left, by Leonardo in 1507. The first I knew about its coming up for sale was when news leaked into the press in September 1980 that Lord Coke was going to offer it at Christie's. Neither Lord Coke nor the directors of Christie's had informed me of the matter. The auction was to take place in December; time was short if anything was to be done. I resolved to do all I could to save it. I consulted Lord Charteris at the National Heritage Fund, who was enthusiastic in his support, but unfortunately his enthusiasm was not matched by that of other trustees, and in the event he was not able to help.

The sale aroused great interest in the press, and some wildly inflated figures of what the manuscript was likely to fetch circulated. An estimated value of £4 million passed into general currency, and there was even a suggestion in *The Times* that the figure could be £6 million. I was sure that these estimates were wide of the mark and endeavoured to persuade Lord Coke to offer the manuscript to a national institution like the British Library; I argued that with the tax concessions available in the circumstances, he would probably receive a larger sum than from its sale at open public auction. In the event this proved to be the case. When the manuscript came up for auction at Christie's in December it was knocked down to the oil magnate, Mr Arnold Hammer, for only £2 million. Thus Mr Hammer could claim to have struck the bargain of the century. I tried to see if there was any chance of raising the money for the British Library, but manuscripts do not have the 'appeal' of pictures, and my efforts were fruitless. I was resigning myself to its departure when, as I was doing some Christmas shopping in the Portobello Road, a brainwave came to me. I had met Mr Hammer in the United States and knew him to be both a generous supporter of arts causes and a great friend of this country. As it was only the day after the auction had taken place, he was likely still to be in England. I rang Claridges, and this was indeed the case. He agreed to see me. I went straight up to his rooms, and in half an hour we had struck up what I considered to be an excellent deal. An export licence would be granted, but a condition of this would be that the manuscript should be exhibited in Britain at the Royal Academy for three months in each year. This arrangement would be for his lifetime and afterwards would be continued in consultation with his trustees. So, at no cost to ourselves, we would have the manuscript in England for a considerable part of the year, and many people would be given an opportunity to see it who would never have been able to do so while it was reposing in the vaults of Holkham Hall. Only one point disturbed me. Mr Hammer was anxious to exhibit the manuscript, sheet by sheet, in perspex display cases and kept employing an Americanism, declaring that he intended to 'take it apart'. To me this sounded an unfortunate phrase, and I persuaded him to say that it was his intention to restore it to its original condition. The sheets had, in fact, not been sewn together until a comparatively late date. The manuscript was exhibited in Washington as part of President Reagan's inaugural celebrations in January 1981 and made its first appearance in Britain later that year. I noted with interest that in the catalogue the manuscript was no longer described as the Codex Leicester; it had been transmogrified into the Codex Hammer!

CONCLUSION

Shortly after I was appointed Arts Minister by Mrs Thatcher in 1979 I drew up, in consultation with my officials, a five-year plan for the Arts Office. I found that we had achieved it in less than two. I was working on a new five-year plan when my reign came to an end. In particular I was looking forward to two projects. I wished to help the British film industry, and I planned to improve arts courses in schools and in adult education. I had, in fact, opened negotiations with Mr John Nott, then Minister for Trade, with whom I shared the oversight of films, and a transfer to the Office of Arts and Libraries seemed likely to be agreed. Negotiations were far advanced when we both departed to other spheres. *Sunt lacrimae rerum et mentem mortalium tangunt.*

PART TWO

The Earthly City

3

Government by Discussion

Parliamentary government has been one of the major contributions of the British nation to world civilization, yet the very phrase 'parliamentary government' is a misnomer and can give rise to profound misconceptions. At no time in its long history of seven hundred years has Parliament governed, nor has it ever made any claim to do so. The executive function has been exercised successively first by the king, then by the Cabinet and today—some, at any rate, would maintain—by the Prime Minister. Parliament's function has been a different one: to subject the executive to certain limitations and controls, to protect the liberties of the individual citizen against the arbitrary use of power, to focus the mind of the nation on the great issues of the day by the maintenance of continuous dialogue or discussion and to impose what I may call parliamentary conventions on the whole political system. Parliament also makes a major contribution to political life by ensuring that the political system enjoys legitimacy, a concept essential for government by consent. It provides continuity, not by the imposition of the rule of a single class or caste but by providing a means by which power can pass peacefully from one class to another without the upheaval and disorder of revolution. It further ensures the reality of government by consent by bringing governors and governed into close relationship and enabling the views of citizens to reach their rulers and vice versa.

Government by discussion, understood in the limited sense just outlined, has been a reality in Britain for hundreds of years. The classes taking part in the dialogue have varied, as have their relative contributions, but the discussion, whoever the participants, has been continuously maintained. In the nineteenth century the franchise reforms represented by the first and second Reform Acts (1832 and 1867) brought first the middle classes and then the working classes into the fullest participation in the political dialogue and so prepared the way for the rise of the modern democratic state, with its redistribution of economic influence and power, which exists today. Parliament was the means by which education, economic opportunity and security were widely diffused in society, so that Britain is able to offer the world the most stable and mature citizen democracy that has so far been created.

How does government by discussion work? What are its shortcomings and limitations? How can it be improved and reformed to meet the contemporary technological challenge and the renewed demand for 'participation' caused both by the spread of education and the fear of subjugation by the massive bureaucracy and huge interests rampant in present-day society?

I start with the presumption that government by discussion is worth having and that the parliamentary system still provides it. There are those today who deny both these premises, but there is nothing new about this. Impatience with parliamentary government was expressed intermittently in the nineteenth century in terms remarkably similar to those employed today. Walter Bagehot (1826–77), whose analysis *The English Constitution* became a classic,[1] identified and demolished the argument with succinct economy in his equally insightful but less well-known work *Physics and Politics* (that 'golden little book', as it was described by William James).

> Their great enemy [wrote Bagehot, referring to the anti-par-liamentarians] is parliamentary government; they call it, after Mr Carlyle, the *national palaver*,[2] they add up the hours that are consumed in it, and the speeches which are made in it, and they sigh for a time when England might again be ruled, as it once was, by a Cromwell— that is, when an eager, absolute man might do exactly what other eager men wished, and do it immediately. All these invectives are perpetual and many-sided; they come from philosophers, each of whom wants some old institution destroyed; from new eraists, who want their new era started forthwith. And they are all distinct admissions that a policy of discussion is the greatest hindrance to the inherited mistake of human nature, to the desire to act promptly, which in a simple age is so excellent, but which in a later and more complex time leads to so much evil.[3]

Bagehot valued government by discussion because it enabled changes to be made slowly and cautiously after full consultation of public opinion.

---

[1] As I have remarked in an earlier chapter, other people have written more learnedly about the English constitution, but no one else has been able to make it amusing. What other treatise on the constitution written in the mid-nineteenth century is available in a paperback today?

[2] Dickens was another, more tedious critic of parliamentary government in the period of disillusionment following the first Reform Act.

[3] *Physics and Politics*, *Works*, vol. 7, pp. 126–7.

Such circumspection was particularly necessary in an old society such as England's:

> all-important English institutions are the relics of a long past; they have undergone many transformations; like old houses which have been altered many times, they are full of conveniences and inconveniences which at first sight would not be imagined. Very often a rash alterer would pull down the very part which makes them habitable to cure a minor evil or improve a defective outline.[4]

The thrust of the alternative attack on government by discussion is the contention that Parliament is unable any longer to discharge its functions. The value of the end is conceded but the efficiency of the means denied. Parties, runs the thesis, dominate the Commons, while the House of Lords is a nullity; the Prime Minister has subjugated the Cabinet, and the executive, backed by the vast resources of the modern Civil Service, has escaped from any control, dialectic or otherwise, by Parliament. There is undoubtedly some substance to these contentions, especially until recent times the latter, but they represent exaggerations which do not accord with the facts, and there is a real danger that their uncritical repetition will lead to the establishment of a new mythology of the impotence of Parliament.

In fact, Parliament still discharges remarkably well its unique function of educating the nation. The Prime Minister, in one sense, is nothing else than the national headmaster or headmistress. In the course of the parliamentary year every subject of political importance, whether domestic or foreign, will be debated in the Commons, and a duplicating process will take place in the upper chamber. The Commons debates are widely reported in the press and by television and wireless, and the public—or that portion of the public which takes an interest in politics—is able to follow the issues, normally presented from two different points of view. This may not be an ideal philosophical way of reaching the truth, since the opposite points of view are presented by passionate partisans, but the public knows this and is able to do some discounting for itself, as can the commentators of the various mass media. The existence of two major parties, on the other hand, and the consequent cut and thrust of debate, dramatize the issues and make them interesting.[5]

The critics of Parliament claim that its dialectic functions have been taken

---

[4] Ibid., p. 312.

[5] If there are strong parliamentary personalities leading the two parties, the dramatic impact is much enhanced. The politics of the middle three decades of the nineteenth century were dominated by the duels between Gladstone and Disraeli; in more recent times Harold Macmillan and Hugh Gaitskell were both outstanding parliamentarians and evenly matched. Lately, the charisma seems to have evaporated (a worldwide phenomenon), but it will come back again. Political like artistic genius comes in waves and is intermittent, not constant, in supply.

over by the parties; the discussions in the debating chamber have become a sham; the results of debates are known in advance; such is the tightness of party discipline that on any major issue the number of Members prepared to vote against their party is rarely more than a handful; the important decisions and discussions take place not in the debating chamber but in private party meetings 'upstairs'. Party has triumphed completely over Parliament. Such is the charge.

Once again, there is some truth in the developed thesis, but it presents only an aspect of the situation. In the first place, party influence may have increased since the 'classic' parliamentary period of the mid-nineteenth century, but the parties remain adjuncts of the parliamentary system. The centre of gravity of power still lies in the parliamentary parties, not in the mass parties of supporters outside of Parliament.[6] This was shown quite clearly in 1965, when the Conservative Party for the first time adopted a democratic method of electing its leader. The electoral decision is taken by Members of Parliament, who are the only individuals who have a vote. Their choice is then presented to a wider meeting composed of representatives of the mass party, the House of Lords, etc., but the function of this larger meeting is purely formal—to ratify the effective choice that has already been made by the elected Members.

The textbook writers tend to refer to 'secret' party meetings that take place in the committee rooms of the House of Commons, where decisions are taken and attitudes formulated, later to be reflected automatically in the chamber 'downstairs'. If one looks at the facts, a different picture emerges. The press, it is true, is excluded from the party meetings, but the debates and decisions are widely reported just the same. The entire proceedings, when any issue of substance is involved, are fully 'leaked' to the representatives of the mass media. This comes about because every speaker fears that someone else will leak to journalists his own version of what was said and so distort individual contributions; in self-defence he leaks his own version of what he said and what others contributed. Parliamentary journalists have developed skills of sifting and re-construction that are remarkably accurate, and if any inaccuracy does occur in reporting, the convention of secrecy binding party members is relaxed. Furthermore, the whips themselves have taken to the custom of releasing the full text of major speeches by leading figures in the party. 'Secrecy' in these conditions becomes a myth.

There is a further point. Voting in the Commons may be dominated by the whips, but speeches are not. The Speaker decides who will be called in debate, not the party managers, and the Speaker is always anxious to see that the full spectrum of opinion is represented in debate. Dissenters have a built-in advantage, since in a debate limited in time—the average

---

[6] For an assessment of recent developments in the Labour Party, see p. 103.

parliamentary debate lasts between six and seven hours—they have a much better chance of 'catching the Speaker's eye' than do orthodox Members. The habit is growing among Members of supporting their party with their feet by walking through the lobby to register their vote but making speeches in opposition.

To some this appears reprehensible, but it is understandable, given the convention that a Government defeated on a major issue in the Commons is required to resign. In practice such defeats rarely occur. There has only been one example of a Government ejected by parliamentary vote since the first part of this century, and that was in May 1979.[7] The truth is that it is not the function of the modern House of Commons to dismiss Governments; that is a prerogative of the electorate, which is exercised at not more than five-year intervals.

Furthermore, it must be remembered that the doctrine that a parliamentary defeat means dissolution is a two-edged weapon. Members supporting a Government do not want an election in circumstances of party division, since this will mean almost certain defeat for their party and may (much worse) lead to the loss of their own seats. Yet the Government also has its own interest in survival and hence will not press its supporters beyond a certain point. For the Prime Minister a threat of dissolution which may involve his own elimination can be a hollow one. This point was well illustrated by the Wilson Parliament. The Cabinet was obliged to abandon its legislation on a compulsory incomes policy, as well as its proposed reform of trade union law involving the fining of unofficial strikers, when the Chief Whip reported to the Prime Minister that he could not guarantee a parliamentary majority. If he had been defeated on this legislation, the Prime Minister would have been bound to ask the Queen for a dissolution. Mr Wilson preferred discretion to valour and never put the matter to the test. The offending Bills were withdrawn.

Again, backbenchers on both sides of the House showed that they were far from mere lobby fodder when the Bill to reform the House of Lords appeared during 1969. The Bill would have created an entirely nominated upper house (nominated life peerages on the advice of the Prime Minister, with salaries to boot) and was supported by the leaders of all three parties. Backbenchers were appalled by the measure, the left wing of the Labour Party because it would perpetuate the House of Lords, the right wing and some of the centre of the Tory Party because of the extension of the powers of patronage of the Prime Minister. They waged a procedural war of attrition against the Bill, forming for the occasion an unholy alliance. Rather than jeopardize its legislative programme for the session, the Government abandoned the Bill.

[7] Even in the crisis of 1940, the Chamberlain Government maintained a majority in the Commons, yet the scale of Conservative abstention was such that Chamberlain fell.

The party organizations in the constituencies are also said to represent a threat to the independence of Members and to prevent them from speaking their minds. It is true that the power of these organizations has greatly increased through the polarization of the electorate into supporters of the two major parties. It is almost impossible to get into Parliament without a party label; its confiscation can bring about political extinction.[8] The selection of candidates for Parliament is, for all practical purposes, in the hands of local party associations; the central party organizations have a veto but little else. Since over two-thirds of the parliamentary seats are 'safe' and do not change sides at elections, the selection of a candidate for the party holding these seats is tantamount to election. Since Britain has no system of primaries, the selection committees in these seats wield great power. It might be thought that as a result Members of Parliament are the mere puppets of their selection committees and local party oligarchs, but it does not work out like this in practice. Other aspects of the situation have to be filled in to give a complete picture. One moderating factor has been the Burkian view of the status of a Member of Parliament, still widely accepted, that he is elected not as a party delegate but as a representative commissioned to use his judgement on the affairs of the nation as they come before him in Parliament.[9] Another can be the personality of the Member. Some Members seem to be more persuasive than others. A third factor is the importance of local affairs. A Member who is zealous in pursuing local interests will have more discretion than one who neglects them. Furthermore, the Member has his own ultimate deterrent; he can always threaten to stand as an independent at the election if denied the official party nomination. In many cases this would mean the loss of the seat to the party.

[8] One development in the Conservative Party is worth noting. Before the war it was customary in the safer Tory seats for the candidate to finance the local association as part of the price for nomination. A former Tory Cabinet Minister informed me that he was asked as a young man by the first association to which he presented himself whether he would subscribe £2,000 to the local association funds. When he declined, he was dismissed with the words: 'In that case we do not wish to ask you any more questions.' The next aspirant agreed and was selected, paying over £2,000 but never gave them another penny. On being approached for his 'annual subscription' a year after election, he pointed out that his undertaking was to make one payment, not a series. After the war a new rule was introduced forbidding Tory Members to pay more than £50 a year to local party funds. This has democratized the party but has led to an increase in the power of local associations. Formerly, the Member bought them; now they buy him. Payers of pipers tend to call tunes.
[9] Since my election to Parliament in 1964, I have not found my own independence unduly restricted. I voted with the Government for sanctions against Rhodesia and against the Kenya Immigration Bill, which was supported by the Opposition. I declined to vote against the Race Relations Bill and have supported such reforms as the abolition of capital punishment (which most of my constituents seem to want to extend especially to students, rather than abolish). I supported homosexual law reform (here I had no trouble mainly, I suspect, because the constituents did not think it a very 'nice' subject to discuss in public), sponsored the Bill to abolish censorship of the theatre, etc.

Pressure from constituents is a normal part of parliamentary democracy, but there have been sinister recent developments in the Labour Party.[10] In many cases local Labour parties have been reduced to a handful of members, and this gives scope for infiltration and take-over by the far left. Taken in conjunction with the adoption of the need for re-selection before each general election, this represents a real threat to parliamentary democracy and is a principal reason for the steady stream of Labour Members abandoning the party, to which they have given many years of devoted service, for the SDP. The fact of their taking such a drastic step is convincing evidence of the totalitarian element that is now seizing control in so many Labour constituencies.[11]

The most important function of Parliament is to check the executive, to scrutinize not only legislation but also the policies that lie behind it and to call the executive, both Ministers and civil servants, to account. There is no doubt that over the past hundred years the balance of power and influence has been steadily shifting away from Westminster to Whitehall. The executive was becoming more and more professional, while the legislature remained dismally amateur. Although the powers and resources of Whitehall had increased immeasurably, the resources available to Members of Parliament had remained static and unchanged. I became convinced that the old instruments of Question Time and the Adjournment Debate, while retaining some usefulness, had become totally inadequate as a means of parliamentary control of the executive. The increasingly confrontational atmosphere in the Commons debating chamber made matters worse, since questions, especially at Prime

[10] The Labour Party outside Parliament has had more influence than the equivalent organization on the Tory side. This is in part for historical reasons. The Conservative Party outside Parliament was created by Disraeli as an aid to the parliamentary party, but in the Labour Party the process was reversed, the Labour Party in the country preceding the creation of the parliamentary party.

[11] Three changes have drastically shifted the balance of power in the Labour Party away from the parliamentary party to the mass party outside Parliament. (1) *Method of choosing leader* The Leader is now chosen by an electoral college made up of a 40 per cent weighting by trade unions and other affiliated organizations (e.g. socialist and co-operative bodies) and a 30 per cent weighting each by the Parliamentary Labour Party (PLP) and the constituency parties. (From Special Rules Revision Conference, 24 January 1981) (2) *General election manifesto* The party's National Executive Committee (NEC) alone, after consultations with all sections of the movement, takes the final decision as to the contents of the Labour Party's general election manifesto. (Under the previous constitution, the manifesto was drawn up jointly by the NEC and the parliamentary committee of the PLP.) From the Labour Party's Annual Conference, 1–5 October 1979) (3) *Reselection* Mandatory reselection is now Labour Party policy. Mandatory reselection is the process whereby sitting Members of Parliament must undergo reselection by their constituency parties in order to remain their party's candidate at the following general election. Furthermore, if a constituency is represented by a Labour MP, then the normal process for selecting a prospective parliamentary candidate should be initiated not later than thirty-six months after the preceding election (not less than eighteen months after the previous election where the MP is serving his or her first term). (From the Labour Party's Annual Conference, 1–5 October 1979; drafting inconsistencies amended, Labour Party's Annual Conference, 29 September–3 October 1980)

Minister's Question Time, seem more and more designed to provoke gladiatorial combat and to make party political points rather than to elucidate information and provide effective scrutiny of ministerial activity.

Many other parliamentarians had reached similar conclusions. In 1976 a procedure committee was appointed to see how the effectiveness of the Commons in controlling the executive could be improved. It reported its conclusions in 1978. It favoured a wide-ranging series of reforms, including the setting up of a comprehensive select committee system to shadow government departments, a new Public Bill procedure, better financial control of monies voted by Parliament under the aegis of the Comptroller or Auditor General, as well as a series of minor reforms.[12]

The report was debated in 1978, while the Labour Government was still in office, and pressure was building up for implementation of the report's recommendations. The Conservative manifesto of 1979 contained an undertaking that the Commons would have an early opportunity to come to a decision on the report's proposals, and after the return of a Conservative Government to office in May that year the House of Commons approved a series of procedural reforms on 25 June 1979.

The package of reforms, which was approved overwhelmingly by the House, set up a system of fourteen select committees to cover every department of state, with the exception of the Lord Chancellor's department which, because of its judicial functions, was excluded.[13] The committees have wide investigative powers but no executive or legislative functions. They have power to send for persons and papers and to request (but not to order) Ministers to attend before them. Members are appointed for the whole of a Parliament, not by the whips but by Parliament itself through its committee of selection. They are empowered to elect their own officers and to appoint specialist advisers to assist them in their work. I pledged the Government to full co-operation in these words:

> I give the House this pledge on the part of the Government that every Minister, from the most senior Cabinet Minister to the most junior Under-Secretary, will do all in his or her power to co-operate with the new system of committees and to make it a success. I believe that declaration of intent to be a better guarantee than formal provisions laid down in standing orders.

I described the setting up of the committee system as the 'most important parliamentary reform of the century', and experience has justified the words. The House of Commons has been able to exercise a

[12] *First Report from the Select Committee on Procedures, 1977–78*, No. 588–I.
[13] The committees' terms of reference were 'to examine the expenditure, administration and policy of the principal government departments and associated public bodies'—see *Liaison Committee Report* (1982), p.8.

measure of influence over government policy which has not been seen for a hundred years. The influence of the committees has been felt throughout Whitehall and, like other constitutional checks, operates in advance. Ministers have co-operated fully with the committees, and no Minister has declined to appear before them. A liaison committee of committee chairmen was set up in 1980 to resolve difficulties, and as Leader of the House I acted as a mediator in any disputes and difficulties.[14]

Since their inception the committees have investigated a wide variety of issues.[15] Thus the Home Office Committee has examined the working of the 'sus' laws (arrest on suspicion) and the deaths of prisoners in prison: the Employment Committee has conducted a dialogue on the need for trade union law reform with the Secretary of State for Employment: the Energy Committee has investigated gas-pricing policy: the Welsh Committee, employment opportunities in Wales; the Education Committee, the organization and funding of courses in higher education. The Defence Committee has completed a major inquiry into strategic nuclear weapons policy. Most influential of all has been the Treasury Committee, which has examined public expenditure and proposed cuts, Civil Service pay and cash limits provision, and monetary and macroeconomic policy. The committee has adopted the principles of Government economic policy for methodological purposes and has judged its results in the light of its own policies. The Chancellor of the Exchequer has been a regular visitor to its proceedings.

The committees have sometimes submitted long reports after lengthy inquiries but at other times have quickly produced short ones in order to influence events. As the Liaison Committee concluded, the flow of information to the House has greatly improved as a result of the appointment of the committees. Thus the Chancellor of the Exchequer now makes an annual Autumn Statement on the financial situation, on which his Budget will eventually be based. Again, draft copies of the supplementary estimates are provided to the committees in advance of publication. The committees have had a direct effect on parliamentary opinion.

Members will be aware [concludes the Liaison Committee report] of the

[14] The Liaison Committee published its first report on its activities in December 1982. It concluded that the select committee system had 'considerably extended the range of the House's activities, strengthened its position relative to that of the Government, and deepened the quality of its debates' (at p. 8). It pointed out, however, that the £360 million of public expenditure represented by the Law Officers' department and the Lord Chancellor's department was not subject to committee scrutiny, and it recommended that it should be so in the next Parliament. The principal point of criticism was that of the reports issued by the committees over three years of activity, only five had been the subject of substantive debate.
[15] These include the arts, education, the Theatre Museum, the Brandt Report, the British Library, British Leyland, budgetary reform, Concorde, monetary control and monetary policy and nationalized industries accounting.

many cases in which recent committee reports have directly affected
Government policy or parliamentary debate. From the amendment of
the 'sus' law to the sensitive debates on the Canada Bill, from efficiency
in the Civil Service to 'misinformation' in the Falklands campaign, from
the promenade concerts to Concorde and nuclear technology, and at
countless other points, Members' attitudes have been affected by what
committees have done. (At p.9)

The Foreign Affairs Committee's report on the British North American
Acts made an important contribution to the 'patriation' debate in Canada
and influenced the approach of both the Canadian and the United
Kingdom Governments to the issue.

Fears had been expressed that the setting up of the committees would
have an adverse effect on attendance in the chamber; this was a principal
argument used against them. Such accusations have been repeated since,
but the Liaison Committee shows that they are without foundation.

The fact [it states] that more than 300 Members are currently engaged in
select committee work has led to occasional assertions that it has
emptied the Chamber for many debates. We question this. The decline
in attendance on the floor had been noticeable some time before the
present Parliament, and in any case the assertion does not square with
an examination of the times of committee meetings. In a recent six-
month period (January—June 1982) 490 meetings were held. Of these,
143 (or 29 per cent) took place in the mornings, when the House was not
sitting. Most of the remainder took place between 4 p.m. and 6 p.m. on
Tuesdays (20 per cent) or Wednesdays (31 per cent). If there was a
simple correlation between attendance in committee and attendance on
the floor, one would expect the effects to be noticeable in those two
periods but not in others, and this has not been the case. (Para. 30)

In 1982, after three years of the new committees' work *The Economist*
made an assessment of their value. At their inception, it noted, great
claims were made for them. Were these right?

In the main they are. . . . No big new policy is undertaken in the
Treasury or Home Office these days without Ministers and mandarins
anticipating the information the Treasury and Home Affairs Committee will seek.

After a searching examination of their work the paper concluded:

The committees are usually defended on grounds of principle. Luckily
they also win support for baser reasons. They offer a real job of work
and some welcome publicity to over 100 MPs. The press has welcomed
the committees themselves, and the information coming out of them.
In service on select committees several rising young politicians have

improved their political education far more effectively than they could have done in weary years of opposition or in the tedium of junior office. They have found that it is more fun to pester Permanent Secretaries than to defer to them. Westminster is witnessing a renaissance of backbench power.[16]

A second instalment of minor reforms in procedure, including an experimental first-time limit placed on Members' speeches in second-reading debates, was implemented in October 1979. Eight outstanding reports of the Procedure Committee, a number of which had been hanging about for years, were also debated and disposed of. I also introduced a motion which enabled the Opposition to vote on its own motions on supply days. In 1967, under Richard Crossman, there had been a change in procedure which had unintentionally prevented this. Governments nearly always put down amendments to such motions, and from 1967 the vote took place on the motion 'That the amendment be made'. Thus the matter was disposed of without the substantive motion being put. In October 1979 the form of voting was changed, and it took place on the motion 'That the original words stand part of the question'. This enables the Opposition to vote on its motions. The wording of a motion could be especially important in a minority Parliament.

The third major innovation came, after a sharp struggle in October 1980, with the bringing into operation of a new Public Bill procedure, by which a special committee system was set up to consider certain non-party uncontroversial Bills. The committee sits first as a select committee to hear evidence from experts, civil servants and interested parties and then turns into a legislative committee to discuss and amend the substantive provisions of the Bill.

The fourth phase began with the setting up of a new procedure committee to consider the manner in which the House of Commons grants financial supply. This had long been a source of complaint, since the traditional twenty-nine supply days are used, in the main, no longer to discuss the estimates but to debate topics which the Opposition selects. Huge sums of money are voted through without debate, and the constitutional foundation of the Commons' control of the executive has been gravely eroded. I left office before the procedure committee reported but was able to give evidence before it. Its first report, issued in 1982, suggested that eight special days should be set aside to consider the estimates and that estimates should be submitted to the select committees for their consideration, but that the principle that increased expenditure can be proposed only by the Government should be maintained. The report was debated in the House of Commons in February 1982, and the

[16] 'Backbench Power Lives Again', *The Economist*, 14 August 1982, pp. 20–1.

Government agreed that three estimate days should be provided in the future. This is not sufficient, but it provides an important new point of departure. Reform of Commons supply procedure has got off to a good start, but more remains to be done.

Other issues of importance are now being discussed. The Procedure Committee is taking evidence on four major topics: parliamentary control of public borrowing, parliamentary control of long-term expenditure projects, parliamentary control of non-supply expenditure, and budgetary reform in the light of the recommendations of the Treasury and Civil Service Committee.

The matter that has commanded the least favour of, and support from, the Government has been reform of the auditing procedures and the means of establishing public accountability for nationalized industries and other publicly owned corporations and companies. The Commons Select Committee of 1977–8 recommended that legislation should establish the principle that 'the accounts of all bodies in receipt of funds voted by Parliament should be subject to examination by the Comptroller and Auditor General' and that audit staff should be regarded as servants of the House.[17]

A review of the situation was begun by the Labour Government, and in June 1979 its Conservative successor announced that it would be continued. A Green Paper was published by the Government in March 1980; it recommended that new legislation was desirable but that the Comptroller and Auditor General should not cover the nationalized industries. The Public Accounts Committee of the House of Commons, in a special report published in February 1981, made sweeping recommendations for change, but the Government's reply to this was unforthcoming, as was its contribution to the debate which took place in November of that year.[18]

There the matter might have rested for the duration of the present Parliament, but in November 1982 I drew second place in the ballot for Private Members' Bills and decided to introduce a Bill to give effect to the recommendations of the report of the Public Accounts Committee. The Bill provided statutory backing for the first time to the Comptroller's economy, efficiency and effectiveness audits and extended the range of his inspection powers to undertake such examinations of nationalized industries, public corporations, publicly controlled companies and all public-sector and private bodies mainly supported from monies provided

---

[17] The Report of the Expenditure Committee (1976–7) had earlier recommended reform.
[18] Green Paper, *The Role of the Comptroller and Auditor General*, Cmnd 7845, 1980. *First Special Report from the Committee of Public Accounts, 1980-1*, No. 115–1. *The Role of the Comptroller and Auditor General*, Cmnd 8323, 1981. Debate of 30 November 1981. Hansard, 1981–2, vol. 14; cols. 39–112.

by Parliament. It further laid down that a national audit office should be set up, of which the Comptroller and Auditor General should be the head, and it altered his status and method of appointment. While preserving his independence, the Bill made it clear that he was an officer of the House of Commons and was in future to be appointed not by the Crown on the advice of the Prime Minister but by the Crown after an address by the House of Commons tabled by the Chairman of the Public Accounts Committee.[19]

The provisions extending the Auditor General's powers from government departments to nationalized industries were bitterly opposed by the heads of the nationalized industries, backed up by sponsoring Ministers *within* the Government. Nevertheless, when the Bill was debated in the Commons on 28 January 1983 it received overwhelming support in the debate.[20] The closure motion was carried by 112 votes to nil, and the Bill was then given an unopposed second reading.

My troubles, however, were only just beginning. In March the Bill went into committee, where I had a reasonable majority. But the Achilles heel of all private Members' legislation is not the committee but the report stage. The Bill then returns to the floor of the House, and it can normally expect only one day of parliamentary time. Thus a Bill will start to be debated on a Friday at 9.30 and proceedings will close at 2.30, five hours later. Since the Speaker will normally grant a closure only after between one and a half and two hours' debate, even a single Member, by putting down a series of amendments, can effectively kill a Bill. The most important reform of procedure that should now be introduced is to give to private Members a power which has hitherto been the prerogative of the Government, the ability to suspend the time limit for debate by affirmative resolution. This would revolutionize the position of the private Member and would enable him, if sufficiently determined and resourceful, to get major legislation on to the statute book.

With the principle of the Bill approved, I extended an olive branch to the nationalized industry chairmen, declared that I felt sure that they would accept the principle of parliamentary accountability now that it had been approved by the House and suggested talks so that their reasonable objections could be met. At first these made little progress, and the Government, through the Treasury and the Department of Industry, remained intractable. These would offer no advice on the nationalized

[19] In its final statutory form the address is to be moved by the Prime Minister with the *agreement* of the Chairman of Public Accounts.

[20] As it had done previously in the press, receiving two leading articles in support from *The Times* (30 November 1982 and 28 January 1983), the *Daily Telegraph* (1 December 1982 and 17 January 1983) and the *Guardian* (27 January 1983), as well as from more popular papers such as the *Daily Mail* (2 January 1983). A further leading article in support of the modified Bill was published by *The Times* on 13 April 1983.

industry clauses of the Bill beyond declaring that they should be dropped. However, on 28 February a breakthrough came at a meeting with Ministers, when it was suggested that value-for-money audits should be carried out annually under conditions agreed by the Committee of Public Accounts, to whom the auditors would report as well as to Ministers, but the audits should be carried out by the private auditors to the industries concerned and not by the Comptroller and Auditor General. This was not ideal, but it seemed to me an advance on the previous 'non possumus' attitude, and I agreed to put it to the nationalized industries' chairmen. This I did on 10 March but with an alternative proposal that audits should be carried out by the Comptroller and Auditor General with the consent of the relevant industries. The hostility of the chairmen to the Auditor General was, however, implacable and an accommodation was reached along the lines suggested by the Government.

Both I and my two principal sponsors, Mr Joel Barnett, Chairman of the Public Accounts Committee, and Mr Edward Du Cann, Chairman of the 1922 Committee, remained convinced that the right person to carry out the audits was the Auditor General. So was he. Mr Gordon Downey, who had been more than generous in the support he had personally given to the Bill, as well as placing the resources of his office behind us also expressed misgivings. However, on balance we thought that the private auditors would be better than nothing and a step in the right direction. I consulted the eleven other sponsors of the Bill, and all save two agreed that we should accept the Government compromise.

The way ahead seemed clear, but these two sponsors and other supporters of the Bill on the committee expressed fierce opposition to the idea of private auditors entering the field. They declared that they would rather drop the nationalized industries provisions from the Bill altogether rather than let in private auditors who, they felt, would block the Auditor General from ever being able to carry out reviews. They then threatened to kill the Bill at the report stage. My strategy throughout had been to obtain a Bill which would emerge from committee as an agreed measure. I had had difficulties with the Government, with the nationalized industries, with Members representing the trade unions in the industries, and all had to be placated. Now I had to deal with my own so-called supporters as well! After an abortive attempt to get the Government to give extra time to the Bill or else to take it over as a Government measure, the controversial clause came up for a vote in committee on 20 April. By then the Chief Secretary to the Treasury had ceased to be a hostile sceptic and was now an enthusiastic supporter of the Bill. The clause was deleted, and the Bill then went on to its report stage, which was scheduled for 13 May.

All appeared to be going well when on Monday, 9 May 1983, the Prime Minister announced that she was going to call an election on 9 June and that Parliament was to be dissolved on 13 May, the very day I had selected for report and third reading. At first I was despondent about the matter and feared that everything was lost, but by the following day I had rallied, encouraged by Mr Edward Du Cann, and approached the Government Chief Whip, Mr Michael Jopling, to see if some means could be found of saving the Bill. I also approached the Opposition Chief Whip, Mr Michael Cocks, through Mr Joel Barnett and Mr Robert Sheldon. Mr Jopling did not feel able to give it Government time but kindly agreed to put it down at the end of business on Wednesday, 11 May, under a little-known procedure by which a Bill can go through 'on the nod'. If a single Member objects, however, the Bill is lost.

I sat there biting my nails and looking anxiously around the chamber at the fifty or so Members present. The Queen had to give her approval to the Bill in advance as it affected the royal prerogative. When the Deputy Speaker asked formally whether it had been given and there seemed to be no sound from the Treasury Bench, fearful that the Bill would be lost, I cried out, 'Signified', thus unintentionally usurping the function not only of the Chief Secretary but of Her Majesty as well! Report and third reading were called, and no Member uttered a squeak.

The Bill was through the Commons, but the hurdle of the Lords still lay ahead. I had arranged with Lord Boyd Carpenter to steer it through the upper house, but he was away in Australia; Lord Renton, at the prompting of the Government Chief Whip in the Lords, Lord Denham, came to my aid and took it over. As a Privy Councillor I was entitled to attend the debate, seated on the steps of the throne. (Mr Jopling commented that in view of what had happened in the Commons the night before, he was surprised that I was not sitting on the throne itself.) On Thursday, 12 May, it went through all its stages in the Lords, and on Friday, 13 May, as the last act of the Parliament, the royal assent was signified by Mr Speaker Thomas. Thus the National Audit Act[21] passed on to the statute book. Friday, 13 May, had proved my lucky day after all.

Parliamentary manners, the all-pervasive influence of Parliament as such on the way in which Britain conducts her political affairs, have as their foundation the doctrine of the supremacy of Parliament. Furthermore, no one can hold office under the Crown unless he is a member of one of the two Houses of Parliament. This has had a profound effect on the whole way in which political life is conducted. A parliamentary statesman emerges only after long years of apprenticeship, served first as a candidate, then as a Member, then as a junior Minister, finally as a member of the Cabinet. The qualities required at one stage of the process are not necessarily those demanded at another, so that a continual winnowing and sifting takes place. Thus an 'unrivalled average of continued ability' is brought to the service of the state. Parliamentary

[21] It had originally been entitled the 'Parliamentary Control of Expenditure (Reform) Bill but the name had been changed in committee.

government tends, save in moments of crisis, to exclude the greatest; those with far-seeing minds and resolute wills do not take kindly to long apprenticeships. On the other hand, it also excludes the fools. Sheer incompetence cannot survive the daily glare of the Dispatch Box. Parliament is an acute judge of character. No one, from Prime Minister to backbencher, is valued at anything more or less than his worth and this despite the limitation that only the public performance of Members is seen. Their private life is obscured, like the dark side of the moon.

Parliamentary debates are now broadcast on the wireless, and a campaign continues to televise Parliament. This would entail obvious risks but seems to me a desirable reform. Television has become the most important means of mass communication, and it would make more sense to get the television cameras to go to Parliament than to continue the present system of getting the politicians to go to the television. Furthermore, parliamentary debate has all the ingredients of good television—drama, conflict and a wide and changing range of characters. To televise Parliament would, at a stroke, restore any loss it has suffered to the new mass media as the political educator of the nation. It is all the more vital at a time when there is widespread feeling that Parliament is remote from the people and when the gap between governors and governed is being filled by a whole range of protest movements, some merely cranky but others highly sinister, a threat to the future of democracy itself.

In the Commons television lottery there would be prizes for all. Ministers and their shadows would be given opportunities to communicate their views to the people, but backbenchers would be the principal beneficiaries. No longer would a handful of MPs with access to the television studios be more equal than others; what has until now been the privilege of a few would become the right of every backbencher who cared to exercise it.

What, then, are the objections to change? Some Members fear that television would trivialize Parliament. The intimate atmosphere of a club would be destroyed. But the Commons is a club with a difference; it exists not for the benefit of its members but to serve the people. Others are afraid that it will cause MPs to play to the gallery, but those so inclined do this already, and posturings are unlikely to pay off under the critical gaze of the electorate. The one consequence of televising the proceedings of the House that can safely be prophesied is an improvement in parliamentary behaviour, since the public would simply not put up with the rowdyism and intolerance that is unhappily becoming a part of our debates.

There are now few technical difficulties. Technology has advanced so far that cameras and lights need not be obtrusive. Continuous transmission would not be desirable; the normal format would be a half-hour programme late at night, but great occasions like Budget Day could be televised live and in full. The nation would have greatly benefited had it been able to see as well as to hear the dramatic Falklands debate.

Parliament is undoubtedly divided fairly evenly on the issue. When the matter was debated in 1980 there was actually a tied vote: 201 voted in favour and 201 against. The Liaison Committee has suggested that select committee proceedings should be televised, and this could offer a way out of the impasse. It would provide some hard evidence to work on without committing the House of Commons.[22]

The pervasive influence of Parliament can also be seen in the creation of news and the attitudes of the press. Journalists centre themselves on the House of Commons in a way that they do not cluster around Congress. In the American system most political news comes from the White House; in England the position of No. 10 Downing Street is not comparable. It is *primus inter pares*, but that is all. By its close connection with the press, Parliament is able both to reflect and to shape public opinion. It keeps closely in touch with it but is not its slave. Thus Parliament was aware when it abolished capital punishment that the majority of the public apparently wished to retain it (80 per cent, according to the public opinion polls) but refused to allow this to be the determining factor. Normally, however, Parliament will not flout the general opinion any more than Governments will. The most valid criticism of Parliament is that because of its sensitivity to public opinion it does too little rather than too much. Yet by its connection with the general opinion Parliament is kept close to those middle principles which, while they are the despair of intellectuals, are the best guarantors of political stability. Novelty does not impress English parliamentarians. ('I never heard of such a thing,' says the average Englishman, and imagines that he has answered the question.) Parliament needs to be brought into contact with new masses of opinion, especially the opinions represented by the young, but that has been done in part by enfranchising voters at 18, and they are now involving themselves more directly in institutionalized politics.

Parliament is not perfect and needs continual renewal, but along with the monarchy, the holding of fair elections, the existence of an impartial and incorrupt Civil Service and the political instinct involved in the character and the tradition of the people, it makes its contribution to government by consent. Parliament has never governed, but it controls, restrains and influences Governments. That is no mean achievement.

---

[22] On 13 April 1983 a Ten Minute Rule Bill was introduced by Mr Austin Mitchell, Labour Member for Grimsby, to allow precisely this. I was a sponsor of the Bill, which was passed by 153 votes to 138. Ten Minute Rule Bills are expressions of opinion and have little chance of reaching the statute book. Mr Mitchell brought his Bill forward again on 2 November 1983. Once again it was passed but with a reduced majority of 5 votes (164 to 159). A suggestion that the Lords Debates should be televised was made at this time and the Upper House may well admit the television cameras first.

4

Toryism: Yesterday, Today and Tomorrow

MORALS AND POLITICS

Politics is undoubtedly in part about the pursuit of power. Disraeli called it a 'great game'. The adjective in that phrase is, I believe, even more important than the noun. Politics is the pursuit of power for great ends, and once that has been said one is out of the realm of politics, technically so described, and into that of morals, into the sphere of what is good and what is bad, what is right and what is wrong. Politics is more than a sporting event—although it is that; it is also a crusade. It is this nexus which prevents politics from becoming boring, trivial and distasteful. The pursuit of power, like patriotism, is not enough. The lowness of the motivation makes *Macbeth* one of the least attractive and least instructive of Shakespeare's plays. Principle apart, if citizens are to be attracted to politics, it must be on a basis wider than the faction which makes Hanoverian politics so repellent. A pragmatic party like the Tory Party, holding in its hand as its strongest card its competence to govern, faces the real danger that its moral basis will not be sufficiently projected and understood. The Labour Party, with its doctrines and defined theoretical aims, finds less difficulty in getting over its ideals, yet the moral ethos of the Tory Party is equally strong, although more subtle and complex than that of its rival.

In politics, as in the rest of life, there should be no disjunction between principle and practice. The politics that are implemented by a political party in Government should flow and draw their strength from the moral views which it holds and which bind its members together. Conservatives should not argue that principles are those things that are spoken of annually at the Conservative Political Centre Conference lecture and that they have little do to with what central and local government politicians do in Whitehall or town hall for the rest of the year. Tory political principles are not a sort of camouflage for expediency which we occasionally feel obliged to bring down from the attic. Those, therefore, who argue that Conservatism cannot be explained in terms of a firm commitment to a particular approach to economic management should not be tempted to go on to say that in Conservatism there is no commitment to anything at all, that Conservatism is only about getting on, or getting power or getting through next week. This was not how, say, Disraeli or Salisbury or Baldwin (to take three very different types of Conservative leader) would have viewed their Conservatism, though all of them would have appreciated that a political party's principles are of largely academic interest unless it is in office periodically in order to implement them. I cannot imagine any one of them subscribing to the view which was recently fashionable among some people that ideological purity and rigour should not be qualified by electoral interests.

A moral justification for political activity is essential for the self-respect of human beings and is also vital for electoral success. You cannot mobilize a mass electorate without party and a party cannot command the hearts and minds of men without a moral base. The electorate must be able to perceive clearly the moral views for which a political party stands if that party is to be given lasting support, and they cannot do this unless the leaders of the party themselves grasp, articulate and project the ethical values of their own tradition.

In this enterprise what Ministers say is important, but how they say it is of equal importance. It is a matter not only of content but also of style.[1] Style in our culture is often dismissed as frivolous: the French are wiser and know better in this respect. I am thinking not about the packaging of policies for electoral consumption, about which I know little, but about something rather different. I would sum it up as regards my party in particular, though it applies to any governing political body, as the duty of Government and Ministers to give effective public expression to the citizens' sense of their shared national identity.

TORIES AND TRADITION

Of all the political parties in the state the Tory Party owes most to history. As custodians of a tradition, not of dogma, it would be especially foolish to attempt to reject our own past. It would be a mammoth task, too, since we have been around the longest. Those who argue that true Conservatism was born in May 1979 are obliged to reject not only the whole post-war Tory tradition, from Winston Churchill onwards, but the party's pre-war history as well. There is, in fact, a clear line of succession moving forward from Baldwin and Chamberlain to Butler and Heath, and backwards to

[1] For example, I often wish that Government Ministers, when discussing the supreme issue of nuclear warfare, would show a little more awareness of the dangers for mankind and the fears in the minds of so many people.

Salisbury, Disraeli and Bolingbroke. The Tory Party is an historical party or it is nothing. The experience of being born again is no doubt a psychological fact of considerable personal importance, but you can base neither a religious nor a political structure on such an essentially private happening.

The Tory Party has had its dogmatic moments, but they have been departures from the norm. In the end, dogma has always had to give way to the facts of life. Protection at one time appeared to be an article of faith, but it was a Tory Prime Minister, Sir Robert Peel, who repealed the Corn Laws. Again, for many years imperialism was an ascendant principle in the Conservative cosmos, but it was always modified and held in check by other perceptions and commitments. The point was put admirably by the present Prime Minister, Mrs Thatcher, when she declared: 'Free enterprise has a place, an honoured place, in our scheme of things, but as one of many dimensions. For Tories became Tories well before the modern concept of a free market economy meant anything, well before it became a matter of political controversy.'

The richness and diversity of the Conservative tradition cannot be reduced to a single doctrinal principle. 'Monetarism', as Sir Keith Joseph has made clear in a pamphlet bearing the title, 'is not enough'. It is not only not enough: isolated from its political, social and moral context, it is positively misleading and dangerous as an indication of party attitudes. In isolation it lends itself both to distortion and misrepresentation and to crude but politically damaging caricatures. If Conservatives are to counter the socialist projection of the party as the paradigm of hard-faced selfishness and callousness, then monetary policy has to be set squarely in the wider setting of traditional Tory social concerns and traced to its roots in moral values.

MONETARISM AND MORALS

Britain may or may not be a nation of shopkeepers—the point has been argued since Napoleon's gibe—but we are certainly not a nation of economists. When practitioners of the dismal science descend on us, Lord Home is not the only one to reach for the matchbox. I do not believe that the average voter understands very much about the theory of monetarism, and it is hard to blame him for that. When the high priests themselves are in dispute about the essentials of their faith, a certain amount of agnostic confusion among the small fry is pardonable. Nothing is more difficult to communicate than an arcane creed over the tenets of which the custodians are in conflict. So let us turn from the hermeneutics to the facts, a course which, in moments of crisis and dispute, the Prime Minister has often wisely counselled.

The Tory Party was returned to power at the election of 1979 not because a monetarist conversion of Pauline proportions swept across our suburbs and shires but principally because the Prime Minister, with her inspired gift for common sense, succeeded in articulating the thoughts, fears, anxieties and aspirations of the majority of the people. And Margaret Thatcher was given her opportunity because the winter of discontent— obligingly supplied by Mr Callaghan's sublime electoral miscalculation— had led the nation to the moral conclusion that we had reached the end of the road, that the excesses and abuses of union power could no longer be tolerated in a free parliamentary democracy, that inflation had become a deadly threat to our wellbeing, our institutions and our mode of life itself, and that a new way forward must be found. So from those bleak winter months of 1979, popular convictions and resolves emerged that the rake's progress needed to be halted; that public expenditure had to be reined back, not as an exercise in masochism but to create room for the expansion of the wealth-producing private sector; that taxation needed to be reduced to provide incentive and encouragement to enterprise. This was not so much an advance to a new monetarism as a return to old values, to appreciation that life is a struggle, that for nations as well as individuals there is no escape from the necessities of thrift, hard work and change if happiness and prosperity are to be achieved.

Monetarism, then, is a means, not an end. It is a technique, not a moral objective. And it is one of a number of techniques, not a panacea. Neither the high monetarists nor the pure monetarists take this view. They maintain that, provided the money supply is controlled, the level of wages is irrelevant. That is an interesting academic view, but it is not the view of the Government. While we look to the Treasury and the Bank of England to control the money supply, the whole weight of the Government has been thrown behind a campaign to secure lower wage and salary restraint in both the public and the private sectors. This campaign was launched in the final phase of the pay round of 1980, the example being set by Members of Parliament and other public servants who accepted substantially lower increases than those recommended by the Top Salaries Review Board. To achieve this end Conservatives expect, and indeed welcome, the co-operation of the trade unions because in the long run wage restraint is as much in the interests of their members as those of anybody else.

The point of emphasizing all this is to stress the intrinsic flexibility of Government economic policy. It is not a mechanistic exercise in economic logistics. Great Britain is not the scene of a gigantic experiment to prove the truth or falsity of academic economists' controverted theories. We are in politics, not in economics. The demands of economic theory have to be moderated by their application to the practical world of politics. Thus the Government accepts that during the period of readjustment of industry we will have to go through a period of high unemployment, but that is quite different from accepting high unemployment as a permanent instrument of policy. There is no inconsistency between accepting, reluctantly, the need for a transitional period of unemployment and modifying its impact on those who are bearing the brunt of the burden by giving special help to hard-hit areas and intervening with steps to help the young unemployed.

Of course, there will be argument and discussion within the Government to reconcile different policy aims, to set the boundaries of one in relation to the demands of another. There must be the fullest and frankest exchange of views on the points at which the requirements of economics have to give way to the needs of the body politic. That is what the Cabinet is for.

The Conservative aim is to achieve economic success. Failure has dogged Britain, with only brief flashes of achievement and success, since the end of the war. As a result, the nation is pessimistic, lacking in self-confidence and demoralized. Without economic achievements we cannot fulfil our wide aims: compassion is nothing more than a sentiment unless we have the means to transmute it into positive policies.

Inevitably, Britain's economic decline has meant that most political debate in the last two decades has hinged on economic issues. We have had to translate our principles into policies which specifically address our major economic problems: our poor record of productivity; our loss of markets at home and abroad; the increase in the proportion of our national product that has been consumed by the state; the destructive power of trade unionism; high inflation; high marginal rates of taxation and high unemployment. It seems to me unlikely that there is one simple key which will unlock all these problems or that, even if there were, it would open the door to our entire political philosophy. Conservatism is not, therefore, synonymous with some technique for running the economy, however glitteringly fashionable it may be.

A few years ago incomes policy, planned growth and tripartism were all the vogue. I did not think then, nor do I think now, that an outline of those policies amounts, *tout court*, to a statement of Conservatism. The same might be said of monetarism. I would personally regard a description of someone as a monetarist—or even a Keynesian for that matter—as less significant than a description of him as, say, a Christian or a Conservative.

This point needs to be made emphatically. We have been told, for example, that there exists something called the 'new Conservatism' and that this Conservatism rests on the twin beliefs that the quantity of money determines the rate of inflation and that the government can control the quantity of money.[2] It seems to me that as a dyed-in-the wool, true-blue,

[2] See Nigel Lawson, *The New Conservatism*, London, 1980.

100 per cent Tory, you could either accept or reject those notions without being one iota less a Tory. Of course, a sensible Conservative—a sensible socialist, for that matter—would accept that a substantial excess of growth in money over growth in output accommodates inflation and that rapid changes in the amount of money in circulation disrupt the economy. I think that such a Conservative might also believe that it would be foolish to underestimate the effect on our economic lives of the post-Vietnam explosion of commodity prices (and particularly the price of oil) or of the collapse of stable international monetary arrangements.

We might question whether the West has given sufficient attention to seeking political solutions to the problems that have resulted from these developments. But, above all, the sensible Conservative would doubt the wisdom of testing his colleagues' or his predecessors' ideological soundness by the answers they gave to these Lockeian questions about the money supply.

I have concentrated on this point of the inadequacy of monetarism as a definition of Conservatism for two reasons. First, no one denies, I think, that the consequences of reducing inflation are bound to be painful. There is plenty in our traditional Conservative philosophy that we can draw on to help alleviate that pain, to limit the loss of jobs and output over the years to come and to retain public consent for our policies.

I doubt whether, if we were to see politics solely in terms of the quantity theory of money, such options would come as readily to mind or hand. So even while we pursue a broadly monetarist policy to abate inflation, we can—and, I am sure, will—pursue other Tory goals. We will put forward more positive measures to help the young who have no jobs. We will recognize in our policies that there is no concentration between, on the one hand, being determined not to prevent industrial change and, on the other, being prepared to play a part as a Government in making such a change easier. We will take a lead in encouraging greater realism in pay bargaining so that more jobs are saved as the recession deepens.

The second reason for refusing to accept a mechanistic and narrow definition of Conservatism has to do more with political than with economic management. I have no doubt that the Conservative Party will be able to take the strain. But that will be more of an effort if, at the very moment when the breadth and generosity of our traditional beliefs are most needed, we seek to redefine them in a morally limited and intellectually stunted way. Part of the strength of the Conservative Party has been the balancing of the Liberal and Tory traditions of liberty and order. I am not sure which of those is 'wet' and which is 'dry', but I do know that if we try to ignore one or the other, or if we waste our time and our energy attacking the legitimacy of either, we shall finish up like the Labour Party: submerged in the soup.

Iain Macleod had a masterly grasp of economics. He attained the highest economic office of all, Chancellor of the Exchequer, but he never forgot that economic and social structures are inseparably connected and that, while they may be prised apart for methodological purposes, they cannot be isolated from each other for purposes of political action. Furthermore, while politics were for Iain certainly a matter of conviction, they were also profoundly concerned with conversion and persuasion.

The theory of monetarism may or may not be true. I am an agnostic on economic theology, but I am wholly convinced that, painful though it may be, there is no alternative to cutting back public expenditure and that to roll back the frontiers of the state, and so to cut down on our enormous and swollen state and local government bureaucracy, is a positive good. Welfare capitalism is now facing a profound crisis—how is it all to be paid for without impossibly high levels of taxation?

Yet I am equally convinced that the reduction of public expenditure is a means, not an end. The achievement of strength through misery has never, as far as I know, been a Tory doctrine. Indeed it was Bagehot who declared: 'the essence of Toryism is enjoyment.' The ends are provision of incentives for the creation of wealth, the supply of investment for the modernizing of our industry, the removal of the blocks which prevent the gifts and talents of our people from realizing their full potential. These are the purposes which we must stress and present as offering hope for the future. The Tory theme is not that public provision of social services is too high, but that our economy is so structured that we cannot afford the level of social service that we need. We have, in the words of Peter Jenkins, become 'a poor but expensive country', and it is that situation which the Government is attempting to change.

What general political attitudes do we need to carry through our economic and other policies to success? We do not want to counter dogma with dogma and offer a mirror right-wing image to that of the doctrinaire left. One of the most important themes of Conservative philosophy has always been its rejection of Utopias and its insistence that politics is an empirical activity in which there can be no absolutes when it comes to what is either possible or desirable. Utopias are not for us. That, of course, does not imply that Conservatives have no political objectives other than the attainment and preservation of office. As a party we may be short on dogma, but we are long on values. One of those values is a recognition of the variety of human nature and of human beings and an appreciation of the need for political flexibility. Burke's is the classic statement of the Conservative position: 'Circumstances (which with some gentlemen pass for nothing) give in reality to every political principle its distinguishing colour and discriminating effect. The circumstances are what render every civil and political scheme beneficial or noxious to mankind.' Nowhere do circumstances change more swiftly or more unpredictably than in the realm of economics. The strategy of the Government will have to be pursued resolutely and over a long period if it is to succeed, but as a party we must avoid the danger of elevating our economic priorities to absolute moral principles from which it is impossible to deviate, or which it is impossible to develop, in any circumstances. We need, in other words, a stabilization programme, without which there can be no hope for the eventual stimulation of the private sector. However, as John Biffen pointed out in a prophetic article in the *Sunday Times* in 1974, 'Arguments may then proceed about the level at which the budget should be balanced and what ought to be the component items of public expenditure and taxation.' We must always be prepared to adjust our measures to take account of events which, in the nature of things, could not have been foreseen when the measures were initially formulated.

So it is balance that should characterize Conservative economic policy, and this has deeper philosophical roots. The need for balance arises from two Tory insights into the human condition: the unique worth of the individual, and mankind's inherited mistake. Ultimately, these *aperçus* have a religious foundation. Christianity provides a theological basis for them both. The value of the individual arises from his relationship with God and his eternal destiny, but this bright picture is shadowed by his capacity for evil and the depth of his sin. Liberal economics is based on an appreciation of the value of the individual and, accordingly, possesses a profound truth. Furthermore, the Tory Party must always recall the necessity of carrying the support and consent of the public when it plans to make changes.

GOVERNING BY CONSENT

The constitutional history first of England, and then of Great Britain, is the history of government (in different forms and degrees) by consent. Kings had to rule with the consent of the baronage, then the barons with that of the gentry, then the gentry and middle class with that of the common people, and so our present parliamentary system ultimately emerged. Our system of government has drawn its strength throughout the centuries from the breadth of this consent. It has been continually modified and adjusted to secure the broad support of those outside the ruling group. I believe that this process—the development and extension of consent—holds a lesson for us today.

No one denies that the fundamental changes that we have to make can be accomplished without sacrifice and difficulty. There is, for example, no way in which we can abate inflation without losing jobs and output in the short run. In order to get through that period we shall need public understanding, public consent, for what we are doing. But, just as important, that consent is essential if the changes we make today are to last until tomorrow and the next day. We could not base a new beginning for Britain on grudging and sullen acquiescence.

We have good foundations to build on. Mrs Thatcher's Government was elected in May 1979 as a result of a dramatic change of opinion among the electorate *as a whole*. Moderate trade unionists appalled by the scenes of the previous winter, council tenants longing to buy their homes, parents wishing to raise educational standards—all rallied to the Conservative Party, often for the first time. Conservatives obtained a higher swing from Labour than at any time since 1950.

The consent was renewed in the election of 1983, which returned Mrs Thatcher's Government with a record post-war majority. Yet the election statistics contained a warning: the Conservative percentage of the vote dropped several points from that achieved in 1979. The Conservative victory was not an outright one—it owed as much to the division of its opponents as to any other factor.

It is imperative that consent, having been gained, is retained. We must explain that our policies are aimed at securing and retaining it. Our sensible and well-judged reforms in employment law—modifying the closed shop, encouraging secret ballots, outlawing secondary picketing—are intended to bring trade unions back to their proper role of responsible wage bargaining and to help to make their leadership more accountable to their members. These reforms are supported by the great majority of trade unionists.

Similarly, by securing wider ownership—through encouraging home ownership, through share option schemes, through the disposal of public assets—we are laying the groundwork for wider consent throughout British society. By dispersing property and ownership we will ensure that it is not just the wealthy— or the Exchequer—who benefit from economic revival; it will be British families. By sheltering those on pensions and supplementary benefit from the ravages of inflation we have demonstrated our sense of responsibility to the old, the sick, the disadvantaged. By creating the fiscal and monetary framework within which the business of wealth creation can go forward we will be able to provide social services and benefits comparable with those currently enjoyed by our wealthier, more successful competitors. `Even now, under severe financial constraints, we are actually funding the NHS more generously than did the Labour Party.

This is a moderate, responsible programme. It is a balanced approach which combines the easing of controls with a concern for the 'condition of the people'. What could be more traditionally Conservative?

There is no doubt that the societies which have relied on fostering man's self-interest have reaped great rewards in terms of freedom and high living standards. This is the justification for capitalism: that under it the ordinary person is freer and better off than under socialism. The case for the free market economy is reinforced because, in Reinhold Niebuhr's words, 'there is no one in society good or wise enough finally to determine how the individual's capacities had best be used for the common good or his labour rewarded.'[3] The man in Whitehall definitely does not know best. Self-interest may not be normative, but it constitutes a reality which has to be recognized and for which there is no substitute.

So far so good for the market economy. But there comes a point at which the good Conservative must part company with the liberal enthusiast: it is allied to the theory that justice, harmony and the highest common good are automatically achieved by the operation of the free market.

The whole history of the nineteenth century in Britain and elsewhere refutes this assertion, as does the history of the 1930s both in Britain and in the United States. Mr Callaghan's rather moving 'valedictory' speech at Blackpool in 1980 indicated that his Labour Party membership rested not on Marxism but on his personal experiences during that period. Property, as the Fathers of the Church knew well enough, has a Janus face and can be a source of injustice as well as a defence of individual rights against exploitation by others. The intervention of the state is thus required to restrain individuals and to promote justice. The art of Conservative politics is to strike the right balance and to permit the fostering of self-interest without exposing weaker individuals to exploitation and the community to disruption. The equilibrium of the free market is a myth because it regards man as an economic rationalist, ignoring his motives of pride, ambition and self-aggrandizement.

Tory realism thus sets its face against the Utopian and sentimental politics of the liberal right and the socialist left. No doubt, if faced with a choice between evils, the right-wing alternative would be preferable, since individual injustice is never as oppressive as the centralized authoritarian version, but the Tory path is a true *via media*. Faced with a clash of warring creeds, the Tory response is to mix them and somehow to synthesize them.

Conservatives tend to go for the middle principles in the country, where the middle principles matter. And why not? The English, after all, have a temperamental incapacity for absolutes. The one metaphysical principle that we have been able to imbibe is to be against the Pope, and even that is beginning to weaken.

Conservatism, as Mr T. E. Utley has pointed out, is a broader concept than capitalism.[4] Central to Conservative thinking is the idea of community, which moderates the rigours of the clash between individual and state. Conservatives have faith in social spontaneity and organic growth. They see society as a true *koinonia*, the manifestations of a life of co-

---

[3] See Gordon Harland *The Thought of Reinhold Niebuhr*, Oxford, 1960, p. 250.
[4] T. E. Utley, 'Capitalism: The Moral Case', *Politics Today*, (Conservative Central Office), 29 September 1980.

operation and reconciliation shared by those who hold certain ideas in common. The common good is a complex, not a simple, concept. Public order and civil peace, the security of the young, the protection of the weak and the old and the inexperienced, the maintenance of the civilized decencies of public behaviour—all are included, but the common good extends beyond these to other moral and social values. Together they constitute the wisdom of a great society transmitted over generations, which furnishes the intuitional *a priori* of both the rationalities and the technicalities of public and private law. These values are so widely accepted and so tenaciously held that if they are challenged by the exercise of power, public opinion, drawing upon them, is able to energize political action to defend them. This is precisely what happened in the winter of 1979 and in the subsequent general election.

A CHURCH, NOT A SECT

A characteristic of the Conservative Party which flows from its synthesizing role is that, like the Church of England, it is comprehensive. It is indeed a Church as opposed to a sect. The party is based not on formulae or dogmas but on certain broad principles which, precisely because of their breadth, are capable of differing interpretations. Thus in their day Mr Enoch Powell and Sir Edward Boyle had, and in our own day Sir Ian Gilmour and Sir Keith Joseph, have, despite distinctive intellectual approaches, good and equal claims to describe themselves as Tories. This broadness of approach leads to a spirit of tolerance at every level of the party. The witch drives and heresy hunts of the left are, happily, unknown in Tory circles.

There is no means of withdrawing the Tory whip from a recalcitrant Member of Parliament, although he may resign it if he wishes to do so. Other agreeable side-effects are that dirty political linen is not often laundered in public and that splits and fissures in the Cabinet have, on the whole, been healed or concealed in Tory administrations. Of course, should things change and should the party become committed to a doctrinal system, this harmony would be likely to become weakened or to be replaced by dissonance and discord.

This comprehensiveness of the party is mirrored in its electoral support. I suppose that the majority of industrialists and the well-to-do are Tories, but the party has never been the creature of the Confederation of British Industry in the way that Labour has been, at times, the puppet of the unions. The genius of the party has been to hold on to its traditional supporters, like farmers and country folk, while adding new recruits from the urban and industrial classes. This process was seen at work at the election of 1979. As every Conservative candidate knows, there has always been a nucleus of Tory working-class support on council housing estates, but at the election of 1979 the swing to the Tories on the council estates was unprecedented in its sweep and strength. This movement, as the election of 1983 showed, was cemented by the opportunity to buy their own houses afforded by Mr Heseltine's Housing Act and strengthened still further by the extraordinary action of the Labour Party in insisting that councils be given the right in future to buy back houses sold at their selling price. It was all summed up by Disraeli, who understood the Tory Party better than any other of its leaders, when he declared: 'Unless it is a national party it is nothing.'

Disraeli put the same point graphically and clearly in 1868. His words deserve pondering and repetition:

> In a progressive country change is constant; and the great question is not whether you should resist change which is inevitable, but whether that change should be carried out in deference to the manners, the customs, the laws, and the traditions of the people, or whether it should be carried out in deference to abstract principles and arbitrary and general doctrines. The one is a national system. . . . I have always considered that the Tory Party was the national party of England. It is not formed of a combination of oligarchs and philosophers who practise on the sectarian prejudices of a portion of the people.[5]

The Conservative Party has succeeded better and lasted longer than any other party in the democracies of Europe and North America because it has usually taken that wise advice.

PATRIOTISM

The Tory Party is the party of patriotism. In Britain patriotic sentiment runs deep but is to a large extent hidden. Our imagination is strong but suppressed. Patriotism is a potential rather than an active force. It can become positive and creative only if our citizens are vividly and often reminded of their shared heritage and of their mutual dependence. The remarkable capacity of the Royal Family to identify itself with the country as a whole and thus to create national harmony is one of the happiest and most successful features of post-war British life. We cannot, however, any longer leave that function to be discharged exclusively by what Bagehot called 'the dignified parts of the constitution'; it must be taken up by what are called (perhaps, one may think, inappropriately) the 'efficient' parts of the constitution as well. Politicians who want to promote identity with the

---

[5] See Robert Blake, *Disraeli*, Eyre & Spottiswoode, 1966, p. 482.

nation as a whole have to impose on themselves a self-denying ordinance and to observe certain limits when criticizing political opponents. A Government which wishes to evoke national unity must be self-restrained: the nation has a rooted distaste for 'yah-boo' politics which, however appropriate to Eatanswill, are out of place in a mature political democracy. I am, of course, suggesting not that Tories have a monopoly of patriotism but that the values of the party are pre-eminently those of Queen and country. You can see that at Conservative meetings in a hundred village halls, where it is the Union Jack, and not the Red flag, that swathes the table; you can hear it at the adoption of any Tory candidate, where the meeting always concludes with the national anthem, not the 'Internationale'. It is reflected in a deep love of the countryside, of the fields and villages and hamlets which the party is concerned to protect from urban destruction and pollution.

The Tory Party is the party of national pride, the party that cares about Britain's role in the world, the party not of little England but of Great Britain—a fact that was clear enough during the Falklands war in 1982. This was the impulse that led the party to support entry into the EEC and that keeps it faithful to its commitment. It is only from within a wider grouping that British influence can be exercised effectively today. Realism, rather than idealism, makes Conservatives pro-Europe. We accept a European framework as essential for Britain's economic prosperity and, above all, for her successful defence from external attack.

Realism dominates the Conservative approach to foreign policy, which is seen primarily as a means of advancing and protecting British interests. This approach is not as narrow as it at first appears, since as a trading nation we have a paramount need for peace and stability. The promotion of these benefits not only Britain but the rest of the world as well. Realism makes Tories cool about the United Nations, not because we do not believe in international organizations, but because we look at what these organizations are actually doing (not what they say they are doing) and hence see their limitations. This approach may at times appear cynical, but a cynic's merit is to see the facts.

As to the internal politics of other countries, whether South Africa or the Soviet Union, a Tory tradition which goes back to Castlereagh and Canning is based on the premise that the character of the regimes of foreign countries is not a primary concern of foreign policy. This attitude has its dangers, but it spares the party the moral contortions which the Labour Party has to go through to reconcile its principles with common sense, and it rules out crusades. Only a tiny minority of Tories approve of apartheid, but an equally small number think that moral condemnation of apartheid entails a boycott of South Africa over trade and defence.

One of the dangers of the current stridencies of the cold war, originating in the White House but reverberating in Downing Street, is that they prevent the really crucial issue of foreign policy being raised, let alone answered. Can the Soviet Union and the United States exist peacefully together? This is a question that Conservative foreign policy needs to resolve before all others.

LIBERTIES UNDER THE LAW

Conservatives are concerned not only with the country but also with the individuals who make it up. Liberty as an abstraction has never had much appeal, but the particular and traditional liberties of a country's subjects are another matter. 'Law and order' is an unfortunate phrase with particular racialist associations, but what Conservatives are concerned about is something rather different—the preservation of liberties under the law. Hence there is nothing Eldonine about the Tory distrust of demonstrations, no panic fear, but a hardheaded assessment of a position in which extremists are using the right of demonstration not to reform institutions or to extend liberties but to destroy them.

One liberty to which Conservatives attach particular importance is freedom of choice. This principle can be seen at work in both social and economic policy. Conservatives would rather that individuals did the saving necessary for the nation than that the Government should do it for them: hence the emphasis on reducing direct taxation. They would rather see an individual making provision for his own old age than the Government: hence the insistence on the right to contract out of state pension schemes, provided alternative private facilities are available. A basic Tory approach is that the state should do nothing for the individual which he is able to do adequately for himself.

This principle is balanced by a concern for the condition of the people, which is an intrinsic part of the party's tradition. Unlike the Republican Party in the United States, the Tory Party in Britain has not encountered much difficulty in distinguishing between socialism and social welfare. The party can invoke not only the shades of Shaftesbury and Disraeli but also those of Baldwin, Chamberlain and (if shade is the right word) Macmillan as well. Conservatives instinctively want to see voluntary service and self-help encouraged, but no Tory wants to see a dismantling of the welfare state.

Ultimately the basis of Conservatism is a recognition of both the possibilities and the limitations of human nature. Tories believe in original sin, although not all would give it such a precise theological formulation. Belief in the pefectibility of man is a delusion of the left, not of the right. Accordingly, Conservatives have a lively appreciation of the value of limited government, knowing that there is much that government cannot do, much that individuals and families have to do for themselves. No Tory believes that politics can create the good life; politics can provide only for its possibility. Variety, choice, freedom, enjoyment—these are the Tory watchwords, and they correspond to deep needs in human nature. When the Labour Party is no more than a dim historical memory, the Tory Party is likely still to be going strong.

THE PRESERVATION OF OUR INSTITUTIONS

Tory patriotism is expressed in pride in our institutions, especially those of the monarchy, Parliament and the courts. Tories are, however, animated by more than sentiment in this respect: there is a hard-headed assessment that in a democracy it is these institutions which provide necessary protection against the tyranny—so feared by Mill—of the majority will or the naked and brutal exertion of power by either bureaucracies or strong but minority interests.

Disraeli was fully seized of the point: in his constitutional reflections in his Crystal Palace speech of 1872, he referred not to 'defending our constitution' but to 'maintaining our institutions'.[6] Furthermore, he was urging not so much their maintenance as their restoration.

Here the Tory record has been good. Concern for efficiency in government, for an overhaul of government departments, for a reformed prime ministerial office springs, then, from an antique root, and indeed interest in efficient administration goes back beyond Disraeli to the Toryism of Pitt and Peel. The party has set its face against a unicameral legislature, believing that this would open a Pandora's box of dangers to individual liberty, and is gradually espousing the reform of the second chamber as a response to Labour's threat of abolition.

The only reforms of the Lords in recent years have been carried out by Tory Governments, the most notable and effective being Mr Harold Macmillan's taking up of Bagehot's suggestion and making it possible to create life peerages. Equally, it has been a Tory Government, the present one, which has set about a systematic reform of the House of Commons. This process must continue if parliamentary government is to be made effective once again. The new and expanded committee systems which we have set up—the implementation of the reforms suggested by the Procedure Committee—the new Public Bill procedure and the suggestions for a more effective exercise by Parliament of its historic prerogative of withholding or granting supply constitute reforms wholly consistent with the Tory tradition. They have already brought the Commons back into the centre of effective political life.

[6] 'Conservative and Liberal Principles', 24 June 1872.

ETHICS AND POLITICS

There is an intrinsic connection between ethics or morals and political freedom. The threat of totalitarian and extremist ideologies, whether of left or right, still menaces free society today, but an even greater danger is a collapse into an anarchy which is amoral and valueless.

A generation could quickly grow up ignorant and uncertain of our ethical and cultural heritage. This I characterize as the threat of a new barbarism. Today's barbarian is not outside the city walls but within them. He wears no bearskin and carries no club; he may be armed with nothing more lethal than a ballpoint pen. The nearest he may get to the primeval forest is the quadrangle of an Oxford (or a Cambridge) College, but he is a barbarian none the less if he undermines the religious and moral values on which our traditions of civility are based.

This undermining may occur in a number of different ways. Moral and spiritual issues may be judged and resolved solely by their practical results, or they may be reduced to the status of linguistic problems and disposed of by an analysis of language, or they may be treated as matters of wholly subjective feeling. All these approaches would reject, implicitly or explicitly, what for centuries has been the foundation of Western society: the belief in an order of values both objective and universal, the following of which constitutes the good life and its rejection the bad. The rejection of reason as a sure guide in human affairs destroys not only liberty but equality and fraternity as well. There can be no liberty without self-restraint, no equality without the recognition of others as endowed with reason and rights like ourselves, no fraternity without a sense of shared values. Without brotherhood, society is reduced to a conglomeration of colliding atoms, in which conflicts are decided by force, not law. Warfare such as this destroys, in the end, the very idea of community, that form of society in which what is shared is more important than what divides, and in which men remain locked in arguments but not in battle or fratricidal strife.

Society's concern with moral values springs, then, not only from their intrinsic worth but also from the perceptions of the connection between the moral and social orders. One rests upon the other. The state borrows from above and below itself: it looks upwards to religion and morality as well as downwards to history and sociology. An earlier age produced the aphorism 'No bishop, no king'. Our own would do well to ponder on another: 'No morality: no law'. To deny or to lose sight of the ethical nature of political freedom is folly, but it is a folly characteristic of our time. It was the Federation of Conservative Students, of all bodies, that voted enthusiastically for the vulgar slogan that people should exercise the same freedom with their private parts that they already enjoyed in relation to their private property, in total and unhappy ignorance of Lord Acton's definition of freedom as 'not the power of doing what we like but the right of being able to do what we ought'.

The essence of a free society is that order is not imposed by force from the top but emerges spontaneously from within in obedience to restraints and imperatives that stem from inwardly possessed moral principles. Democracy is thus much more than a mechanism, more than a political experiment. It constitutes nothing less than a spiritual and moral enterprise. Those who would be politically free have constantly to control themselves. Without that self-restraint which springs from a sense of values, internally acknowledged and accepted freedom cannot survive. Emerging within society as a shared possession, this moral force alone has power both to discipline the destructive powers of men and at the same time to overcome the inertia, indifference, boredom and triviality which more and more seem to be the mark of our time. A paramount duty of the Tory Party as Labour disintegrates into a welter of fads and fancies, of faction and fratricide, is to maintain and renew the moral consensus of the nation on which our political institutions ultimately rest.

5

Religious and Moral Values in Schools

To be concerned with education is to be involved in values. The purposes of education are varied—to impart knowledge, to inculcate skills, to fit people for work in adult life—but perhaps the most important of all educational aims is to help young people develop as full human beings, inclined and equipped to lead the good life rather than the bad. In this task religious and moral values are inevitably involved.

What, then, are schools to teach in these vital and intimately related spheres? Private schools will be concerned with the objects of their particular foundation; maintained Church schools will pursue denominational ends;[1] but what of the maintained non-Church schools, the 'state' schools of popular parlance? What values should they seek to transmit? I believe there can only be one answer: the values of the society by which they are supported and those of the parents from whom they derive their mandate and legitimacy and to whom the right to educate their children inalienably belongs.

These values can certainly be ascertained. Solipsism is a concept of metaphysics not of politics or sociology. Members of every society hold certain ideas in common concerning the individual, the state, religion and morality: indeed, one can describe the essence of civilization as the agreement to live together in peace and amity, respecting certain ethical values.

The importance of our schools in transmitting, and so preserving, our moral inheritance cannot be over-estimated. They play a co-ordinate role with the family in this vital task, on the successful discharge of which so much of our future depends. The educational system remains the foundation of the civilization of the dialogue which differentiates free and

---

[1] 'Aided' schools now receive all their running costs from the state, including the payment of teachers' salaries and 85 per cent of their capital costs. To seek higher financial aid than this could constitute a threat to the independence of Church schools. I would also hope that in the special context of the Northern Ireland situation, the Churches could make progress in finding ways of educating children of different faiths together.

responsible men from animals on the one hand and criminals on the other. Wolves don't discuss the merits of hunting in packs, and guns never argue.

Such is the case for giving a high priority to the teaching of moral values in schools, but we cannot stop there and are driven on to raise other questions: where do these values come from? On what ultimately do they rest? The answer is religion. To say this is not to deny the contribution of secularism and rationalism to morality. Much less does it reject the proposition—supported by the facts—that morality can exist without religion. But it is to assert that within the British tradition morality has drawn its inspiration, its strength and its sanctions much more from Christianity than from the Enlightenment. It could, of course, have been otherwise: the *philosophes* might have been our prophets, and Hinduism or Mohammedanism might have been our spiritual inspiration (and one day may be), but in fact they have not been so. Christianity is the soil in which the roots of our morality have been planted. Cut them off from this and the morality is likely to die.

Freedom, democracy and morality in Britain are all three heavily indebted to Christian insights. Of course, good theology is no guarantee of good government—otherwise Roman Catholics would be placed in a nice dilemma by the history of the Papal States. Yet Christianity has provided the individual with a profound sense of his own worth. It has given him an alternative source of authority by which to judge and delimit the authority of the state. At the same time, by recognizing the reality of man's sinfulness as well as his dynamic towards virtue, it has contributed to the creation of those institutional and constitutional checks which protect him from the abuse of naked power. On this view the British office of the Leader of the Opposition, which takes into the constitution itself the principle of resistance to government, is a very Christian institution. As Reinhold Niebuhr has put it: 'Man's capacity for justice makes democracy possible; but man's inclination to injustice makes democracy necessary.'

The case for the teaching of religion in our schools is not, then, primarily a theological one—although theology and its adherents may provide some useful ancillary troops—but cultural, historical and social. Christianity has got into the foundations on which our house has been built, and it cannot be taken out without a grave risk of the house falling down.

But how is the end to be achieved within the context of the British schools system? This was the problem facing Lord Butler and Archbishop Temple in the 1940s, and their answer to it was contained in the religious settlement clauses of the 1944 Education Act. The religious schools, Anglican and Catholic in the main, were given an honoured and honourable place in the new national system of education, while in the non-religious state schools religion was guaranteed a limited but important place through an undertaking that non-denominational religious instruction was to be provided and time set aside within the school timetable for worship.

The Butler–Temple clauses have been criticized (most sharply on grounds of their compulsory character), but they have stood the test of time. No political party today proposes their formal alteration. They were intended to stand not on their own but within the context of schools themselves, providing an ethos of ethical and moral values. This too was surely right. To seek to confine moral and religious education within set periods is misconceived: such work, if it is to be done, must be discharged by schools as a whole. Contemporary critics have also concentrated their fire on the worship clauses, taking the view in many cases that while obligatory religious education is acceptable, 'compulsory worship' is not. This line of criticism, while superficially convincing, cannot, I think, be rationally sustained. The justification for including religious instruction in the school curriculum is, as I have endeavoured to show, not theological, but if justice is to be done to the subject educationally, there must be experience of worship: this is the affective side of it. To attempt to understand religion without worship is like being an astronomer who has never seen the stars. Worship is a feature of all religions: it is the attempt to make the divine power felt as a reality within individual lives. The compulsory provision for opening the school day with an act of worship should then be seen not as a form of forced prayer but rather as an opportunity for experiencing an essential part of the subject.[2]

It is true, of course, that much will depend on how the subject is handled. Young people object much more to boredom than to compulsion. School assemblies, then, like marriage ceremonies, should

---

[2] The report of the House of Commons Select Committee on Secondary School Education, which reported on 16 December 1981, had this to say on the subject:

> Our evidence was rather less clear-cut on the question of assemblies. The Church of England Board of Education accepted that there is difficulty at the present time of 'implementing the law relating to a daily act of worship', and noted that 'some schools disregard the law, some perfunctorily observe it, while others have with imagination revolutionized the atmosphere of the assembly.' Cardinal Hume thought that the larger size of schools created obstacles to the implementation of valid 'acts of worship'. The Archbishop of Canterbury felt that more flexibility was required. He was concerned that schools needed an element of carefully planned uplifting experience, but he thought that this purpose could be better served by 'a sort of molecular structure . . . perhaps small group experiences of prayer or silence . . . or sacred music'. Mr Macarthur of the Free Church Federal Council supported the call for flexibility and endorsed the Archbishop's view that quality was much more important than quantity: his view was that it would be better if the provision were carefully planned and possibly occurred once a week. In their written evidence the Church of England Board of Education say that they would 'welcome an opportunity to discuss with the Secretary of State a revision of the clauses in the 1944 Act relating to assemblies so that more flexibility both as regards the frequency and the nature of acts of worship might be possible in the future'. The Free Church Federal Council added that more research is required into current failures and successes in school worship before decisions can responsibly be taken as to future policy.

be as cheerful as circumstances allow. Music, drama, relevance, opportunity for participation, variety—all are important, for without them there will be no religious experience for most pupils, and that is the point of the provision. The decline in church-going is sometimes put forward as a reason for discontinuing religious assemblies, but the opposite conclusion may equally well be drawn. If children do not gain the experience of worshipping together in school, they will be unlikely to get it anywhere else.

It is often maintained that conditions have changed radically since the passing of the 1944 Act and that therefore the religious clauses have lost relevance and should be altered or repealed. This is an exaggeration. What I believe has changed is the attitude to religion of religious people themselves. They are much more 'open' in their approach to their beliefs and practice than they were immediately after the war. The decline of fundamentalist Christianity, the effects of the permissive revolution of the 1960s, the advance of the ecumenical movement among Protestants and the profound changes brought about among Roman Catholics by the Second Vatican Council have led to an extraordinary openness and flexibility among Christians, a development largely welcomed by non-church-goers. This is the major change that has taken place since 1944.

If I am correct in this, there is no case for altering the provisions of the 1944 Act, although there is a real need for new approaches and

---

The report concludes:

> We support both these suggestions. It appears to us that the whole concept and intention behind the school act of worship is in danger of falling into disrepute and that schools are badly in need of considerable guidance. We recommend that the Secretary of State should now begin discussions with all interested bodies, including the Church authorities, about guidance to schools. These discussions should include the possibility that legislative changes may be necessary. We also recommend that HMI should survey current practice in schools as an aid to furthering these discussions. (*Report*, 5.36)

The General Synod of the Church of England Board of Education, in its submission on religious education had this to say:

> *Church* or *ecclesia* means a gathering, an assembly, and communal worship is an essential feature of religions. There is great point, therefore, in regarding assemblies at schools as part of the process of acquiring skills that will be needed in church for religious assemblies. The art of gathering for a common purpose, sharing common endeavour, savouring and participating in common patterns of ritual, using shared song, words, movement or dress, using reflective silence in assembly—all these are precursors to a true and fulfilling participation in worship. Those who make simplistic statements about the need for assemblies to be 'Christian' at school, must be aware of the basic skills that ought to be acquired before one can fully participate. Some assemblies certainly ought to introduce pupils to Christian hymn, song or prayer; some, it would seem to this Board, ought to flow more from aims that are educational than liturgical. There is considerable room for imaginative and careful experiment in this field and the Board wishes to draw attention to the counter-productiveness of badly prepared assemblies. (Evidence to the Select Committee, p. 441)

interpretation of its religious clauses.[3] We are less a church-going people today than then, but church-going was not the basis of the claim that England should be considered a Christian country in 1944. What, then, is meant by the phrase? It means, I think, that we are a people with profound religious and ethical instincts, a people with a long, rich and varied Christian tradition, which is held in esteem by the majority and for which a sizeable minority is part of a living Church tradition. We are a secular society in the sense that civil society has come of age, that it has emancipated itself from ecclesiastical and theological tutelage, but we are certainly not a secular society in the sense that we have made a choice of a rationalist, agnostic model of society, from which all public association with Christianity should be excluded. We are a Christian society in the sense that we are benevolently inclined to the Christian religion, wish it well and at moments of importance and crisis seek its help.

This general attitude is reflected in the public attitude to the teaching of religion in schools. The evidence of polls and surveys is overwhelming: the vast majority of parents want their children to be taught about the Christian religion in our schools. The problem is not one of whether but of how, a more complex problem.

There are a number of ways in which religion should *not* be taught to children. The starting point for religious and moral teaching in schools should be not doubt but certainty. Society has a duty to pass on its experience and knowledge from one generation to another. Thus it would be self-defeating for teachers to give children the impression that they were unsure about what is right and what is wrong, what is true and what is false, and leave children to make up their own minds. Reflection and possibly rejection can come later, but to put it in its crudest terms, children have a right to have something to reject. Furthermore, the method of teaching will vary with the age of the young people being taught: there is no point in teachers having the same attitude to primary schoolchildren as to sixth-formers. All this may seem obvious enough, but there is a school of educational thought which insists that all moral conclusions, as well as decisions, should be left to children from the earliest age. In practice the results of such an approach are chaos and confusion.

A second method to avoid is that of reducing religion to lowest common denominator terms. To try to reduce all religious experience and belief to certain shared concepts is to travesty the special contributions and insights of particular religious faiths.

A third method, favoured by some, of taking children on a kind of rubber-necking tour of the great religions of the world is more likely to

---

[3] The House of Commons Select Committee on Education (1981) recommended that the phrase 'religious instruction' in the 1944 Education Act should be replaced by 'religious education' and that the 'continued existence of voluntary denominational schools with the maintained sector be guaranteed' (London, HMSO, 1981, 116–I, at pp.xlix, lii).

leave them confused and uncertain than anything else. In the limited time available for religious education in the school timetable, this approach is condemned from the start to be superficial and unsatisfying.

What, then, is the best way to teach religion to young people in contemporary schools? The method, I would suggest, has to be both open and committed. It should be made clear to children that the religious approach is a way of looking at the world and interpreting and ordering experience. Religion is not an easy way of finding final answers but a continuing search and quest for God, the infinite and the never fully knowable. The nature of religious education as a quest was stressed in the Crowther Report of 1959:

> Teenagers [it declares] need perhaps before all else to find a faith to live by. They will not all find precisely the same faith and some will not find any. Education can and should play some part in their search. It can assure them that there is something to search for and it can show them where to look and what other men have found.

The Newsom Report of 1963 also laid great stress on spiritual and moral development as a central goal of education, but the Plowden Report of four years later was more ambiguous and failed to give the religious education of children up to 12 the attention and examination which is its due.

The purpose of religious education in county schools today should not be indoctrination. It should strive to awaken children to the spiritual dimension of life and to the possibility of making religious choice and commitment. In this way the lives of young people are potentially enriched: if they are denied the opportunity or live in ignorance of it, they are diminished as human beings. Religious education should seek to set things seen in the context of things not seen. The stress should be on the freedom of faith—a gift freely bestowed and freely taken up. No man can be forced to believe. Furthermore, religious education is education, not evangelism: the latter is a matter for the Church, not the schools.

It is thus essential to stress the general purpose of religious education. As the Durham Report of 1970 states:

> Religious education has its place on the school curriculum because it draws attention to a significant area of human thought and activity. A curriculum which excluded religion would seem to proclaim that religion has not been as real in men's lives as science, or politics or economics. By omission it would appear to deny that religion has been and still is important in man's history.

Yet in one sense there is no such thing as 'religion' as such; there are only 'religions'. All religious thought and experience has arisen or developed within particular traditions. Religious education has to take account of that crucial fact. Religion is not abstract but concrete.

Thus in the teaching of religion there has to be an actual religious model, and the model that should be used in Britain, for cultural and historical reasons, is a Christian one. Christianity has shaped our history and is the form in which the spiritual has come to the majority (although not all) of our people. Our culture lies within the Judaeo-Christian tradition.[4]

The distinctive point about the Christian religion is not only that it is a system of ethics but also that it centres on a person. The heart of Christianity is God's activity in Christ, admirably summed up in the Prayer Book blessing: 'The grace of the Lord Jesus Christ, the love of God, and the fellowship of the Holy Spirit'.

This uniqueness of Christianity and its (in one sense) exclusive claims has to be at the centre of any teaching about it, yet there is nothing inconsistent between this point and asserting the desirability in religious education of comparison with other faiths. In the restricted time available, this should be done. It would be a misunderstanding of Christianity to hold that it asserts that knowledge of God and his laws can come only from Christian revelation: to do so would be to reject the whole of the centuries-old natural law tradition.

But if the model is to be a Christian one, what form is it to take? The 1944 Education Act laid down that religious instruction was to accord with an agreed syllabus drawn up after consultations between the Church of England, local authorities, teachers and other religious bodies. It is easy to deride 'agreed-syllabus religion', and indeed it was so treated by the late Archbishop Downey of Liverpool, who once described it as 'the religion of nobody, taught by anybody and paid for by everybody', yet the purpose of the syllabus was sensible. It was to import some degree of objectivity into religious education and to protect children from the excesses and enthusiasms of religiously inclined (or disinclined) teachers. Voices are once more being raised against the device of the agreed syllabus, but until something better is found to put in its place I would counsel that it should be retained.[5]

---

[4] So, in 1982 the Archbishop of Canterbury, Dr Runcie, told the National Society for the Promotion of Religious Education that Christianity should be central to the religious education of all pupils, regardless of their cultural background: 'While recognizing that a truly pluralistic society should not merely tolerate diversity but value and nurture it, I must also express a fear that at times we seem tempted to sacrifice much of our native Christian tradition on the altar of multi-culturalism.' Christianity, he went on, still held the allegiance of most people in Britain; other faiths were espoused by quite small groups distributed somewhat unevenly throughout the country. 'Hence Christianity should be the main perspective studied by most pupils. I think all children, of whatever cultural background, need to understand Christianity, its nature and spirit, its truth and claims, and its pervasive influence on their present and our past' (*The Times*, 18 March 1982).
[5] This was also the conclusion of the report of the House of Commons Select Committee on Education, already referred to. The Committee endorsed the qualification expressed by

Religious education, as I have stressed, has to justify itself on educational grounds. If it is to do this, it has to reach the standards of other subjects in the curriculum. It needs the support of tests and exams; above all, it requires dedicated and professionally trained teachers. Of these, despite the denials of Education Ministers, there is now an acute shortage.[6] The situation has been made worse by the wholesale closure of education colleges and the drastic reduction in the number of Church-connected colleges. An urgent and swift inquiry is needed into the numbers and training of religious education teachers. The real threat to religious education today is not assault from without but decay from within, and local education authorities need to address themselves urgently to what has to be done to renew religious education in our schools.

Religious education teachers need adequate initial and in-service training in their specialized task. But they need more than this: they require commitment. As Mrs Mary Warnock has said of moral education: 'You cannot teach morality without being committed to morality yourself: and you cannot be committed to morality yourself without holding that some things are right and others wrong.' This judgement is applicable equally to religious education. I do not say that you have to be a Christian to teach religion effectively, but you do have to be committed to a religious view of life. I should have thought that the Church colleges could make a particular contribution in this sphere. In 1944, for better or for worse, the Church of England made a conscious decision to give up many of its secondary schools or to accept controlled status for them and to

---

Cardinal Hume concerning the dangers of treating religions *à la carte* at the expense of searching for the essence underlying different religious beliefs: 'Given our reservation, we welcome the new generation of agreed syllabuses, and we recommend that those authorities which have not already done so should prepare revised syllabuses in consultation with the religious leaders in their communities.'

[6] In March 1982 I tabled a series of Parliamentary Questions to the Secretary of State for Education, over sixty in number, to establish the extent of the crisis in the provisions for religious education (see *Hansard* for 11 March, 18 March, 23 March and 8 April 1982). The figures given illustrate how deplorable the present staffing position is. The Secretary of State's reply showed that 59 per cent of all teachers teaching RE are without formal qualifications in the subject. This compares with only 16 per cent unqualified among those teachers currently teaching biology in maintained secondary schools in England and Wales. There are 12,300 teachers of RE in our secondary schools who have no qualifications in the subject and only 4,800 whose highest teaching qualification is in RE. Twenty-two per cent of primary school and 33 per cent of middle school teacher trainees will receive no course in RE, and the rate of turnover in the staffing of the subject is one of the worst: 43 per cent of secondary RE teachers have five years' experience or less.

Table 8 of the DES Bulletin 6/80 shows that in secondary schools the percentage of pupil periods given to RE is as follows:

First year 4.1%   Fourth year 2.7%
Second year 4.1%   Fifth year 2.6%
Third year 4.0%   Sixth year 1.9%

concentrate on the teacher-training colleges in order to provide 'a Christian presence' in the schools. Religious education is above all where this presence is needed today.

Such a 'presence' has nothing to do with proselytism: rather, it is the provision of a service to others. To teach religion fruitfully in schools today requires rare qualities of openness, tolerance, sensitivity and tact. Those engaged in this sphere should take to heart Gide's reproach of Claudel: 'He uses the crucifix as though it were a bludgeon when it ought to be a lamp.' The more I study the complexities of this subject and reflect upon it, the more I am convinced that the key to the future is in the hands of the teachers. Religious education, and indeed education as a whole, will be as good as the men and women whom we can recruit to this high vocation.

Such is the depth of the moral and religious crisis through which our society and our schools are passing that we can no longer afford to take the High Whig line of Mr Harold Macmillan, who once declared that matters of religion were best left to the archbishops. Religious education is both too important and too threatened to be left to the professionals. It should be the first concern of all those who regard life, with all its opportunities and all its beauties, as a God-given gift, who see man's course as a trajectory not confined to time and space, who are repelled by the foolishness and aridity of materialism and who are concerned that the great spiritual and ethical achievements and traditions of our country should not be lost but passed on to enrich future generations.

One of the main contributory factors to the shortage of RE teachers is the lack of a proper career structure. It is not surprising that the rate of turnover in this subject is so high. Bishop David Konstant, Auxiliary Roman Catholic Bishop in Westminster, has himself pointed out that because there are too few RE teachers, there are inadequate opportunities for teaching religion at the higher levels in the schools, and this means in turn that few people are available to enter the teaching profession as teachers of religion.

The report of the House of Commons Select Committee on Education in 1981 referred to the Archbishop of Canterbury's concern about the comparatively small number of specialist advisers in RE in local education authorities. One of the Committee's principal recommendations was that more properly qualified religious education teachers and inspectors should be appointed (Recommendation 17, *Report*, para. 5.37).

6

The Arts and Society

———————

The arts—be they popular or fine—constitute some of the greatest achievements of the human spirit. This is not to say that I elevate art or the arts into a religion. The drama is not the Messiah: the arts will not save us, but they do perform for society some of the functions which religion discharged in the past. That is one reason why they are so important; they also show us what is happening in the society in which we live, and they identify the directions in which we are all moving. They teach us most effectively truths about human beings. One can learn more about old age by looking at a portrait by Rembrandt than at countless blue books.

In a technological society in which material plenty is matched by spiritual starvation the arts remind us of the existence of a higher order of values, and the artist keeps us in touch with those mysterious powers in man and in the universe before which we can only stand in awe and gratitude. And what is artistic and creative genius but a gift which comes unheralded and uncovenanted?

The arts give us insights and help us to impose unity on the endless and apparently meaningless flux of our personal existence. The task of a Minister for the Arts is an important but humble one: it is to help to create and to preserve a framework within which the arts can flourish. He is a trustee of the possibilities of civilization. He is in the position of Bagehot's constitutional sovereign—he has the right to be consulted, to encourage and to warn.

We are not, I suppose, at the most self-confident period of our history. World power has passed from us and is unlikely ever to return; while some find this more depressing than others, we are all affected by the fact. We are facing many industrial troubles. British industry is not in an ideal state: we are all aware of that. What we as a nation are not perhaps as aware of as we should be is that there is one sphere in which we still lead the world: the arts. In literature, drama, painting, sculpture, music and poetry the British contribution is substantial and continuing. Our great post-war successes have been in the arts. Furthermore, although power has passed from us, influence has not. The establishment of the English language throughout the world has been our one permanent imperial conquest. How foolish, then, the counsels of those who bid us cut down our investment in the British Council, which does such a magnificent job, on slender resources, of spreading knowledge of our language and culture throughout the world, or of those who wish us to reduce the number of foreign students who come here to learn about our culture and institutions. The time for us to get worried is not when such students come here but when they do not.

Our artistic achievements bring us prestige throughout the world, but we do not value them enough. Medieval folk were wise: at a time when religion still held sway every town with a claim to impress had its own hermit as a necessary status symbol. Would that that were so with artists today.

THE ARTS: PAYING THEIR WAY

The arts are not justified only on their own merit: they pay their way. All the arts, from literature to painting, earn money for Britain, but this is especially true of the performing arts. Our earnings from tourists amount to over £3,000 million a year, and over two-thirds of tourists give as their reason for coming to Britain their desire to avail themselves of our arts facilities.[1] In 1981, in the West End alone, the theatre—that excludes Stratford, Glyndebourne, Edinburgh and the other great regional centres—contributed £21.8 million directly to the balance of payments.[2] One has only to look at Broadway, New York, where so many of the shows running are British, to realize what a financial contribution the theatre is making to our export drive. Our exports of books earn us over £250 million—and so I could go on, but enough has been said to make the point.

These considerations should make us as a nation generous in our public support of the arts. One of the major causes of Britain's economic decline has been the willingness of successive Governments to invest in declining industries, to shore up the inefficient, to press crutches on lame ducks, and the result has been to starve our growth industries of the capital they need for expansion and re-equipment. We have, in short, invested in failure rather than in success. We have to change this course if we are to arrest our national decline and to restore slashed living standards. One sphere that, because of its record of economic success, has a unique claim on public investment is the arts.

[1] See British Tourist Authority's *Overseas Visitors Survey, 1977–78*.
[2] In 1981 of an estimated 6.9 million visitors, 49 per cent said they intended to visit the theatre during their stay; see *Overseas Tourism on the West End Theatre* (1982).

Yet I return to the topic of the intrinsic value of artistic activity as a justification for public support. As Lord Bridges put it in his Romanes Lecture of 1958:

> The heart of this matter is surely that the arts can give to all of us, including those who lack expert knowledge of any of them, much of what is best in human life and enjoyment; and that a nation which does not put this at the disposal of those who have the liking and the capacity for it is failing in a most important duty.

The contemporary view of the state in Britain is that it exists to promote the welfare of all the people, and an essential part of that welfare is the opportunity for spiritual development that the arts facilitate.

The arts in Britain, however, have their enemies, and battle has to be joined. Public opinion, if not hostile, is apathetic; it has to be aroused and interested in the problems of the arts in contemporary society. Then there is official myopia and political indifference. Political parties do not give the future of the arts a prominent place in their programmes: with a handful of honourable exceptions, politicians tend to be Philistines. There is the greed and the cynicism bred by a consumer society, of which we are all to some extent the victims. This in turn encourages artists to isolate themselves from a society which they find heartless and uninterested: an internal immigration can be effective as an external one. The arts have to contend as well with an educational system which is inadequate in its response to the arts and frequently unimaginative. Finally, there is the cultural sterility of so many urban residential areas. As Dr Ulsar-Gleichen observed once, at a symposium on the arts in Berlin:

> This environment lacks the factors which might be biologically re-conciling, might permit leeway for human peculiarities, might create cosiness and security, might permit accidental encounters—in a word, we are lacking the essential environmental conditions in which a cultural life can prosper.

Increased public expenditure on the arts may ameliorate these problems, but it will not provide a radical answer. The first essential is to create an enlarged constituency for the arts so that they become a social and hence a political force, in the sense that they have to be taken seriously by those in positions of power in our society. I fear that the cultural boom and expansion in which many of us put our faith is more of a myth than a reality. The market for culture may well be as low as 3 per cent of the population, and there is little evidence of expansion among those who traditionally have taken no interest in the arts.

Of course, there are those who are prepared to accept that culture, of its very nature, must remain a minority interest. Culture, by definition, derives from the biological principle of selection from undifferentiated matter to produce a coherent, developed strain, and this will always be a minor strand. The significance of a major opera house, according to this view, is not that two thousand people on any night will have the opportunity to attend a performance, although that is important, but that the opera house constitutes a centre of excellence which is of benefit to the whole of a nation's musical life.

I believe that one can accept the premise of the importance of centres of excellence for the arts without being driven to the conclusion that one must accept a static role for them and must give up any effort to expand the arts constituency. The Ark of the Covenant must be safeguarded, but there should be missionary endeavour as well. How, then, is knowledge and appreciation of the arts and culture to be spread?

First, one must take a broad view of the nature of culture and the arts. One should perceive and project their social role in creating a fully human environment, doing something to redress, and in the future to prevent, the hideous failures of our planners and social administrators, who have created sterile townscapes without any regard for the encouragement of community. This thought is in line with that of Lord Eccles, who in an article on the role of culture in *The Times* wrote:

> Everyone in some degree can share in an attitude of mind which through the choice of personal experience enriches his life inwardly and outwardly through what he and his friends make of the environment in which they live. Such an attitude of mind could be called a religious view of life. Unless I believe that truth and beauty are better than lies and ugliness, why should I make the effort to refine my taste? Unless I believe that a unified community is better than a divided community, why should I look for common ground between my neighbours and myself? So the question that must first be answered is 'Can we live by bread alone, and if not, by what else can we live?'[3]

I say 'Amen' to that manner of presenting the argument.

The second point that flows from this is that when we consider the arts we must move outside the 'ceremonies of culture' which act as bulwarks, which certainly keep the minority in but equally surely keep the majority out. As I said in my Richmond Lecture at Downing College, Cambridge: 'We must present the arts in settings where the barricades set up by opera houses, concert halls and art galleries are at least scaled down. The arts should not be a fortress but an open city.'[4] Thus one of the best things that ever happened to the ballet in Britain was the strike of scene shifters some years ago that forced the Royal Ballet Company out of the Opera House into a tent in Battersea Park. A whole new audience for the ballet came

[3] *The Times*, 4 August 1977.
[4] 25 November 1977.

forward once the art form was presented on the level of their own lives and the need to scale the Capitol was done away with. A similar success was enjoyed by the Béjart contemporary dance company in Paris when it put on its performances in the unlikely setting of the Palais des Sports. Opera Houses are necessary and have their place, but we must move out from them, away from *die Stimmung der Heiligkeit* (the odour of sanctity) which keeps so many at bay. By a happy technological development, we have in television a medium ideally suited to transmitting the essence of opera and ballet performances, and of orchestral music as well, and projecting it beyond the class and cultural barriers of the past. In Britain we are most fortunate of all, having in the BBC an independent corporation with a flourishing cultural tradition and a group of independent companies spurred on by a variety of motives to emulate its achievement. Surely here is a field where the unremitting labour of an Arts Minister would produce worthwhile fruit?

Looking back, we now see as one of the great achievements of the nineteenth century the adaptation and transmission of a culture, aristocratic in origin, to the new industrial and commercial classes that became dominant as the century progressed. Our century must do the same for the new classes of our time, or we shall end up not with a civil society but with that foreshadowed by *The Clockwork Orange*. The medium we can use is television and, to a lesser extent, the wireless. That is why I have consistently supported the televising of Parliament and urge now its extensive use in all our traditional cultural institutions. In this way they will be able to defend themselves against the charge of being nothing more than expensive cultural anachronisms: the Opera House, far from being 'dead', will receive a new lease on life. Opera and street theatre will no longer be Dives and Lazarus—the gap between the two worlds will be bridged. If the Minister for the Arts devoted a substantial part of his time to constructing this causeway, it would be time well spent.

My third point is this: we are moving—indeed, to a certain extent have moved—towards a leisure society, in which work occupies only a proportion of people's lives, and this is likely to be a continually diminishing one. In such a society spending on the arts is not an optional extra but as vital in its contribution to the quality of life and the promotion of human happiness as expenditure on health or education. There is thus a duty on the state to bring the arts within the reach of all, but because of the spiritual and cultural values which are involved this must be done in such a way that the integrity and independence of the arts and the artist are respected.

On these foundations we must build a powerful new constituency for the arts: that is the only way in which progress can take place in a free, democratic society. The principal recommendation of the late Lord Redcliffe Maud's admirable report on the arts, that local government should become the major arts patron of the future, is a desirable one in theory, but who, looking at the dismal record of local government in the arts in the past, can have any confidence that it is likely to fulfil this role any better in the future? What has been lacking is any sense at the local election level of a pressing problem, affecting all citizens, which requires an urgent solution. Our task is to build up a climate of opinion through a powerful arts lobby at every level of the national life which will create this sense, so that both local authorities and central government will regard the promotion of culture as a service to the community that is as indispensable as hospitals or housing. And we should be helped in this by the multi-racial character which our society has now assumed, for the arts can play a unique part in breaking down barriers of prejudice and mistrust between the races and in both preserving and dignifying different cultural traditions.

In this endeavour we should call in aid a wide range of interests and groups in our society. We should enlist the help of the trade unions, which should become as active in the arts field as they have been in that of education; we should interest the youth groups in all forms of artistic endeavour; we should see that the needs of pensioners and old people are identified and met. Above all, we should use our education system, for it is from the schools that the arts audiences and participators of the future will come.

ARTS AND THE SCHOOLS

In schools three Rs are not enough: we need not three but five: reading, writing, arithmetic, religion and arts. The situation is reasonably encouraging in our primary schools, where music, dance, drama and painting are flourishing. Nothing has impressed me more than this during my visits to primary schools, but by comparison our secondary schools are a desert. In 1981 only 5.1 per cent of CSE subjects and 4.1 per cent of O-Levels were in the arts. These figures are the more alarming in that they mark a continuing decline over a period of years: in 1975 the figures for CSE were 6 per cent and for O-levels 5 per cent.

There is an acute shortage of drama and music teachers, and the situation has been made worse by the foolish policy of cutting down on the employment of practising artists as teachers in our schools. Far from being frowned upon for misplaced reasons of professional *esprit de corps*, artists should be encouraged to come into our schools because they bring a unique practical experience and perspective to the classroom.

Drama is also a field ripe for expansion and more intensive use in education. The training of teachers needs to take into account the role of the arts as a matter of urgency; for too long teacher training has been isolated from the world of the practical artist and of art colleges and institutions. And when school is left behind there arise the great challenges and opportunities of adult education, when missed opportunities can be regained and life can be enriched by learning sought freely from the standpoint of maturity. Art education could hold the key to the future, and it is all the more extraordinary that the Arts Council has not attached a higher importance to this vital area.

Those, then, are my long-term perspectives for the future—a prophetic view, if you like, of the way the arts should develop in Britain. We need to evolve something we have never really had: a *consistent* policy of public support for the arts. The principal reason for this neglect has been suspicion and dislike of government patronage. 'God help the minister that meddles with art,' declared the great Lord Melbourne to Benjamin Haydon, who was one of the most persistent meddlers of his time. Art has always had to justify itself to the British public on grounds other than its own intrinsic value. The French have been more fortunate, and art has been able to fight its battles on its own ground. 'Un drame n'est pas un chemin de fer,' Gautier once remarked acidly,but that is precisely how it has often been treated in England. It has had to improve morality or design, or manufacture or, as today, to benefit the balance of payments. *Ars gratia artis* has been about as meaningful to Great Britain as to Metro-Goldwyn-Mayer.

Of course, there are dangers in governmental support of art which have to be guarded against. In my view, censorship is not, in Britain at any rate, the principal one. In many ways the private patron is a greater threat to the freedom of expression of the artist than the public one. Paradoxically too, the more the Government supports the arts, the freer they are likely to be. Minimum government intervention is likely to promote official culture: maximum does not because of the different institutions that are supported and the different formulae that have to be involved to meet different cases. The more insidious danger is the creation of a bureaucratic apparatus which is inflexible, establishment-minded and promotes only the tried, tested and accepted. Innovation becomes more and more difficult.

That is why I supported so strongly Sir Norman Reid and the Tate Gallery in the slightly absurd 'bricks' controversy. It was not that I thought the bricks a work of art—I did not. I felt, however, that the risks arising from supporting experimental art were much smaller and much less dangerous than those of supporting only accepted modes of artistic expression. If one supports those who innovate, one sometimes makes mistakes, and directors of art galleries are not infallible.

Anyhow, in Britain we are fortunate to have the Arts Council which, along with the University Grants Committee, has surely been one of the happier inventions of the post-war period. The Arts Council is far from perfect, but it has been successful in solving the central problem of how to reconcile public support for the arts with the integrity and independence of the artist and the exclusion of political influence. This has been a remarkable achievement. Sir Hugh Willat's words, those of a former Director General of the Arts Council, may be taken not as a fitting epitaph but as a fitting encomium for the Arts Council:

> I believe that the great increase in artistic provision in our country in the past thirty years has been mainly due, first, to the liberty given to the Arts Council which, though a government agency, was free to create its own policy and method; and, second, to the widespread response among artists and citizens to the opportunity given by the system, created by their own disposals and individual effort in the knowledge that public money, encouragement and advice was available.[5]

So where do we stand today? Some progress has been made. The Arts Council does exist, and its government subsidy has increased over the last ten years from £21 million in 1974–5 to £92 million in 1983–4, although much of this represents compensation for inflation. The National Theatre is at last a reality. Yet how typical it is that the same theatre, pride of Britain and envy of the world, should be sinking deeper into debt because it has not been provided with adequate funds to maintain its building.

The arts today face as grave a challenge as any in our history. Private patronage has been destroyed by social policies, and rising costs in the arts steadily and cumulatively outstrip inflation elsewhere in the economy. Unless this fact is recognized, the arts seem doomed to a state of perpetual financial crisis. If we continue to try to run the arts on a shoestring much longer, the shoestring will snap. At present, by dint of scrimping and saving, we can hold our own in the world of international opera, theatre and music, but I doubt if our major national companies will be able to cope with inflation much longer, unless the attitude of central government towards the arts undergoes a radical change.

After all, how much money is at issue here? The Arts Council grant is currently running at about £92 million. Total central government expenditure on the arts for 1981–2 (excluding public libraries and the upkeep of historic houses) is estimated to be more than twice that amount—£202 million. In the context of central government expenditure these sums are tiny. Indeed, they can hardly be said to affect public expenditure at all. And, as Kenneth Robinson, a former Chairman of the Arts Council, has said, 'There is hardly an area of spending where each extra million pounds can make a greater impact.' By the same token, I would add that there is barely an area of spending where each cut of a million, a thousand or even a hundred pounds can have a more disastrous

[5] The Alport Lecture, 1977.

effect. If you cut into arts expenditure, there is little or no fat to cut through before you are down to the bone.

Because the amounts under consideration are so small, and because the arts need a real increase year on year if they are to keep pace with their higher rate of inflation, arts spending should be a nugget that is unaffected by across-the-board public expenditure cuts. Much more needs to be done if worthwhile projects are not to be stillborn or to wither away after a brief period of life.

England, Disraeli noted, does not love coalitions and she cares for revolutions even less, but the one sphere in which one would be desirable is in our attitude to the arts. Plato at least paid them the compliment of taking them seriously. He considered them to be so dangerous and subversive that in *The Republic* he counselled that they should be either banned or subject to rigid control. If the attitude 'The arts are not for us' is to change, then those promoting them need to be less high-falutin' in their approach. People should be started 'where they are at'. To start at the highest point is likely to evoke a response only from the few. Marghanita Laski, who is a firm exponent of the former approach, has given some examples of the materials that might be used, those through which most people's artistic responses first come and from which they can work upwards.

> An ounce of example [she writes] is worth a pound of theory, and I offer, from my own first remembered experiences of this kind, Watts's 'Hope', Jackie Coogan in *The Kid*, the song 'I dreamt that I dwelt in marble halls', Noyes's 'Come down to Kew in lilac time'; on to adolescence and the painter was Breughel, the poet Dowson, the composer Ravel, the film *Congress Dances* and so on. Anyone who is not a genius in sensibility can produce similar examples. For most of us, responses to art are a matter of development, like all other education, and many factors besides sensibility may play a part: for instance, fashion (a word I always use neutrally not pejoratively) and social inspiration (trying the new because admired people use it).[6]

Miss Laski is, accordingly, a strong believer in the importance of popular song, I have a similar feeling about brass bands.

What the arts provide for the individual are experiences which greatly enrich his personal life, and society benefits as well. As Alexander Solzhenitsyn wrote: 'Art extends each man's short time on earth by carrying from man to man the whole complexity of other men's life-long experience, with all its burdens, colours and flavour. Art recreates in the flesh all experience lived by other men, so that each man can make this his own.'

[6] From 'A Popular Approach to the Arts, or By Steps to Parnassus', an unpublished paper by Marghanita Laski.

7

Art, Morality and Censorship

————◆————

Censorship is what the linguistic philosophers would call an emotive word. The mere mention of it is liable to produce apoplectic rather than Socratic reactions in the minds both of those who are obsessed by the frailty of other people's morals, and therefore want to censor everything, and of those whose only concern seems to be that statements should be made and opinions published whatever be the truth or value of their content. These are the battle lines along which the rival forces engaged in the contemporary censorship struggle are too often rigidly drawn, as they have been for so many decades.

Censorship is interesting not in itself, since censoring is a negative and rather dreary activity, but because of its involvement with the moral values, literary taste, legal concepts and, indeed, the whole extent and limits of rational freedom in a liberal society.

Let me consider the topic first from the point of view of the creative artist and writer. After all, he is the *sine qua non* of the censor's activity. Authors have, I believe, a right to communicate their thoughts and to work freely. They must feel free if they are to give of their best. And they cannot feel free if they live in perpetual fear that either they will be prosecuted or their books will be suppressed. Such freedom is not divisible, and it must extend to every sphere of conduct, including that of sexual morality and behaviour, which is the only sphere (apart from blasphemy and sedition) in which freedom of expression is restricted in Western liberal societies.

The need for such freedom is greater than ever today, when literature, and especially the novel and drama, is so closely concerned with psychological problems and a realistic, or naturalistic, presentation of life. The Victorian solution, which was drastic and simple—namely, to omit sex entirely from literature, or else to confine its representation to relationships of such impeccably regular kinds that even the most severe reverend mother could contemplate them with equanimity—would be of small assistance to writers such as William Faulkner, Erskine Caldwell, James Jones or Iris Murdoch in solving their particular literary problems.

Authors have, I believe, rights which are peculiar to their position as expositors, possibly ultimately preservers, of the culture of a given society. But, of course, they also have duties. They are not writing in a vacuum; they are writing to be read. And if a great literature cannot be created without freedom, neither can it be sustained without a sense of responsibility on the part of the authors. The greater the power, the greater the need for interior sanctions which are voluntarily imposed. This machinery of self-censorship is not often considered when freedom of expression is discussed; emphasis is generally concentrated instead on external restraints.

The first interior restraint is, as I have indicated, prudence. The author must accept responsibility for influencing the thought and behaviour of his readers. That is a consideration which appears foreign to the minds of those thinkers who believe that it is a fundamental freedom that every opinion and viewpoint may be put forward with respect neither to moral values nor to truth. These same enthusiasts, aided and abetted by the social psychologists, maintain further that there is no scientific evidence of any causal connection between reading and behaviour, and that until some generous foundation, presumably American, has expended millions of dollars to enable some zoologist or entomologist to establish some statistical relationship between the two, we must suspend belief in the all but universally accepted proposition of common sense, that we are affected for good or for ill by what we read.

On this point I would offer a statement of another author, Bernard Shaw, who in his preface to *Mrs Warren's Profession*, a work which was denied performance in the public theatre for thirty years, expressed his conviction that 'Fine art is the subtlest, the most seductive, the most effective instrument of moral propaganda in the world, excepting only the example of personal conduct.' We can all think of authors who have changed our own perspective on life. There are some authors, such as André Gide or Teilhard de Chardin, whose books have changed the outlook of a whole generation.

The second interior restraint is imposed by what I might call the natural law. Natural law theories have, in the main, been articulated by Roman Catholics, at least in this area. But the conviction that there are certain moral values, both objective and universal, must, I think, be posited by every Christian and even by many agnostic humanists. Indeed, if this pattern of human nature—and it is in that sense that I use the words 'natural law'—did not exist within us, neither history nor a transmitted culture would be even a possibility. Much less could we comprehend the great creative works of the past, for the existence of this pattern is what Alexander Pope has called at once the source and the test and the end of art.

Of course, these values will be expressed differently in different periods, but I do not believe that their essence alters. The moral sublimity of *Antigone*, for example, is not dependent on a knowledge of Greek burial rites, though they may call for a footnote in explanation. Its appeal depends on its presentation of the human predicament, the conscious involvement in a world which is both good and evil. The contest between the demands of morality and the demands of law is a problem which has been with the human race across the ages.

The third interior restraint, closely connected with morality but not co-extensive with it, is the discipline imposed upon the creative artist by the work of the art itself. Cleanth Brooks has suggested that the artistically defective tends also to be the morally offensive. Of course, to take such a view one concerns oneself primarily with works of art not as direct reflections of actual ethical systems but rather as worlds of their own, organized on their own terms, the evaluation being shifted from one of external correspondence to that of inner coherence. Works of art therefore, from this point of view, are to be judged not by their messages but by their self-consistency. This is a sophisticated standpoint, which I think contrasts sharply with the naive didacticism of morally orientated organizations, which condemn works as immoral if they fail to conform to a particular set of ethical norms. Some bodies, accordingly, draw no distinction between a novel by D. H. Lawrence, which is consistently true to its own moral evaluations, and a work of pornography, which has no coherence, moral or otherwise. Of course, by insisting on a conventional, moral ending to a film—one of the major aims of the old Legion of Decency in the United States—based on a different values system, such organizations do not purify it, as they imagine; they simply render the whole thing incoherent.

Coherence, however, is not the only standard on which to insist. We may ask that works of art should present us with credible responses and human behaviour which we know is not in flat contradiction to human nature as we ourselves experience it. That, of course, is to relate a truth of coherence to a truth of correspondence, even if that correspondence is to human nature in general and not to a system of ethical propositions. This is related to what I said about the natural law.

The sensational, the monstrous, the pornographic are thus both inartistic and immoral because they violate the values of works of art, which themselves must be ultimately grounded in human nature. The average work of pornography posits an impossible masculinity and an equally impossible femininity and brings them together in a totally incredible conjunction.

A work, then, is to be condemned not on the basis of the material which it uses but on the way in which it uses them. That, I think, is in accord with Cardinal Newman's view that a sinless literature of sinful man is itself a contradiction. I think that one can extend that view theologically and regard the whole of literature as one of the more agreeable consequences of original sin. If there had been no original sin, there would have been very little to write about.

It is jejune, then, to look upon art, as some people do, as though it were a species of embroidery to illustrate moral principles. One can, however, legitimately expect that if an artist uses vile materials, he will relate them to a fully human context and that he will make them subserve some purpose wider than the excitement of horror or prurience; in other words, there is a burden on him to transmute dubious materials into art.

Now, you may say that internal restraints may be sufficient for the genuine and dedicated artist, but what of the imposter and the pornographer? Are they to be restrained by dissertations on moral values or the inner coherence of works of art? The answer, of course, is that they are not, and society cannot abdicate its responsibility for what I may call the minimum moral welfare of its members, any more than it can contract out of their defence from internal violence or external assault. But what that minimum moral welfare and that minimum moral standard may be is bound to vary as one age succeeds another.

How are society and the law to deal with a phenomenon such as pornography? Pornography, I should have thought, is a self-evident social evil, although we lack reliable information as to its incidence and extent. I regret to note that it seems that it is men rather than women who buy and read pornography. When some years ago a group of women graduates were the subject of an investigation into the sources of their sex knowledge, only 72 out of the 1,200 questioned mentioned books. None was of the pornographic type. One was Motley's *Rise of the Dutch Republic*! Asked what they found most sexually stimulating, 95 out of 409 answered, 'Books.' A much larger number, 208, to their great credit replied, 'Men.'[1]

I have referred to pornography as an evil, but views have been advanced in its defence. Havelock Ellis, for example, maintained that the conditions of contemporary, highly conventional society require relief from restrictions, just as the conditions of childhood create the need for fairy stories. Obscene books are, therefore, not aphrodisiacs but safety valves, protecting society from crime and outrage. The average reader of pornography is not socially undesirable but a quite harmless creature, some university professor or Member of Parliament perhaps, who, deprived of this outlet, would turn to others more directly harmful to society. St Augustine uses similar arguments when he counsels against the Roman state's suppression of prostitution.

Against that opinion may be set the views of Sir Anthony Absolute, as expressed to Mrs Malaprop in Sheridan's play *The Rivals*. 'Madam,' he

[1] See Alpert, *Harvard Law Review*, 1938, pp. 73–4.

says to her, 'a circulating library in a town is an evergreen tree of diabolical knowledge. It blossoms through the year!—and depend on it, Mrs Malaprop, that they who are so fond of handling the leaves, will long for the fruit at last.'[2]

The role of the law, as opposed to its formulation, seems to be clear on general principle. It is to reconcile a genuine clash of social interests. Authors have an interest in writing freely, and the public has an equal interest in being able to choose what to read. Society in general, however, also has an interest in preventing the exploitation of literature by those who wish to make money by the stimulation of base appetites and passions. Racketeers are especially tempted today by the emergence of a new public which can read but which in fact is only semi-literate.

The difficulty occurs in the formulation of the legal restriction. It is not as simple as some authors would have us believe. Here, I think, one must glance briefly at the different stages through which the law has passed to see what guidance it affords.

THE HISTORY OF CENSORSHIP

The English censorship laws have a long history behind them, but not as long as some people think. Before the Reformation there was no developed system of censoring books by either Church or State. The medieval Church certainly concerned itself from time to time with heresy, but its interdicts were issued haphazardly. With obscenity it hardly concerned itself at all, and Ovid's works, for example, were freely studied in English monasteries. When *The Decameron* did finally fall under the papal ban in 1559, this was not because of its obscenity but because it satirized the clergy. The Church authorized an expurgated edition, but the expunged references were those relating to the saints and the clergy: the obscenities remained. Accordingly, monks became magicians; nuns were turned into noblewomen; and the Archangel Gabriel was transformed into the King of the Fairies. A full ecclesiastical censorship was not instituted until after the Reformation, at the Council of Trent.

As in the Church, so in the State legal censorship was not introduced until after the Reformation. The first decree licensing the publication of books was issued by Henry VIII through Star Chamber in 1538 and required permission from the Privy Council for the publication of all books 'in the englyshe tongue'. The decree does not appear to have been enforced. In 1556 a decisive step was taken, destined to influence the whole Tudor and Stuart censorship, when Philip and Mary incorporated the Stationers' Company. In return for the charter, which confined

[2] *The Rivals*, Act I, sc. 2.

printing, apart from special licences, to members of the Company, the members undertook to search out and suppress all undesirable and illegal books. This was a royal master stroke, since the Company was the one instrument by which the Crown's policy could be successfully carried out. Besides ordering the destruction of books, the wardens were empowered to commit to three months' imprisonment anyone who attempted to hinder them in the exercise of their duties. In addition a fine of 100 shillings could be imposed, one half of which went to the Company and the remaining half to the Crown. In 1559 the charter was confirmed by Queen Elizabeth, and the system continued until the expiration of the licensing laws in 1695.

The Elizabethan and Stuart censorships were theological and political rather than moral, and the records of the Stationers' Company reveal that only a very occasional work was refused a licence for obscenity. Even the King's printers sometimes fell foul of the law: in 1631 Barker and Lucas were fined for improving the fifth commandment in their edition of the Bible to 'Thou shalt commit adultery.' The licensing system came to an end not because Parliament became imbued with liberalism but because of the growth of a general conviction that the law was unenforceable.

After the lapse of licensing the government turned to the libel law, and especially to the law of seditious libel, to control publication. In 1727 a powerful new weapon was created with the recognition of a new offence at common law, that of publishing an obscene libel. In 1708 an unsuccessful attempt to establish the offence had been made in Read's case. Read had printed a pornographic book, *The Fifteen Pleagues of a Maidenhead*, and was indicted, but the case was dismissed as being within the exclusive jurisdiction of the ecclesiastical courts. However, twenty years later, in Curl's case, this decision was overruled, and jurisdiction was assumed by the common law. Curl was a contemporary pornographer and plagiarist who had enjoyed immunity until he overreached himself with the publication of *Venus in the Cloister or the Nun in her Smock*. He was sent to the pillory, but as the state trials record:

> Being an artful, cunning (though wicked) fellow, he had contrived to have printed papers dispersed all about Charing Cross, telling the people he stood there for vindicating the memory of Queen Anne: which had such an effect on the mob that it would have been dangerous even to have spoken against him; and when he was taken out of the pillory the mob carried him off as it were in triumph to a neighbouring tavern.

Curl was condemned for publishing a pornographic book, not a work of literature, and throughout the eighteenth century no attempt was made to prosecute publishers of books of literary merit. The only approach to such action was the unsuccessful attempt to arrest the circulation of Matthew

Lewis's *The Monk* by means of an injunction. During the same period pornographic works circulated freely. John Cleland's *Fanny Hill, or The Memoirs of a Woman of Pleasure* was written in 1748; although he was summoned before the Privy Council, he was granted a pension of £100 by Lord Granville on condition that he abstained from such writing in the future. As late as 1780 Harris's *List of Covent Garden Ladies*, a publication made up of erotic descriptions of various whores who used it to advertise their charms, was generally available. In 1795 a new magazine, *Rangers*, was founded, which combined a directory of prostitutes with ribald stories of seduction and other frolics, together with a great number of bawdy anecdotes.

Such freedom is not surprising when the robust masculine literary taste of eighteenth-century England is taken into account. By the end of the century, however, things were changing, and nothing is more fascinating to trace than the transformation of eighteenth-century robustness into mid-Victorian podsnappery and squeamishness.

Queen Victoria is often blamed for this transmogrification, but the great Queen was not in fact responsible. Her accession to the throne in 1837 was confirmation rather than cause of the movement which bears her name. In 1803 the Germans had coined a word, *Engländerie*, to convey the same meaning as our 'Victorianism'. Bowdler and Plumptre were active a decade before the Queen came to the throne. They 'improved' Shakespeare in a great burst of self-confidence. Some of the 'improvements' are a little dubious. One springs to mind. Shakespeare wrote:

> Under the greenwood tree
> Who loves to lie with me?

In the 'improved' text those lines became:

> Under the greenwood tree
> Who loves to work with me?

Prime responsibility must be placed on the evangelicals who strove so manfully to reform morals and taste. They worked partly by persuasion but also by coercion. In 1802 the Society for the Suppression of Vice was founded in order to enforce the moral laws, especially those against obscene books. Sydney Smith said the last word on all such societies when he called it 'a society for suppressing the vices of those whose incomes did not exceed £500 p.a.'. Evangelical distrust of literature was re-enforced by the other great seminal movement of the period, Benthamism. As Dicey has shown, they were both individualist, humanitarian and anti-traditionalist.[3] Above all, they both propagated a restricted view of life, whether the achievement of spiritual salvation or of material happiness, to

---

[3] A. V. Dicey, *Law and Public Opinion in England*, London, 1914, pp. 397–404.

the attainment of which literature and the arts were equally irrelevant. Mill reproached Hume for allowing himself to become 'enslaved' by literature, 'which without regard for truth or utility seeks only to arouse emotion'. Further aid came from the upper classes which, in fear of the French Revolution, began to reform their manners and to pursue virtue as a means of safeguarding their property.

As the nineteenth century progressed, taste grew more severe, and moralism in literature swiftly degenerated into an excessive prudery. The law kept pace with the critics, becoming more oppressive, and in 1857 Lord Campbell's Act was passed. This Act was intended to suppress the pornographic book trade which was centred in London, somewhat inappropriately in Holywell Street. It created no new criminal offence but gave magistrates the power to order the destruction of books and prints if, in their opinion, publication would amount to a 'misdemeanour proper to be prosecuted as such'. The measure was vigorously opposed as a threat to literature, but Lord Campbell assured the critics that the measure 'was intended to apply exclusively to works written for the single purpose of corrupting the morals of youth and of a nature calculated to shock the common feelings of decency in a well-regulated mind'. Lord Lyndhurst's comment on this was prescient: 'Why, it is not what the Chief Justice means but what is the construction of an Act of Parliament.' The subsequent use to which the Act has been put to suppress the books of D. H. Lawrence, Radclyffe Hall, Havelock Ellis and others would seem to have justified his forebodings.

In 1868 came the second great nineteenth-century contribution to the obscene libel law, when Sir Alexander Cockburn in Hicklin's case laid down the first definition of obscenity. 'The test of obscenity', said Sir Alexander 'is whether the tendency of the matter charged as obscene is to deprave and corrupt those whose minds are open to such immoral influences and into whose hands a publication of this sort may fall.' This definition was adopted by the American courts, and its wording is still preserved in the present English Obscene Publications Act of 1959. Accordingly, it has had a profound influence on the law. It meant, in its original formulation, that a book could be judged obscene on the basis of isolated passages read out of their context and with no reference to the author's intention.

In 1877 an attempt was made to extend the obscene libel law further when Charles Bradlaugh and Annie Besant were prosecuted for publishing Charles Knowlton's tract on birth control, curiously entitled *Fruits of Philosophy*. Hitherto prosecution had been confined to pornographic books, which had been attacked for their language rather than for their theme. The trial aroused great public interest and lasted for many weeks. Finally, both the accused were convicted, only to be acquitted subsequently because of a defect in the indictment. The only effect of the prosecution was to raise the sale of *Fruits* from a few hundred a year to many hundreds of thousands. Chief Justice Cockburn remarked: 'A more ill-advised prosecution has never been brought.' In 1888 Vizetelly, a London bookseller, was sent to prison for publishing Zola's *La Terre* in translation. In France, three weeks before the prosecution, Zola had been awarded the Legion of Honour for writing it. In 1898 Havelock Ellis's medical classic *Sexual Inversion* was destroyed by order of the courts. 'It is impossible', said the magistrate 'for anybody with a head on his shoulders to open the book without seeing that it is a pretence and a sham, and that it is merely entered into for the purpose of selling this obscene publication.' After the First World War, during which D. H. Lawrence's *The Rainbow* was ordered to be destroyed by the courts, standards relaxed somewhat, but in the 1920s, when Sir William Joynson Hicks was Home Secretary, a return was made to repressive policies. Radclyffe Hall's *The Well of Loneliness*, the first English book to deal with a homosexual relationship, was destroyed as obscene and corrupting.

When one reflects that the offending words in *The Well of Loneliness* were, 'that night they were not divided,' one realizes what a long way we have travelled from what seems to us an excessive reticence to the explicitness of so much of today's literature. A later victim was *Ulysses* by James Joyce, which was destroyed by the United States Customs in 1923. The first inroads into the repressive American laws were made in 1933/4, when the ban on *Ulysses* was lifted and the book was first allowed into the United States. In the District Court Judge Woolsey declared he could find nothing in the book which he would describe as 'dirt for dirt's sake' and, applying the test of the reasonable man, he allowed the book to be admitted into the country. The United States Appeal Court upheld his decision. Judge Hand made it clear that he judged the book as a whole, and on its motivation and purpose, not on isolated passages.

> We believe [he said] that the proper test of whether a given book is obscene is its dominant effect. In applying this test, relevancy of the objectionable parts to the theme, the established reputation of the work in the estimation of approved critics, if the book is modern, and the verdict of the past if it is ancient, are persuasive pieces of evidence, for works of art are not likely to sustain a high position with no better warrant for their existence than their obscene content. . . .[4]

In England, in 1929, an exhibition of D. H. Lawrence's paintings at the Warren Gallery was closed after intervention by the police. *The Times* records that it was replaced by an exhibition entitled 'Art Forms in Nature Taken from Vegetable Growths', which apparently gave less offence.[5]

[4] See *US* v. *One Book Entitled 'Ulysses'*, 72F (2d) 705 (2nd Circ.) 1934.
[5] 9 August 1929. A folio of Blake was also seized but later released.

Sporadic attempts to suppress books were subsequently made by the police from time to time, but it was not until 1954 that a major assault was mounted on serious authors and their work.

In that year five prosecutions were brought against more or less reputable publishers, of whom two were convicted of publishing obscene libels and two were acquitted; one case resulted in disagreement. The books condemned were *Julia* by Margot Bland, a worthless volume, and *September in Quinze* by Vivien Connell; those acquitted were *The Philanderer* by Stanley Kauffman and *The Man in Control* by Charles McGraw; and the book over which there was disagreement was Walter Baxter's *The Image and the Search*. After two juries had been unable to agree, the proceedings were dropped. At the same time the Swindon magistrates distinguished themselves by ordering the destruction of *The Decameron* as an obscene and corrupting work.

Alarmed by this threat to the freedom of the pen, the Society of Authors set up a committee, under the chairmanship of Sir Alan Herbert, to amend the law. This committee drafted the Bill which, in a much changed form, was to become law as the Obscene Publications Act 1959. The purpose of the Act was to enable juries to distinguish between out-and-out pornographic works and books of literary value which might contain incidental obscene passages necessary for their theme. In the words of its own long title, it was intended 'to provide for the protection of literature and to strengthen the law against pornography'. To achieve this, the Act brought about three major changes in the law. It laid down that books should be judged as a whole and not by isolated passages. It then went on to create a new defence of publication for the public good. A person, says the Act, is not to be convicted of an offence of publishing an obscene book 'if it is proved that publication is justified as being for the public good on the ground that it is in the interests of science, literature, art or learning or of other objects of general concern'. To establish or to negative this defence, the opinion of experts as to a book's 'literary, scientific or other merits' was made admissible. The Act also laid down maximum penalties for the offence and provided the bookseller with a special defence that he had no reasonable cause to suspect that a book sold by him contained obscene matter.[6]

The Act was in essence a compromise and therefore an imperfect piece of legislation. It reached the statute book only after a struggle lasting five years, during which a principal clause, making the intention of the publisher or of the author of the book attacked a necessary ingredient in the offence, had to be dropped. Thus even its sponsors were dubious about whether the Act would work in practice. The prosecution of Penguin Books for publishing *Lady Chatterley's Lover* in 1960 provided an

[6] Obscene Publications Act 1959, ch. 66.

admirable test case. The first lesson to be drawn from the acquittal is that the Act worked. It effectively protects some works of literature. Whether it would protect every work of literature is doubtful.

The case of *Lady Chatterley* also established various important points of law. The judge ruled that the intention of the author or publisher is irrelevant to the question of publishing obscene matter, but the author's intention is relevant when considering whether the book is a work of literature, published for the public good. He further held that the mere fact that a book is of literary merit is not enough to establish the defence; the obscenity and the literary merit must be weighed in the balance and the verdict given according to the way the scale tips. The experts who were admitted were primarily experts on literature, but testimony was also allowed as to the book's moral value and its psychological merits. In practice, in giving their evidence the experts were allowed a great deal of latitude.

Sensible administration of the law is crucial. Most prosecutions are, in fact, brought by the police, who are obliged, under regulations made in 1946, to consult the Director of Public Prosecutions before any action is taken. They are not under any obligation to accept his advice, but its rejection is unusual. No obligation even to consult the Director exists when the police wish to apply for a destruction order, but such consultation is also usual in practice. Complaints about books by private individuals are frequently received by the Director's Office, as well as information sent by societies and organizations such as the Public Morality Council. An important reform of the law (originally in the Society of Author's Bill) would be to make all proceedings involving obscenity subject to the Director of Public Prosecution's or the Attorney General's consent.

One development in the law has disturbing implications for authors: the decision of the House of Lords in the case of the *Ladies Directory* (May 1961) that a conspiracy to corrupt public morals is still a criminal offence at English law. This crime is so loosely defined that it gives judges virtually a free hand to punish or suppress whatever happens to arouse their moral indignation at a particular time. It also means that all the protections provided by the Obscene Publications Act could in theory be by-passed. The Act declares that obscene publications shall not be prosecuted at common law, but the House of Lords has now held that this does not exclude prosecution for immoral conspiracy.

CENSORSHIP OF PLAYS

Censorship of the drama in England has had a long, if not an especially honourable, history. The Tudors were the first English sovereigns to attempt control of the stage and made use of a royal official, the Master of the Revels—whose function since 1374 had been 'to sett fourthe such devises as might be most agreeable to the prince's expectation'—to carry out their wishes. By Stuart times he had become firmly established as official licensor, but Parliament deprived him of his occupation when it closed the theatres in 1642. At the Restoration he resumed his functions but was superseded when statutory censorship, under the Lord Chamberlain, was set up in 1737. Immorality and obscenity were charges that had been constantly levelled against the stage, but when theatres were finally brought under control the reasons were political, not moral. Gay in *The Beggar's Opera* and Fielding in *Pasquin* and *The Historical Register for 1736* had viciously attacked Walpole; the Government retaliated by passing the Licensing Act, the main provisions of which were re-enacted in 1843. One of the reasons for the later Act was the ingenuity of those who had devised schemes for its avoidance. Thus at the Strand Theatre no charge was made for admission, but purchase of an ounce of lozenges for 4 shillings at a neighbouring confectioner's secured admission to a box, while pit patrons bought peppermints for 2 shillings. The 1843 Act, through a careful definition of the words 'for hire', closed this loophole in the law.

Plays have been banned on political, religious and—since the first half of the nineteenth century—moral grounds. A typical example of political censorship was the banning in 1924 of J. E. Cairns's play *In the Red Shadows* because it dealt with the Black and Tan atrocities in Ireland. The most absurd was the prohibition of *The Mikado*—twenty years after it had been written—for fear that it might offend the Japanese. At the time the music was being played aboard Japanese ships paying an official visit to Chatham! Any representation of the reigning Royal Family was strictly taboo, and at times the ban was extended to cover sovereigns long since dead. Housman twice fell foul of the censor, first for his play *George IV and Queen Caroline* and then for *The Queen's Progress* because it featured Queen Victoria.

Discussion of religious topics on the stage was also severely restricted. At one time the Lord Chamberlain's office prohibited the portrayal of any scriptural character, and although the rule was eventually relaxed, no representations of God or Christ were allowed on the English stage. George Moore's play *The Passing of the Essenes*, adapted from his novel *The Brook Kerith*, accordingly never received a licence.

In post-First World War Britain most plays that were banned were suppressed for moral reasons, and the importance the Lord Chamberlain attached to this part of his work was shown by his licence, which expressly guaranteed that the play did not 'in its general tendency contain anything immoral or otherwise improper for the stage'. One of the earliest plays banned on this ground was Shelley's *The Cenci*, which had to wait a hundred years for a public performance. Ibsen's plays were licensed only after a bitter struggle, and *Ghosts* remained under a ban until 1914. Shaw, as might have been expected, was censored, and both *Mrs Warren's Profession* and *The Showing Up of Blanco Posnet* were denied licences. Lady Gregory put on the second play in Dublin, where, strangely enough, there has never been any theatre censorship. *Salome*, despite repeated applications for a license, was banned for many years, as was Edward Garnett's *The Breaking Point* and Granville Barker's *Waste*. In the 1920s Marie Stopes was unable to present her play *Vectia* because it dealt with birth control, while other banned plays included *Vile Bodies*, *Young Woodley*, *Desire under the Elms*, Edward Bourdet's *La Prisonière* and even Pirandello's *Six Characters in Search of an Author*. More recently, public productions of Lillian Hellman's *The Children's Hour*, Gide's *The Immoralist* and Tennessee Williams's *Cat on a Hot Tin Roof* were forbidden.

One reason why such an oppressive censorship was tolerated for so long was that, however much it was detested by authors, managers gave it their whole-hearted support. They preferred the certainty of the Lord Chamberlain's imprimatur to the uncertain danger of being prosecuted for indecency. Censorship also protected them from the risk of adverse publicity and reduced clashes with the author to a minimum. In the last century the three parliamentary committees appointed to investigate the censorship all recommended its retention. In 1909, however, a fourth committee, under the chairmanship of Herbert Samuel, reached a different conclusion. 'Secret in its operation,' declared the report, 'subject to no effective control by public opinion, its effect can hardly fail to be to coerce into conformity with the conventional standards of the day dramatists who may be seeking to amend them.' The committee recommended the abolition of the existing censorship and its replacement by a voluntary system, of which managers could avail themselves if they wished. This recommendation, like those of the 1908 Committee on the law of obscene libel, was ignored.

In July 1966, however, a joint select committee of both Houses of Parliament was appointed to consider the Lord Chamberlain's jurisdiction over plays.[7] The committee could have recommended a number of courses of action: the maintenance of the *status quo*; the setting up of another pre-censorship body, with or without the right of appeal; the establishment of a voluntary system of censorship; or the complete abolition of pre-censorship. In the event, it opted unanimously for the last of these. In 1968 the Theatres Act was passed, implementing this recommendation, and the Lord Chamberlain's long history as a censor finally came to an end.[8]

---

[7] Members of the committee included Lord Kilmuir, Lord Brooke, Lord Annan and Lord Goodman from the Lords, and Mr Michael Foot, Mr Andrew Faulds and myself from the Commons. See HL 255/HC 503.

[8] I moved an amendment at the committee stage to forbid representation of members of the existing Royal Family on the stage, but it was rejected.

CONCLUSION

The question now arises of whether the present law on obscenity should be kept on the statute book or whether there should be further reform. It is a difficult and perplexing problem. One does not have to align oneself with Mrs Mary Whitehouse or Lord Longford to see that a problem is presented by pornographic literature. I myself doubt whether the law can do very much that is useful in the sense of applying a test of what is moral or immoral. For a law to be successful, there must be some agreement in society about standards of morality. In the sexual sphere, in Britain, it hardly exists. There is agreement, it seems, but it is one that differs from group to group. To some people homosexuality is wrong; others would accept it as a natural deviation from the norm. Some people take the view that all sexual intercourse outside marriage is wrong; others think it acceptable; others again regard it as desirable.

In such a society an effective law, the enforcement of which depends on some kind of moral consensus, is usually impossible either to draft or to administer. For this reason, I think it might be sagacious to abandon the effort altogether and to treat the question of pornography as part of the law of public nuisance. The law should remove itself from the impossible task of trying to establish tests of what is moral and what is not and should confine itself to two things: first, preventing people from being annoyed by pornographic books as they go about their business—in other words, there should be no display of pornography in public places, shop windows and so on; secondly, there should be no sale to minors under 16 or 18. Subject to that, the law should remove itself from this sphere and leave the matter to private judgement and private choice.

I was able to put my principles into practice when I was Arts Minister. In October 1980 Sir Horace Cutler, Leader of the Greater London Council, was shocked by the play *The Romans* at the National Theatre, with its scene of simulated rape, which later led to a private prosecution by Mrs Whitehouse. I was asked to intervene but declined, saying that it was no part of an Arts Minister's job to be a censor. Politicians, civil servants and theatre directors sped away from the issue as though it were the plague.[9]

Prudence in the administration of the law is as important as the law itself. Unsuccessful prosecutions of a book serve only to raise sales. We are still in the unhappy position that an old lady may be shocked by a book in a library and set the whole machinery in motion against publisher and author, though it is liable to be an expensive and uncertain business. Dr Johnson, the great lexicographer, disposed of all such busybodies in a terse phrase. 'Doctor Johnson,' said a lady, 'what I admire in your

---

[9] I was reminded of the 'fleeing' of the monks in Carpaccio's painting of the monastery garden when St Jerome enters with his pet lion on a lead. This painting still delights thousands of visitors at San Giorgio Degli Schiavoni in Venice.

dictionary is that you have inserted no improper words.' 'What!' replied the Doctor, 'You looked for them, Madam?'

One final reflection is perhaps not entirely out of place: the problem of obscene or immoral literature is only a part of a much wider problem of the sexual mores and ethical outlook of a society. St Paul, in his Epistle to the Romans, connects, in an intriguing passage, the spread of sexual aberrations with the adoption of a wider false morality.[10] Pornography is a symptom, not a disease. It would be a pity to substitute the occasional pursuit of the outrageous for a sane and rational attempt to rectify what I think is an infinitely more horrifying and dangerous thing—the exploitation of sex for the purposes of sales by a commercial society. As for works of literature which are ethically incoherent and may seem to us to lack the moral integrity of the works of other ages, should we not reflect, before we give way to a burst of righteous indignation, that our ire against them may well be nothing more than the rage of Caliban who sees his own face reflected in the glass?

[10] Romans 1:25.

PART THREE

The Heavenly City

8

What Religion is About

The importance of religion, from both the intellectual and the affective point of view, is that it attempts to answer the ultimate question of what life is about. The Church too has a simple purpose, which is not to act as a kind of useful social cement—although it may well have this effect in practice—but to arouse and keep alive the spiritual faculties in man. If one stands back and looks at the activities of other human beings, or indeed one's own, there is something depressingly ant-like about them. People scurry from one chore to another, obsessed with trivial or seemingly important tasks, engaged in a hectic round of futilities. There is something not only absurd but also horrifying about this prospect. Ahead lies an inevitable extinction. *Accidie* threatens. I see the issue otherwise. Life without the spiritual dimension would constitute a desert. Religion unifies and gives meaning to the endless daily round. It saves one from despair.

Deprived of God, modern man is perpetually teetering on the verge of hopelessness. As he becomes aware of the gigantic size of the universe and of what lies beyond, his own insignificance increases. Cosmically dwarfed, he is subjected to relentless, reducing pressures by the advance of technology on his own planet. The paradox of the advance of science is that its promise of freedom from want is accompanied by a threat of the subjugation of man by the means necessary to bring it about. To compensate him for the loss of the spiritual dimension, man is being offered two nostrums, both forms of materialism.

The first, which equates the end of life with happiness and conceives happiness as the possession of a wide range of creature comforts, has been castigated by Reinhold Niebuhr as the final vulgarity. Man cries out for bread and is offered prefabricated stones. Now it seems that even this tawdry promise may not be honoured as world economic activity declines.

The second form of materialism, more sophisticated than the first, has been formulated by Sir Julian Huxley.[1] He tells us that despite this separation from God, contemporary man is not alone. Thanks to Darwin, he knows he is not an unique phenomenon cut off from the rest of nature.

> Not only is he made of the same matter and operated by the same energy as all the rest of the cosmos, but for all his distinctiveness he is linked by genetic continuity with all the other living inhabitants of his planet; animals, plants and micro-organisms, they are all his cousins or remoter kin, all part of one single branching and evolving flow of metabolizing protoplasm.

What kind of consolation is this for the soul of man gasping for the infinite and reaching out for that point of absolute commitment and submission which is its deepest need? Can one pay homage to protoplasm, however metabolizing? Can the words which Sir Julian uses so freely, such as love, compassion, spiritual effort, sacredness and transcendence, be meaningful when they are separated from their religious roots? The absurdity is that acceptance of Huxley's idea of triumphant evolutionary man requires an act of faith just as radical as that commanded by Christian revelation, although his theory is presented as the culmination of rationalism. His concept is essentially visionary and mystical, in contrast to which the Christian theological system seems the epitome of sober reason.

Acceptance of the Christian faith does, of course, require a certain 'sacrifice' of the intellect. The soul in search of God, at a certain point in its reasoning struggle, escapes from the turmoil. It leaps, as Kierkegaard put it, into the arms of God. The act of faith is extra-rational but it is not non-rational. The intellect is not given up but voluntarily restricts itself within a certain framework of postulates which it accepts as true. By doing this it does not deny itself but concentrates its forces in a given field and so becomes effective. Hence the appeal of an organization like the Roman Catholic Church to so many thinkers from Thomas Aquinas to Newman and beyond, since it offers the opportunity to reconcile freedom and order.

Religion bridges the gap between human ideals and human achievements which is present at every level of life and experience. Human nature is not totally corrupt but deeply flawed. The Christian doctrine of original sin, its positing of a fallen state from which man is always struggling to recover, with varying degrees of success, enshrines a profound truth about human beings. Human nature at its worst takes on a demonic element, seen most clearly when men are in conflict with one another over passions and principles. Humanist optimism seems an extraordinarily superficial and unsatisfying creed when confronted with

[1] In a collection of essays edited by Sir Julian entitled *The Humanist Frame*, London, 1961.

the brute facts of human behaviour. How is it that human beings can rise so high or fall so low? There is a mystery here which only religion can explain and penetrate; religion integrates both the tragic and the sublime.

Religion enhances rather than diminishes life. Only those who do not believe in God have any reason to be permanently gloomy. Life really is like a play, a play in which the real meaning is different from the apparent one. There is a part to perform and, having found out by a process of trial and error what it is, one should play it out with zest. One has also to remember that at any moment the play may come to an end and that one's part may be summarily concluded. If we are to be in touch with reality, we should always be conscious of the skull beneath the skin.

To put it another way, religion provides a means of evaluating external life and activities: one is able to stand aside and assess them by another yardstick. It gives one detachment and hence increases enjoyment of life. It provides an inner set of values and prevents that identification with external things which dehumanizes man. Materialism is a singularly dreary and repellent philosophy. Ideally, and if one were a saint, all one's exterior activities would flow from interior moral and spiritual attitudes. As we are (most of us) not saints, we have to put up with some disparity, but this can be of value in itself. We live with the paradox that while, in the light of eternity, life is of the greatest importance, the outcome of worldly endeavours is of singularly little moment. On this theme Newman wrote one of his most profound sermons, 'The Greatness and Littleness of Human Life'. If one believes in the four last things, death, judgement, hell and heaven, achievements and failures are put into their proper perspective.

The religious tradition in which I happen to have been brought up is that of Roman Catholicism. This is both a declaration of interest and an important fact, though not necessarily one of paramount significance. The break with Rome made in 1534 by Henry VIII makes me part of a minority in Britain, but I have always been conscious of the universal nature of the Catholic Church. The breach, temporarily healed by Queen Mary but confirmed by Queen Elizabeth I on her accession in 1559, was the decisive development in the Reformation struggle.

At the time it did not seem like that. England was a small, struggling country on the edge of Europe, insular and troublesome, but from Rome's point of view of only minor importance. Spain, by contrast, loomed large. Spain was the greatest Roman Catholic power of the period, bestriding the world with a great empire in the Americas and Africa, a country of incomparably greater significance than puny Britain. That is undoubtedly how it appeared to the sixteenth-century papacy, but Rome, not for the first time, was wrong.

Spain had already passed its zenith: the future belonged to England, a country just beginning an ascent in power and influence, both political and cultural, which was destined to continue unbroken for more than three centuries. This grand historical progress of increasing wealth and power was to be brought to an end only in the twentieth century under the impact of two world wars. Furthermore, it was from England that the North American continent was principally to be colonized. Thus, the culture of the nation destined to emerge as the greatest and most influential in the twentieth century, the United States, was to be overwhelmingly Protestant, albeit with a strong and growing Catholic component.

The far-off events of the sixteenth century meant that the identity of English culture and indeed of the English nation was to be indissolubly associated, if not with Protestantism as such, certainly with 'No Popery' and with anti-Roman attitudes. The national identity was to be established by conflict with the political and to a certain extent with the theological claims of Rome. Just as Irish nationalism identified itself with Catholicism, so English nationalism drew strength from its Protestant foundations. The Catholic religion was proscribed, recusants were fined, and until Catholic emancipation in 1829, Roman Catholics were debarred from any kind of office or service in public life.

Of course, Catholicism remained a part of English culture: the Church of England was never the Presbyterian Kirk, and it was its proud boast to be both Catholic and reformed. Elizabeth I and the Stuarts after her were determined that Anglicanism should be a *via media*, but it was a *via media* with a decisive turn against Rome. Thus it was that many of the symbols that we think of as being peculiarly English, such as the cathedrals, the great parish churches, Parliament and indeed the Crown, although retaining their Catholic ethos were severed from their Roman roots. It was only in the nineteenth century that the Oxford Movement, pursuing the logic of its own Catholic principles, ended up by reverting to Rome. In so doing, it entered a national cul-de-sac, and even today the lasting influence of the Oxford Movement is to be seen more in the Church of England than in the Church of Rome.

When the Roman Catholic hierarchy was restored in England in 1850, the resultant anti-Roman outbreaks that led Parliament to pass the foolish and unenforceable Ecclesiastical Titles Act, forbidding Catholic prelates to use their titles under the threat of heavy penalties, showed that 'No Popery' was still an intrinsic part of English culture.

Yet there were signs of a change. Walter Bagehot noted the strength of the anti-papal feeling in Britain in the 1850s but treated it with a note of detachment and mockery which heralded changes to come. 'Tell an Englishman that a building is without use,' he wrote in 1852 in his essay on Oxford, 'and he will stare; that it is illiberal, and he will survey it; that it teaches Aristotle, and he will seem perplexed that it don't teach science, and he won't mind; but only hint that it is the Pope, and he will arise and burn it to the ground.' Even better is his treatment of Gibbon's conversion to Catholicism in the previous century. 'It seems now so natural that an Oxford man should take this step', he wrote, 'that one can hardly understand the astonishment it created. Lord Sheffield tells us that the Privy Council interfered; and with good administrative judgement examined a London bookseller—some Mr Lewis who had no concern in it. In the Manor house of Buriton it would have created less sensation if *dear Edward* had announced his intention of becoming a monkey. The English have ever believed that the Papist is a kind of *creature*; and every sound mind would prefer a beloved child to produce a tail, a hide of hair, and a taste for nuts, in comparison with transubstantiation, wax candles and belief in the glories of Mary.'

Royal visits to the Vatican have helped to bring about a change of attitude, the latest being a state visit paid by the Queen and Prince Philip to Pope John Paul on 17 October 1980. The Pope, wearing the stole which he dons for the visits of the heads of other Churches, paid tribute to the Queen and singled out 'the great simplicity and dignity with which Your Majesty bears the weight of your responsibilities'. In return Her Majesty expressed her pleasure at the Pope's forthcoming visit to Britain and gave the first royal commendation of the ecumenical movement.

What really matters today is whether one takes a two-world-centred or a one-world-centred view of things. Faced with this critical division, denominational differences can be seen in perspective. Intellectually, I have found my religion satisfying and stimulating. I know that many people think of Roman Catholicism as imposing an intellectual straight-jacket, and certainly some people allow it to do so. Yet one has to start one's religious thought somewhere: life is not long enough for most people to work out an entire religious creed of their own, and the advantages of being a member of the Roman Catholic Church is that over two thousand years of preparatory work have been done. Membership of the Church provides a discipline which I suspect most people need, but it does not override conscience or private judgement.

Man always remains essentially free: that is the human condition. Being a member of a Church and also an individualist sets up a tension which can be creative. The reconciliation of Catholicism and liberty has been for me a principal intellectual preoccupation over the years.

The Church is often referred to, in an apt metaphor, as a 'mother', but just as one has to pass from a relationship of childlike dependence to one of adulthood with one's real mother, so the transition has to be made in relation to the Church. If one has to grow up physically, one must do the same spiritually. For myself, and for many other liberal Catholics, a turning-point came with the calling of the Second Vatican Council by Pope John XXIII. What the Council achieved, among other things, was the establishment of a legitimate pluralism in the Catholic Church, a freedom not enjoyed by Catholic thinkers since pre-Reformation times. Thus it is now possible to be a Catholic without having to accept, for example, all the arguments and contentions of Pope Paul VI's encyclical on birth control, *Humanae Vitae* (1968). One can be a good Catholic and discuss freely the meaning and implications of such matters as papal infallibility, transubstantiation or the Catholic attitude to the priestly orders of other Churches.

Religion, and especially Catholicism, provides a moral framework for life which is useful but can be given an exaggerated importance. Morality, after all, is only part of man and only part of religion. Walter Bagehot once wrote:

> Nothing is more unpleasant than a virtuous person with a mean mind. A highly developed moral nature, joined to an undeveloped intellectual nature, an underdeveloped artistic nature, and a very limited religious nature, is of necessity repulsive. It represents a bit of human nature—a good bit, of course, but a bit only in disproportionate, unnatural and revolting prominence.[2]

By far the most important part of the Catholic religion lies in its theological doctrines. The Catholic Church's doctrinal system appeals to the intellectual—or, at any rate, a certain type of intellectual—but it would be a gross distortion of the role of dogma if it were treated as a purely intellectual formulation. Catholics accept such doctrines as the Resurrection, the Virgin Birth and the Assumption as historical facts, but these also have profound psychological and symbolic significance. Their religious effectiveness depends on a symbolism which transcends the intellect and appeals to the whole man, the heart as well as the mind. Hence the uneducated peasant is able to participate as fully in the Catholic religion as the most intellectual schoolman. This is a point of major relevance for Catholicism in the modern world. Dogma, far from being 'musty' (whatever that may mean) is efficacious in providing those transcending symbols and archetypes which the contemporary world lacks. The doctrine of the Assumption of the Lady, which caused such umbrage among so many otherwise sensible people when it was finally defined by Pius XII in 1950, provides a good example. Outside critics seem so hypnotized by their own materialist vision of the body of the Virgin floating somewhere in space that they miss its symbolic significance altogether. They fail to see that through the doctrine of the Assumption the Catholic Church is associating the feminine principle in an especially intimate way with a Godhead which has been defined by theologians in exclusively masculine terms.[3] The honour paid to Mary within the

[2] *Wordsworth, Tennyson and Browning, Works,* vol. 2, p. 351.
[3] See my discussion of the Assumption in chapter 11.

Catholic Church may well in time be a vital point of contact between the faith of the West and the great religions of the East, which conceive of the Godhead as feminine.

The Catholic Church was recognized by Jung as possessing a symbolic system of unparalleled richness and complexity, and although he failed to accept her historic claims, he fully recognized her therapeutic value. Doctrines, sacraments, symbols, simple externals like statues and pictures, all have one common purpose, which is to lead men into the reality of the spiritual life, in essence a close personal communion with the Lord. Certain doctrines have to be accepted by all members of the Church (although there is room for differences of interpretation), but not every cult or devotion is intended for every member. The diversity of devotions has developed precisely to suit individual needs and tastes, just as the diversity of religious orders is the Church's answer to the needs of different vocations. Doctrines and devotions are the means by which mankind can come to know the deity and his purpose for mankind. 'In the attainment of that purpose,' writes Father Victor White, as did St Thomas before him, 'alone lies man's *salus*—his ultimate health and weal.'[4]

If religion is to be effective, religious people have to try to understand the spirit of their own age. We may look forward with anticipation to the twenty-first century or backwards with nostalgia to the nineteenth, but either is a singularly futile occupation: both are beyond our grasp. To settle in the nineteenth century, like an illegal immigrant, may be personally satisfying but is not much help to other people; neither is soothsaying or a vain attempt to see into the future. The twentieth century, poor thing though it may be, is our own—the one age which we possess, the only one we are able to redeem.

We need the past to give us a sense of proportion, to make us reflect that we are children of our own time and that no age has a monopoly of insight or knowledge, but the past should be a corrective, not an escape, and the future a reminder of the responsibility, not an imperative to day dream.

For religious men and women—by which I mean those who accept the reality of two worlds and are concerned with the need and means to penetrate one with the other—the obligation to read the signs of the times is primary. Unless that is done, no one can co-operate in God's plan or accomplish the true human purpose, which is to play a part in redeeming the age in which we live. We have to study the signs of the times in both the secular and the ecclesiastical perspective, especially the secular, because in a world emancipated from the Church the secular world has a greater influence and importance for religion than the ecclesiastical world as such. The secular influences the ecclesiastical; the ecclesiastical has all but ceased to influence the secular, and its influence over the religious is in

[4] Victor White, *God and the Unconscious*, London, 1952.

dramatic decline. What Christians have to do today is to seek out those aspects of the religious which have reality and appeal for contemporary man and to exemplify them in their lives so that those who have not yet found the Kingdom will be lead towards it.

The greatest single need of religion today is authenticity. By this I mean that if religion is to interest, to grip the individual and appeal through him to others, it must be inwardly experienced, felt and lived; it must be inner-directed and inspired, not imposed from without. There is an immediate conflict between that notion of religion—imposed by authority from without—and the kind of inner spiritual adventure, highly individualist in pattern, to which many people effectively interested in religion are being called today.

Authority, as traditionally presented, has lost its sanction and its appeal. Modern man is interested not in sanctions imposed from without but rather in disciplines experienced and lived from within. This is especially true of the young, who are thought lawless but, in fact, are looking for a law which will be meaningful for them to obey. The kind of authority needed today is not that of power and sanction but of spiritual service which respects the interiority and uniqueness of vision of each individual soul. This must mean the tolerance of a much wider degree of diversity in belief and practice than previous ages could envisage. They could not afford diversity: we cannot afford to disregard it.

As the Christian looks out from within himself at the world around him today, he, like other men, is half-blinded and bewildered by the distressing paradoxes which he sees on every side. On the one hand, there is the flight not only from spirituality in the conventional sense, from religion, from the Churches as we have known them, but also from all the old-established values of society, consecrated by religion and experienced over the ages. He seems to see a collapse into a kind of personal hedonism of which sexual emancipation is only a part, dominated by a refusal to accept any limitation on the relentless pursuit of personal happiness and self expression.

Yet at the same time he sees a deep dissatisfaction with a material way of life, a striving and a concern for unself-centred values and a compassion for the suffering of others which, for the first time, embraces the whole of the human race. There is today a world consciousness and conscience which is unique in the history of human beings. We all suffer with those, for example, in Latin America or in India who are enduring lives of appalling want and need, with those in South Africa who are being denied elementary human rights. The indiscriminate rejection of society's values, which have been developed by a painful process of trial and error over the centuries, is foolish, but who can doubt that a great part of the criticism of modern industrial society, which has created so much horror and ugliness, is justified? We should be dense indeed if we were not moved to protest at the twin prospects which now face the world—either a nuclear holocaust or, if that is staved off, a polluted planet on which the human race will not be able to survive. The two issues are interconnected. The effort and the money which is going into the arms race is precisely that which is needed to neutralize the polluting effects of modern industrialism, to conserve our countryside and rebuild our cities, and to help those nations that are trapped in poverty to reach the threshold of industrial take-off which alone can bring relief to their suffering populations.

The horrifying alternatives which now face mankind have led to widespread anxiety and despair and a loss of faith in existing social structures. If capitalism has been a false god, so too has communism which, far from being a liberating force, has turned out to be a more ruthless and tyrannical form of capitalism of the state variety, crushing out personal liberty and dignity. Mankind is left today in no danger of being dazzled by a myth of inevitable progress but is more likely to lapse into the paralysis of despair.

The Church's mission is primarily spiritual, but because it is spiritual it affects man's whole behaviour and therefore has moral and social effects. The Catholic Church has always held that what one believes affects what one does, a view that does not appeal to contemporary Britain, where all forms of belief tend to be looked on as being as good (or as bad) as one another and equally irrelevant to practical life. Yet if history proves anything, it is that men are affected for good or ill by what they believe. The horrors of Nazi Germany could never have been perpetrated had not men first lost belief in the Christian doctrine of man as a creature, intended for an eternal destiny and therefore endowed with sacred and inalienable rights. The course of recent history and the actions of the Soviet Union are directly traceable to the Marxist doctrine of the inevitable triumph of world communism. Continental Europe has been resuscitated by a revival of belief in European unity. Only in Britain, where institutional and family life has remained strong, can trust still be placed in the fallacy that belief and behaviour are not connected.

Yet there are signs of a Christian third way emerging. Latin America, for example, is the Catholic continent of the future. Of the world's Catholic population of 700 million, over half will be found there when we reach the second millennium. All the problems which confront the Third World— poverty, malnutrition, excessive population growth, tyranny and exploitation—are to be seen in Latin America. It constitutes a vast zone of depression and deprivation, yet it has some of the richest resources available to the human race. These conditions have produced horrific violence. Over a thousand priests have been murdered in recent decades, a process which reached a blasphemous climax in 1979, when Archbishop Romero of San Salvador was gunned down as he raised the chalice during the celebration of mass.

I have been able to see the situation in Brazil for myself. São Paolo is typical of the modern city—no longer the centre of the *civilitas* of the ancient world but a sprawling mass of concrete, bursting with people, without a tree or a blade of grass in sight, every hectare built on and developed, a species of monetarist paradise. The city is ringed by *favelas*, hideous slums where millions of people live in sub-human conditions, without adequate shelter, with little or no drainage, where new-born babies emerge from their mothers' wombs to take their chance against the effluent arising from open sewers. Such poverty spawns crime, violence and, above all, hopelessness.

How have the *favelas* grown up? They are of recent origin, the degrading fruit of too rapid social change, undirected and uncontrolled by any government intervention. Peasants and small farmers have been driven off their land as speculators have flocked to the cities, their numbers swollen by drop-outs and the unemployed. Brazilian peasants have no title deeds: they clear a little patch of jungle, grow their bananas and breed their scraggy chickens and microscopic pigs. It is a hard life with no extras, but at least it is rooted and its ways are known; it has some dignity and generates a sense of community. Squatters' rights exist, but the people are ignorant of them or do not know how to enforce them. The only people who show any concern for the poor—the governing class is both callous and contemptuous—are the priests and the bishops.

Cardinal Arns, the Archbishop of São Paolo, a Franciscan living out the evangelical counsels in sharp contrast to his triumphalist fellow cardinal in Rio de Janeiro, gives leadership and prophetic witness. Most impressive of all are the Irish missionaries, many of them Holy Ghost Fathers stemming from one of the most conservative and clerical Churches of the world, who have emancipated themselves dramatically from the restrictions of their formation.

This is the background against which liberation theology has developed. It is fundamentally a social gospel. It starts not with abstraction but with the actual social situations in which people find themselves and the problems that they face in their lives. It then looks to the Gospels to see how Jesus and his followers confronted contemporary problems and seeks to apply those principles in the conditions of today. Thus it transcends the limitations of a specific historical situation and goes, in the words of its founder, the Peruvian priest Gustavo Gutierrez, 'to the very root of human existence: the relationship with God in solidarity with other men'. Liberation theology is a community approach inspired by Gospel insights. As Father George Boran put it to me when I was in Brazil: 'The kingdom of God is the deep-down dream that every man has, that a society of justice, of peace, of love is possible—a people can really be brothers. That is the Kingdom, and that is salvation.'

In liberation theology social justice is given a higher priority than personal piety: the 'option for the poor' takes precedence over private devotions. The theology is not content with relieving the symptoms of poverty but looks behind them to identify and eradicate its causes. For this reason authoritarian regimes are hostile to it and brand it as subversive. The instrument chosen to transform society is the basic Christian community. The parish structure remains in Brazil, but it is wholly unsuitable for the conditions which prevail in the *favelas*, so a chain of small groups has been set up, comprising normally between twenty and fifty people and in no circumstances more than 100, modelled on the sharing groups which are described in the Acts of the Apostles. A handful of these were formed in the 1960s; today there are 80,000 throughout Brazil. Members of the groups help one another in their problems; they pool their meagre resources; they act together to improve the appalling social conditions in which they live.

During my stay in Brazil I visited a number of Christian communities and found them deeply revealing. On some days each group meets for a Eucharistic service. The priest says mass in his church and then brings the sacred elements to the meeting place in the *favela* where the Eucharist is to be held. This is presided over by the leaders of the local community, both men and women: the priest is present but remains inconspicuous at the back. Extemporary prayer is widely used, and the sermon is replaced by a question-and-answer session. The purpose of all this is to give to people who have been downtrodden for centuries a feeling of their own worth and a sense of responsibility.

Their appreciation of their own intrinsic dignity thus flows directly from their religious experience. All this takes place in a non-political context, but the Government fears, and no doubt rightly, that what has started in an ecclesiastical setting will spread and reverberate in the wider secular world. And this is ultimately why the communities are of such profound social importance. The outlook for the peoples of Latin America is bleak. They are caught between the opposing forces of *capitalisme sauvage* and the equally ruthless followers of the Communist Party. Through Christian social action a third way is opening up which could be decisive for the future of the continent and could rescue the people from the tyranny of ideologies.

I was able to discuss these matters with the present Pope at a private audience in Rome. I explained to him that I had never before realized what the Christian Gospel meant until I saw it being lived out in practice in Brazil. The Holy Father told me that he himself had visited the *favelas* and had preached on the theme 'Blessed are the poor in spirit', perhaps the greatest of the Beatitudes. He did more than this. In Recife, during his visit to Brazil in June 1980, he declared that the land belonged to the people; in São Paolo he stood up in the stadium with 150,000 workers and identified himself with their cause. He sat up until the early hours of the morning rewriting the speeches drafted for him by curial officials.

Typical of the efforts being made by the Church to improve the conditions of the people is the night school conducted in São Paolo by the Holy Ghost Fathers. This is a school to which young men come by day or after their day's work (if they have any) to learn a skill or acquire a qualification. This is of crucial importance for their future. If they join a union or even show independence of thought, they risk losing their jobs. Unskilled workers have no mobility, and once a job is lost the only alternative is to sink back into the degradation of the *favelas*. If they have a qualification, their prospects are different, and they can seek alternative employment. At the school they are taught not only to help themselves but also to help one another—a truly Christian formation. They have a chance, at least, of escaping from the treadmill of poverty, the lot of so many of their contemporaries, and of living a better life in the future.

9

Devotions and Doctrines

———————

PRAYER

It was St Augustine who wrote nearly 1,600 years ago, 'To work is to pray', crystallizing an eternal truth in a minute phrase. For the Christian the whole of life is in one sense prayer—our activity is a reflection of a divine dynamism, and everything we do, provided it is not expressly sinful, can be made into participation in the life of God. Yet at the same time human beings have a need for prayer in a specific form—we need to communicate with God in a special way, and we can do so. I am not thinking here of public prayer, when we offer ourselves to God as a community of men linked with one another, although that is necessary and valuable— indeed, we have the specific promise of Christ that when even two or three come together in His name He Himself will be there too. I have in mind the prayer that is essentially personal and private, when the individual places himself in confrontation with God, the God who is, in fact, 'out there' in the sense that He is other than us but who at the same time is to be found in the depth of our souls.[1] This sort of prayer can be disturbing as well as consoling: God is infinitely great and we are pretty small beer. Private prayer brings us glimpses of the divine light, and, conscious of both our insignificance and our imperfection, we may want to shield our faces from it and hide under any sheltering stone. How can our pettiness survive in the presence of divine majesty? The answer is that as soon as we are cast down by the magnificence and grandeur of God, we are lifted up again by his loving care for every individual person.

The first purpose of prayer is praise and thanksgiving—praise for the One who has brought us out of nothing into the joy and potential of being. 'What do I have to give thanks for?' people sometimes ask. One answer is: the light which we see when we open our eyes each morning. However,

---

[1] Thus Cardinal Newman speaks of the individual in these terms in one of his sermons: 'No one outside him can really touch him, can touch his soul, his immortality: he must live with himself for ever—he has a depth within him unfathomable, an infinite abyss of existence.'

the most common form of prayer is that of petition, in which we approach God, requesting Him to fulfil our needs. This is not a high form of prayer, but there is nothing wrong with it—indeed, we have the example of the unfortunate widow in the Gospels whose pestering is explicitly commended by Our Lord.[2] This kind of prayer can go wrong if we treat it as a form of magic by which we seek to make God serve our needs rather than His, to fulfil our will instead of His purposes. We are right to ask— how far there will be a direct intervention we cannot know—but what is essential is to be content to leave the response to God. We cannot, in fact, write both sides of the equation. We are entitled to make our requests but not to determine the manner of the response. Very often a response will take a form that is different from that which has been requested. This may be a disappointment, but often we are able to see that it has been for the best. Praying for others in this manner is a slightly higher form of the same activity. It constitutes a form of companionship. Holding our friends in prayer is to be with them.

We are right, then, to ask for the satisfaction of our needs and those of others, both temporal and spiritual, but the prayer of petition is a primitive form of prayer. Prayer is presence rather than power. In this kind of payer we simply open ourselves to God and let Him do His work. God needs only the opportunity to come in, and that man has to provide, but once that has been offered, God does the rest. To open ourselves to the divine we must be a little quiet: Christ Himself tells us to go into a room alone to pray, and that is more necessary today, not less.[3] Traditionally, the Church has favoured the early morning for private prayer, and modern life, with all its complexities and interruptions, has validated this precept. Such prayer should be real contemplation. Unfortunately, we have become rather nervous of the word: we think in terms of mystical ecstasies, of which the Church has traditionally been suspicious. We may think too that we must be perfect before we can contemplate and experience the presence of God. This is a misapprehension. Everything is gift: God gives to whom He chooses, not because of any merits of their own but simply because He is Love.

In prayer we should bring everything to God. Devout people have a tendency to present only those parts of themselves which they find acceptable. In fact, it is absurd to seek to leave anything out. After all, God knows it all much better than we do ourselves. He knows the secrets of men's hearts. It is no use pretending with God, so we might as well give it up. He is not waiting for us to be good before He loves us. If we think in these terms, we are liable to arrive in God's presence with a label round our necks reading, 'All my own work'. Prayer is by no means always

---

[2] Luke 18: 1.
[3] Hence the practice of setting up monasteries and convents in peaceful settings. There is a holiness of places as well as of persons.

consoling, as I have remarked, although consolations are agreeable things to have. We have to remember that if God shows us His face, He is there, but He is equally there when He hides it from us. Sometimes the highest form of prayer is simply to endure.

Contemplative prayer is intensely private, which is not the same as being selfish. Its purpose is to open oneself up to God and become a channel of his power so that it can be used in the service of others. As we are told, we cannot love God unless we love our fellow men, but we can love them much better if we also love God. Life, as the Anglican mystic Charles Williams puts it, is a web of exchange, and all the currency comes ultimately from God. We give and receive every day of our lives. Prayer should make us more conscious of the existence of this web; it should embed us in the world, not separate us from it. The need today is for a holy worldliness, not an unholy and priggish other-worldliness. Despite all the manuals that have been written on the subject, there are no rules for prayer. We should talk or be silent according to how we are moved. The essence of prayer is to set oneself down in front of God and to let him take possession of one.

It is prayer that not only the individual but also the world needs, especially our own semi-affluent society, obsessed with the material, and unconscious that we are lapped about by great mysteries from the cradle to the grave. Society is suffering from spiritual starvation, which can be alleviated only through the channels opened up by the mystics, leading their hidden lives of union and devotion. The Christian Church's failure to meet this need has led to a multiplication of exotic religious fads and fancies. Seekers after meditation and contemplation have had to turn to the East to find what they are being denied in the West.

One of the great exponents of contemplative prayer was St Teresa of Avila, who despite the gap of 400 years which separates her from us, is very much a saint for our times. St Teresa does, in fact, bridge the gap between contemplation and activity, for out of her mystical experiences sprang a campaign of reform which was to revolutionize her own order of Carmelites. She has, therefore, a double appeal and links up with two dominant demands of religion in our age, the signs of the times: the desire to see Christianity simply practised, as witnessed by the life of such saints as Mother Theresa of Calcutta, and the longing for direct experience of the transcendence of God. This latter is the desire which, however imperfectly directed, lies at the heart of the drug-and-sex culture of the younger generation.

The gap, then, between St Teresa and a contemporary hippie is narrower than might be supposed. True, there are certain features of St Teresa which are not attractive to the contemporary mind. It never occurred to her to question the theological orthodoxy of her own time, for example: she was content to see heretics burned and Lutherans persecuted; she was obsessed with her own shortcomings, which seem fairly trivial to most of us (but then she was seeing them in the light of the immediate presence of the Other). Yet these things are of little importance when compared with the quality of her mystical experiences, her ability to reflect on them and to articulate what she felt. She is a splendid teacher: her image of the garden watered by grace is illuminating to the simple and sophisticated alike.

St Teresa's contemplative form of prayer went beyond the intellect and consisted in the direction of the whole personality and will towards God. Through its practice she was lifted as though, as she puts it, by a 'powerful eagle rising and bearing you up on its wings' into a world of rapture and ecstasy. It was not that she had visions with her physical eyes, to the disappointment of some of her spiritual advisers, but that she saw things internally with the eyes of her soul. God acts directly upon the unconscious of the mystic, and images of Him are clothed in the experience of the person to whom the illumination is given. Like so many mystics, St Teresa turned to light to provide a description of her experiences of God.

> It is not a dazzling radiance but a soft whiteness and infused radiance [she tells us]. The brightness and light that appear before the gaze are so different from those of earth that the sun's rays seem quite dim by comparison and afterwards we never feel like opening our eyes again. It is as if we were to look at a very clear stream running over a crystal bed in which the sun was reflected and then to turn to a muddy brook, with an earthy bottom, running beneath a clouded sky.[4]

St Teresa's experiences of God seem to have been less passionate than those of her friend, St John of the Cross: in the mystics' world there are many mansions, and each seems able to grasp an aspect of God according to his or her particular gifts and temperament. For St Teresa God was not so much lover as king: she always refers to Him as His Majesty.

Yet all Christian mystics have one thing in common, a sense of the magnificence and power of the love of God, in contrast to the dazzling hues of which worldly attachments fade into a brown sepia. I think in this connection of the moving final lines of the Father Superior in Henri de Montherlant's play *La Ville dont le prince est un enfant*, when he speaks of the love of God and concludes with, 'Auprès duquel tout le rest n'est rien'.

PRAYER — BUT TO WHOM?

Conversation with people is easier if we have some idea of their character and personality. It is the same with talking and listening to God. With

---

[4] See *Life of St Teresa*, translated by S. M. Cohen, London, 1957.

people we are helped by seeing them, hearing them, evoking a verifiable response. The difficulty is that we cannot do this with God. He does not act like that. Those who claim a 'hot line' to the Holy Spirit, some form of direct communication with the Deity should be regarded with a little suspicion. They may be talking only to themselves.

There are clues and guidelines scattered throughout scriptural and devotional literature which help us on our way. The beginning of wisdom is not to strain to see things clearly and to recognize that we are in the realm of mystery, which goes beyond human reason while in no way contradicting it. In his Gospel St John gives a helpful insight into the problem. In the first chapter he writes: 'It is true that no one has ever seen God at any time. Yet the divine and only Son who lives in the closest intimacy with the Father, has made Him known.' St John points here to the ultimate unknowability of God. No one save the Son has looked upon the Father, but it is through the Son that knowledge is mediated to men.

Because God is a pure spirit, He provides no material for the imagination to work on, and this is of particular difficulty in our own country. As Bacon has put it, 'The English mind likes to work on stuff.' In the absence of primary materials, one has to revert to secondary substitutes. These tend to be highly unsatisfactory, made up of the bric-à-brac left over from various stages of mental development. There is the father remembered from early childhood, or the authority figures of youth, or the iconography gathered during early visits to art galleries and other forbidding places. So most people, if they visualize God at all, see Him as the stern judge, or the old man with the beard, or the angry octogenarian. It is clear that God is not like that at all. God is Love, as we are tremblingly told in St John's epistle. Furthermore, there is nothing angry about Him. The fourteenth-century English mystic Mother Julian of Norwich tells us: 'It is impossible for God to be angry.' Anger is not compatible with love. But when God is said to be Love, what is actually meant by such a statement? We are saying that God constitutes the very essence of love, burning, incandescent and all-consuming, so that it is impossible to come into contact with Him without a distancing. Without that, it would be like a moth flying into the heart of the sun.

It seems that this love is so great that it overflows outside the Godhead into acts of creation. Hence spring the world, animals, plants and ourselves. Both St John and St Paul connect creation specifically with the Second Person of the Trinity: 'He is the first and upholding principle of all creation. He is before all things and in him all things hold together.'[5] Furthermore, it is the Second Person of the Trinity who becomes man. One reason, among others, why He does so is in order that we can see what God is like in terms that we can understand.

[5] St Paul, Letter to the Christians at Colossae, 1:15.

The Incarnation took place in the person of Jesus. What was he like? We do not know physically very much about his appearance, but we can deduce a majesty there because it affected even the cynical and worldly Pontius Pilot. Individuals were converted merely by seeing Him. Evidently he was rather different from the gibbering idiot of Dennis Potter's play. The Gospels, of course, were written fifty years after the death of Jesus and are therefore as much an account of the post-Resurrection Christ as of the historical Jesus. Jesus, we sometimes have to remind ourselves, was really a man. He was not God dressed up as a man, which is the image conveyed in so much of what passes for religious education, but a real man, Jesus of Nazareth.[6] We know very little about his psychology, but one thing we can say with reasonable certainty is that he did not go about thinking to himself that he was the Second Person of the Trinity. That definitive knowledge came to him as a man after the Resurrection, not before it.

Before we can see him as a man for all times, we have to see him as a man of his own time. While we have no biography of Jesus, the signs of what he was like are present in the Gospel narratives. He was obviously loving and compassionate to individuals. This contrasted with his firmness in enunciating general principles. He had no time for the establishment of the time—the excoriated Pharisees. He had his measure of worldly wisdom. He did not allow himself to be trapped until his moment had come. The outstanding feature of the character of Jesus was his total obedience to the Father. It was through the obedience rather than the suffering that the Redemption was brought about. He evidently had enjoyed a father experience of unique love and intensity, and it was his fidelity to that revelation which led on to his suffering and death and eventually his resurrection and glory.

In the person of Jesus we catch sight of God's universal mercy, shown in the Son's stretching out to sinners, his willingness to embrace social and religious outcasts, his indifference to the past of individuals provided they turned now to the Father. He submitted to being washed by Mary Magdalene, an act which the Jews at the time found both incomprehensible and intolerably provocative. This ever-present love, always manifesting itself, always seeking a response, has nothing to do with either anger or fear. If we want to know what God is like, we must study the Incarnation, but we must also look at all of his Creation, for this gives us glimpses of himself. God is beauty as well as truth. We see him in the highest aesthetic achievements of man—in the arts, in music, in architecture. We see him in nature, the garment of the creator, in sunrise and sunset, in the oceans and in the evening star. We see him, above all, in the triumphs of the human spirit, in the self-surrendering, self-sacrificial,

[6] The best modern attempt to disentangle the two is contained in Edward Schillebeeckx, *Jesus: An Experiment in Christology*, New York, 1981.

unselfish love which has marked out some men in all ages, in the love and friendship which we ourselves experience.

One type for modern times is Maximilian Kolbe, a Franciscan friar who volunteered to take the place of a married man who was to be starved to death in the condemned cell at Auschwitz. He did this partly to help the man and his children but more so that, as a priest, he would be able to minister to the nine others who were facing a similar dreadful end in the concentration camp bunker. The point was stressed by the then Cardinal Woytyla, later John Paul II, after the beatification of Father Kolbe in Rome in October 1971:

> It was as a Catholic priest that he accompanied his wretched flock of nine men condemned to death. It was not a question of saving the life of the tenth man—he wanted to help those nine to die. From the moment that the dreadful door clanged shut on the condemned men, he took charge of them, and not just them but others who were dying in cells nearby and whose demented cries caused anyone who approached to shudder. . . . It is a fact that from the moment Father Kolbe came into their midst, those wretched people felt a protective presence, and suddenly the cells in which they awaited the ghastly final dénouement resounded with hymns and prayers.

It is in acts like these that we get some slight measure of the intensity of the love of God.

SOME REFLECTIONS ON THE FEASTS OF THE CHURCH

The teaching of the Christian religion, for the majority of people, lies not so much in the formalities of the classroom as in the liturgical life of the Church. In the Anglican Communion, for example, hymns are a principal means of conveying doctrine. In the Catholic Church, as Augustine Birrell put it, 'It is the mass that matters.' Thus the great feasts of the Christian Church provide much on which to reflect.

CHRISTMAS

Christmas is both a pagan and a Christian celebration, but we should not be disturbed by this. Grace builds on nature. The feasting, the giving and receiving of presents, the reunions with family and friends, the imaginative and moving picture of the child in the stable watched over by the ox and the ass and visited by the three Kings, are all things good in themselves, but in the light of the Incarnation they are lifted up and transformed into a lasting joy.

The Christian is at all times two-world-centred but at certain moments more obviously so than at others. Christmas is one of these. The greatness of Christmas is that it is a supreme moment of interpenetration of one world by the other. We stand in adoration and awe before the crib, recalling the moment when the Almighty, the God of majesty and power, the creator and sustainer of the universe, stooped down towards the world which he made and reduced himself to that most helpless of creatures, a new-born babe. In that embodiment of gift and condescension and love, we get a glimpse of what God is really like, a being whose nature it is to love and who can do no other. At Christmas that fiery furnace is transubstantiated into the gentleness, the meekness and helplessness of a tiny child.

In the Christian cosmology there stands God and there stands man, bearing the burden of his individuality for ever. The Incarnation brings the two together. The difference between them is that He is sinless and men are steeped in sin, subject to pride and selfishness and lust—and not only their own but also the accumulated sinfulness of the human race. Mankind is caught in the structures of sin, in the Church, in the State, in individual lives, unable to free themselves save through the mediation of that child. Without Jesus the whole human race, individually and collectively, is trapped by sin: but this is the child who lifts the intolerable burden from mankind and carries it for him, who bears the burden of guilt and evil on his own shoulders and who in the end will carry it, actually, in the form of the Cross. Even as the Wise Men hasten towards Bethlehem, filled with indescribable joy by the sight of the star, as Matthew tells us,[7] the shadow and the glory of the Cross are seen in the stable where the child lies, the child who has come to save his people from their sins.

From that moment, the great work of redemption is set in motion, redemption not only of the individual but also of the whole human race. It is the race, and not the individuals alone who compose it, that is to be saved. The theology of redemption highlights the evil of racialism, which implicitly denies it. And in this work of redemption, so secretly and humbly set in motion, every individual has his or her part to play, so that in the end the new creation, described by St Paul, comes to fruition. So the Church is right at Christmas to give thanks for this greatest of gifts of God to man, to bid us fall to our knees in adoration and praise in the stable filled with the light of that heavenly child.

ST CHARLES THE MARTYR

'Remember' was the last word uttered by King Charles to Bishop Juxon before his execution. Having said that and handed his George, the insignia of the Garter, to the bishop, the king lay down on the scaffold

---

[7] Matthew 2: 1.

which had been erected outside Inigo Jones's Banqueting Hall in Whitehall and placed his head upon the block. The events of that freezing January day more than 300 years ago are still remembered by some in the services which are held every year on the anniversary of the martyrdom, 30 January.[8]

But what do they remember? The events took place centuries ago, and the old ideological battles have long grown stale. No one today would subscribe to King Charles's words on the scaffold, referring to the people:

> Truly I desire their liberty and freedom as much as anybody whomsoever; but I must tell you their liberty and freedom consists in having of government, those laws by which their life and their goods may be most their own. It is not for having a share in government, sir, that is nothing pertaining to them. A subject and a sovereign are clear different things.[9]

Today the monarchy has evolved in a manner King Charles never foresaw: power has steadily passed from monarch to Parliament, from Parliament to Cabinet and from Cabinet to Prime Minister.

What we remember is something rather different. First, there is the personal tragedy of the king. E. M. Forster has written that it is only private life that holds up the mirror to eternity, but although the king's final drama was played out in public—indeed, it was essential that it should be, from his persecutors' point of view, since they were making a public point, otherwise he would have been secretly murdered—behind these externals stands the private man. It is his personal tragedy that fascinates posterity.

---

[8] The feast of St Charles the Martyr is observed by some Anglicans. It has found a place in the list of 'lesser festivals and commemorations' in the *Alternative Service Book* of 1980, but no sentences, collects or readings are provided in the book. Nevertheless, the feast is celebrated in some 650 churches throughout the Anglican Communion. King Charles's day was observed after the Restoration as a black-letter day with the approval of the restored Charles II. Queen Victoria, however, after debates in Convocation and the House of Lords, removed the feast from the Prayer Book in 1859. It was revived by the Society of King Charles the Martyr, founded by Mrs Greville-Nugent and the Reverend James Fish, and services are held every year in the Whitehall Banqueting Hall and at St Mary-le-Strand. Wreaths are placed at the foot of the statue of King Charles at the top of Whitehall. A number of hymns have been written to commemorate St Charles, of which the following verse is not untypical:

Royal Charles, who chose to die
Rather than the faith deny,
Forfeiting his kingly pride
For the sake of Jesu's bride;
Lovingly his praise we sing,
England's martyr, England's king.

[9] This and subsequent quotations are extracted from C.V. Wedgwood, *The Trial of Charles I*, London, 1964.

King Charles was a devout and a holy man. During his imprisonment at Carisbrook, his trial at Westminster Hall and on the eve of his execution he spent much of his time in meditation and prayer. The day before his execution he received the Sacrament, listening to the Gospel, taken from the twenty-seventh chapter of Matthew, which recounts the passion of Our Lord. By chance or providence, it was allotted to the day. King Charles's serenity during his suffering has been caught for ever in the painting executed by Edward Bower of the king at his trial. It shows him attired soberly in black; round his neck hangs the glittering George on its blue ribbon; and his cloak bears the great silver star of the Garter. His mind was concentrated not on worldly tribulations but on God. He had even given up his favourite dogs, the greyhound Gipsy and the spaniel Rogue, since he found them a distraction. At the scaffold he was upheld by that inner power which comes to so many martyrs. He appeared to be communing with God in a special way. At his trial the stutter and impediment of his speech from which he had suffered throughout his life vanished, and he was able to speak fluently. 'I fear not death,' he declared. 'Death is not terrible to me. I thank God I am prepared. I go from a corruptible to an incorruptible crown, where no disturbance can be, no disturbance in the world.'

We see in the king a type of the suffering servant of Isaiah. He was a sensitive man. For four years he had been separated from his wife, his children and his friends. Handed over to hectoring Puritan divines, he must in those last days have thought of the words of Shakespeare's Richard II:

> I live with bread like you, feel want,
> Taste grief, need friends:—subjected thus,
> How can you say to me—I am a king?

The second thing we remember is that the king died for the rule of law. The court which tried him was not constitutional. As he himself pointed out, Parliament may be a high court but the House of Commons alone is not. Furthermore, it was the Army, not Parliament, that was effectively in charge of the trial. The judicial process was a sham: no court, even if it were properly constituted, had power to try the sovereign. Of the 150 judges only forty-nine in the end signed the death warrant. Throughout his trial the king stood firm and refused to acknowledge the court or to plead. As he said to Bradshaw on the first day of the trial:

> I would know by what power I am called hither. I would know by what authority, I mean *lawful*. . . . remember I am your king, your *lawful* king, and what sins you bring upon your head, and the judgement of God upon this land; think well upon it, I say, think well upon it, before you go from one sin to a greater. . . . I have a trust committed to me by

God, by old and lawful descent; I will not betray it to answer a new unlawful authority; therefore resolve me that and you shall hear more of me.

This went to the heart of the matter, and when Bradshaw admonished the king that he was before a court of justice, King Charles replied ironically, 'I see I am before a power.' Later in the trial the king explained his position further. He declared:

> If it were only my own particular case, I would have satisfied myself with the protestation I made the last time I was here against the legality of the court, that a king cannot be tried by any superior jurisdiction on earth. But it is not my case alone, it is the freedom and the liberty of the people of England; and do you pretend what you will, I stand for their liberties. For if power without law may make laws, they alter the fundamental laws of England, I do not know what subject he is in England that can be sure of his life, or anything that he calls his own.

Today, as ever, it is the law and the institutions of the realm which stand between the individual and the naked power of the state. Law is broken at our peril, and the execution of Charles I can be traced back to that of his Catholic grandmother, Mary Queen of Scots, by her regicide sister, Elizabeth I.

The king died for the Church of England. He gave up his life for its liturgy, its traditions, its episcopacy, its holiness. He could have safeguarded his own position by abandoning the Church, but he declined to do so. The point was underlined at his funeral, which was conducted without any service, the prayer book of the Church of England being forbidden. The Book of Common Prayer was carried before his black-palled coffin, but it remained closed. By the time the coffin had reached the vault at Windsor it was covered not in a black but in a white pall of snow. Veronica Wedgwood catches the irony of his obsequies in her account of the king's burial in the vault at Windsor that already contained the remains of his predecessor Henry VIII, 'his strange companion in death':

> the king who broke the Church of England from the Roman Communion to gain political advantage and to satisfy a sensual appetite and a king who died because he saw in the Anglican faith the best and purest form of the Christian doctrine and the church militant on earth.

As so often, the blood of martyrs turned out to be the seed of the Church. One hundred and fifty years ago the Oxford Movement drew inspiration from the king in its mission to restore 'the Church of Charles and Laud'.

The fidelity of the king to his Church was beyond all doubt. He gave his heir, Charles II, clear instructions that there should be no concessions compromising the Church or the Crown in order to secure a reprieve. At his last meeting with his daughter Elizabeth, he instructed her 'not to grieve and torment [her] self for him, for that would be a glorious death that he should die, it being for the laws and liberty of this land and for maintaining the true Protestant religion'. Almost his final words were about the Church of England: 'I die a Christian according to the profession of the Church of England as I found it left to me by my father,' he said to Bishop Juxon on the scaffold. Yet there was nothing exclusive about the king's Anglican devotion. He declared:

> I am and ever shall be of such moderation as to keep aloof from every undertaking which may testify every hatred to the Roman Catholic religion; nay rather will I seize all opportunities . . . to remove all suspicions entirely; so that as well as all confess one undivided Trinity and one Christ crucified, we may be banded together unanimously in one faith. That I may accomplish this, I will reckon as trifling all my labours and vigilance and even the hazards of kingdoms and life itself.

As Father Charles-Roux has pointed out, these words give the martyred king a claim to be the patron saint of ecumenism.[10]

The king is marked out by his courage, the greatest of the virtues, without which there is no security in holding any of the others. We see him as a man of inner direction, contrasting starkly with the spirit of our own age, which is one of mass media, mass opinion and mass conformity. King Charles lived by internal standards and was guided by the light of faith. We see him too as a man directed outwards, standing for regularity, lawfulness and order in Church and state. His story illuminates the problems which the contemporary world is facing on a scale and magnitude which the seventeenth century could scarcely have imagined. Yet the moral challenge is the same. Today we look back to that lonely, tragic and, in the end, integrated figure for guidance. We remember him as King Charles, Charles the Martyr, St Charles, the Exemplar of Fidelity and Fortitude.

GETHSEMANE AND HOLY WEEK

Holy Week is a time when the Church meditates in a special manner on the sufferings and death of Jesus. For all human beings the anticipation of suffering constitutes much of its horror. Jesus was no exception to this rule, as the graphic account given by St Mark in his Gospel shows:

> Then they arrived at a place called Gethsemane and Jesus said to his disciples, 'Sit down here while I pray.' He took with him Peter, James and John and began to be horror-stricken and desperately depressed.

[10] J. M. Charles-Roux, 'The Sanctity of Charles I', a pamphlet published by the Society of King Charles the Martyr.

'My heart is nearly breaking,' he told them. 'Stay here and keep watch for me.' Then he walked forward a little way and flung himself on the ground praying that if it were possible he might not have to face the ordeal. 'Dear Father,' he said, 'all things are possible to you. Please—let me not have to drink this cup. Yet it is not what I want, but what you want.'[11]

This scene in Gethsemane is imprinted indelibly on the Christian imagination. Those who visit Jerusalem can still see the garden where it took place, with the olive groves, the gnarled and wise old trees deeply rooted in time and history. Encapsulated in St Mark's description is a vital part of the Christian message: the necessary confrontation with death and suffering, the real humanity of Jesus epitomized in his fear and dread, and his obedience to the will of the Father, a submission essential for the world's salvation. At this point in Holy Week, as the Paschal moon begins to rise, the mind of the Christian world is concentrated on that lonely figure, prone in the shadow of the olive trees, suffering an anguish so intense that, as St Luke tells us,[12] his sweat was like great drops of blood falling to the ground. Christian artists have sentimentalized the scene, but there is nothing sentimental nor aesthetic about descending into the depths of suffering, facing the horror, the dryness, the loneliness and the abandonment. This age is fascinated by the humanity of Jesus, and here we have it. We have Him who is placed higher than the heavens facing what is an essential part of being human, pain, suffering and death. When one calls to mind the suffering of mankind one can reflect that no human being has suffered more at the hands of men than their Creator.

So it is to a meditation upon death that the Church calls us at this time—our own death, the one predictable fact of our existence. It brings to mind the death of others and indeed the death that is the common experience of the entire human race, befalling the good and the bad, the just and the unjust, the rich and the poor. Death is the great fact before which the contemporary world is silent, appalled and horrified, finding it obscene or absurd. Only the good news of the Gospel can make it at all sensible and bearable.

In Gethsemane Jesus came to fulfil the purpose for which he was born, as the gift of myrrh at his birth had foretold. In Gethsemane the shadow which had lain across the lives of both Jesus and his mother for so many years became a reality. He was taking up not only the burden of his own suffering but also that of every member of the race. What was even heavier was the carrying of the accumulated sinfulness of mankind from the first moment of Creation to that of the Second Coming. What the Lord was facing was the violence, the injustice, the wickedness, the atrocities not of

[11] Mark 14: 32.
[12] Luke 22: 35.

one age but of the whole of time. He was taking them on his own shoulders, lifting them up away from others, freeing and liberating men from both death and sin. Thanks to this, death is no longer a stone wall that bleakly and brutally bars all our hopes and aspirations but becomes a gateway through which we, and arguably the whole of Creation, pass to a new birth.

The transfiguration of death into birth, of dying into living, begins in Gethsemane and is accomplished on Calvary. On Easter Day, with a mighty explosion, the stone is rolled away from the tomb. So, symbolically, the redemptive power of God is released into the world, a process which Paul describes so eloquently for the Christians at Ephesus.[13]

These events succeeded each other in time, but to grasp their significance Christians must see them all at once—death, Resurrection, the Cross, glory and, at the centre of them all, Jesus. Gethsemane, with its agony, is the essential prerequisite for Easter Day, with its message of hope for every individual.

Holy Week, then, is resplendent with both suffering and hope. We see the reality of our destiny, eternal life, so different from the physical appearance—extinction in the grave. Instead of a cold and unfeeling universe, indifferent to men's sufferings and struggles—at once pitiless and absurd—we observe a world transfigured and transformed by love, made alive by it. This love is at the same time so powerful and so general that it has called the whole universe out of nothing into the light of existence, and so particular, so gentle, so intimate that it confers something special, something unique, upon every human being.

Yet Christian hope is not confined to individuals; it encompasses the whole of the human race. The race itself is to be redeemed, and Easter provides the means by which—through the activity of millions of unseen, humble wills, conforming themselves to the will of the Father as revealed through the Son—the world can and will be saved from the spirit of evil. Hope gives the insight, the power, to see behind the apparent triumph of evil in the world the ceaseless working of grace in the establishment of the Kingdom. Thus the victory of righteousness is assured if only human beings open themselves to God. And with hope comes joy, the state of mind both tranquil and ecstatic which springs from the knowledge that beneath the disordered appearance of things everything is safe in the hands of God,[14] everything, in the words of the great English mystic,

---

[13] Ephesians, 1: 15.

[14] Wir alle fallen. Diese Hand da fällt.   We are all falling. This hand's falling too—
Und sieh dir andre an: es ist in allen.   all have this falling-sickness none withstands.

Und doch ist Einer, welcher dieses Fallen   And yet there's always One whose gentle hands
undendlich sanft in seinen Händen hält.   this universal falling can't fall through.

Rainer Maria Rilke, from 'Autumn', in *Requiem and Other Poems*, trs. J. B. Leishman, London, Hogarth Press, 1935.

Mother Julian of Norwich, will be 'all right'. Through hope we know that the mighty river of love will not be defeated by the pathetic barriers that human beings seek to erect in its way, that the Church will not founder, but as Ezekiel saw, the dry bones will live.[15]

EASTER DAY

Easter is the greatest feast of the Christian year—more vital, if less touching, than Christmas, more exclusively religious, less pagan, and mercifully, less commercialized. Christmas marks the possibility of man's redemption, but at Easter he rejoices in its fulfilment. Redemption comes about not through the Cross as such but through Christ's perfect submission to the will of the Father, which entailed the Crucifixion. God, after all, is the Father of love, not a Moloch to be propitiated. If Christmas is the festival of charity and love, when we meditate on their supreme manifestation in the fact of the Incarnation, Easter is pre-eminently the celebration of hope, when we see more clearly than at any other time the triumph in Christ of God's intentions for the salvation of the human race. After the suffering of Gethsemane and Calvary comes the glory—the triumphal exit from the tomb, the vanquishing of the last enemy. Easter invites reflection upon a central doctrine of the Christian faith: the resurrection of the body. Christ's own Resurrection points the way which all shall follow. The fact of the Resurrection is what is important. The empty tomb and the appearances are evidence of this; they are not the fact itself. I wonder, however, how many Christians take the resurrection of the body seriously, giving it an effective rather than a notional assent? St Paul, in that wonderful passage in the fifteenth chapter of his first Letter to the Corinthians, develops the theme of resurrection, using what are clearly inspired insights, returning again and again to his subject, but stressing always that the body will be not only raised but transformed: 'It is sown a natural body; it shall rise a spiritual body. If there be a natural body, there is also a spiritual body.'[16]

The body, then, after death remains a real body, but it will be, as some theologians put it, a 'glorified' body. We can see the archetype operating in Christ himself after His Resurrection. My own belief is that the resurrection of the body takes place immediately after death. I do not see how a disembodied soul can exist at all, suspended as it were, waiting for a body to come along to inhabit. This does not accord with the facts of human nature, which is not soul plus body but soul-body. What, then, of the general resurrection of the dead? I see it as some kind of recognition of the final working out of God's plan for the world, a glorious manifestation

[15] 37: 1.
[16] 15: 35.

of a new future for the whole human race, when the earth itself and all those who have lived on it have passed away.

The Christian religion accords the body a higher place than does any other world religion. In this sense Christianity is the most materialistic of religions. The body, as Charles Williams has put it, is holily created, holily redeemed and is to be holily raised from the dead.[17] From the Incarnation onwards there is something very concrete about the Christian religion: it is related all the time to flesh and blood, not to abstractions. How strange, then, that a religion which accords such importance to the body should in practice, over long periods, have rejected it altogether. In popular Christianity, at any rate, the idea is prevalent that somehow the body has fallen lower than the soul, an idea which finds its ultimate vulgarization in the notion that the sin of Adam was a sin of sex. In fact, we do not know how the Fall came about: what we do know (and the evidence is on every side, both in ourselves and without) is that it took place. Human nature is not irretrievably damaged, but it is certainly flawed. Yet somehow, over long periods of Church history, heretical notions about the body have held sway. Who is to blame? The Church fathers? The pagan Greco-Roman world into which Christianity came and against which it reacted? Misunderstanding of St Paul, who is thought by many to have condemned the body when he condemned the 'flesh'? The object of his censure was not the body but the spirit centred on this world instead of the two-world-centred spirit which Christianity manifests Victorian culture and its rejection of the body? The list could go on.

The contemporary world, on the other hand, has rediscovered the body but seems to have forgotten about the soul. In the rock musical *Hair* there is a lyric 'I love life', which is a more or less pagan glorification of the body. It recalls Charles Williams's essay, 'The Index of the Body', but that is written from the Christian point of view.[18] 'The imperial structure of the body', he writes, 'carries its own high doctrines—of vision, of digestion, of mysteries, of balance, of movement, of operation.' Every part of the body has its own unique function from the eyes, the windows of the soul, down to the lowly feet on which the whole 'imperial structure' rests. The body is, in fact, our only true possession, from which death alone separates us; but as soon as we have lost one, we gain another. The body is an essential part of human beings, who are not carcasses animated by ghosts. The body is good, not evil—although, like everything else that is human, it can be used for base purposes. Easter brings to mind the high destiny not only of the soul but also of the body, and proclaims that body and soul are properly one entity, torn apart by the unnatural event of death, which itself is the penalty of sin. Easter is the one time at which

[17] See Charles Williams, *The Image of the City*, Oxford, 1958, pp. 80–7.
[18] In *The Image of the City*.

triumphalism is justified in the Church, but the triumph is not that of human beings, save vicariously and in promise: in essence, it belongs to the Redeemer.

Easter is a festival ignored by the contemporary world, and yet the world has greater need of the Easter message today than perhaps at any other time in history. The temptation of modern man is not pride but despair: belief in the perfectibility of man has vanished from the West, to be replaced by fear of his capacity for self-destruction. The problems confronting the human race are indeed daunting: the affluence of the minority is rebuked by the poverty of the majority; the technological progress which offers mankind a chance to escape want; offers a parallel threat to life and dignity at the very moment when it seems able to aid man to become fully human. Our eyes and ears are daily assaulted by the accounts of the horrors of human behaviour in every part of the world. Constantly we are presented with agonizing moral dilemmas, which the rush of events prevents us from reflecting on. Barbarism seems to be triumphant in the world; the forces of enlightenment and humanism are everywhere in retreat. Where, then, can mankind look to be saved? Only to the empty tomb, the enclosing rock thrown forward by the power that upholds the universe, channelled into human history through the person of Jesus.

The violence, the injustice, the tyrannies and the atrocities of our contemporary world should not surprise us. They have always been there. The difference today is that they confront us more immediately. The truth is that the world is permanently caught up in sin. We live and move in the structures of sin built up by our parents and forbears; we add daily our own measure of disorder to that already present in the world. We are, in truth, trapped in sin—until, that is, we glimpse that figure so transfigured by the glory and the joy of sacrifice that death itself is overcome. At Easter we celebrate the fact that Christ has overcome physical death, and we reflect that what is apparently the end of all affection and endeavour is merely a doorway through which we pass to the fullness of life. As Maurice Baring has put it, death will be like opening an envelope and finding the letter inside. Yet the conquest over physical death does not constitute the essence of the Resurrection: it is a reflection only, of the ultimate triumph, which is that of Jesus over sin. So he opens the gateway and passes through it as leader and head of the race, followed by the millions of human beings who have suffered and sinned and whom he has liberated through love.

WHIT SUNDAY AND THE HOLY SPIRIT

Whit Sunday is the anniversary of the birthday of the Church, but it is somewhat of a low-key celebration. In the West—until recently—the

Holy Spirit has been the neglected person of the Holy Trinity: He is not given the place of honour accorded Him in the Orthodox world. Perhaps those in authority are rather nervous of His unpredictable activity. Theologians and official artists have combined to tame Him. The modest little tongues of fire which are portrayed in so many paintings as hovering demurely over the heads of Our Lady and the Apostles are a poor representation of what seems really to have happened on that far-off Pentecost. The Holy Spirit must have manifested Himself as a terrifying and revolutionary experience. In the Acts of the Apostles we are told that there was a great sound from heaven, reverberating throughout the house 'like the rush of a mighty wind' and that flickering flames descended on the Apostles.[19] Then came the gift of tongues in which they babbled and sang their responses from the depths of the unconscious and then dashed out into the street to spread the good news of the Gospel. From that moment the Church, although she has faltered from time to time, has never abandoned her mission.

The downgrading of the Holy Spirit is all the odder because the Lord himself attached the greatest importance to the coming of the Spirit, giving this as a reason for His own departure, without which the Holy Spirit would not be able to move among men. We are told in the Gospels that we shall not be left 'orphans' but that the 'Comforter' will be there with us to fill the void left by the Ascension. We know by faith, then, that the Holy Spirit abides permanently within the Church, constantly guiding and inspiring the whole people of God as He moves through history towards the goal of ultimate salvation. At the same time, we know by observation that at certain times in the Church's history the Holy Spirit has been more obviously present and active than at others. One such period was at the first Pentecost and during the apostolic period of the Church's life, when the gifts of the Holy Spirit seemed to have been scattered among the faithful in an especially lavish and generous way.[20] Another was at the period of the Reformation which, seen in the light of history, was a providential event that in some respects went wrong. The Catholic Church of the period was both corrupt and torpid and so unable to adapt itself to the changes taking place in the world around it. Luther was a prophetic figure, calling the Church and its members back to the paths of righteousness, but unfortunately, partly because of the defects of Catholics, partly because of his own failings, he succeeded not only in purifying but also in disrupting the Church. The parallels between the Reformation period and our own are striking. Once again the Church is having to adapt herself to a new world, and once again the signs of the

---

[19] Acts 2: 1.
[20] The gifts of the spirit are ninefold, according to St Paul—namely, love, joy, peace, patience, kindness, generosity, fidelity, tolerance and self-control.

activity of the Holy Spirit, assisting the Church to make the transition, are evident and manifest.

The need of the Church today is to absorb new insights and to cast off much of the baggage with which she has been lumbered by past ages. The prognosis is more optimistic than at the Reformation. The spiritual life of the Church is strong; there is little of the corrupt worldliness that led to the disastrous outcome of the first Reformation. Men and women of the highest personal probity are found on all sides of current theological controversies. The twentieth-century Catholic reformers are also determined to remain within the Church and not to be separated from Rome. This makes talk of a 'schism' within the Church not only unwise but out of keeping with the facts. Certain individuals may fall away, and that is inevitable in difficult times, but there is no indication of a repetition of the rending events of the Reformation. If there is a threat of 'schism' today, it comes not from the periphery but from the centre, from those who would deny the local Churches their legitimate autonomy and would impose optional matters as though they were issues of faith.

The existence of the Holy Spirit reminds us, at a time when there is rightly so much emphasis on the social and relational aspects of Christianity, that we also need a positive and unequivocal notion of the transcendence of God. God is Love, and the life of knowledge and love which are the two truly human activities are a participation in the life of the Trinity. That is very different from saying that love is God and identifying him with a mere activity. This is the error into which the 'death of God' theologians have fallen, mistaking the manifestations of God's love for God himself. To do this is really to reduce Him to vanishing point and Christianity to mere benevolence. It also robs eternal life of meaning, since the essence of life after death is a continuing growth in the knowledge and love of God. As Christians we share in that eternal life now, but through the veil of the flesh; then, as St Paul tells us, it will be face to face. The life will be the same, but the mode of apprehension will be different; yet we will never be absorbed into God. We carry our own individuality, which is something placed over and against the individuality of God for the whole of eternity.

TRINITY SUNDAY

On Trinity Sunday[21] we commemorate the most important and fundamental doctrine of Christianity, that God is both One and Three.

One point about the doctrinal formulation of the Trinity is that it presents us with an idea of Godhead which is not passive and static but active and dynamic. It tells us that within the Godhead an intense life of

[21] Trinity Sunday is eight weeks after Easter Day.

love is proceeding that expresses itself in persons. St John describes it with admirable economy in the opening lines of his Gospel: 'At the beginning God expressed Himself. That personal expression, the word, was with God. And was God, and He existed with God from the beginning.'[22] The love between Father and Son is such that it is expressed in a Third Person, the Holy Spirit. In this life of love we are able to participate through grace.

Trinitarian life throws some light on another mystery, that of Creation. It seems that the love is so great that it overflows outside of the Godhead in acts of creation. Both St John and St Paul connect Creation specifically with the Second Person of the Trinity. He is the first and upholding principle of all creation: 'He is before all things and in Him all things hold together.' In one sense all the writings of a thinker like Teilhard de Chardin are but an extended commentary on that central Pauline thought. It indicates the reason for the Incarnation: 'Our relation with the Son is accomplished through the historical Jesus.'[23] The possibility of this relationship constitutes the uniqueness of man. Creation as a whole reflects the love and the glory of God, but only man can take conscious part in it.

The love within the Trinity makes possible the love among men which constitutes our real and lasting life, and men can live in love because they are made in the image of the Trinity. There is no contradiction, then, and no necessity for choice between God 'out there' and God acting in the midst of creation; they are two manifestations of the same principle. Private prayer links us directly with Trinitarian life—good works do the same, indirectly, through service to those others whom God has also created.

The Trinity, then, is not merely an abstract but also a very practical doctrine: without it there would be no link between men. The great exchanges of love which take place for ever within the Godhead, the reverberations of which we pick up on our spiritual antennae, are the basis for similar exchanges, on an infinitely smaller scale, which are going on in the world of men. We can, if we wish, decline to make exchanges. The declining on the part of millions of individuals over the centuries constitutes the disorder in our world. We can add to that disorder or create new harmonies of redemption: that is the point of our humanity.

The Trinity illumines not only metaphysics but also Christian living. Take, for example, chastity (both within and without marriage), at present an unfashionable virtue. The scholastics commended it on the basis of natural law and an analysis of the character of physical organs, an apologetic which does not appeal to modern scepticism and relativism. Christian moralists might be more convincing if they showed that the evil

---

[22] 1: 1.
[23] John 1: 1, and Colossians 1: 15.

of lust and sensuality lies not so much in their violation of the alleged fixities of the order of nature as in their shutting out of the vision of God, which is the beginning of participation in Trinitarian love. Furthermore, Trinitarian belief regulates all dogma by its unique profundity. It does not abolish other doctrines but allows them to be seen in perspective: it is not an absolute but a constitutional sovereign. An effective belief in the Trinity, for example, is incompatible with Mariolatry.

Finally, the Trinity is the fount of the theological virtue of hope, which is so conspicuously absent from our world. Rationalism in the last century was marked by over-confidence and pride; its successor today is defaced by despair. In many ways the predicament of modern man is terrifying. Some of the terror is justified, but much is not; it is fostered by a limited vision which distorts the picture. A glimpse of that majestic, incandescent and never-ceasing life of love restores a sense of proportion. Perhaps the doctrine of the Trinity is not quite as academic after all.

THE TRANSFIGURATION AND GLORY

Each year, on 6 August, the Feast of the Transfiguration is kept by the Church. It is the occasion on which she commemorates that extra-ordinary moment on Mount Tabor, when, as all three synoptics record, the glory of the Godhead suffused the humanity of Jesus, filling with dread and awe the Apostles who witnessed it. The moment chosen was when Jesus was midway through his course, the Gallilean ministry lying behind him and Calvary ahead. Perhaps it was intended to strengthen the Apostles for the trials before them.

One of the many losses occasioned by the Orthodox schism is that the Western Church has never attached high liturgical importance to this event. It was not treated as a general feast day until the fifteenth century, when in 1457 Pope Callixtus ordered its observance throughout the Church; today its occurrence is noted only by the rather more than normally devout. In the Church of England it is still only a black-letter day, although in the Episcopal Church in America and Canada its status has been raised.[24]

Very different has been the treatment afforded the Transfiguration in the East. It counts as one of the twelve great feast days of the Orthodox year, ranking with Christmas, the Epiphany, the Ascension and Pentecost; only Easter Day itself exceeds it in solemnity. These differing

---

[24] The Church in Wales, disestablished from the Church of England in 1920, also keeps the Feast of the Transfiguration as a red-letter day. The Collect, however, is not that suggested by the 1928 Prayer Book but reads: 'Almighty and everlasting God, who before the passion of thine only-begotten Son didst reveal his glory when he was transfigured on the holy mount: mercifully grant unto us such a vision of his divine majesty that, purified and strengthened by thy grace, we may be transformed into his likeness from glory to glory: through the same Jesus Christ our Lord.'

liturgical emphases highlight a major difference between the Christianity of East and West, the different theological appraisals of Cross and glory that have been made within the two traditions. The Western Church has exalted the Cross, so that at times it seems to stand isolated from the other mysteries of the Christian faith; the Eastern Church, by contrast, has so bathed the Cross in the glory of the Resurrection that it is possible to underestimate the intensity of the sufferings of Christ. One sees the Western approach most clearly depicted in the crucifixes and Crucifixion paintings of German, Flemish and Spanish art, that of the Orthodox East in the triumphant liturgy of Good Friday. Orthodox theology stresses the victorious aspects of Christ's life, the Redemption he accomplishes at both the individual and the cosmic level, the mysterious nature of Christianity; while the West has been more concerned with society and morality, with precepts and law. It has closed its eyes to the glory which, explains the neglect of the Transfiguration. St Paul reconciles the opposites by bidding us keep our eyes fixed on the Cross, but even as we do so we see through him the branches of that tree, suffused in glory.

The Transfiguration is an event of paramount importance in Christian revelation. From this starting point it is possible to develop a whole theology of glory, which can illumine both the nature of the human condition and the great truths of salvation and redemption. 'Glory', in its original Hebrew sense, meant the riches or distinction which marked out the identity of a man or a nation. The glory of God is akin to this, in that it is a word which strives to convey something of the inmost reality of God, His character and nature. As applied to God, therefore, it is a highly complex notion amalgamating ideas of sovereignty, holiness, love and beauty.

The glory of God, its contemplation by the saved, will constitute the life of the world to come. The darkness and shadows of this world will finally be rolled away in a great onrush of joyful light. As St Paul tells us in his First Letter to the Corinthians, we see now 'as in a glass darkly' but then 'face to face'. The glory, then, will be fully revealed only the other side of death, but we do see something of it now—or can if we wish. After all, the glory of God is shown in all created things: there is a witness to, or sign of, God in the beauty of the world, acknowledged by the nature mystics, who have penetrated behind the garment of the Creator to find the Creator himself. As the poet Francis Thompson has put it:

> Turn but a stone, and start a wing!
> 'Tis ye, 'tis your estrangèd faces,
> That miss the many-splendoured thing. . . .
>
> Yea, in the night, my Soul, my daughter,
> Cry,—clinging Heaven by the hems;
> And lo, Christ walking on the water
> Not of Gennesareth, but Thames!

We catch glimpses of glory—glimpses only because we must not be dazzled into belief and therefore it is for the most part hidden—in our prayers, in the love of friends, in the sacredness of places and in the holiness of the heart's affections. We see too reflections of the glory of God in all human accomplishments and achievements, in art and music and technology. Provided always one recognizes that the ultimate source of this magnificence is not man but God, it is right to rejoice in them. The glory is there. It is a reality. It has been given to man, but it is not for man, or not for him alone. Yet when that has been said, the glory we can see in this way is reflected, not original; for the source itself we have to look elsewhere, and it has been given us in the Incarnation. One stands awestruck at the grandeur, the magnificence, the generosity of that act by which God divested himself of His glory, only to be offered it back again through the perfect obedience of Jesus to His Father's will. By that act is glorified not only God but the whole human race, individually and collectively, in that all are given the possibility of participating in a new glorified Creation which is yet to come.

An essential part of redemption through faith is that the glory should be hidden. Nevertheless, the glory is there; we should not be surprised if it does break through from time to time, and here one comes to the central importance of the Transfiguration. For a few moments the Apostles saw the Son as he really was, then the veil was replaced and they saw 'only Jesus'. The point of the Transfiguration is that it does away with any false dichotomy between Cross and glory. The Cross is glory, and glory is the Cross. That is the ultimate truth of the matter.

THE ASSUMPTION

The Assumption, one of the great feasts of the Church, is celebrated on 15 August. Yet this feast is much more than a celebration: it constitutes a stumbling-block, a scandal in fact, for many Christians. This should not surprise. Since the definition of the Virgin as 'Theotokos', Mother of God, at the Council of Ephesus in 531, Marian doctrines have been a source both of strength and of division in the Church. The great definition of Ephesus constituted the exaltation not only of the Mother but also of the Son: what was ultimately protected by the definition was the belief in the divine personality of Jesus.

The definition of the doctrine of the Immaculate Conception by Pio Nono in 1854 was a logical step in the development of Marian devotion, but it has been the source of constant misunderstanding ever since. The movement for the definition had gathered pace in the seventeenth century, but it was the appearance of the Blessed Virgin to the young novice Catherine Labouré at the Convent of the Sisters of Charity in the rue du Bac in Paris in 1830 that gave it the final impetus. The vision included the inscription 'O Marie, conçue sans pêche, priez pour nous qui avons recours à vous.' (The chapel at the rue du Bac, incidentally, is open daily to visitors and to this day has an aura of holiness which is almost tangible and very un-Parisian.) Pio Nono himself came to the papal throne with a strong personal devotion to the Virgin Mary, and the definition was one of the high points of his pontificate, commemorated by the beautiful pillar which he caused to be erected in the Piazza di Spagna in Rome, crowned by an effigy depicting her as she appeared in the rue du Bac.

Pius IX set an important precedent in the manner of the definition of 1854, which was closely followed by Pius XII when he came to define the sister doctrine of the Assumption in 1950; both popes made the definition *ex sese* (on their own authority), but only after the widest consultations among the episcopate had shown overwhelming majorities both holding the beliefs and favouring the definitions.

The definition of the Assumption as an article of faith came as a shock and surprise to many, despite the antiquity of the feast in both the East and the West. There is, of course, no direct scriptural warranty for the Assumption. The first Father of the Church who, we know, subscribed to the doctrine was St Epiphanius (*c*.310 – 400). However, the feast dates back to the beginning of the fifth century and was celebrated with even greater solemnity in the East than in the West. It was in the East, after all, that the event occurred (if indeed it did), and pilgrims can visit the spot high above Ephesus in Asia Minor where the Assumption is said to have taken place. I visited the little house myself some years ago,[25] as well as the tomb of my patron, St John the Evangelist, who is buried at the foot of the hill. While I arrived sceptical, I came away convinced.

The difficulty of the Assumption for many people is its particularity. An icon of the Blessed Virgin, floating artistically heavenwards surrounded

---

[25] It has a curious history. The building is called 'Meryemana', which means 'Mary's House'. Until the end of the last century it was known only to a few local peasants, but then in far-off Germany a crippled woman, Catharine Emmerich, had a vivid dream about Turkey, a country which she had never visited. She saw, as though in a vision, a small stone house where Mary lay dying, supported in her old age by St John. The dream was so clear that Catharine was able to record every detail, including the existence of a spring of water nearby. She wrote about the dream in her *Life of the Blessed Virgin*, which was read by two Catholic priests, Fr Jung and Fr Poulin. They recognized Ephesus from the description, followed her directions, began excavations and found the ruins of a small house in 1891. They discovered that to the local people this was known as 'Mary's House' and that they came there to pray and had done so for centuries. Nearby the priests came across the spring which is said to have miraculous healing qualities. John wrote part of his Gospel at Ephesus and, according to the peasant tradition, brought Mary here after the Crucifixion and often climbed the mountain to visit his adopted mother. Another local name for the spot is 'Panaya Kapula', which means 'The Doorway of the Virgin'. The basilica at Ephesus was dedicated to the Virgin Mary. Contemporary canon law allowed a church to be dedicated only to saints who had lived or died in the place itself. In 1967 Paul VI knelt and prayed at 'Meryemana'.

by a cloud of angels, is one thing; the image of an actual woman of flesh and blood being lifted up and translated heavenwards is quite another. To many it is at this point that the borderline between faith and superstition is crossed. What may or may not have been a fact has become a matter of faith. Yet the scandal of particularity is one that attaches to the whole of the Christian religion: the synoptic evangelists were intent on placing Jesus in his historical setting: St Luke, for example, pinpoints the exact moment of the Lord's birth by reference to the census of Caesar Augustus: what could be more particular than the resurrection of the Lord himself? The whole doctrine of the resurrection of the body in which Christians profess their faith is an affirmation of belief in the particular. If one can believe in that, one can believe in anything!

The ultimate significance of the Assumption, however—again, like that of other Christian truths—lies not in its particularity (although, given our humanity, this is essential) but in its universality. As the late Father Victor White, OP, put it in a famous article on the Assumption published in 1950: 'The rehabilitation of nature and of woman, and the redemption of our body, is completed, but also pre-typified, in the taking of Mary, body and soul, into the glory of the divinity.'[26] The woman, the feminine, is an intrinsic part both of human nature and of religion; and in the Assumption one finds not only an actual historical incident but also the embodiment of an archetype hidden in the depths of the psyche. The archetype is a living one, and it is no accident that the Eastern Church, which has retained Mary, has also retained its Catholicity, while in the Protestantism of the West the expulsion of Mary and of Catholicism went hand in hand, to be painfully brought back into the Church of England together (on this point Faber—who had an extravagant devotion to Mary, whom he always addressed as Mama—was surely right) at the time of the Oxford Movement.[27]

[26] See 'The Scandal of the Assumption', in *The Life of the Spirit, Blackfriars Review*, vol. 5, November/December 1950, pp. 199–212.
[27] Marian devotion has revived in the Church of England, but it has had its difficult moments. One of them has been immortalized by Hilaire Belloc's poem 'Ballade of Illegal Ornaments', which combines irony and deep feeling in unique proportions.

BALLADE OF ILLEGAL ORNAMENTS

. . . the controversy was ended by His Lordship, who wrote to the Incumbent ordering him to remove from the Church all Illegal Ornaments at once, and especially a Female Figure with a Child.'

When that the Eternal deigned to look
  On us poor folk to make us free,
He chose a Maiden, whom He took
  From Nazareth in Galilee;
  Since when the Islands of the Sea,
The Field, the City, and the Wild
  Proclaim aloud triumphantly
A Female Figure with a Child.

These Mysteries profoundly shook
  The Reverend Doctor Leigh, D.D.,
Who therefore stuck into a Nook
  (or Niche) of his Incumbency
  An Image filled with majesty
To represent the Undefiled,
  The Universal Mother—She—
A Female Figure with a Child.

The Assumption may well prove to be of the deepest ecumenical significance, forming a bridge to reunite East and West, and not only the two branches of the Church but also Eastern and Western religion. As Father Victor has suggested, perhaps the definition will lead the Church to closer consideration of the deep mystery of the Motherhood of God.[28] As he wrote a quarter of a century ago: as Christ, ascending to heaven, leads the way to God our Eternal father, perhaps Mary, assumed into the same heaven, will lead us to deeper knowledge and love of God our Eternal Mother.[29]

His Bishop, having read a book
   Which proved as plain as plain could be
That all the Mutts had been mistook
   Who talked about a Trinity,
   Wrote off at once to Doctor Leigh
In manner very far from mild,
   And said: 'Remove them instantly!
A Female Figure with a Child!'

Envoi
Prince Jesus, in mine Agony,
   Permit me, broken and defiled,
Through blurred and glazing eyes to see
A Female Figure with a Child.

I heard it for the first time recited from memory by Sir Duff Cooper, when he came to the Oxford Union to debate one of Belloc's quatrains and to unveil his portrait by James Gunn on 5 December 1950. I recall his words clearly:

> Posterity may wonder that the country whose language he chose to enshrine his genius should have conferred on him no recognition of any kind. Even his own college of Balliol ignored him. But I think tonight, as he sits in the quiet of his Sussex home listening to this debate [it was broadcast], this presentation of a portrait by the present generation of undergraduates will give him more pleasure than any handful of silver he might have had from the state or ribbon to stick in his coat.

The quatrain was:

The question's very much too wide,
And much too deep and much too hollow,
And learned men on either side
Use arguments we cannot follow.

Those taking part in the debate included Sir Duff Cooper, Mr Godfrey Smith, the retiring President making his farewell speech, and myself.

[28] See Victor White, 'The Scandal of the Assumption'.

[29] Pope John Paul I, who flashed across the ecclesiastical firmament in thirty days like a bright meteor, referred in one of his addresses to 'God our Mother', a revolutionary statement. He also made a major contribution to ecumenism by abolishing the papal tiara and presenting the Pope not as sovereign but as first bishop.

10

Christian Humanism

'All things work together for good for those that love God.'[1] This text of
Paul has a marvellous comprehensiveness: it draws everything together
and leaves nothing of human experience out. So often the theology of Paul
has been misunderstood. He is thought to have posed an intrinsic
opposition between this world and the world of the spirit. He is thought
also to have rejected and condemned the body. In fact, when Paul
opposes *flesh* and *spirit*, he is not opposing them in the sense of prescribing
a contrast between body and soul, but he is contrasting the spirit that looks
only to this world and that which looks beyond it. This form of distortion
appears in the current dispute between humanism and Christianity. One
can accept such an opposition for colloquial, code or methodological
purposes, but it reflects no actual reality. The point is that there is only one
true humanism—Christian humanism.

To claim to be a humanist is to claim to be an understander and lover of
mankind—to know, in other words, *what* man is. This is the question that
all generations ask, but modern man poses it urgently and insistently.
What am I? Why am I here? Have I a purpose? Fewer today are likely to be
satisfied with Louis MacNeice's lines:

> It's no go the Yogi-Man, it's no go Blavatsky,
> All we want is a bank balance and a bit of skirt in a taxi.[2]

The starting point for our own generation is psychological, not philosophical. We find ourselves in an absurd position, perched on a globe
whirling through the Universe, which itself appears to be set in unending
space. With the limitations of our mortality heavy upon us, we experience
aspirations and hopes that have no limit. Confined in our little tank of
time, we reach out to beyond the stars. The paradox is there—the
foundation of both comedy and tragedy. There is a contradiction between
the human mind and its employments. As Walter Bagehot put it:

[1] St Paul's Letter to the Romans 8: 28.
[2] From 'Bagpipe Music', *Louis MacNeice: Collected Poems 1925–1948*, London, 1949.

How can *a soul* be a merchant? What relation to an immortal being have the price of linseed, the fall of butter, the tare on tallow, or the brokerage on hemp? Can an undying creature debit 'petty expenses', and charge for 'carriage paid'? . . . The soul ties its shoe; the mind washes its hands in a basin; the eternally destined mounts the omnibus: all is incongruous.[3]

Christianity alone resolves this paradox, which lies at the heart of human existence. It tells us both the facts and the secrets of our being. It declares, yes, you are in time but not of it; you are created by God to be with Him for ever; you are free to move towards Him or away from Him— you will never be compelled one way or the other. So life, in Newman's phrase, is both great and little. It is totally insignificant, yet charged with meaning which will have eternal consequences. Christianity goes further and tells us that the divine image is impressed on the soul of everyone. The threefold stigmata of the Trinity, printed indelibly on the depths of human nature, are waiting to be released and to rise into consciousness, if only they are allowed to do so. Thus the destiny of each human being is to be a tiny yet scintillating mirror, reflecting back for ever the beauty and the goodness of Him who made us. So Christianity tells us *what* we are. We cannot start to be human beings until we know that.

The second thing that Christianity confirms is our humanity. It informs us that we are human beings—unique combinations of body and spirit. Man is not pure spirit; he is not an angel. Nor is he a mere body; he is not in essence animal. He is, in fact, both. Too often we think of our nature as a soul imprisoned in flesh, released from incarceration at death. We regard the body as a carcass which we drag about with us for seventy years (unless there is a bonus), until the ghost is let out of the machine. Whatever religion this belief may reflect, it is not Christianity. Christianity teaches that both body and soul are necessary to men. When we rise from the dead the body will rise with us. But do we believe that effectively? Those who do not have no claim to be Christians. It follows that the body is good. The rejection of the body has nothing to do with Christianity. The body may be rejected for Victorian reasons or Irish ones, or because of inhibitions or a prudish nature, but none of these derive from Christianity. One of the positive things about the age in which we live is that it has rediscovered the body. That is a gain, but it is not enough, and we have to reunite it with the soul.

For the Christian there are two ways of coming to God: the way of affirmation and the way of negation. To some degree, they are combined in individual lives, but in certain ages some people are more attracted to one way than to the other. The beginning of wisdom is to see the destiny to

---

[3] 'The First Edinburgh Reviewers', *Works*, vol. 1, p. 338.

which one is called. The way of Christian humanism is the way of affirmation. The need of our age is a need for affirmation. The need is not for separation from the world but for immersion in it, while never becoming of it. The type of saint for our time, therefore, is not a cloistered reverend mother but someone—such as Dietrich Bonhoeffer—who comes to spiritual serenity through being submerged in the world of great events. The Christian humanist, therefore, rejects neither the world nor himself as evil—although he recognizes the evil tendencies there—but he looks to see if what at first sight seems evil cannot be transformed into good. Our task, therefore, is to be not less human but more, to rejoice when there is a time for rejoicing, to mourn with those who mourn, to weep if others are weeping. Christians feel human joys and sorrows as intensely as others, but their religion sets their feelings within a framework and saves them from both euphoria and despair. Our duty is not to deny our humanity, our individuality, which is our only and most precious possession, but to transfigure it in Christ. The Christian humanist has in Jesus the model of the perfect man who was also God. And we have Christ's promise, recorded to St John,[4] that He, with the Father and the Holy Spirit, will come to live in the man who follows his teaching. This does not deny human personality; rather it confirms and exalts it. It enables human beings to escape from the cul-de-sac in which they can be trapped by the past, by misfortune, by unsatisfactory parental relationships. It frees them from fighting old battles and enables them to leap into the world of disinterested love. Thus the Christian humanist becomes more, not less, himself.

So we see that wonderful personality of Jesus as a model. We see his courage and forthrightness—the prophetic strength which showed itself against the Pharisees. We see worldly wisdom in its proper place and his use of it. We see his concern and understanding for the individuals he knew, and above all we are able to observe that love which gave itself so freely and without thought or care for return. Life, then, is a great gift, for which one should offer thanks and praise. The combination of life with the Christian faith, however, is a blessed one because it is only this which offers man the possibility of being fully human.

[4] 14: 15.

11

Hope

St Paul is the first major theologian of Christian hope. In his Letter to the Christians at Rome he sums up, in a remarkable sentence, a whole theology of hope: 'May the God of Hope fill you with joy and peace in your faith, that by the power of the Holy Spirit, your whole life and outlook may be radiant with Hope.'[1]

Paul establishes first the intrinsic connection which hope, like the other two theological virtues, faith and charity, has with God. Second, he draws attention to the fruits of hope: joy and peace here and now amidst the troubles of this life, a sense of proportion, confidence and contentment. Third, he stresses the power of the Holy Spirit, who gives courage to continue along the path towards God and, through hope, imparts patience, endurance, stability and self-control. So one's whole being is rendered not merely hopeful but radiant with hope. There is nothing timid or shrinking about Pauline hope—it constitutes a lustrous sign which shines out to encourage others.

The theological virtues acquire their name because they are free gifts of God. They are not of man's making or achievement but are a direct imparting of Himself. Like all virtues, they are attitudes freely adopted by beings endowed with intellect and will. Yet that attitude or disposition is created and supported by God's self-bestowal. Only the theological virtues are dynamic enough to characterize the freedom of the self in its full dimension. For purposes of methodology, we may divide them up: faith is based on intellect and the facts of revelation; charity is concerned with the will and the affections, with the goodness of God; hope is based on trust and confidence in God, the boundless expectation of good, the conviction of His fidelity, the knowledge that, provided we co-operate with grace, we will assuredly attain our ultimate goal of salvation, eternal life, union with the Trinity. Methodology can be helpful, but it can also be misleading. The acts of faith, hope and charity are different, but they are

---

[1] Romans 15: 8.

all of them commitments, not of part of man but of the whole person, to the One who sustains him in the depth of his being and at the same time stands over against him for ever.

Hope is a supernatural virtue, meaningless outside a religious structure, fully meaningful only within a Christian one. The ancients, it is true, had an idea of hope, but it was rather a different one from our own. It had none of the certainty of Christian hope. There was a hovering ambiguity; it was never clear whether hope was real or a delusion, whether it was good or evil. We are told that when Pandora opened that box she let all the *other* evils out, leaving only hope inside. Nevertheless, we should never forget the saying, 'Grace builds on nature.' If God did create human beings, we would expect to see reflected in their nature signs, traces, penetrations, of that divine nature itself. So, in fact, we observe that there is something in the human condition itself which cries out for hope. It is there at the personal level. The past has slipped from our grasp, embalmed and entombed. The present is too fleeting, too slippery, to hold. Only the future remains always available to us. So all human lives are directed ahead. People have ambitions, plans, aspirations, dreams for themselves or for their children or friends. They believe that things can get better and take responsibility for their actions. Without that hope, which we take for granted, life would be grim indeed. Old age is often sad because hope tends to wither and die. Youth is the natural time for hope.[2]

As at a personal level, so too at a national one. Nations need hope. A. C. Benson linked hope with glory in his famous chorus. Today there is so much failure in Britain that as a nation we are in danger of becoming hopeless, despairing. As a people we need hope more than ever.

To be human, then, is to hope. Human beings need hope. Life is difficult for everyone, even for those whose outward circumstances seem most fortunate. Happiness is vulnerable; health may be lost; so may friends or security or money. Overnight love can give way to bereavement and mourning. Hope can be replaced by despair, which itself may be brought on by lust and worldliness, as St Paul warns.[3] Finally, death comes, the end of all hope, the separation and the silence—the verdict

---

[2] Thus Emerson: 'Hope writes the poetry of the boy, memory that of the man.' St Thomas Aquinas also reflects on the relationship between youth and hope:

> Youth is the cause of hope on these three counts, namely because the object of hope is future, is difficult, and is possible. For the young live in the future and not in the past, they are not lost in memories but full of confidence. Secondly, their warmth of nature, high spirits and expansive heart, embolden them to reach out to difficult projects; therefore, are they mettlesome and of good hope. Thirdly, they have not been thwarted in their plans, and their lack of experience encourages them to think that where there's a will, there's a way. The last two factors, namely good spirits and a certain recklessness, are also at work in people who are drunk. (*Summa Theologica*, 1A–2AE,L6)

[3] Romans 2: 11.

from which there is no appeal. One is left with the stoic handclasp of some attic stele.

That is where Christian hope comes in. It confronts the future. It challenges it. It grasps hold of it, transforms and redeems it. It does not foretell the future: it is not magic, nor clairvoyance, nor palmistry, nor astrology. These are hope substitutes—Odiles, not Odettes. It does not determine the future: to attempt to do that is not hope but presumption. Yet hope enables us to shape the future. It is, to borrow that expressive Italian word, an *aggorniamento*, both a renewal and a reformation, plus some untranslatable extra.

How does hope work? It has, paradoxically, already happened. For Christians, their hope is behind them—the intervention of the Incarnation has already taken place. The Old Testament looks forward in promise only. The New Covenant looks forward because it can look back also to the fulfilment of that promise. We look, Janus-like, to the person who has vanquished both sin and death and has taken the burden on his shoulders. We marvel at the majestic procession from stable to Cross, through the Resurrection to the glory of the *Parousia*, the Second Coming. This is he who embodies hope. With Him we have confidence that we can change ourselves, overcome our weaknesses and vices, progress in virtue and grow in love. With Him we can (as recounted in the Ninety-Third Psalm) walk unscathed over the asp and the basilisk and tread upon both the lion and the dragon. We need no longer stand in dread of the ferocious and terrifying creatures of the unconscious, for Jesus has dominion over them too. Love casts out fear and drives its horrors into the open, so that they dwindle and shrink in the light of day. With Him we can change society—redeem it as well. The future is not out there in another world but here and now. We must penetrate one world with the other and exercise a creative responsibility for the future. Let it be liberalism, or conservatism, or socialism, according to our judgements, but let us not ask too much from these ideologies, rather submit them to constant reappraisal and criticism in the light of commitment to the One who is incalculable and not subject to our control.

Faith, hope and charity, these abide: so says St Paul in mysterious words. Hope is not a transient mode of the other two. There is hope in heaven. When we see face to face, we will not comprehend God but will go on knowing and loving for all eternity. Hope continues as the ground of our salvific knowledge of God in this life and the next. Human beings need, then, constantly to make acts of hope and to give thanks and praise for this lovely gift—the anchor which holds us to reality, which gives us courage and tenacity and leads us ever onwards into joy and light:

In the long vista of the years to roll
Let me not see our country's honour fade:

O let me see our land retain her soul,
    Her pride, her freedom; and not freedom's shade.
        From thy bright eyes unusual brightness shed—
        Beneath thy pinions canopy my head! . . .

And as, in sparkling majesty, a star
    Gilds the bright summit of some gloomy cloud;
Brightening the half-veil'd face of heaven afar:
    So, when dark thoughts my boding spirit shroud,
        Sweet Hope, celestial influence round me shed,
        Waving thy silver pinions o'er my head.[4]

[4] From Keats, 'To Hope'.

12

Ecumenism

For me the most splendid development in twentieth-century Christianity has been the growth of the ecumenical movement, by which members of the different Christian Churches have drawn together. I was ecumenical in spirit and feeling long before it was fashionable so to be. The purpose of ecumenism is not to convert or proselytize but to learn and grow together and so help to create a common conscience for all mankind. Thus religion reflects the growth of a sense of unity among the nations of the world which exists despite all the conflicts.

I have never been other than loyal to my own Church, and I accept her claims, but I am drawn to other Churches, especially to our national Church, the Church of England, with her beauty, her order and her holiness. I rejoice that I have lived to see the time when Roman Catholics, without denying their own patrimony, are able to begin to take up in part the heritage of Canterbury from which for too long they have been cut off.

The foundation of my ecumenism is simple: I have found holiness in those who are not of my faith. My experience has shown me that Christ is present in others who do not acknowledge Rome in the sense that I do. I have received much spiritual enlightenment from Christians outside my own communion. In discussing religious matters with other Christians, I am conscious of differences but of no real division. We walk along different spiritual paths, but our faces are set towards the same goal. The invisible unity conferred by baptism is already achieved; only the visible dimension is lacking.[1]

God is present everywhere in the world. After all, it is his world not the devil's. Christ is not everywhere in the same sense, yet he is present in the separated Churches. The sacraments of the Church of England, for

---

[1] The Roman Catholic Church takes the view that inter-communion is the goal or sign of unity and not a means to its achievement. There are, however, Catholics who take a contrary view, building their position on the importance of baptism. They argue that once it has been conceded that baptism admits to the mystical body of Christ, then it follows logically that the members should also be admitted to Holy Communion. There are not two bodies, one baptismal and one Eucharistic, but only one, the mystical body of Christ.

example, are clearly channels of grace. How does one reconcile such a viewpoint with the exclusive claims of Rome? That is the task of ecumenical theology, which is still in its infancy. I am writing here of the validity of my own experience.

The obstacles to ecumenical progress are pride and fear. It takes humility to give up the stiff-necked attitude of superiority of the Pharisee and to get down on one's knees with other Christians and pray to the God who is Father of all. It is humbling also to have to admit that there are corruptions and defects in one's own Church, to which one has given loyalty and assent. An attitude of *Noli me tangere* ('Don't touch me') is much more satisfying to *amour propre*. Humility is required to recognize that every Church today is incomplete, in that there are whole areas of spirituality and culture which have developed outside one's own particular communion and from which one is cut off.

Fear is another matter but is equally destructive. Many Roman Catholics are afraid that by following the ecumenical road they will lose the unity they already possess and that their Church is threatened by dissolution. Equally, there are non-Catholic Christians who regard ecumenism with suspicion because they see it as merely the latest manifestation of a Roman imperialism which has altered in form but not in name, namely the spiritual and jurisdictional subjugation of others by the Holy See. To these fears there is no wholly rational antidote. They can be met only by the transcendence of love. Love does cast out fear.

Ignorance is yet another obstacle. Men can grow together only by working together. Four hundred years of separation, as is the case with the Catholic and Anglican Churches, cannot be exorcised by formulae but only by working and sharing together. Hence the importance of new churches that are being built for more than one denomination to use.

When we talk or think about Christian unity, we tend to do so in terms of dialogue, negotiations, discussions or treaties. Yet the essence of ecumenism—true ecumenism—is that one is already there. The barriers have been transcended. The truly ecumenical person has arrived at a point of inner spiritual unity and, looking back from that, asks the experts to explain why the barriers over which he has hurtled are still standing. In this connection the words of Pope John to the observers for the other Christian Churches at the Second Vatican Council are relevant: 'We do not intend to conduct a trial of the past. We do not want to prove who was right and who was wrong. All we want to say is: Let us come together. Let us make an end of our divisions.' Pope John was not a silly, benevolent, sentimental old man. He had spent years of his life in pastoral work and had eventually risen to one of the highest posts in the Vatican diplomatic corps, that of papal nuncio in Paris. He had suffered for his views, which were ahead of his time, and before his appointment to France he had been exiled to Bulgaria and Constantinople.

Pope John was well able to conduct not only a political dialogue but a theological one as well. He adhered to the great truths of the Christian faith with tenacity, but his life embodied a true spiritual ecumenism. The final phase of the dialogue constituted a leap—a great leap into unity through love.

Why unity? Why bother? The answer for Christians is that it is God's will. It was clearly the will of Jesus. St John shows that in his magnificent account of the last Passover, the supper in the upper room which occupies several chapters of his Gospel.[2] He records the final prayer of the Son to the Father: 'That they may be one, as we are one—I in them and you in me, that they may grow complete into one, so that the world may realize that you sent me and have loved them as you loved me.'

First comes the call to unity, since this accords with reality, the reality of the Trinity. Second, unity is enjoined for the sake of credibility, so that the world will be enabled to believe the Christian message. The Trinity provides a model of the unity that should be sought—not uniformity but diversity within unity. So ecumenism starts not with the Church as institution but with the Church as mystery, with the mystical body of Christ joined in the life of prayer and love with the Trinity. Significantly, the Second Vatican Council's dogmatic constitution on the Church starts at this point too—with its epoch-making declaration not that the Church of Christ is co-extensive with the structures of the Roman Catholic Church but that it *subsists* in them. So the way has been opened for a new ecclesiology which declares that the mystery of the Church is found in its fullness in the Roman Church but is present in all the Christian Churches. The barriers to reunion have thus been cleared away. Reunion is based not on a common denominator, Christianity, but on the renewal of the spiritual life within each individual. As people strive for holiness and experience conversion, so they live their faith more deeply and, in fact, become one. On that spiritual foundation new structures will arise.

In ecumenism there are no losses but only gains. All are added to, not diminished. Rome has the keys, and that is what she has to give; Canterbury has the *Geist* of liberty and openness and free inquiry, equally essential if Christianity is to redeem the contemporary world. Our eyes must also be turned to the East if we are not to lose the sense of religion as mystery and if we are to avoid the danger of being stranded on a too rationalist shoal. The reconciliation between Rome and Canterbury could well come through Constantinople. The tendency of Anglicanism, for example, is to minimize the role of Mary and to reduce her status; Rome veers in the other direction and exalts her individual position to such a pinnacle that there is a danger—I put it no higher—of separating her from her Son. In the iconography of the East one finds a resolution of this

[2] Chapters 12–17.

dichotomy: the *Theotokos*, the Mother of God, is fully honoured but is almost invariably jointly represented with the person of her Son.

The Orthodox attach a special importance to the first seven general councils of the Church. It was at the third of these, Ephesus in 431, that the doctrine of the *Theotokos* was definitively proclaimed. In doing so the Council was defending not only Mary but also the doctrine of the Incarnation. This had been challenged indirectly by Nestorius, when he maintained that Mary was entitled to be called 'Mother of Christ' but not 'Mother of God', since she was the mother of Christ's humanity but not of His divinity. To have accepted this would have destroyed the doctrine of the Incarnation, since one would have to conclude that God in fact never really became man, or not in any normal human way.

The ruins of the Greco-Roman city of Ephesus still straggle along the coast of Asia Minor, more impressive and complete than those of the forum in Rome. Still standing and clearly recognizable is the great double church in which the assembled fathers gathered 1,600 years ago to proclaim and protect one of the great truths of salvation. In Ephesus too, with its idolatrous worship of Diana, is found the clue to why Marian devotion emerged so late in the Christian Church. The early Christians feared that devotions to Mary would be confused with the pagan fertility cults to Diana and other goddesses. Only after these had declined could a development of doctrine safely take place, and to Ephesus fell the honour of formulating the definition which has so vitally affected Christendom across the centuries. As Charles Williams remarks: 'Such remote Cristological quarrels in the slums and the boulevards of the Near East are not without interest today. It was the real nature of perfection as credible and discoverable by men that was then in question and it is still perfection that we are at.'[3]

The common ground shared by the Orthodox Church of the East and the Roman Catholic Church of the West is extensive. At the same time there are striking differences of approach and mentality between the two communions, but in an ecumenical age these different perspectives, far from constituting insurmountable barriers, can be of benefit to both Churches, opening up new lines of thought which, given good will, can converge and create unity. It is a sad paradox that whereas the dialogue between the Catholic Church and the Protestant Churches, divided by much greater doctrinal gulfs than those which separate Catholicism and Orthodoxy, has made rapid progress, the movement of reconciliation between the Churches of East and West has only just got under way. As I have remarked, it may well be that it is here that the great prizes of ecumenical encounter will be found in the future.

Pope John Paul II's first priority in the ecumenical field is reconciliation

---

[3] See Charles Williams, 'Anthropotokos' in *The Image of the City*.

with the Orthodox Churches. For Rome, Orthodoxy presents itself as 'the problem of problems'. Some argue that it was the schism of 1054 which led directly to the Reformation and thus to the split in the Western Church. Had the rift with Orthodoxy not occurred, Rome would not have made the attempt to impose juridical uniformity which led directly to the Northern European revolt.

In November 1979 the Pope visited the Patriarch of Constantinople in Istanbul. The Patriarch, Dimitrios I (elected to his office in 1972, as the successor to the Patriarch Athenagoras), and the Pope participated in a joint liturgical celebration at the Phanar in the Patriarch's own church of St George. The following day the Pope attended the mass celebrated by the Patriarch for the feast of St Andrew, the first visit of a pope to an Orthodox mass since the schism. The Pope's presence acknowledged the authenticity of the Eucharistic celebration, although he was there as a witness and not as a participant, and the occasion was given an added symbolic significance since it coincided with the feast of St Andrew, patron of Constantinople, the younger brother of St Peter. St Andrew is also the patron saint of the entire Orthodox Church. The long-awaited theological dialogue between the two Churches opened on the islands of Rhodes and Patmos in June 1980.

Orthodox popular devotion is strikingly similar to that of Catholicism. Orthodox churches are alive in the same way as Catholic churches, filled with worshippers and those who use the church buildings for their private prayers. The use of votive candles is as popular in the East as in the West, the only difference being that in the East they are used to venerate ikons instead of statues. In Orthodoxy ikons seem to have an even greater doctrinal significance than images in Catholicism. They are thought to safeguard the full doctrine of the Incarnation. God cannot be represented in His eternal nature, but the Incarnation made a representational religious art possible: God is able to be depicted precisely because he became a man. To see the devotion with which men and women kiss ikons in the Orthodox Church is a moving experience. It has nothing in common with idolatry. As John of Damascus writes in his treatise on ikons: 'I do not worship matter but I worship the Creator of matter, who for my sake became material and deigned to dwell in matter, who through matter affected my salvation. I will not cease from worshipping the matter through which my salvation has been effected.'

Orthodoxy can also throw some light on the perplexing questions of Church structure and order which loom so large at the present time. Orthodox experience may reassure Catholics who fear the loss of the Church's doctrinal treasure because of the decline in the centralized authority of Rome and the eclipse of canon law. Orthodoxy has preserved all the great doctrines of Christianity—even, in vestigial form, that of the Roman primacy—without recourse to such aids. And what is collegiality in the Western Church today but a return to an insight which has been commonplace in Orthodoxy over the centuries? It is the correcting of the false emphasis of some Roman theologians by a return to the insights of the early Eastern fathers of the Church. The essence of collegiality is contained in the seven short letters which St Ignatius, Bishop of Antioch, wrote in 107 as he journeyed to Rome to be martyred. 'The bishop in each church', he wrote, 'presides in place of God. . . . Let no one do any of the things which concern the church without the bishop. . . . Wherever the bishop appears, there let the people be, just as wherever Jesus Christ is, there is the Catholic Church.' St Ignatius saw the Church, as did the Second Vatican Council, as subsisting in the local community, which realizes its true nature when it comes to celebrate the Eucharist.

As the Church of the West works out the implications of collegiality and hopefully the old temper of Roman authoritarianism disappears, the way will be prepared for reunion between East and West. The West is moving forward, with occasional convulsions, to a Church structure which is both old and new. The task of Orthodox theologians is to think out fully what is meant by the declaration that they accept the primacy of Rome. To be meaningful, this must be more than an historical accident of primogeniture. The content must be more than an empty honour. The obstacles of pride, fear and past history are there and at times seem insuperable. To many Orthodox, the fourth Crusade is still a living affront, but mutual understanding and reflection can pave the way and provide for a bridging of the unbridgeable by love. Rome, Constantinople and Canterbury: I see them not as rivals but as a Holy Trinity, complementing each other in a loving and balanced harmony, a reflection of the living God they serve.

The only institution around which the Christian family of Churches can unite is the papacy. There is no other comparable centre. But if the papacy is to play this role, it must change. It must be shorn, for this purpose, of the 'accidents', the inessentials, the curia, canon law and even the college of cardinals. It must become a papacy not seeking to dominate, not demanding the primacy of honour which the Archbishop of Canterbury, Dr Runcie, has generously offered, but rather giving a primacy of service, the one primacy worth having, and acting as a catalyst through the witness of its love and disinterestedness.

Pope John Paul II gave substance to this vision during his visit to Britain in May of 1982. He turned out to be an evangelist of such simplicity and profundity that one has to go back in English history to the days of John Wesley to find a fitting parallel. With the Falklands war at its height, the Pope issued a series of prophetic warnings on war and peace which climaxed at Coventry, when in unforgettable words he dismissed the medieval scholastic theory of the 'just war' and called on the nations to abandon war as a means of settling their differences. 'Today,' he declared, 'the scale and the horror of modern warfare, whether nuclear or not, makes it totally unacceptable as a means of settling differences between nations. War should belong to the tragic past, to history: it should find no place on humanity's agenda for the future.'

An equally important feature of his visit was the stress placed on achieving Christian unity and on the value of the ecumenical movement. He by-passed possible opposition by referring to himself not as Pope but as Bishop of Rome, thus avoiding the controversial quagmires of papal infallibility and anchoring himself in the firm, historic ground of the Roman primacy. Thus he turned what has been used as a diminishing insult into an encomium. The theme of Christian unity roused the most enthusiastic applause in the cathedrals of all denominations. The ecumenical high point was reached on the second day, when the Holy Father and the Archbishop of Canterbury walked together to the high altar of Canterbury Cathedral with applause rippling up the aisle until silence came as they knelt side by side in prayer. Then the Pope went forward to embrace in fraternal love virtually every member of the Anglican bench of bishops. At that moment the Anglican Communion was caught up into the Universal Church and recognized publicly, in the words of Paul VI, as a 'sister Church'.

Anglicans saw the Pope with new eyes and he them: Pope John Paul knew about Orthodoxy from his Polish pastoral experience, but it was not until he arrived at Canterbury that the closed book of Anglicanism was opened. The fruit of this meeting and also of that with the Moderator of the Church of Scotland was evidenced at Bellahouston Park in Glasgow on 1 June 1982, when in unforgettable and spontaneous words the Pope committed himself without reservation to the cause of Christian unity, saying: 'We are only pilgrims on this earth, making our way towards that heavenly kingdom promised to us as God's children. Beloved brethren in Christ, for the future can we not make that pilgrimage together, hand in hand?' Thus the Pope provided a transforming symbol which sums up and transcends the essence of ecumenism. The visit became a manifestation of the threefold Christian vocation: *martyria* (witness), *koinonia* (unity) and *diakonia* (service).

13

Science and Faith

———————

The phrase 'science and faith' has a somewhat nineteenth-century ring, and not inappropriately, since it was over a hundred years ago that one of the most famous clashes in the long-drawn-out Victorian struggle between science and religion took place. It was at Oxford in 1860 that Bishop Wilberforce, led astray by the dangerous vice of frivolity, attempted to worst the prophet of evolution by ridicule and ended by being severely discomforted himself. He asked Huxley whether he claimed descent from a monkey on his grandfather's or his grandmother's side and was met by Huxley's devastating retort that he would rather have a monkey for his ancestor than 'a man who used great gifts to obscure the truth'. Disraeli dismissed the whole controversy by saying that if he had to choose between the apes and the angels, he was on the side of the angels.[1] This remark outraged the contemporary intelligentsia, and they never forgave him for it.

The incident is worth mentioning because it has had an effect out of all proportion to its true significance. It has distorted the British imagination when it seeks to visualize the relations between the Church and science, which it sees as a drama in which science is cast as the champion and the Church as the obscurer of truth. The way for the formation of this attitude had been prepared many centuries before with the case of Galileo. Whatever did or did not happen to Galileo—and we should remember that the heliocentric theory of the Universe had first been put forward by Copernicus, a Catholic cleric, in 1540 and accepted by the Church—the handling of his case set the myth of a necessary struggle between scientific enlightenment and ecclesiastical obscurantism on a trajectory which has still not finished its course.[2] Yet there is no incompatibility between faith and science.

[1] The remark was made on 25 November 1864, when Disraeli was addressing a meeting of the Society for Increasing Endowments of Small Livings in the Diocese of Oxford. He said: 'Is man an ape or an angel? Now I am on the side of the angels.'
[2] The censure of Galileo has now been rescinded by the Vatican.

The chasm between the Church and science was opened in 1830, when Lyell published his *Principles of Geology*, in which he expounded the history of the world as seen through the medium of rocks. He showed conclusively, through the examination of fossils and rock formation, that the history of the world should be reckoned in millions of years, contrary to the general ecclesiastical belief that it could be numbered in thousands. Indeed, one Protestant divine had fixed the date of the creation of the world (on careful biblical calculation) as 4004 BC. Lyell's conclusions made nonsense of any literal interpretation of the account of the Creation given in Genesis. Far from the earth having been created by God in one day, its structure had been gradually formed over billions of years by the action of natural forces, whose activities were still continuing. This apparently insoluble conflict between religious and scientific truth set many Victorian intellectuals on the path to loss of faith which was to cause them so much anguish. But worse was to come. The very year after Lyell had published his researches, Charles Darwin set off on his voyage on the *Beagle*, which was to last five years. Another five years were spent in accumulating every fact which had bearing on the problem of the origin of species, and it was not until 1844 that Darwin formulated his hypothesis.

It was truly a theological blockbuster. Darwin concluded that, far from the species having been formed all at once by one creative act of God, they had evolved by purely natural processes from a handful of simple forms or, possibly, from one. Another fifteen years were to pass before his conclusions burst upon the Victorian world, but burst they did in 1859, with startling effect.

> I am fully convinced [proclaimed Darwin in his *Origin of Species*] that species are not immutable; but those belonging to what are called the same genera are lineal descendants of some other and generally extinct species, in the same manner as the acknowledged varieties of any one species are the descendants of that species. Furthermore I am convinced that natural selection has been the most important but not the exclusive means of modification.

Here was another body-blow at the whole mosaic concept of Creation, and worse, it carried the implication (not explicitly stated) that man himself, like every other species, must be descended from the primeval form. At one stroke Darwin, whether he intended to do so or not, had removed God from the *mise-en-scène* and levelled man with the brutes. No wonder the Victorians were anguished. Their harmonious and beautiful picture of nature as a living proof of a divine intelligence, in which every need of every species was provided by benevolent design, vanished and in its place was substituted a horrid vision of a world where all this was brought about by chance and the ruthless operation of the principle of the survival of the fittest.

Darwin himself was not an atheist. At the time of writing *Origin of Species* he was not even an agnostic but a vague theist. He was never a metaphysician and was content to leave the precise origin of his first forms vague, but others were not so restrained. They saw that the choice lay between an original act of creation and an eternity of matter, and they chose the latter. Thomas Huxley extended the battle. 'Clericalism', he declared, 'is the deadly enemy of Science.' On the other side theologians were no less virulent. The *Witness*, a Christian magazine, was denouncing Darwinism in 1862 as 'the vilest and beastliest paradox ever invented in ancient or modern times'. What is important to bear in mind, however, despite the sweeping generalizations of the protagonists, is that the clash was not between the whole Church and science as such but between some scientists and some churchmen. That Darwinism and the theory of evolution are quite incompatible with fundamentalist Christianity is true, but it is equally true that there is no intrinsic conflict between Christianity and evolution, provided a literal interpretation of the account of Creation in Genesis is not insisted upon. One may well, as a Christian, hold with the whole theory of evolution, provided one believes that the evolutionary process had a divine as opposed to a chance origin. Indeed, one could argue that since evolution shows greater economy of wisdom than direct creation, it is the more probable agency of divine action.

This point was not lost on all Darwin's opponents and, indeed, was alluded to defensively by Darwin in his book. Pusey, who was one of Darwin's most formidable opponents, conceded it in a sermon in 1878, 'Unscience, Not Science, Adverse to Faith'. But Pusey put his finger on the real threat of Darwinism, which was not that it denied God but that it ignored Him. He has eliminated Him, declared Pusey, 'from all interference with the works which he has made'. Here in microcosm is revealed the essence of the nineteenth-century undermining of religion. It was never frontally assaulted; it was by-passed. Theology was not violently dethroned. There was never any French Revolution. Her regiment was allowed to wither away. Philosophy in due course has met the same fate. Metaphysical propositions have not been challenged; they have just been ignored.

This, then, was the essence of the nineteenth-century challenge to religion, a denial that religion had anything relevant or useful to say outside the realm of private devotion, which people could indulge in or not, as they pleased. The significance of the clash between science and religion was that it helped this view to triumph by making religion look ridiculous. But this was brought about not by any intrinsic incompatibility between science and religion but rather by the postures adopted by the controversialists. However real the conflict may have seemed to Victorians, it does not seem more than a pseudo-conflict to us looking back. After all, as early as the fourth century, in his *De genesi ad litteram*, St

Augustine had shown the way out of the dilemma when he had declared that when some established fact of science or history was at variance with the natural interpretation of some biblical passage, it was necessary to reject the natural interpretation. The theory of evolution itself had been anticipated by Augustine, at least in relation to the vegetable and animal kingdoms, since in his commentary on Genesis he writes that on the third day the earth was given power to produce grass and trees *causaliter* (i.e. it was endowed with a potency for producing different species), and this interpretation was approved by the greatest of the schoolmen, St Thomas Aquinas. The true lesson to be drawn from the nineteenth-century experience, then, is not that Christianity and science are incompatible but that if there is a conflict between them, it is only apparent. Both present truths about man, and therefore if they clash, either the scientific facts are not facts at all or religion has extended itself beyond its proper sphere. When a clash occurs it may take time for the illusory nature of the conflict to work itself out, and those caught in the thick of the battle will be blinded and will suffer, but the significant point of the nineteenth-century experience is that it illustrates that even in the fiercest of conflicts an eventual reconciliation is possible. Whose religious faith today is undermined by a reading of Lyell's *Principles of Geology*?

The nineteenth-century lesson is worth learning, since the situation may arise again, but the present problem of the relationship between science and religion is a rather different one. It is part of the wider problem of the relationship between scientific and humanist culture. There is no conflict—peaceful coexistence, perhaps, but little communication. Of course, in some way this is the right relationship. Theology and science each have their own competencies, and much of the nineteenth-century troubles were caused by ignoring this. Had the doctrine of the two spheres been applied as successfully in the intellectual world as in the Victorian home, the conflict would never have arisen.

Science is concerned principally with the 'how' of things, not with the 'why', which is the province of the metaphysician and the theologian. What is required is not an overlapping of the spheres but communication between them, and here the barrier of language is formidable. Few scientists know any theology: few theologians know any science: the average layman is equally ignorant of both. The situation is not encouraging. What we need today are men who are able to feel at home in both worlds. We need scientists who can write out of a background of theology and theologians who have mastered modern scientific knowledge. One man has in modern times managed to lift the iron curtain. I refer to Pierre Teilhard de Chardin, the palaeontologist whose book *The Phenomenon of Man* was published in England in 1959.

Teilhard de Chardin was born near Clermont, in France, in 1881; he died in New York in 1955. The two dominant interests of his life appeared early:

his passionate interest in science and his strong religious bent. At the age of 17 he joined the Jesuits and was ordained a priest. After this he served in the French army as a chaplain during the First World War and after demobilization was able to pursue his scientific studies at the Sorbonne, specializing in geology and the study of plants. He was appointed a lecturer at the Institut Catholique in Paris, but his superiors took fright at the boldness of his speculations and removed him from his academic post to exile in the Far East. He was allowed to go on writing but was subjected to a rigorous censorship.

It has been clear for over a hundred years that the traditional Christian view of the book of Genesis is essentially that suitable for a primitive tribe, not for modern, sophisticated and scientific man. Theologians and men of science had realized this long before Teilhard, but until he wrote, evolutionary views about man had not been effectively baptized. That is the essence of his achievement. He finally liberated theology from its imprisonment in the static world view of Aristotle and moved it into the dynamic, evolutionary universe of today. His thought complements that of Cardinal Newman, who demonstrated that development and evolution are intrinsic to theological doctrine.

Another feature of Teilhard's work which appeals especially is his glowing optimism about man and his prospects. I am not in sympathy with those Christian pessimists who think it the primary function of religion to flee from and condemn the world. Teilhard saw the material world not as something to be despised and rejected but as something good, truly the work of God's hands. No one could be less 'churchy' than Teilhard. For him the Holy Spirit acted through matter as much as through the Church. He was, in short, a Christian humanist.

Nowhere are his humanism and his optimism seen more strongly than in his essay on the explosion of the atom bomb, written in 1946. For him this heralded not the end of the world but the opening up of immense and exciting possibilities for man's development. For those scientists who wished to close down the whole project he had nothing but scorn. He saw the explosion as the prelude to a great advance, man's understanding and control of the energy which lies at the heart of matter. He looked forward eagerly, instead of with dismay, to man's forthcoming control of genes and chromosomes, and, therefore, his power to control heredity and sex, and to the liberation of the soul 'by direct action upon springs brought to light by psychoanalysis'. As for man's political development, Teilhard felt that the invention of the atom bomb had turned the unity of man from an ideal into a necessity.

The significance of *The Phenomenon of Man*, is not that it is a theological treatise but that it is a scientific and, in part, mystical treatise written by a man who was also a trained theologian. It symbolizes the healing of the old breach between science and religion, for in it he puts forward not a plea for a contingent acceptance of evolution but a demand for the acceptance of adopting an evolutionary point of view if we are to understand the universe in which we live. The pendulum could have not swung further from Bishop Wilberforce. The point is suitably underlined by the fact that the French Jesuit's greatest work is prefaced by an introduction from Sir Julian Huxley. How Thomas Huxley and Bishop Wilberforce would rub their eyes!

One great heresy of the last century, from the effects of which some people are still suffering today, is scientism, by which I mean a belief that the methods of natural science can provide a solution to every type of problem. Allied to this view one often finds the conviction that it is ignorance rather than sin which is the basic human problem. If ignorance can be dispelled, all will go well. This naive illusion is found more often on the left than on the right in politics, since it rests on a fundamental revolutionary principle, belief in the perfectability of man. Conservatives, on the other hand, have a healthy respect for the doctrine of original sin, although they will not always give it a theological formulation. The basic objection to scientism is that it ignores the facts of human existence—not only sin, imperfection, moral evil, call it what you will, but also experience. As Reinhold Niebuhr has pointed out, it ignores the fact that the methods of science have been 'singularly deficient in generating wisdom in human affairs'. Furthermore, it ignores a basic distinction: the social and historical sciences can never command the exactness of the natural sciences because their study is not matter but man. The human person, being free and autonomous, is not determined in his actions, and is therefore not predictable. A basic principle of the natural sciences is that they can predict the future by using an analysis of the past. If one carries out experiment A under condition B, then one can be certain that C will result. This the historian or sociologist cannot do. It is not a matter of these disciplines being in their infancy—and history, in any case, is a fairly aged child—nor a matter of their one day being able to predict with certainty. They cannot achieve certainty by the very nature of things. The human person is involved in them, as he is not in the natural sciences. He is within the historical or social process and therefore, of necessity, is biased. Objectivity can never be achieved.

We today, with the bitter experience of two world wars behind us and the prospect of nuclear dissolution lying ahead, are less likely to be taken in by the specious over-simplifications of scientism. In fact, since Hiroshima many have tended to look upon science not as God but as the devil. Both attitudes are equally erroneous. At first sight a distrust of science might seem to be favourable to religion. The world is full of fear, and when man is afraid he turns to religion. If we accepted that view, we should be exposing ourselves to the taunt of Voltaire and Nietzsche, that the Christian religion is a religion for the enslaved and the craven. To regard science as an evil is contrary to the Judaeo-Christian tradition, which regards the natural world as something good. The evidence is there in, for example, the opening chapter of Genesis, with its account of Creation and its reiterated refrain 'and God saw that it was good'. In the same chapter we are told that dominion over the earth and its creatures has been given to man. So for the Christian the advance of science, the increase of man's control over his environment, is in itself in accord with God's plan for the world. But we also know from the third chapter of Genesis that there is an ambiguous element in knowledge, that if there is knowledge of good, there is also knowledge of evil. After all, our first parents brought disaster on themselves and on us by eating the fruit of the Tree of Knowledge. But here again it is important to be precise. It was not knowledge itself which brought about their ruin but the inordinate desire for knowledge, the worship of knowledge and its conscious selection as being preferable to God.

The religious man, therefore, finds no ally in a modern revival of medieval obscurantism. On the contrary, he welcomes science as the means of raising all the human race to standards of material wellbeing which every past age known to us has confined to the few. At the same time he is not blind to the destructive potential which science has placed in his hands. This potential in itself is neither good nor bad; it acquires moral character from the use to which it is put. But in so far as it prevents *hubris*, an unwarranted and unlimited pride in human achievement, it can be an agency for moral good. If the horror of this destructive power at man's disposal drives him towards religion, not in panic but in humility and confidence, in order to strengthen his moral nature so that he can make the best use of his discoveries, then it can be a force for good as well as for evil. Already we have seen in the international sphere the contingent good in the existence of atomic weapons, which has prevented minor conflagrations from becoming major conflicts. It may be—but this is only speculation—that world peace is based on surer foundations when it rests on the fundamental instinct of self-preservation than when it is based on idealism, a naked desire for peace and international order unclothed by effective institutional forms. If so, there is something to be said for the obscene atomic armoury which both imperialisms are feverishly accumulating.

Religion has a further important function to play in relation to contemporary science: it keeps technology under control. Here I think we should bear in mind a distinction between two types of science. The science of dead matter has almost reached the end of a cycle; the science of living matter is still in its early stages. Ahead stretch limitless possibilities, including the possibility of commanding the secret of life itself. Mary Shelley's Frankenstein monster may well, within a few generations, be translated from fiction into fact. How is this knowledge to be used? For guidance on this question we shall look in vain to the vague though widely diffused goodwill which for so many people today constitutes their only principle for ordering life. But the Christian religion, precisely because it has a view of human nature, because it can essay an answer to the question 'What is man?', possesses ordering power. The Christian view that man is not absolute master of his own fate but holds his life and body on trust for other purposes, evokes little response in an era which places a supreme value on personal emancipation and has provided man with the means of its achievement. But the technology which promised a paradise now shows signs of delivering a hell. Against the tyranny of scientific techniques the emancipated man finds himself defenceless. He has rejected the Christian view of human nature which, if it places limits on man's independence by stressing that he is the user, not the proprietor, of life, also preserves his humanity by erecting barriers beyond which technology cannot pass. The scientific humanist may be repelled as much as the Christian by the prospect of the replacement of the family by the stud farms of artificial human insemination, but unlike the Christian he has no final argument against it. If the power is there, why should it not be used?

I conclude by stressing once again the potential for good which science presents to mankind. On the natural plane science or discovery is truly the vocation of man, and to pursue this vocation fully requires human unity. It requires a sharing of knowledge, a sharing of resources and effective acknowledgement of the common humanity of all the peoples of the world. Driving us on towards this unity, despite ourselves, is the nuclear threat. Surely world government is the only ultimate guarantee of safety from instantaneous and unheralded destruction? In the long and painful achievement of this goal, not in the over-simplifications of the uni-lateralists, lies the hope of mankind. The error of the unilateralists is really a simple one. They treat a highly complex political problem as though it presented a clear choice between good and evil. In politics, as any politician will tell one, there are very few such simple choices. Normally one has to select from a number of competing, contingent evils. The choice is not a naked one, that between being sovietized and being atomized, but is a choice between the risks of these events occurring. Among these shoals we have to shape our course. I do not wish to fall into the same error as unilateralists by suggesting that world government would be easy to attain. To achieve it will require generations of organic institutional and moral development in the international sphere, for which history has no precedents. But if it is to be achieved, then religion has a vital part to play in its construction by moderating the passions of men and pointing to ideals higher than purely selfish or national interest. Science has made human unity necessary. Perhaps it will fall to religion to make its achievement possible.

PART FOUR

Some Earlier Offerings

This was the first article I had published. It appeared in the Westminster Cathedral Chronicle *of October 1947.*

Impressions of Monte Cassino

Along the modern motor road sped the bus from Rome. The day was hot, but the Italian summer with all its oppressive warmth still lay two months in the future. All around us spread the flat expanse of the Campagna, not yet dusty, but fresh and green in the full flush of spring. In the distance appeared the dark blue shapes of the Alban Hills. As we bowled along through this peaceful countryside it was difficult to believe that it was here that some of the bloodiest battles of the late war had taken place. But as we neared Cassino the signs of the armies' passage became more marked. By the roadside a battered gun would lie abandoned, in the fields were scattered rusty tanks, and every now and then a pile of bricks or gutted ruin showed where church or humble peasant dwelling had formerly stood. Our eyes were strained to catch the first glimpse of the Abbey ruins,[1] and quite suddenly they appeared crowning a steep mountain to our left. The massive foundations still seemed to be intact, but the walls had crumbled. Of the beautiful domed church there was no sign. All that remained was a jagged and spiky silhouette against the blue of the morning sky.

At the foot of the mountain the bus drew to a halt. As we dismounted the conductor with a dramatic gesture indicated the Abbey and the town, adding bitterly, *Fu Cassino.*[2] In another minute the bus was gone and we were left to ascend the hill. Turning our backs on the town which consisted of a number of ruined houses intermingled with some prefabricated modern structures, we commenced the long and arduous climb.

The mountain-side had formerly been covered with thick woods, but of these nothing remained. Shards, flints and pebbles lay everywhere. Rocks jutted up in front of us, and the only living things to be seen were the lizards which scurried away at our approach, or an occasional flowering shrub which had survived the blasting of the bombs and shells. On and on we toiled, now by the road, now up the face of the mountain. Shell cases, mortar bombs, husks of hand grenades, shreds of boots and parachutes showed the hell that this now quiet and deserted hillside had once been. The sun beat down on us and we grew tired and parched but the thought that it was this way that St Benedict had ascended encouraged us. In just over an hour and a half we stood at the summit, and turned round to look over the way we had passed. In the valley beneath lay the town Cassino, its new houses looking strangely white and out of place. A blue river wound its way slowly along looking from our view-point as if made of glass. The neighbouring mountains swept down in majestic lines of green and brown. On one was perched the plain obelisk placed there in memory of the troops who died in the battles round its slopes. On another could be made out the cruciform shape of the Polish military cemetery centred round a massive Polish eagle. We turned and approached the Abbey.

---

[1] The abbey of Monte Cassino was founded by St Benedict in 529 about 80 miles south of Rome. It was here that the famous Benedictine Rule was written. On 15 February 1944 it was destroyed by an air raid.
[2] 'This was Cassino'.

We passed bands of Italian pilgrims inconsequentially chattering, some were singing, others were dancing. The sight of these people apparently so ignorant of the sacredness of the spot where they were standing, infuriated me. Then I remembered the *Canterbury Tales* and realized that it was not only the Italians who were remiss in the matter of pilgrimage behaviour. But my attentions were distracted by the sight of a Benedictine monk making his way towards us from the Abbey. My joy at seeing him was great. I had half feared that the Abbey would have been totally abandoned, but here was a real monk in the familiar habit. He was most courteous and at once offered to show us what remained of the Abbey. Then came the saddest part of the journey. The damage was even greater than one would have suspected from the ground. The walls that were standing were a mere shell. Inside was complete ruin and desolation. Where once were beautiful courtyards, lovely fountains and graceful arches, nothing could be discerned save heaps of rubble. The simple cells of the monks had completely disappeared. The seminary, the novitiate, the secular college—of these also nothing remained. But most tragic of all was the site of the church. The Abbey church had been one of the glories of Christendom. Even in Italy, a land of lovely churches, it could safely be said that 'none could be found like unto this'. Built when the Renaissance was at its height, richly decorated, its walls encrusted with precious marbles and irreplaceable frescoes, it yielded pride of place not even to St Peter's itself. Below the church was the crypt, gorgeous with gold, marvellous paintings and inlaid marbles. Of all this glory all that remained was dust, rubble and a few broken pillars. Solid blocks of marble, tiny pieces of mosaic and painted plaster lay scattered everywhere. It was a depressing sight.

Yet although one felt depressed, and indeed ashamed, one did not feel hopeless. I was at a loss to analyse this feeling but at last found its cause. It was the attitude of the monk who was our guide. Without any vain regrets or complaints he took us cheerfully through the scenes of so much former splendour to the tomb of St Benedict. And here indeed was more reason for hope. The church, the Abbey, the riches, all had gone, but the body of St Benedict remained and his spirit lived on in the monk at my side. Over the tomb of the saint mass was being said as it had been said before for centuries. Priest followed priest as in the old days of the Abbey's greatness, Englishmen, Frenchmen, Germans, all anxious to celebrate the holy sacrifice in this hallowed place. And furthermore, miraculous to relate, one tiny part of the Abbey remains unharmed. This is the room occupied by St Benedict, when he founded the Abbey so many centuries ago. Here the community of monks hold their services and sing their office. Here also the spirit of the founder and the work of the Abbey goes on.

My kindly guide led me round to the other side of the Abbey and there I was amazed to see a new Abbey. There was nothing resplendent about the buildings either inside or out, but they had a simple dignity, and they showed that the monks had already started the work of reconstruction. Here I met the Abbot. He was most considerate and answered all my questions. 'No, there had been no Germans in the Abbey until after the bombardment. Only three hundred civilians from the town beneath, all of whom had been killed. . . . Yes, the manuscripts had been preserved and all the monks had escaped from the monastery in time. . . . Yes, the work of reconstruction had begun. The Italian Government had given some workmen; it would be a long task, but monks were never in a hurry'.

I left Monte Cassino with mixed feelings. The futile tragedy of its destruction and the loss of its treasures weighed me down. But on the other hand there was the fact that the body of St Benedict was safe; that the monks were still there; that there was no pessimism or bitterness, but an attitude of cheerful optimism and stern resolve to meet the future, and repair the ravages of the past. Would St Benedict have been satisfied with this? I think he would.

In 1948 I attended a course for undergraduates at Swinton, the Conservative College of the North, which at that time was presided over by Reginald Northam. A commission was set up on Conservative Principles as part of the course. This report was the result.

Conservative Principles

The rise in recent years both at home and abroad of ideologies and political faiths alien to the historic tradition of Western civilization has rendered urgent a restatement of the fundamental and enduring principles on which Conservatism has always been based. Only by the acceptance and understanding of these principles can the prosperity of the nation as a whole be ensured. While we consider they find their fullest and most complete expression in Conservatism, which is best equipped to defend them, we do not claim them as exclusive property and concede that many individuals outside the Conservative Party accept them. These principles make up no mere party doctrine but are of the essence of the British way of life.

The Conservative philosophy is based on the acceptance of a natural law over and above that which is merely man made, and on the divine origin and end of human personality, and the Christian ethic. We recognize that man by his nature possesses certain inalienable rights, such as the right to life except in just punishment for crime and the right to follow the dictates of conscience. But every right involves an equal and corresponding duty. At all times the exercise of rights must be limited by respect for the rights of others and duty to the community, for man is not only an individual but also a social animal.

We value tradition as representing the accumulated wisdom of past generations, while recognizing the necessity for continuing development in accordance with the needs of succeeding ages. Duty to the community combined with the value of tradition has led, in Conservative belief, to love of country and loyalty to the Crown, as being the best way in which the British people can contribute to the good of the wider community of nations. The Conservative Party regards the Empire as a family bound together by love and the spirit of common service.

A cardinal principle of Conservative faith is the recognition that man by his nature as a social animal has a right to own property. The exercise of this right is not absolute but is limited by the Christian ethic, the needs of the community and the rights of others. The right to own property springs directly from man's natural dignity and his need for self-expression. By this right Conservatives do not mean merely the ownership of chattels but ownership of the means of production, distribution and exchange. Thus the normal means of conducting the affairs of the community is through private enterprise. Nevertheless a measure of state control is justified and indeed necessary in specific cases.

Conservatives do not regard nationalization as being inherently immoral but believe that it should only be employed where there is conclusive proof that private enterprise has failed to serve the best interests of the community. In every case there must be full compensation for existing owners.

In general Conservatives are not in favour of private monopoly but do not condemn it in particular instances where its value to the community can be proved. Monopolies harmful to the community should not be tolerated and the field should be opened to private enterprise.

The right to determine the disposal of property after death is implicit in the concept of ownership. In the case of excessive concentrations of property in private hands detrimental to the interests of the community as a whole, limitations of this right are permissible by means such as death duties.

Private property then is one of the fundamental bases of society. A society can thus only be healthy where there is the widest possible distribution of property. Opportunity to own property should be made available to all. As means to this end co-partnership in industry and ownership by the individual of his own house are particularly recommended. Through such distribution a wide diffusion of power is obtained which contributes to the essential balance and stability of the community. These ideas find their ultimate expression in the concept of a property-owning democracy.

The full spiritual and cultural development of man can only be made possible by the continual improvement of material standards. All men must have equal opportunity to develop fully their several abilities and the opportunity to use them when developed. A minimum standard of subsistence must be ensured for all. Wages and salaries must allow for the exercise of the right to marry, to raise a family and to make reasonable provision for the future. Above this minimum, payment should bear relation to experience, initiative and effort. Certain social services provided by the state are essential for the health and welfare of the community. It must be emphasized that the extent of social services which can be provided, is dependent upon the material prosperity of the community. Social security is also essential for stability and prosperity. . . .

The individual has a duty of loyalty to the state and community. He must bear a fair share of the responsibility of government and not seek to overthrow lawfully constituted authority. While his primary duty is to work for his own family and dependents he must act with regard to the interests of other families and the good of the community as a whole.

By the acceptance of these principles and their application to practical problems the true balance between the individual and the family on the one hand, and the community and state on the other, can be successfully maintained.

Tradition, of itself and for its own sake, has no absolute value: a thing simply because it is old does not acquire any particular value. However in as far as tradition is the accumulated wisdom of past generations it has a positive value which is not lightly to be cast aside.

Although great age is not necessary, age is an essential of the concept of tradition. A generation in relation to tradition has no fixed duration in time.

A basis of tradition is a prerequisite for continuity, without which there can be no development. Development is diametrically opposed to revolution. Revolution introduces the new only at the price of the old; development preserves what is good in the old while adding what is good in the new.

Since every tradition is native to the community in which it was formed, neither individual traditions, nor the total tradition of a community can be transferred.

An institution is defined as a body which is set up by a community to carry out a specific function and is continued for the carrying out of the same or other functions in the form in which it was originally set up. Thus, while the functions of an institution may change, form and potential remain the same.

British institutions have a particular value by reason of their place in the life of the nation. The absence of a written Constitution leaves the way open for the supremacy of the legislature. The traditional working of British institutions and the observance of constitutional conventions provide the essential safeguards against tyranny. The maintenance of the rule of law is dependent on tradition. Furthermore the preservation of the Christian ethic, largely divorced from organized religion, is only possible by means of the traditions of the family and public morality. Our position as a commercial nation makes stability essential, and here again tradition plays a vital part.

Thus it can be seen that our conception of spiritual and material values depends, for its continuance, on tradition without which the British way of life would not long survive.

I attended both Cambridge and Oxford and was in statu pupillari *at both. These reflections were published in the* Spectator *on 17 September 1951.*

Oxford and Cambridge

I never realized when I first decided to go to Oxford and Cambridge the seriousness of the step I was taking. One might have gone to Eton and Harrow and got away with it. Devotion to those establishments is the privilege of an esoteric circle about whose rivalries the mass of the people care little. Oxford and Cambridge, however, are a national passion. Father is divided against son, mother against daughter, aunts against nephews and nieces, by a fierce emotional conviction that they are either 'Oxford' or 'Cambridge'. Residence at one of the universities is the least qualification for entertaining such feelings. Indeed, it seems stronger amongst those who have not attended them than with those who have. The crowds that throng the tow-paths of the Thames on Boat Race Day, sporting their various shades of blue, are only the outward manifestation of what St Augustine or Dr Jung would have styled an archetype.

In this glorious rivalry I can never take part. An invisible barrier separates me from my fellow-men. It is exhilarating to respond to the ever posed question, 'Oxford or Cambridge?' with an enigmatic 'Both.' But the thrill is only momentary, and is rapidly dispelled by the look of shocked disapproval on the face of the questioner. At my club, appropriately enough 'The Oxford and Cambridge', I feel that less scandal would have been caused had I been at neither. Perhaps one would fare better at the 'United University', but no doubt the name is deceptive.

Suffering can, however, be borne, and is at any rate refining. What is intolerable, and even degrading, are the jokes which relentlessly pursue me. Everyone permits himself the luxury of one, little realizing that it is a privilege of which countless hundreds have already availed themselves. I am constantly told that you can tell a Cambridge man from an Oxford man by the way he talks of our two great universities. Alternatively it is impressed upon me that when an Oxford man enters a room he looks as though he owned it, whereas a Cambridge man looks as though he couldn't care less who owned it. Cambridge is the capital of the fens, while Oxford is described as the Latin quarter of the Cowley works or the city nestling on the outer fringes of Lord Reading's marquisate.

Nevertheless, when all has been said, the unique advantage remains of being able to survey both the universities from an inner standpoint. Similarities, of course, are many. The college system creates a solidarity and sociability which Red Brick can never achieve. An ancient tradition of centuries is shared by both, and the baleful threat of modern scientific education is equally felt. Scientists throng King's Parade as much as they do The High. They scuttle into the laboratories by day and out again by night. Rigid requirements of work, overloaded syllabuses, endless and mysterious experiments preclude them from the more genial activities of university life. They form a vast, silent, Nescafé-drinking mass. Government grants and state scholarships foster an unhealthy sense of duty which demands imperiously a steady second or a brilliant third. Utilitarianism is an unattractive philosophy and reduces a university education to the status of one more lever in the struggle for social advancement.

If similarities exist, the differences are deeper marked. The most striking contrast is the difference in ethos between the two. Cambridge is a matter-of-fact, down-to-earth, sensible university. It is still defiantly progressive and somewhat less defiantly Protestant. Oxford, despite the impact of Lord Nuffield, is very much the city of dreaming spires, the home of lost causes, Catholic and conservative in its deepest roots. Eccentricity is frowned on at Cambridge; at Oxford it is a cult. Poetry flourishes at Oxford; philosophy finds its home in Cambridge. Oxford undergraduates have a certain brilliance; their conversation sparkles; they are intimately concerned with their inner reactions and feelings. Cambridge undergraduates are more concerned with their relations with their fellow-men; they get on with the job and leave the devils, or the angels, hidden away inside. To sum it up in psychological jargon, Oxford is introverting whereas Cambridge is extroverting. Generalizations are inevitably faulty. Oxford types may be found in Cambridge and vice versa; individuals exist who defy any classification; yet by and large the distinction is true, although it is a differentiation of shades rather than a contrast of hues.

Oxford is undoubtedly—to use an unpleasant word—the more fashionable university. Rich undergraduates, a rapidly diminishing class, tend to go there. Oxford is news in a way that Cambridge never is. Ever since the unfortunate 'King and Country' motion the Oxford Union has enjoyed a certain notoriety. Americans always want to go to Oxford. They fill the streets; they flock into Christ

Church; they 'do' Oxford in a way that they never 'do' Cambridge. This has advantages and disadvantages. Dons mix easily with Cambridge undergraduates; at Oxford they sit in an ivory tower. Port is drunk in Oxford; light table wines and sherry at Cambridge.

Is Oxford more beautiful than Cambridge? The question is unanswerable. Oxford is an architectural treasury of the Middle Ages; Magdalen, with its slender tower, shady cloisters and stately deer-park, is an enchantment; the grandeur of Christ Church Hall and Tom Quad, the eighteenth-century magnificence of Peckwater could hardly be surpassed. Yet there is nothing to equal the loveliness of the backs at Cambridge in the height of summer, the nobility of King's College chapel, or the elegant and perfectly proportioned Senate House. Architecturally, Cambridge is to Oxford what Paris is to Rome. In Cambridge, as in Paris, everything is on show, and the whole is laid out to the best advantage. Oxford, like Rome, abounds in beauty, but it is a hidden beauty that must be sought for.

Cambridge is a delightful county town with restaurants and shops generating that easy, convivial atmosphere that can only be found in small English towns. Oxford bears the unmistakable marks of a modern industrial city, with its seething crowds of shoppers and rash of chain and other stores. What Cambridge is on a Saturday afternoon, Oxford is all the week, and only on a Sunday, when the roar of the buses and traffic has ceased, does Oxford become a university town. Industrialization has forced the university to retreat into itself and so be saved from city inundation. College loyalties are thereby strengthened, but between town and gown there is a severance and a tension that Cambridge has never known.

I have always been told that it is dangerous to write about places until one has left them, and I have an uneasy suspicion that this contains some truth. This short account can claim to be nothing more than a subjective impression, with all its shortcomings and defects. And if any reader should happen to wonder what would be my reaction to the most searching test of all, namely, to which university would I send my son, I can swiftly set his heart at rest. I intend to remain a bachelor. The question therefore does not arise.

In 1955 I spent two months in Vienna writing a novel which was never published. This article in the Spectator, *published on 4 November 1955, gave my impressions of the city.*

Vienna

In 1945 Dr Karl Renner, then President of the Republic, described Austria as a light skiff occupied by four elephants, unwelcome but apparently permanent guests. Today the elephants have gone and the skiff is on the high seas, but the course is still undetermined since it is only a few weeks since the last elephant—the red one—left the capital to the accompaniment of Russian speeches, folk dancing and the discreet applause of the citizens. Today Vienna retains no mark of the Russian occupation save for the gigantic monument of a Russian soldier in the

Schwarzenbergplatz (at present Stalinplatz) holding aloft a burnished shield which the Viennese maintain contains 40,000 of their stolen watches.

In Austria as a whole the end of the occupation has been greeted with mixed feelings. Natural gratification at the recovery of independence has been tempered by knowledge of the pressing economic problems that must now be solved. In Salzburg province alone the withdrawal of the American troops has meant an annual loss of 680 million schillings, and the story is similar in other parts of the country. In Vienna, however, the end of the occupation has hardly been noticed, since the zones, unlike those in Berlin, were never rigidly separated, while the old city, the cultural and historic centre within the Ringstrasse, was internationalized. The only practical difference from last year is the increased number of prostitutes in the Graben who, to the chagrin of their Viennese sisters, have migrated from Salzburg, where the withdrawal of the American forces deprived them of their livelihood.

Vienna is to Austria what Paris is to France, partly because of the lack of any independent provincial cultural life and partly because nearly one-third of the entire population is concentrated in the city. Since 1945 Vienna has made an astonishing recovery which still surprises its own inhabitants, who refer to it as the 'Austrian Miracle'. The scars of war can still be seen, but they are less noticeable than in London, and it is difficult to conjure up the picture of ten years ago with the streets piled high with rubble, the Opera and the Stephansdom ablaze, no electricity, no transport, and famine just around the corner.

The charm and geniality, the *Gemütlichkeit*, for which the Viennese have always been famous, is as marked as ever, and in no other European capital does one feel so swiftly at home. Even some of the gaiety associated with the names of Lehar and Strauss remains, although narrowly circumscribed by the realities of post-war life. The Viennese go to work earlier and work harder than ever before, and as a result go earlier to bed. In any case they have little money, and after ten o'clock the city closes down, even London being lively by comparison. Only at weekends is there any night life, when the citizens go out to Grinzing to drink the *Heurigen* (new wine), and even on Saturdays the last tram leaves just after midnight and carries the remaining drunken revellers back to their homes. A rival to Grinzing is Sievering, where Anton Karas plays the 'Harry Lime' theme on his zither—but not after ten, the deadline fixed by harassed local residents.

Early rising has also meant the decline of café society, a symptom of which has been the recent closing of Dobner's, once famous as the centre of Vienna's theatrical life. You can still linger over your coffee in any of the many coffee houses, reading your newspaper attached to its bamboo frame, but they are very often empty; while the new espresso bars, with quick service and no time for conversation, are nearly always full. The most popular café is the Old Vienna in the Kärntnerstrasse, whose American juke boxes, Italian coffee machines, and pin-tables, make its name a bad joke. On the other hand, Sacher's and Demel's are unchanged. At Sacher's you can have the best food in Vienna, including a *Salzburger Nockerl* of unforgettable richness and lightness, and eat it in the gilt and red-brocade dining-room over which the portrait of the late Frau Sacher presides. At 83, her sister still sits at the cashier's desk at Demel's and supervises the serving of coffee with *Schlag* and the best pastries in Europe as she did in the far-off days of imperial splendour when courtiers from the neighbouring Hofburg dropped in with their ladies. The Viennese never seem to eat a full meal, and at the same time they never stop eating. In what other city would hot sausages be served in the principal banks at half-past ten in the morning, or sandwiches be placed on the counters of the department stores? The results as recorded by the feminine figure are, however, unfortunate.

Apart from snacks, the main Viennese relaxation is the cinema, of which there are over 200 in Vienna, most of them of great age and correspondingly appointed. A new tax is now being levied to assist in the cost of modernization, and CinemaScope has just begun its inroads. Continuous performances are unknown—the Viennese cannot see the point of seeing a film when it has run half through—and one result of advance booking is a flourishing black market run by the Vienna teddy boys, who buy up all the tickets for popular films. When Marlon Brando's film *The Wild One* was being shown, the only tickets available were being sold outside the cinema at double price.

Music, of course, flourishes, which is only fitting in a city renowned for its composers, and where Beethoven had more houses than he wrote symphonies. The Opera House, which was given priority in the rebuilding programme, is to reopen on 5 November with a performance of *Fidelio*, and the company will return from its exile in the Theater an der Wien, where it has been cramped for the past ten years. Theoretically, tickets can be obtained for anything from fifty to 5,000 schillings, but in fact they were all sold out twelve months ago, mainly to those who inundated the box-office with blank cheques for the management to fill in. *Fidelio* will also be the first transmission of Austrian television, about the control of which the politicians are still wrangling. No one appears to consider it of importance that hardly anyone in Austria possesses a television set.

Apart from such issues, the Viennese show no interest in politics, and this is not surprising, since the coalition of Catholics and Socialists has meant that all available political energy has gone into dividing the spoils of office—a game indulged in to the last degree of mathematical accuracy, and extending even to a division of the typists in the various ministries. The latest suggestion is that university appointments, which at present are made on a basis of friendly nepotism, should in future be made by a committee with members from the Ministry of Agriculture, the Ministry of Education and the trade unions. The universities are not to be represented. As for anti-Semitism, the dominating factor in pre-war Viennese politics, it exists no longer, for the best of all reasons—the destruction of its object. A bearded rabbi can still occasionally be seen in the streets, but he arouses only curiosity, not hostility.

About the future the Viennese are mildly optimistic. The dreams of reviving the days of imperial glory, either through a restoration of the Hapsburgs or union with Germany, have gone for ever. Vienna's galling experience as a provincial city administered by Prussian nominees is vividly remembered; nor is it forgotten that their German brothers fired the city in 1945 as a parting benediction. Everyone talks gaily of Austria as a second Switzerland, but the only justification for this is the high prices of hotels and pensions which hoteliers, intoxicated by this year's influx of tourists, have sent rocketing skywards. Viennese *Schlamperei*, the muddle-headedness which alone made the Hapsburg despotism tolerable, has little in common with Swiss clockwork efficiency. Besides, Vienna has too much grandeur, too much history, too much culture, to make such an object either worthy or attainable. A parallel with Venice would be more exact. That Vienna will attract an ever increasing number of tourists no one can doubt. Whatever the realities, it is still for foreigners a city of romance, and despite the peeling façades, the deserted cafés and the early nights, the sway of the past is too seductive to resist. Nor can anyone who has listened to the Vienna Symphoniker playing 'Roses of the South' on a summer evening in the Arkadenhof, with Eduard Strauss conducting, believe that the past has gone for ever, or resist for long the exhilarating illusion that Vienna is a city where all one's dreams will be fulfilled.

This article was first published in Vogue *and was included in* Travel in Vogue *(London, Macdonald/Futura, 1981).*

Rome

Some cities pull at the heart strings, like lovers they inspire rapture but they also make demands, and Rome is the most demanding of all. Once she has cast her spell, she never lifts the enchantments and one is permanently enslaved, condemned always to return with longing in a vain attempt to sound her depths. Not that Rome is the most beautiful of cities, Paris can lay a courtesan's claim to that, nor the most romantic, Venice carries off that palm, nor the most nostalgic, Vienna has the crown, and certainly not the most stimulating, New York wins hands down, but Rome more than any other has time and history at her command. Rightly she bears the title of the eternal city, the dust of monarchs, popes, emperors and dictators mingles in the soil, and still the fount of civilization, law and religion, she flows like the Tiber timelessly on. The city is one great theatre of marble and brick where the play is life and only the cast is ever-changing.

Rome is at her loveliest in October when autumn touches her domes and palaces with gold, suffusing the streets with lambent light, while the branching plane trees by the Tiber drop their russet leaves. If you cannot visit Rome in autumn then go in early summer, in the latter days of May or the early ones of June, when the sun is warm and lifegiving but not yet fierce, and the Borghese gardens, still unscorched by the glare of July and August, are a variegated pattern of green, and the wild roses are blooming on the Palatine. Easter, of course, has its claims for pilgrims but it's really too early for Rome and, as I know to my cost, it can be biting cold.

The great set pieces, St Peter's dome and Bernini's colonnade, the skyline saints of St John Lateran, the crumbling crenellation of the Colosseum, the jagged outlines of the Forum are well known enough to everyone by sight or vicarious postcard so I will let them be, and dart off along some byways. My first call is oddly enough a graveyard, the Cimitero Acattolico, otherwise known as the English or the Protestant cemetery, which nestles around the base of the pyramid of Cestius, by the Porta San Paolo, one of the southern entrances to the city. The pyramid itself dates from the first century BC and commemorates a well-known tribune of the period of Caius Cestius. St Paul's eyes must have lighted on it when he was being led outside the walls to execution. In its shadow live today a colony of those rake-like Roman cats who wolf down the spaghetti left for them in newspapers by benevolent old ladies.

I know of no place on earth more beautiful, more peaceful, more deliciously melancholic than this lovely plot of land, remote from the tide of Roman life and traffic which rolls noisily by beyond its walls, which shelters beneath its shady cypresses the foreign dead. Nearly all its inhabitants died in exile save for a sprinkling of Italian Protestants, equally exotic in their way. Unlike the Catholic cemetery of San Lorenzo, far away on the other side of Rome, which paradoxically is a bustling hive of activity (Italians practise an extraordinary cult of the dead), this is a real place of quiet. Poets, sculptors, artists and diplomats lie here side by side; English, French, German and Russians are for once at peace: Goethe's son and Prince Yousopoff's father are curiously united in death. But the stars of the place are the two English poets whose names are for ever linked with Rome, Keats and Shelley, whose remains lie here. Through an aperture in the wall one can glimpse the grave of Keats with its bitter epitaph: 'Here lies one whose name is writ in water.' Next to him is his lifelong friend Severn, sent by Keats to find this last resting place as he lay dying in the tiny *pensione* off the Spanish steps. When Severn returned and told the dying poet that white and blue violets, daisies and anemones were growing wild on the graves, Keats was happy and said he 'already felt the flowers growing over him'. Further up the slope lie the ashes although not the heart of Shelley, which the flames of his funeral pyre would not consume and which was plucked from the embers by his friend Trelawney, who bore it back to England. Here amongst the broken columns and marble fragments covered by trailing ivy and honeysuckle with here and there a fiery red camellia, one can sit shaded by pines and laurels and myrtles and find a little peace. 'It might make one in love with death,' wrote Shelley, 'to be buried in so sweet a place.'

Away in the heart of the city in the Piazza d'Espagna one finds another memorial to the two English poets, the Keats–Shelley house, where Keats spent his last days. The simple, narrow room where he died with its pale blue ceiling and lime-washed walls can still be seen. The house itself stands by the Spanish steps at the foot of the church of Trinità dei Monti where the nuns sing vespers on Sundays and holy days in piping high voices. The house is packed with books and relics of the poets but is not so much a museum as a house of contemplation, presided over by a serene and charming deity, Signora Vera Cacciatore, who has been its curator for many years. During the dreary days of occupation she shuttered the windows and resolutely kept the Germans out and was rewarded on the day of liberation when she threw open the doors and found by happy chance the soldier sent to guard the house by the allied high command was a Keats scholar.

In Rome, museums and galleries can get one down. The Vatican museums are as splendid as the Louvre and equally debilitating. My favourite Roman gallery is the more manageable Villa Borghese, the home of Napoleon's favourite sister, Paolina. There she reclines, immortalized in marble by Canova, a pose of which she later became somewhat ashamed but it was times that had changed, not she. Canova's masterpiece can hold its own with the marvels of Bernini which stand nearby, while above on the *piano nobile* live a choice collection of pictures of which the highlight is Titian's iridescent allegory of sacred and profane love. Spare a moment, too, for the highly idiosyncratic collection of paintings at the Palazzo

Spada near the Piazza Farnese, a gem of settecento good taste, with a splendid *trompe l'œil* garden gallery by Borromini. Pop in also to the Museo Romano at the opening of the incomparable Piazza Navona, where Domitian once staged his chariot races, and you will be regaled by the sight of one of nineteenth-century Rome's most agreeable curiosities, the railway train of Pio Nono with its open and closed carriages complete with papal thrones. The Quirinale is also well worth a visit, especially its magnificent chapel with an intriguing papal squint and its formal gardens. You could also tour Rome's thirteen obelisks starting from the magnificent specimen in St Peter's Square to its homely and diminutive fellow creature, which is mounted on the back of Bernini's delightful elephant in the Piazza della Minerva. But I must stop. As Silvio Negro, one of Rome's great lovers, wrote: *'Roma, non basta una Vita'*, for Rome, a lifetime is not enough.

This article was published in the Daily Express *on 20 February 1982 after my first visit to Australia during the previous year.*

Sydney

Sydney must be one of the better kept secrets of the contemporary world.

A cosmopolitan city, sophisticated and welcoming, with charming buildings and houses, good restaurants and chic shops, all laid out in a beautiful maritime setting, reminiscent of San Francisco.

As the jet swooped over the city I was riveted by the view of the great blue bay speckled with the white sails of the boats, spanned one side by the huge iron girders of the 1920s bridge ('the old coathanger' to true Sydneans), and flanked on the other by the Opera House.

This last landmark is the Danish John Utzon's masterpiece, with its ten gleaming white roof shells, rising out of the waters like some glittering sea monster.

Sydney is not Australia any more than New York is the United States, but it is not untypical of Australian life which is essentially urban.

Australians cherish their nostalgic self image of sunburned surfers and pioneers of the outback, but they are predominantly a town people, crammed into the cities which string out along the coast—less than 15 per cent of Australians actually live in the countryside.

The conquest of the outback may be the Australian reverie and they are proud of their weird variety of marsupials, kangaroos, eucalyptus drugged koala bears, wombats and, of course, the duckbilled platypus (*Ornithorhynchus anatinus*), but most Australians have seen them only in the zoo.

The Australian dream is to migrate to the suburbs not to the back of beyond, and there they sprawl dismal and uniform without cohesion or community.

The British relationship to Australia (and vice versa) is both tense and contradictory. Canada has cut free and fallen under the thraldom of the United States, but no such dubious escape route is open to the isolated southern continent.

New Zealand is too remote to care, but for Australia the old umbilical still binds and there are tugs at both ends.

For the Englishman visiting Australia for the first time it's rather like visiting members of the family whom one has never seen, so he is a little nervous and apprehensive, not quite sure whether he is to be made much of or spurned.

The tension is heightened for those English who have accustomed themselves to look upon Australians as culturally deprived poor relations who then turn out to be rich, prosperous and civilized.

Australians are kind, generous, open and hospitable, but sometimes they seem to be sitting on the edge of their chairs waiting to be offended or patronized. What both sides need is affection mediated through tact and understanding.

Australians have great residual good will towards Britain although the restrictions imposed by the Commonwealth Immigration Act of 1962 still rankle; but they are at the moment particularly determined to be a nation in their own right.

The outcome is a superficial hostility to the mother country. I was hardly through the door of the apartment where I was staying when the tenant's girlfriend let fly with an anti-Pom diatribe which in my jet-lagged condition I accepted with uncharacteristic meekness.

It was only next day that I felt strong enough to counter-attack, but after that we got on very well.

I had some good material as there were no less than seven strikes going on, with piles of rubbish in the streets and even the ballet had hung up their pumps, but I was told it was all the fault of emigrant Pommie shop stewards!

Chauvinism does come to the surface quickly and is made worse by a certain sense of insecurity, symbolized by Australian ambivalence to Dame Edna Everage (née Barry Humphries), whom they are never quite sure whether to laugh with or be ashamed of.

Images of the pale colours of rain-sodden England struggle in their minds for priority with the more garish sun-drenched hues of the Australian outback. Comparisons really are odious and are part of the difficulty on both sides.

I dragged my poor agnostic friend to choral matins at St Andrew's Cathedral and found a splendid choir and no fewer than three anthems, but it was still not St Paul's.

Republicanism is mildly in the ascendant and I now see why Prince Charles cannot go out just now as Governor General, but in ten years' time it will be different.

Happy memories jostle in my brain. I recall the perplexity of the taxi-driver when I dashed into his seat (that accursed right-hand drive) in an attempt not to be stand-offish and his fury when remembering London counsel not to tip I forgot to pay him at all.

Then there was my brief campaign with the beautiful Diane Cilento to save Australia's astonishing arts renaissance from assault from yet another philistine government. I even pounced on the deputy Prime Minister, Mr Anthony, who had the misfortune to sit next to me on the journey home.

I enjoyed being festooned with 'right honourables': Australians are not class-conscious but they make up for it with awareness of status.

Anyhow, I liked them and hope that they liked me. And why shouldn't I? After all, it was in Canberra that they gave me a gold medal for my parliamentary reforms which got me the sack in Britain.

Sensible people the Australians. Good on them!

This article was published in the Wiseman Review *(Dublin) of June 1961. At the time it was written the Roman Catholic Church had not formally accepted the principle of religious freedom. It therefore can claim to be something of a pioneer contribution. The principles argued for in the article were accepted in the Second Vatican Council's 'Declaration on Religious Freedom' promulgated at the Fourth Session in December 1965.*

Catholicism and Religious Toleration

Some notes towards a restatement of the Catholic attitude to religious liberty in a contemporary pluralist society

Can those who believe in a religion based on a revealed truth tolerate other forms of religion? This is a problem of perennial intellectual fascination and contemporary relevance. For English Catholics brought up in the dual traditions of dogmatic faith and liberal politics the question is existential although somewhat academic. Lord Acton felt the problem acutely. 'I find that people disagree with me,' he wrote in a letter to Mandell Creighton, 'because they hold that Liberalism is not true, or that Catholicism is not true, or that both cannot be true together. If I could discover anyone who is not included in these categories, I fancy we should get on very well together.' In the United States, on the other hand, the problem is far from academic and gives rise to sharp political conflicts. Catholics in the United States number 40 million and hence are a powerful political force. Much of the opposition to the election of Mr Kennedy as President of the United States was based on bigotry, but it also rested on a more excusable doubt about the attitude of Catholics to traditional civil liberties and the separation of Church and State guaranteed by the constitution. This doubt is largely caused by the intellectual confusion of Catholics themselves. They feel as strongly about constitutional liberties as other men, but they are not always clear as to the intellectual foundations of their belief. What is required by American Catholics (and by other Catholics as well) is a coherent theology of religious freedom and civil liberty. Until this is thought out, mischievous anti-Catholic propagandists like Paul Blanshard will continue to stir up trouble. A period of history which is witnessing the advance of Catholic ecumenism at an unprecedented pace would seem an appropriate one for its formulation.

Catholic relations with other Churches cannot be securely founded until a Catholic doctrine of toleration is fully developed. Rethinking of Catholic attitudes has begun, but there is scope for further intellectual effort. Man, after all, is born intolerant, and, as John Morley has pointed out, 'of all ideas toleration would seem to be in the general mind the very latest'. Still, one may hope that Catholic thinking has advanced beyond the statement attributed to many Catholic spokesmen, namely, that 'When we are in the minority we demand for ourselves freedom according to your principles; when we are in the majority we refuse you this freedom according to our principles.'[1] Belief that this impertinent distortion constitutes the last word of Catholics on toleration forms part of what Cardinal Newman called 'the stain' on the Protestant imagination, which has to be expunged before the true concept of the Church and her world-wide redemptive mission can be comprehended.

Toleration can certainly be justified on grounds of simple expediency and denied any content of moral value. If rival Churches with conflicting claims are found within the same community they can either strive to exterminate one another or to live in peace. In the Western world the second alternative has been chosen, but only after centuries of fierce religious wars and bitter persecutions. The argument can be shifted to a somewhat higher plane by stressing that civil peace and concord is itself a moral value, and the necessary prerequisite of any advance in civilization.

Persecution can also be condemned on the grounds that it does not work. Ideas, it is said, will always triumph against the sword. This may well be true in the long run, but in the short term persecution can undoubtedly achieve its aim. In England the penal laws succeeded in reducing the old majority religion to a pathetic remnant, and it was only on their repeal that a Catholic revival became possible. In Scandinavia, the effects of legal proscription of Catholics are still obvious, and Catholicism retains only a tiny foothold. In Spain and to a lesser extent in Italy the Inquisition prevented the spread of Protestantism. Persecution can certainly, then, restrict the spread of a particular religion, but it cannot create belief. Indeed, its effect as seen in some Catholic countries has been to create a scepticism amongst the educated classes which has gravely undermined the country's religious character. This is a more convincing argument against persecution than the liberal optimism which presumes that truth will always triumph.

A powerful practical argument against persecution is that it can be used by either side, the upholders of falsehood as well as of truth. In such a situation truth has no advantage, unless it happens to have the sword on its side, but this is accidental. In discussion, on the other hand, truth has an intrinsic advantage, by its very nature. It may also be said that discussion and therefore toleration is necessary for the development of truth. Revelation of necessity sets bounds to discussion in that it presumes certain statements are true but it does not exclude it. Such discussion is in fact necessary for the full development of doctrine.[2] 'Without discussion,' wrote Walter Bagehot, 'each mind is dependent on its own partial observation. A great man is one image—one thing, so to speak—to his valet, another to his son, another to his wife, another to his greatest friend. None of these must be stereotyped; all must be compared. To prohibit discussion is to prohibit the corrective process.'

Man being rational, government by discussion is the most perfect form of government and represents a real progress in social institutions. In primitive

---

[1] The statement is most often assigned to Louis Veuillot, Napoleon III's fanatical admirer, who was certainly capable of making it. It seems, however, to have been manufactured by Macaulay. See Macaulay, the *Edinburgh Review* (July 1 1835), p. 304.

[2] Heretics go to extremes in maintaining their opinions, but it cannot be denied that their challenge has been fruitful theologically for the Church.

societies cohesion is of primary importance. In such societies the overwhelming necessity is to preserve some kind of order. Any order is better than none, and the order is so insecurely founded that discussion is a dangerous luxury. Such societies need one religion and religion becomes the bond of society. But civil society like man himself comes of age, and then the social necessity of one religion is reduced or vanishes altogether. Religious pluralism—such is the lesson of history—inevitably follows.

Such pluralism is not of course desirable in itself, but, given the fallen nature of man, appears inevitable. Man's imperfection affords another powerful argument for toleration. Physical power is always liable to abuse. Power does in fact corrupt. It can be used to enforce uniformity where no uniformity is called for. Religious assent can be demanded to propositions where none in fact necessary. This is an ever present danger for authoritarian religious bodies. Cardinal Manning's erroneous insistence on the necessity of the papal temporal power is a case in point.[3]

Persecution invariably has danger for the persecutors. If the Church uses the state to maintain her doctrines, the state will demand its price. The Edict of Constantinople of 392 which abandoned the tolerant policy of Constantine enshrined in the Edict of Milan (313), and placed paganism under a ban throughout the Empire, was welcomed by the Church as a blessing. In fact it proved a curse, as it laid the foundations of the Caesaro-papism which was to plague the Church for centuries to come. A potent cause of the Reformation was the exploitation of the Church by the state and the overlapping of functions which required Church officers to serve both God and Caesar. When the crisis came many ecclesiastics preferred Caesar, because they were in fact state officials despite their ecclesiastical garb. In 1928 the Church of England experienced the drawbacks of establishment when its Prayer Book, approved by the highest spiritual authorities, was rejected by Parliament. It is no accident that the Catholic Church today is most flourishing in the United States, where the constitution requires the rigid separation of Church and State.

The practical approach to toleration was formulated anew by Pius XII in his address to the fifth national convention of the Union of Catholic Jurists in 1953.[4] The essence of the Pope's view is contained in the following extract:

> Reality shows that error and sin are in the world in great measure. God reprobates them, but He permits them to exist. Hence the affirmation: religious and moral error must always be impeded when it is possible, because tolerance of them is in itself immoral, is not valid *absolutely and unconditionally*. Moreover, God has not given even to human authority such an absolute and universal command in matters of faith and morality. Such a command is unknown to the common convictions of mankind, to Christian conscience, to the sources of

---

[3] Cf. the complaint put forward by Erasmus that in his time heresy had changed its character: 'for any futile reason they shout at once: "Heresy! Heresy!" Formerly someone was considered a heretic if he deviated from the Gospel, the articles of faith or something of similar authority. Nowadays, if anyone differs however little from St Thomas, he is a heretic. . . . Anything that does not please or is not understood is heresy. To indulge in cultivated speech is heresy. . . . I admit that to corrupt the faith is a grave accusation, but all the same one should not turn everything into a matter of faith.' *Opus Epistolarum*, ed. P. S. Allen (Oxford, 1906–47), IV, pp. 101, 102 and 106.

[4] 9 December 1953. *The Pope Speaks* (Maryland), I: 64.

revelation and to the practice of the Church. To omit here other Scriptural texts which are adduced in support of the argument, Christ in the parable of the cockle gives the following advice: let the cockle grow in the field of the world together with the good seed in view of the harvest (cf. Matthew xiii, 24 – 30). The duty of repressing moral and religious error cannot therefore be an ultimate norm of action. It must be subordinate to *higher and more general* norms, which in *some circumstances*, permit and even perhaps seem to indicate as the better policy toleration of error in order to promote *a greater good*.[5]

All these arguments for toleration are reasonable and based on common sense. They are in line with the development of Catholic thought on toleration during the nineteenth century, especially its formulation of the dichotomy of 'thesis' and 'hypothesis'. The thesis or ideal solution to Church–State problems is the establishment and full recognition by the state of the Roman Catholic Church. Other Churches are said to have no true juridical claim to existence, 'error has no rights', and, while discreet private worship should be tolerated, any public manifestation of religious rites or propaganda opposed to Catholic truth should be prohibited. Heretics, those 'ravening wolves' beloved of medieval polemicists, if not incinerated, should be firmly muzzled. The state should accordingly act as an instrument of the Church and enforce her dogmatic and moral teaching by means of civil law. The political and social situation, however, in many countries, prevents the implementing of the 'thesis' and the Church in these countries has to act on an hypothesis, i.e. she avails herself of the freedom conferred by the liberal state, and accepts on a temporary basis, the rights afforded to other Churches.

Faced with this formulation of the Church's views the average, straightforward Englishman feels distinctly uneasy. It puts him in an ambiguous position where he acts (and speaks) one way to his fellow citizens, and thinks differently to himself. This savours somewhat of duplicity. The dichotomy is certainly open to satire. It might be described as 'Heads I win, tails you lose.' The thesis, it was said, of Mgr Chigi, a socially minded nineteenth-century papal nuncio in Paris, was to burn the Jews, but the hypothesis was dinner with M. de Rothschild. It seems a little curious that the Church throughout her history, apart from the brief interludes of the late Roman Empire and the Middle Ages, should have been in a state of permanent hypothesis, and apparently condemned to it for the foreseeable future. It is to say the least odd that the whole free society has nothing more than a contingent basis.

The thesis-hypothesis theory, however, presents less difficulty when one realizes that it can lay no claim to eternal validity but was a product of a particular epoch. Taken out of its nineteenth-century setting it becomes meaningless. The Church in the nineteenth century, it should be recalled, was on the defensive. The French Revolution and its aftermath of illuminism and encyclopaedism had been an even greater traumatic shock than the Reformation. Science was in direct

---

[5] This statement is not a new departure, cf. Leo XIII's encyclical *Immortale Dei* (1885) *The Pope and the People* (London, 1932), pp. 62–3. Both pontiffs advanced well beyond St Thomas Aquinas who allowed toleration of heathens and Jews but denied it to heretics. St Thomas discusses the practical reasons for toleration but finds them outweighed by the danger of heresy spreading. St Thomas had in mind not those born into heresy who had never known the Catholic religion but 'unbelievers who at some time have accepted the faith'. See *Summa Theologica*, II-II, Questions X and XI. On the other hand St Augustine advised the toleration of carnal vice: 'If you do away with harlots, the world will be convulsed with lust.'

conflict with religion and the free institutions which the century developed owed nothing to the Church. Civil liberty was elevated into an absolute, and the supernatural denied any public place in civil society. This was the liberty so severely criticized in the encyclicals of Gregory XVI and Pius IX and even—to a lesser extent—in those of Leo XIII. Catholic political theory was bedevilled by the ephemeral question of the temporal power, and the fate of the Papal States. These conditions have now fundamentally altered and the significance of the papal utterances with them. Much ingenuity has been spent in trying to effect a verbal reconciliation between what was said by nineteenth-century popes and what is being said by contemporary Catholic thinkers on liberty, but such efforts are misplaced. Once the historical dimension is taken into account, the conflict ceases. In any case, the nineteenth-century statement of the 'ideal' in terms of a subservient persecuting state will not be found 'ideal' by many today. As Fr Hartmann has pointed out: 'The ideal ("thesis") which has obviously not been reached, is not the Catholic state, which refuses non-Catholic public worship, but the condition of human society in which tolerance is not necessary because everyone is united in confessing the truth.'

The arguments for toleration on grounds of expediency are powerful, but they do not take one far enough. The question whether toleration can have a positive moral value is left open. In the past those who have tried to show that it has, have too often been reduced to silence by the flourishing of the intellectual bludgeon 'Error has no rights'. Yet this phrase is virtually meaningless. Rights do not inhere in intellectual abstractions but in human persons. The human person should be the starting point of contemporary discussion of religious liberty not ideal truth. When ideal truth in the form of religious doctrine formed the bond of society there was some reason for its use as a starting point, but there can be none today, when human rights not unity of faith, is the basis on which society rests.

The moral basis of Western society, and its chief distinguishing mark from the totalitarian societies of the East, is respect for the human person. The human person is autonomous, free and inviolable. The human person is not explicable in terms of social or religious forms, nor should he be subordinated to their purposes. He transcends them. In so far as society progresses it is principally by enabling the human person to realize itself more fully in relation to other human beings with similar aims. Discipline and conformity are the essentials of primitive societies, but freedom is the hallmark of a mature and advanced society. Man finds himself in a social environment with certain political and religious doctrines, but he cannot be forced to accept them, although outward conformity may be exacted. They can only be adopted by assent. A particular moment of conscious assent is not necessary, although these clearly occur in individuals, but the validity of religious belief depends on a continuing day-to-day assent, which may never be specifically formulated. Once assent is withdrawn religious belief is destroyed.[6]

'It is against the nature of religion', therefore, as Tertullian wrote, 'to force religion; it must be accepted spontaneously and not by force; the offerings demanded, indeed, must be made willingly. That is why, if you force us to sacrifice, you give in fact, nothing to your gods: they have no need of unwilling

[6] Hence Cardinal Newman's remark in his letter to the Duke of Norfolk (1874): 'Certainly, if I am obliged to bring religion into after-dinner toasts (which indeed does not seem quite the thing), I shall drink—to the Pope, if you please—still to conscience first, and to the Pope afterwards.'

sacrifices.' And St Augustine declared tersely: 'Credere non potest homo nisi volens.' Man is essentially a free being and the essence of an act of faith is that it is a free act. 'Freedom', writes Cardinal Feltin, 'lies at the very heart of Christianity, which seen from without might look like a system, but thought and lived from within is a living bond between persons, a religion of the spirit. Faith is the encounter of a free gift and a free acceptance: a call on the part of God and a conscious and submissive response to God's voice.' Thus the contemporary approach to toleration should start not from an abstract 'thesis' but from the act of faith itself, in essence an act of freedom. Faith comes through the Church but is not given by the Church but by God. A coerced act of faith, as the Church has always known, is in a real sense of blasphemy, whether the coercion is carried out by Church or state because it substitutes one or the other for the operation of the Holy Spirit. Since freedom is the essence of the act of faith, the freer it is and the more spontaneous, the more perfect it becomes. The duty of the state is, therefore, to create the conditions most favourable for the possibility of acts of faith. The Church thus requires freedom but she needs no more. There cannot of course be a right in the human person to reject God but there is a liberty to do so. That after all is the human predicament. Man accordingly has a right against the state and the Church not to have God imposed on him against his will.

The point was put clearly by Pius XII in his encyclical *Corporis Mystici*. 'But while we desire', said the Pope,

> supplication to go up unceasingly to God from the whole mystical body, that all those who are astray may as soon as possible enter the one fold of Jesus Christ, we declare that it is absolutely necessary that this should come about by their free choice, since no man believes unless he is willing. Wherefore if any persons, not believing are constrained to enter a church, to approach the altar and to receive sacraments, they certainly do not become true believers in Christ; because that faith without which 'it is impossible to please God' must be the perfectly free 'homage of intellect and will'.

By faith man is able to participate in the redemption, and redemption itself is both given and received by love. Love like faith is a free act. 'When one has known the love of free men,' says Péguy, 'the prostrations of slaves are worthless.' Through grace man is liberated from the servitude of sin and becomes a free man. He enters, says Danielou, freedom in a new sense. 'It means that man's relation to God is no longer merely that of a servant to his Lord but also that of a son to his Father.' Such a relationship is inconceivable unless it is free.

Instead then of basing toleration on social or political expediency, it can be made to depend on the nature of faith itself and to spring from it. This is not to deny importance to historical factors but to allot them a subsidiary role. Religious liberty is seen as the condition in which faith can achieve its purest and fullest form. The act of faith is an interior act, but man cannot be content with interior freedom, since he is not an anchorite but a social being. As a human person he has to live in society and give outward expression to his inner faith. A freedom which cannot express itself is in man's case illusory. Toleration and liberty thus extend from the inner formation of faith to its manifestations. Toleration accordingly becomes a social policy based on the very nature of man. The problems raised by divergent views of what is morally allowable by the law have been considered by the present writer in an earlier article. In the present article the author is concerned only with matters of faith.

The problem of achieving religious liberty in practice, cannot—as has been said earlier—be separated from an historical context. This is the mistake of the 'error has no rights' school, who try to isolate it from any social or historical setting. The same isolationism is displayed by those who draw an analogy between arresting the spread of bodily disease and arresting that of heresy, and conclude that because the state impedes the one (which only kills the body), it should also impede the other (which is worse because it kills the soul). Whether any heretic is in fact damned is a moot point, but the principal error of such analogizers is to see the problem under one aspect only, and to separate it from all consideration of the character of the human person or the nature of religious belief. They also exclude any consideration of the different functions of Church and State. Yet toleration can only be discussed meaningfully when these too are taken into consideration. How far ideal religious liberty can be realized in any particular society will depend on historical circumstances and that society's state of development. In the Middle Ages, for example, St Thomas advocated the punishment of heretics, not because they were denying the Catholic faith, but because they were disrupting society, which was held together by a common Catholicism. But St Thomas's situation was pure 'hypothesis': the 'thesis' is the state of religious liberty.

Religious liberty may then be considered as required by the human person for his full development. The state, which is little more than a mechanism to ensure the safeguarding of the liberties of human persons and their welfare, has no right of coercion in religious matters. The state as such has no direct knowledge of the Church or her mission and therefore places all religions on an equal basis, not because it considers one to be as good as another, but because it has no means of distinguishing between them. The state comes first in time: the Church is first in dignity: but there is no primacy of causality. The state is not the instrument of the Church but has its own defined and limited functions. Given the need of the human person for religious liberty, the state's function is to safeguard it, and not to impede man as he pursues his end of moving freely to God. The state is certainly not indifferent to morality, and its moral policies will be influenced by the moral views of its citizens, but in using coercive power to impose moral notions by law it is always limited by the fundamental autonomy of the human person. In pluralist societies, furthermore, where there is only a limited agreed morality, only what is agreed can be part of the public moral order. Where there is no consensus, the question must be left to be determined in the private sphere.

Intolerance does have a place in religion but it is a limited one. Within the Church there must always be a dogmatic intolerance arising from the Church's mission as teacher of the truth and guardian of the deposit of faith. The Church is bound to defend the truth entrusted to her, but she carries out her duties with prudence and charity. When she must she resorts to her weapon of excommunication, a spiritual not a temporal weapon. In the world, however, the Church has to coexist with other faiths: a necessity which will grow more imperative as the rudiments of a world order are formed and a genuine international society created. She has to lead men to the truth not by the exercise of a coercive will but by persuasion. To fulfil this mission she needs freedom but nothing more. 'It is not the office of the Church', declared Pius XII in his address to the new cardinals on 20 February 1946,

> to include and in a manner embrace, like a gigantic world empire, all human society. This concept of the Church as earthly empire and worldly domination is fundamentally false. She follows in her progress and her expansion an opposite path to that of modern imperialism. She progresses before all else in depth, then in extension. She seeks primarily man himself. . . . Her work is completed in the depths of each man's heart, but it has its own repercussions on all the duration of life, on all the fields of activity of each one. With men so formed the Church prepares for human society a base on which it can rest with security.

In October 1976 John Ogilvie, a distant kinsman by marriage of Princess Alexandra, was canonized in Rome. At the ceremony Princess Alexandra was mistakenly offered Holy Communion, which she accepted. A public controversy ensued. In this article, published in the Catholic Herald *on 29 October 1976, I reflected on the matter.*

Princess Alexandra

The canonization of St John Ogilvie, like many another spiritual event, has brought with it not only peace but a sword. The English hierarchy, with a curious sense of timing and apparently no saving sense of irony, chose the week of the canonization to issue a solemn warning about the 'unlawful' nature of the Tridentine Mass in defence of which the new Scottish saint died.

Archbishop Worlock is reported as stating at a Press conference that 'in all humility the bishops had to admit some responsibility for failing to educate the laity sufficiently about the new Rite of Mass,' but he did not expect the problem to last long.

One might say to the Archbishop with equal humility that the laity do not wish to be 'educated' out of ancient loyalties but rather to be recognized as responsible adults with a right to choose.

Most of the problems associated with the Tridentine Mass are of episcopal making, and if they could be 'educated' on the need for plurality in liturgical matters it would be no bad thing. If there is not to be diversity within the Household of Faith then the outlook for the ecumenical movement in the future is bleak indeed.

The only institution capable of being the centre of a reunited Christendom is the papacy: but hundreds of years of separation cannot be done away with by a stroke of some concordatial pen. Those who have grown apart will have to grow together, and while they are doing so very wide differences will have to be tolerated and in some cases welcomed.

The Church of Scotland reacted with fury to the news of the canonization, claiming that this was the sort of thing that drove Churches and individuals further apart. With all respect to the elders of the Kirk, they have got a false idea of what the ecumenical movement means. It does not mean giving up distinctive approaches but developing a new appreciation of why people come to the altar in different ways.

The Communion of Saints, when properly understood, offers no difficulties to Christians of any denomination, and in fact is a basic tenet of the Christian creed. We have, however, to start looking at these differences of emphasis in an understanding, charitable and tolerant way.

The elders may have boycotted the ceremony in Rome, but the Royal Family was represented by no less a person than Princess Alexandra, the Queen's first cousin, whose husband, Mr Angus Ogilvy, is a relation of the new saint.

I visited the Scots College last month when I was in Rome, where I was hospitably received, and they were all looking forward delightedly to the Princess's visit. In the event they received more than they bargained for.

During the ceremony of canonization in St Peter's, Holy Communion was distributed and a Franciscan friar came along the row where the Princess and her family were kneeling and offered them Communion, which they accepted. For their pains they were denounced by some, according to the Italian newspaper *La Stampa*, as causing 'an ecumenical scandal'.

Canon Purdy, of the Vatican's Secretariat for Christian Unity, is reported to have made a less apocalyptic comment: 'The monk made a complete ass of himself. The organizers should have tipped him off about the people who should receive Communion.' Thank heavens he was not tipped off: a murmur of *O Felix Culpa* is certainly not out of place!

First of all, Princess Alexandra (as always) behaved with that exquisite sense of courtesy and good manners which has made her deservedly one of the most popular members of the Royal Family. To have created a scene by refusing to receive Communion from the enthusiastic friar bearing down upon her would have been quite wrong.

It would have marred the ecumenical character of the proceedings, caused distress, and occasioned hurt feelings and unfavourable comment. Courtesy is the flower of charity, and such blooms are not to be despised.

Yet Princess Alexandra was not only correct in her behaviour: she was fully theologically justified in what she did. Neither the Catholic Church nor the Church of England supports the 'open Communion' which is espoused by some Protestant denominations, and in this they are surely right. Neither does either Church approve of reception of Holy Communion by members of the other Church as a matter of course.

Full inter-communion must wait upon reunion. To have full inter-communion without the organic unity and theological reconciliation which are its foundations would be false.

What, however, both Churches do practise is what I may call 'occasional inter-communion'—that is, reception of the Sacrament by a non-member when there are very special circumstances justifying the exception to the rule.

One such in the Catholic Church is the reception of Communion by the non-Catholic party at a mixed marriage. I, like many other Catholics, have been present on ecumenical occasions when the circumstances have led the participants to communicate together. The Eucharist, we should remember, is not only a sign of unity but a means to unity as well.

Princess Alexandra is a baptized and practising Christian, and as she herself said through her spokesman: 'The Princess and other members of the family accepted that they were in a Christian church participating in a Christian service.' All praise, then, to the Princess, who has shown herself not only courteous and good-mannered, but a first-class theologian as well!

My maiden speech was delivered in the House of Commons on 17 November 1964 (Hansard, 702, 290). The debate on immigration was precipitated by the Expiring Laws Continuance Bill, renewing the operation of a number of Acts of Parliament, including the Commonwealth Immigration Act of 1962.

Immigration

I rise with trepidation to make my first speech in the House of Commons, but I am fortified by the knowledge of the kindness with which it is customary for hon. Members to hear the first speech of a new Member. In the last Parliament, I sat in this Chamber in what was literally, but in no other sense, a higher place, but where to give tongue would have been to court instant expulsion. That is, I hope, a hazard which I shall not run tonight.

I am proud indeed to be a Member of this ancient and honourable assembly and proud to represent the constituency of Chelmsford, which is so typical of modern Britain and which has, I might inform my hon. Friend the Member for Rugby [Mr Wise], a bishop who, while no supporter of the party opposite, has spoken out strongly on the racial issue. I am also very glad to be able to pay tribute to my predecessor, Sir Hubert Ashton, who served the state faithfully for so long and has now gone on to serve the Church. In his new position he is in charge of the investments and properties of the Church of England, so he is in the unique and happy position of being able to serve both God and Mammon. In Parliament he consistently upheld the traditions of progressive Toryism, and that is a path along which I am very happy to attempt to follow him.

This amendment tonight is a rather technical one and I hope I shall remain within the bounds of order, but there is nothing technical about the subject which underlies the subject of our debate, which is, indeed, part of a debate being conducted in every home in the country. It is a debate about the problem of how we are to live in peace and in mutual charity with those who share a common allegiance to the Crown but many of whom are different in colour from ourselves and have different national traditions and different national ways of life. What is at stake in this debate is really the continuance of the amity and civil concord which is at once the basic prerequisite of a civilized society and at the same time its highest achievement.

We have to consider in this discussion whether or not immigration from the Commonwealth should continue to be controlled, and, if so, how it can best be done. This is an issue on which people feel strongly. It is an issue where emotions and passions are involved; and it is, therefore, right that it should be discussed; but I think there is an inescapable duty on all in public life, and, if I may venture to say so, particularly on Members of this Committee, to seek in that discussion to moderate and assuage the force of passion by the counter force of reasonable argument.

One argument which, I trust, will not be put forward to this Committee tonight—I mention it because it is an argument which is prevalent in the country—is that there should be stricter control of immigration because the crime rate and the prevalence of disease are higher amongst immigrants than amongst other sections of our population. Home Secretary after Home Secretary has denied this shameful and baseless allegation. I feel it is the duty of Members not only to refrain from presenting it themselves as an issue but to repudiate those who for electoral gain put it forward on their behalf. I do not think one can stand by on this issue like Pontius Pilate washing, or wringing, one's hands. I think one has a positive duty to dissociate oneself from that kind of support. I am not referring to the situation in Smethwick in particular, because I do not know what went on there at the time: I was busy in my own constituency. I mention it as a matter of general principle.

I trust that our discussion tonight, and any other discussion which is held here, will not be marred by any thought of party advantage or marked by a display of partisan venom, and, if I may be so bold, I would presume to offer the right hon. and learned Gentleman the Home Secretary my own appreciation of the balanced, humane and informative way in which he has dealt with this problem tonight.

In passing—I do not say this for partisan purposes—may I say how much I regret the injection of rancour into an earlier discussion of this matter by the right hon. Gentleman the Prime Minister.[1] That intervention must be at the back of our minds as we discuss this Measure, and, indeed, my hon. Friend the Member for Rugby [Mr Wise] brought it to the forefront. I feel that it is better left in the background. The right hon. Gentleman the Prime Minister made a mistake. I think he is human and, therefore, it is not surprising. I think the temptation now is to exploit that mistake. I think it should be resisted, not out of tenderness for the right hon. Gentleman, because I do not think he needs it, nor, perhaps, deserves it, but because if we persist in keeping the discussion on the level to which it was unfortunately debased it will make it much more difficult to find the solution to the problem which involves not only the peace and happiness of many millions in this country at the present time but, as the Home Secretary has said, of generations of people to come.

Now I should like to say a word about the Act. To me the most that can be said for it is that it is a disagreeable necessity. I do not take very seriously the point made by members of the Government that the basic point at issue is one of consultation with the Commonwealth. I feel that, at the best, this view is wrong-headed, and at the worst a little hypocritical. I believe that there is general agreement that there should be some control, and far more important than the actual provisions of the Act are the manner and tone in which we discuss its provisions tonight and on other occasions.

---

[1] Mr Wilson had attacked the new Member for Smethwick, Mr Peter Griffiths, who had been involved in racial controversy during the campaign in which he defeated Mr Gordon Walker and suggested that he should be treated as 'a parliamentary leper'. The Reverend Mother of the leper colony in my constituency at East Hanningfield wrote to me to protest at the harmful effect of using the word 'leper' in this context. The Prime Minister wrote personally to her apologizing, but not to Mr Griffiths!

My hon. Friend the Member for Rugby criticized the Act because there were loopholes in it, and the right hon. and learned Gentleman the Home Secretary spoke of evasion of the Act and of a level of evasion which would be tolerable. I should like to make this point, that it is precisely because there are loopholes in the Act, because there is the possibility for a certain amount of evasion, that the Act is tolerable. If I may use an illustration, which may not be familiar to the Committee but will be familiar to my hon. Friend the Member for Uxbridge [Mr Curran], it is rather like the Roman index for forbidden books, which is tolerable because to some extent it is unenforceable. If the Act were tightened and were to be made foolproof it could be done only at the price of an intolerable invasion of the very precious and basic liberty of all Commonwealth citizens to visit the mother country freely and with the minimum of interference. A certain amount of evasion, I think, is worth paying for the preservation of this freedom.

I should like to see one liberalizing of the law. It was discussed in relation to the previous question of aliens. I should like to see the establishment of an appeals tribunal for Commonwealth citizens—it should certainly be established if one for aliens is to be established. People excluded from this country on health or other grounds should have an opportunity of appeal against executive decisions to a more impartial tribunal.

Of course, it will be said that we are in danger of being swamped by immigrants. Perils come and go. We had the yellow peril in the past and we have the black peril at the moment. Doubtless there will be some other coloured peril in the future. I do not think that this peril of being swamped by immigrants was ever very much more than a myth. Basically, immigrants come to this country because there is work for them to do, and that is borne out by the very interesting statement of the Home Secretary who said that the rate of unemployment amongst immigrants was 2·5 per cent, a very low figure indeed. There is a built-in economic regulator of immigration, in the actual state of our economy. This was, I think, proved in 1958 and again in 1959, when the rate of immigration fell dramatically when there was a mild recession.

I think it is right that we should pay tribute to the work, the excellent work, which immigrants, on the whole, do. The Home Secretary referred to their work in the National Health Service. Anyone who has been in hospital knows how true this is. If there be prejudice, then let it be prejudice on the side of liberty, and let this Act be liberally interpreted.

Liberalism today—and I say this with a proper sense of respect for the right hon. Member of Orkney and Shetland [Mr Grimond] and his gallant band who occupy nearly three-quarters of the second bench below the Gangway—is not so much a party but a frame of mind. It is an attitude to social and moral problems which is the fruit of centuries of free and ordered government. It is found in every part of this Committee, and I would also like to say on this issue in particular that illiberalism is found in every part of this Committee, too.

One other principle of the Act to which I should like to refer is that, whatever the controls at the ports, once a Commonwealth citizen has been admitted to this country he ranks equally with other citizens. The right hon. and learned Gentleman said that we should not have any second-class citizenship. How much I agree with that. We should deplore any attempt to do so. We should particularly deplore any attempt to deprive immigrants of the full protection of the courts. I know that we are not discussing the deportation proceedings tonight, but may I say in passing that any question of taking the jurisdiction over deportation away from the courts and giving it to the executive authority should be firmly resisted.

If the rights of those who immigrate to this country cannot be assured by the ordinary, normal, social processes, then I believe that there is a case for intervention by the legislature, and I was very interested in the right hon. and learned Gentleman's announcement that it is the Government's intention to introduce legislation to make certain forms of racial discrimination illegal. We must all regret the situation which has created the need for such legislation, but if it be necessary to secure one of the things which make life in this country worth living, namely, equality before the law, we as a legislature should not be afraid to take the necessary steps to ensure the enjoyment of basic human rights.

The right hon. and learned Gentleman gave us a lot of figures, and we are most grateful to him for them. I estimate that under the Act this year the net immigration will be between 70,000 and 90,000, but what folly it would be to admit even one immigrant to this country unless we are prepared to make an intense effort both in housing and education so that the problems of these immigrants are solved. I refer particularly to overcrowding which is a great social problem, and which causes such social tensions.

I am not saying that there should be preferential treatment for those who immigrate to this country, because, if we gave preferential treatment as such, we would merely increase tensions and not lessen them. But, at the same time, it is the duty of local authorities to see that those who come into this country and contribute to our wealth and prosperity are not, by reason of their social position, denied the amenities of civilized life. It is equally the duty of local authorities and other voluntary bodies to do all that they can to help those English residents who suffer most from the inevitable tensions created by new arrivals and who bear the burden of this problem literally on their doorsteps.

We often speak of a multi-racial Commonwealth, and we speak of it with pride. Today, in Britain, for good or ill, we have, and we are, a multi-racial society. Life would be easier were it not so. It would be simpler if we put up the shutters now and said, 'No admission', but I think that we would lose by that more than we would gain.

We should welcome the fact that we are a multi-racial society, because it makes us sharers in the greatest problem, apart from the problem of war and peace, which faces us in the twentieth century, namely, how men and women of different colours and different creeds are to live side by side and to work out their destinies in friendship and goodwill.

Today there are many people who are perplexed about Britain's role in the world. I believe that this debate highlights one contribution which we can make. We can build up a society in Britain which, for fairness, justice, and tolerance on the racial issue will be a model for the rest of the world. If this is successful, it will be a triumph not for power but for example. I believe that, if it can be achieved it will be something worthy to rank with the greatest of our successes in the past.

This poem appeared in the Spectator *on 30 May 1969.*

Norman Conquest

Oh, isn't praying simply great
When even saints are up to date?
Now Christopher's travelling days are done
And Barbara's jumped her last sad gun,
While St Cecilia leaves the stage
To music swinging with the age.
Quitting their altars, they now yield room
To St John-Stevas, I presume.

                                        Christopher Hollis

Anthony Eden died on 14 January 1977. This appreciation was published in the Catholic Herald *later that month.*

A Great Foreign Secretary

The passing of Anthony Eden—and it is surely by this name rather than by the ermined camouflage of Lord Avon that we all remember him—marks more than the death of an eminent man.

It signifies the end of an era and resurrects a past which, so swift is the passage of events in modern times, seems light years ago, although in truth it is only a few decades since he was one of the dominating statesmen on the world stage.

He became Foreign Secretary in 1935 at the extraordinarily early age of 38, when diplomacy was still dominated by the European Powers and when both the United States and Soviet Russia were brooding presences on the sidelines of international politics, of immense potential but whose power and interests were somehow muffled and withdrawn.

'Great Britain' still had a real meaning: the seat at the top table was ours not by courtesy, or by history, but by right. Anthony Eden was the last of the 'great' British Foreign Secretaries in that he was the last who could really profoundly influence the tide of world affairs.

Among the many ironies of his career, perhaps the greatest is that it should have fallen to him, by the fatal miscalculation over Suez, to have revealed to the world what had in effect long been a fact—our decline from that of great to medium power.

Since then the descent has been continuous, and we now find ourselves near the bottom of the second division and still going down. Suez telescoped into a few weeks what it would have taken another decade to demonstrate, namely that the British Empire was gone and had passed beyond the point of recall. Britain's impotence was revealed for everyone to see.

I remember those days well, and although I was not in Parliament at the time was passionately against the intervention on both moral and pragmatic grounds. I ended up by being anti-everyone, anti-Eden, anti-Nasser, anti-American and anti-Russian!

I would certainly not have gone into Suez, but having gone in I would equally certainly not have come out, and longed for the British Forces to press on and reach the other end of the canal.

I was in close touch with Edward Boyle during those weeks and, not for the last time, he represented the liberal conscience of the Tory Party and won both admiration and obloquy.

His resignation from the Government was hailed by many of us as an act of great courage, and I recall that Lady Violet Bonham-Carter arranged a dinner party in his honour which turned out to be something of an anticlimax.

By the time the dinner was actually held, Suez was over, Anthony Eden had gone, Harold Macmillan was Prime Minister and Edward Boyle was back in the Government again! Such are the swift vagaries of politics which make it such a fascinating (I was almost going to say pastime) but will settle for occupation.

Why did Anthony Eden act in such a manner and pursue a policy which was so contrary to his previous record and experience? It was not through lack of knowledge: despite his debonair appearance he had a capacity for hard work and application to problems unequalled amongst his contemporaries.

It was not malevolence: collusion was not in his nature. It was in fact (and this is what makes him such a tragic figure) miscalculation.

He was, as Lord Blake has pointed out, a figure worthy of Greek tragedy—the great man who in the enjoyment of high reputation and prosperity brings disaster on himself not by depravity but by some great error.

He was led to this by his own past experience. He drew the wrong lesson from history, and a parallel between Nasser's seizure of the Suez Canal and Hitler's occupation of the Rhineland.

The situations were different. Nasser was not intent on an expansionist policy and the Egyptians are not the Germans: above all, the relative position of Britain and France had altered.

In 1936 or even in 1938, Britain and France acting together could have halted Hitler: by 1956 no Western nation could act successfully in military matters without the support of the United States, and at crucial moments this was withheld. Eden hated and distrusted Dulles, and with good reason.

Suez was tragic, but the event although it looms large, has not eclipsed the earlier achievements. The obituarists in the newspapers would have us believe that it had (I except *The Times*) but it is not so.

The public, who in these matters are often a much better guide than the professionals, recall him not as the man of Suez but as the gallant officer, the patriot, the statesman who rumbled Hitler and Mussolini and stood up against them, who would not be 'taken for a ride' by Chamberlain and who at the country's darkest hour (which was 1938, not 1940) stood for strength and honour and principle in international affairs.

Anthony Eden was not a great Prime Minister but he was a very great Foreign Secretary. He was also a man of singular charm and attractions—a man of sharp perceptions and great strength of purpose.

England loved and admired him because in a striking way he embodied the best side of the national character: he was in appearance what all Englishmen would like to be: his virtues were English virtues, and that is why he is so widely mourned in his country today.

Lord Rupert Nevill died on 18 July 1982. This tribute to him appeared in the Tatler *in October 1982.*

Lord Rupert Nevill

Lord Rupert Nevill—a beautiful name for a beautiful person. Rupert's charm both fascinated and beguiled. His courtesy and consideration for others conquered hearts: Prince Charming in name and deed. Those perfect manners—the flower of charity; that precious gift of putting people at their ease and causing them to feel magnified rather than diminished in his presence. Charm can be a facile and dangerous endowment, used to hide an inner heartlessness. Rupert's charm was not of that order: it was grounded in true feeling and rooted in genuine sympathy. Hence the sense of real deprivation at his passing: on the day of his funeral the path from Eridge church to the graveside was lined by the flowers of friends. Rupert's capacity for friendship was one of his loveliest gifts. He was an acute judge of character and could be devastating in putting down pretension. His personal judgements were rather like the collective ones of the House of Commons: people got a fair assessment neither above nor below their true worth.

He combined good judgement with good taste. Micky's was the creative hand in the domestic arrangements at Horsted and St James's, but Rupert was never indifferent to what was being done: he noticed, suggested and counselled. Flowers—inside and outside—were for him a continuing delight. He was a genial and welcoming host—Horsted was the setting for a gracious, grand but cosy hospitality, redolent of another era. His sense of fun reverberated happily in that house: gaiety and laughter were the hallmarks. He enjoyed unmalicious gossip and could provide a few titbits himself.

On important matters of state his discretion, as befitted a counsellor of the monarch, was rock-like. He was near the centre of that magic circle, both as servant and as friend, but you would never have guessed that from his conversation. Prince Philip, whom he served so faithfully and well, paid him a rare and right last tribute when he read the lesson from the Book of Wisdom of Solomon at his obsequies.

All his gifts and graces were enhanced by resting on a basis of right values both moral and religious. He was a devoted husband and a loving father. He probably never reflected on the strength and comfort this gave to all his friends. Those forty years of fidelity and love formed a well on which many drew. I think of Tom Moore's line: 'And from love's shining circle the gems drop away.' It is and will be a consolation to us all as the years pass and the shadows lengthen to look forward to the reconstitution of that circle in both memory and hope.

This appreciation of Michael Joseph Canavan (1905–83) was published in the Catholic Herald *on 20 May 1983.*

Michael Joseph Canavan

The name of Michael Joseph Canavan was not a household word; I don't suppose many, outside the little walled garden of the Institute of Charity in England had ever heard of him. Yet his passing on Sunday 8 May at the age of 78 will leave a void in the lives of all those who knew and loved him.

The manner of his death was surprisingly public and dramatic for such a private and inner directed person. It took place at the golden jubilee celebrations of Grace Dieu, the preparatory school for Ratcliffe. There were two guest speakers—Fr Michael and myself. The golden glory was rendered more lustrous by the fact that it was also the fiftieth anniversary of Fr Michael's entry into the Rosminian order.

That morning I had attended his last Mass with him. With the usual English optimism, a triumph of hope over experience, the school authorities had set up the altar for the celebration on Grace Dieu's beautiful lawns.

But the weather too was typically English and Fr Michael and I followed the Mass from the headmaster's study, which thus was transformed into a combination of private oratory and medieval squint. As Augustine Birrell once observed, for Catholics 'It is the Mass that matters', and it matters for a priest most of all. So I was privileged to share such a sacred moment.

Afterwards when he came to introduce me on the platform he chose as his theme the purpose of Christian education, which he declared was not financial gain nor even academic success but, in the words of the penny catechism: 'To know, love and to serve God in this world and to be happy for ever with Him in the next.' These were his valedictory words: immediately afterwards he lost consciousness and that evening he passed into eternity.

No one who knew him could doubt for a moment he is in God's presence. He had a rare combination of gifts, not always found in religious people, that of a loving human kindness with a deep personal spirituality. Most of his life was passed in teaching at Ratcliffe, Grace Dieu and elsewhere and what he imparted was precisely what he outlined in his final words—the primacy of the spiritual.

There must be many men today in different parts of the world who are grateful to him for that initiation into the secret life of the Spirit. As he said himself in his farewell address: 'It is one thing to know about Christ, another thing to know him. You can't teach this: you catch it.'

Michael Canavan was headmaster of Grace Dieu from 1948 to 1956, then after a gap he returned as spiritual director for more than a decade, before finally coming back again in 1979, for what was styled retirement but was full of activity and service to others. He even developed an apostolate in the United States, which he visited every year, and balanced the fevered American extroversion with his own serene contemplative spirit.

So it was at Grace Dieu that his life's work unfolded. He loved the place. He had a delicate response to the beauties of nature and a sense of history.

He appreciated the importance of Grace Dieu as a centre of the nineteenth-century Catholic revival in England, the house which was long the home of the gothic enthusiast Ambrose Phillipps De Lisle and from which the passionate and ascetic Gentili carried out his mission to the villagers of the Midlands, surely one of the most extraordinary episodes of the Second Spring.

There is a holiness of places as well as of persons and in Fr Michael's residence at Grace Dieu they came together.

He was imbued with the serenity of the Rosminian spirit, at the heart of which is found an abiding trust in divine providence. This is not a form of quietism, although it is sometimes misrepresented as such—Rosmini's own tempestuous career gives the lie to that, but a willingness after all the effort and engagement to leave the result to God.

Rosmini never tried to write both sides of the equation: he never forgot that God often prefers to write straight with crooked lines.

So Fr Michael maintained his trust in Providence to the end and received a last gift of graciousness in being granted not only a happy but a painless death. A death in such circumstances might at first sight seem shocking but it was nothing of the kind. It had its own proportion and fittingness. It came at a moment of achievement and fulfilment, amongst the people and in the place he loved.

One looks back to that day not with sadness but joy. His friends will miss him profoundly but they will be consoled by the thought that they have gained an advocate at the court of courts before the King of Kings. *Requiescat in pace.*

This letter on the riots which erupted in different parts of Britain in 1981 was published in The Times *on 15 July 1981.*

Roots of the Riots

Sir,—On Thursday the House of Commons will have the opportunity to discuss the riots which have disfigured our national life over the past weeks. The House is the representative of the nation so may I hope that it will rise to the occasion, transcend party politics and speak for the whole of our people. Nothing would be more damaging to the body politic than the matching of the physical violence which some of our great cities have had to endure with verbal violence at Westminster.

Furthermore, there is no need for it. There is a wide measure of agreement on how the crisis needs to be tackled and the duty of the Commons is to make this clear, not to obscure it. The Prime Minister has been quite right to stress that the first duty of the Government is to resist violence, securing the punishment of malefactors, and restoring the rule of law. In this aim she has the full support not only of the Leader of the Opposition and other party leaders but of every Member of the House of Commons.

There is also a consensus that the root and long-term causes of the riots need to be identified and remedied. Repression in these circumstances is never enough, reconciliation and reform are co-ordinate duties with the upholding of the law. Of course there is no simple or single answer—Brixton, Southall, Liverpool,

Birmingham and Leicester require separate analysis—but there is equally no doubt of the existence of a shared background of urban decay, allowed to proceed unchecked for decades and high unemployment especially amongst the young, which has reached horrendous new heights. I recall the words of Stanley Baldwin, one of Britain's great reconciling Prime Ministers in the twenties: 'Unemployment deprives men of hope: it deprives them of faith: and without faith and hope it deprives them of love—love of home and love of country.' As I warned in the House of Commons debate on unemployment on 24 June: it is a moral evil of the first order which if left unchecked 'will destroy not only the traditions of civility that are so important to public life, but our cohesion as one nation, and ultimately, it will undermine our free institutions themselves.'

Is it not time for a national effort to meet national crisis? Should not the parties come together with the Churches and the employers and the unions to establish common ground on the basis of which we can proceed? I am not arguing for a coalition but for joint effort to meet one of the gravest social challenges we have faced since the war. And surely such an initiative comes naturally to a Conservative Party which over the years has seen society in terms of a trust, drawing its cohesion from the observance of mutual obligation with its rulers ready to employ where necessary the engine of government to promote the wellbeing of the people? We need to get away from the sterile conflict between individual and the state and return to the idea of community and re-establish, especially in our cities, a true *koinonia*, a shared life of co-operation and reconciliation by those who hold their basic ideas in common. Social measures must be based on and inspired by this concept if they are to succeed.

This address was given to the Tory Reform Group at the Conservative Party Conference at Blackpool on 13 October 1981.

Prophecy and Politics: the Tory Future

CONSTRUCTIVE CRITICISM

The conference which opens today at Blackpool is clearly one of the most crucial in our history: its decisions, its style and its tone will deeply influence not only the immediate future of the party but its long-term destiny as well. Those of us who see ever more clearly the dangers which lie ahead and are free to speak out, are morally bound to raise our voices clearly and unambiguously in warning, identifying the perils which threaten us and counselling how they may yet be countered and avoided. Above all our criticism must be constructive not destructive and we must have constantly before our minds the common purpose which animates and inspires all Tories, wet or dry or merely damp—the return of a Conservative Government at the next election able to safeguard the gains which have undoubtedly been made and to guide the nation through the perplexities of the closing decades of the century.

This is the third year in succession in which I have addressed what is so inadequately described as a 'fringe' meeting at our party conference. When I spoke to you at your annual dinner in October 1979, at a moment of justified triumph for the party, I was the first member of the Cabinet to give public warning of the dangers of seeking to separate the economic and the social aspects of our policies and to declare my own agnosticism on the economic theology of monetarism. I stressed then that while I fully supported the policy of reducing public expenditure, that it was as a means and not as an end, and declared the ends to be: 'the provision of incentives for the creation of wealth, the supply of investments for the modernizing of our industry: the removal of the blocks which prevent the gifts and talents of our people from realizing their full potential.' That analysis is as valid today as when it was first made but it would be a brave man who would claim that those ends have yet been achieved. I warned further against what I called 'the danger of elevating our economic priorities into absolute moral principles from which it is impossible to deviate or develop in any circumstances': who can say that that danger has been avoided today?

Last year, while still a member of the Cabinet, I developed this theme, more specifically and more urgently to your fellow organization the Bow Group, during the Brighton Conference.

PROPHETIC WARNING

This year, as the political skies around us darken and the dangers deepen, I once again raise my voice in prophetic warning about the courses we must follow if we are to avoid what I increasingly fear could be an electoral catastrophe. What do I mean by prophecy in the political context? Prophecy does not claim to foresee the future, that is soothsaying, and as the witches demonstrated in *Macbeth*, it constitutes an uncertain science. Neither is there any evidence that politicians are endowed with clairvoyance, rather the reverse. The prophetic voice in politics is rather different but perhaps more important: it interprets the party to itself, it points to key features in the political landscape which its leaders have overlooked, it reminds members of the party of convictions which they may have forgotten they possessed. In government the prophetic voice can be raised but is necessarily muffled by the doctrine of collective ministerial responsibility: on the back benches it can ring out loud and clear. It was for that reason, amongst others, that when the Prime Minister requested me to leave the Cabinet, I declined the offer of another ministerial post and tendered my resignation from the Government. I wished to be free to speak my mind on behalf of the party.

THREE PRINCIPLES

There are three principles which the party needs to hold constantly in mind during our debates this week at Blackpool, debates which will be followed through the media with close attention by friends and enemies alike as well as by those of no fixed party allegiance but who are looking for a political home to afford them shelter and comfort. Let us remind ourselves that this last and crucial group, probably larger than at any other time in our political history, will be following our discussions not with the avid enthusiasm of partisans but with the cool and critical eye of detached observers.

THE CENTRE GROUND

The first point is this: in British politics it is the centre ground that is vital. Those who occupy it win elections, those who vacate it or appear to do so, lose them. It is because our party has never for long lost sight of this efficient truth that we have remained for so long a party of government: a party unique in European, or for that matter in American, experience which dares to glory in the name Conservative and which has nevertheless won the majority of elections which have taken place over the last hundred years. The centre ground is not determinant in other European countries—in France, for example, as General de Gaulle knew so well, the pendulum swings between the discipline of authoritarianism and the delights of anarchy, why should it be so in Britain? The answer, as both Bagehot and Burke knew so well, is that it is the terrain which most accords with the national character, the psychological reality which alters least in a world of ceaseless flux and change. In England it is the middle principles which matter: the English mind as Bacon pointed out likes to work on 'stuff', it is distrustful of extreme theoretical conclusions however logically they may be entailed, it likes to shuffle over the hitches in the argument to arrive at sensible and common-sense conclusions. It is no accident that the fiercest proponents of monetarist theories have been academics from universities either on the Continent or from the United States. And what is all this verbal sparring about 'consensus' and 'conviction' politicians? Are not those who believe in liberality, moderation and compassion in politics as convinced of their value as those theoreticians who would refashion England into a new model with their harsh logic and pitiless economic doctrines— the twentieth-century equivalents of nineteenth-century utilitarians—or 'brutalitarians' as Disraeli branded them. It was another great Tory Prime Minister, Stanley Baldwin, who declared: 'Socialism and Laissez Faire are like the North and South poles: they do not exist.'

THE COMPLEXITY AND HUMANITY OF POLITICS

The second principle I wish to lay before you this afternoon is equally important: to subordinate politics to economics and within that thraldom to select a single economic end, the abatement of inflation, as the one to be pursued regardless of all other values and considerations, is not only to turn politics into a gamble on ground which since the war has been marked not by success but failure, but even worse it is to subscribe to a false and distorted view of human nature. The presentation of man as an economic animal may well be appropriate in a Marxist party but to find such a vision holding sway within the Tory Party, the party in the state which above all others has a clear view of the moral nature of man with all its complexities and imperfections, is indeed strange. There is nothing Tory in subordinating man with his individual uniqueness, his inalienable freedom, his immortal destiny to the demands of production, of market forces, of the creation and consumption of wealth. Who would have thought that we could live to see the day when economic materialism could deck itself out in Tory colours and claim to be not only the authentic voice of Conservatism but its only legitimate manifestation, yet this is precisely the theme of what has been arrogantly styled 'The New Conservatism'.

THE MORAL CONSTITUENCY

The third truth which no Tory should ever lose sight of is that politics is about people of flesh, not about bloodless and impossible abstractions but about men and women who are at one and the same time virtuous, flawed, imperfect, aspiring and struggling. Of course the talented must be encouraged to develop their talents but the talents themselves, like beauty or inherited wealth are given not earned. No merit exists in the endowment although there may be some—and this can be exaggerated—in their development. Furthermore the Tory knows that talent like property is held in trust to be used not for self-aggrandizement but for the good and benefit of all. It is to people then that we address ourselves and to no ordinary people, the British people, a nation with a long and distinguished history characterized save for short and untypical interludes by generosity and kindliness; a nation with institutions of unique continuity and effectiveness supported by a high degree of social cohesion and a sense of community, and which has developed a practical moral sensibility unmatched anywhere in the world. This is the country where the natural virtues still flourish even if the supernatural ones appear temporarily to have withered away. Britain is the country of compassion and concern where no charitable appeal goes unheeded, where care of neighbour, relief of suffering, help to others, are the warp and woof of our daily lives. There is in our country an extended moral constituency made up of citizens who look to public life not for what they can get out of it but for what they can contribute, who will that the quality of life be improved, who care about the health, employment and wellbeing of their fellows, who want to see our hospitals and schools improved and who are proud if our arts flourish.

WORLD PROBLEMS AND THE CHURCHES

Furthermore it is this constituency which regularly raises its eyes to gaze beyond our own moat and which is deeply concerned about the two great problems now confronting the human race, the threat of nuclear annihilation and the ever-growing gap between the rich and prosperous nations of the north and the poverty-stricken and famine-ridden nations of the south. The moral constituency has a major component of young people—we would have cause for alarm if it did not—but it comprises members of all age groups and classes, the mature and reflecting as well as the idealist and impulsive. Can anyone in this hall today conclude that the Conservative Party is today addressing that constituency in the terms and tone worthy of the issues with which its members are concerned? There is one particular sign of the times which we ignore at our peril and that is the growing gap between the Churches and the Conservative Party. It used to be said satirically that the Church of England was the Tory Party at prayer: how badly that joke would misfire today. What have the aridities of monetarism to say to the moral conscience of this nation and its great contemporary interpreters Archbishop Runcie or Cardinal Hume, or the never to be forgotten Barbara Ward? Are we not becoming the prisoners of a rhetoric which stigmatizes many of our fellow citizens as enemies, which like a lightning conductor draws upon our own heads the responsibilities for an economic recession whose primary causes lie in world not national conditions, and which makes us appear indifferent to the social issues and values which have for so many years been at the heart of the Tory tradition?

THE GRAVEST CHALLENGE

This is the background against which we have to confront the gravest challenge which the Tory Party has faced in its long history. I said earlier and I used the word advisedly that we could face an electoral catastrophe: let me spell out what I mean. The British people will not vote for an extremist party whatever its political hue. This means that the present Labour Party will find it virtually impossible to win the next general election. The old constitutional and moderate Labour Party is deader than the dodo. Whatever the cosmetic cover-up at Brighton last month the fratricidal war amongst the band of brothers will continue. The Labour Party has become like Ulster a political territory in which two rival races with different aims and different ideologies are fighting a war to the death in which there can be neither compromise nor conciliation. The Left has lost a battle by a whisker but it has not lost the war and that struggle it is likely to win in the end. At the very moment when the Labour Party is *in fact* turning itself into an extremist organization we have contrived to make ourselves *appear* to be marching to a similar dead end. The only conceivable beneficiaries of this grotesque situation must be the alliance of Liberals and Social Democrats which is heading for the centre ground and offering a soft option to those disinclined to make hard choices.

I well remember the election of February 1974 when the electorate was confronted with a choice between two major parties, both of which it disliked: night after night Mr Thorpe and his Liberal supporters appeared on the nation's television screens offering the seductions of a third way and they very nearly pulled it off. The prize slipped from their grasp for one reason only—the Liberals did not look as if they could form a Government. That trump card is no longer in our hand: the alliance does look like a credible alternative and it could emerge in the next Parliament to hold the balance of power, to constitute the largest single party or even with enough seats to form a Government. In any of these events proportional representation is likely to be introduced with the effect of perpetuating not a right centre accord but a left centre consensus. In such a situation the Conservative Party would be isolated and likely to be consigned permanently to a position of right-wing impotence. That may be a nightmare but it is also the long-term lesson of the polls with their persistent and unprecedented figures of support for a centre grouping. Public opinion polls are not the end of the story but they are certainly the beginning of the argument. To treat what they are saying with scorn or to close our eyes to the conditions which are producing them is the grossest form of folly. I give this solemn warning today at the outset of our conference not to make your flesh creep, much less to issue a self-fulfilling prophecy but because there is still time to save the situation although that time is now beginning to run out. The next twelve months are the crucial ones in which we can pull our party round and through.

MRS MARGARET THATCHER

There is no question of changing our leader: Margaret Thatcher enjoys not only the confidence of the parliamentary party but her courage and resolution still command admiration even amongst those who reject her policies or who have reservations about them. It is not a question either of executing a humiliating U-turn, that *ignis fatuus*, whose baleful glare seems to deprive some people of all sense of proportion, reality and flexibility. What is needed is a modification of policies to take account of changed circumstances since we came to office, namely the deepening world recession, the unprecedentedly high American interest rates, and above all the dreadful surge of unemployment.

A SIX-POINT CHARTER

I have outlined the principles which must guide us and they must lead to modified policies, new initiatives and a change of attitude and tone. I now put forward my suggestions as a six-point charter for the future. Let no one think in terms of disloyalty or faction: there is such a thing as loyal dissent and what we must have in the party is a period of open debate, not in code but in language which everyone can understand.

First, we need a change of tone—we must show by our words as well as our deeds the generosity, compassion and concern which we do in fact feel: the idealism of our party must be on display. The Government must be flexible and show itself to be willing and able to modify policies according to changing circumstances and need. As the great Lord Salisbury maintained: 'The commonest error in politics is sticking to the carcases of dead policies.' Let us free ourselves also of what Macaulay stigmatized as 'the ignorant pride of a fatal consistency'.

Second, we must make a comprehensive and national approach to the problems which confront us. Margaret must draw the different bodies of opinion within the party closer together not drive them further apart. The foolish advice given to her by sections of the Press to try and construct a Cabinet of only one point of view has already proved damagingly counter-productive. The Tory Party is a Church not a sect and a Broad Church at that, not a community of saints following a Messianic vision. In the country we must draw upon our tradition as the party of the nation and make it our first aim of policy to bridge the gulf between north and south. We must seek to associate our policies, as President Reagan has done so successfully in the United States, with the patriotic feelings of the nation as a whole. The monarchy in our constitution is the great unifying force but that reconciling and healing spirit should be drawn on more directly in our political life.

Third, we must recognize unemployment for what it is—a moral and social evil of the first order. Its reduction must now become our primary purpose: if we say we can do nothing about it we will soon be pushed aside by those who will. Let us have some sense of outrage at this conference about the truly horrific unemployment figures which deny man a fundamental dignity, the right to work, and less of what is becoming callous chatter about a leaner fitter British industry. You may be leaner but you are certainly not fitter if you are standing in a dole queue experiencing the degradation, humiliation and diminishment of being out of work. We must not only accept but proclaim that it is the duty and responsibility of government to create the conditions in which people will have the opportunity to work. If this means a moderate degree of reflation and the stimulation of some demand in the economy so be it. We must undertake studies into such matters as early retirement to find long-term solutions to the unemployment problem. A political party must always identify itself with emergent interests and issues.

Fourth, we must address ourselves effectively to the issues of nuclear war and of world hunger. Where nuclear weapons are concerned we must recognize that public anxiety about self-destruction is now world-wide: it is very much more than the hapless Michael Foot reliving the triumphs of his youth. It is as though there is welling up in the human consciousness a foreboding of some cataclysm to come. The moral imperative is not unilateral disarmament, but the urgent seeking of multilateral agreements both for the scaling down of these frightful weapons and their non-proliferation. It is the spread of nuclear weapons which is threatening to destabilize the balance of terror which has so far kept the peace. We need more than a pious genuflexion to mutual reduction of weapons: it must be made a major aim of foreign and defence policy. As to the Third World, far from cutting back on aid we should be seeking new ways of helping their peoples who thanks to the advance of modern technology have for the first time the chance to escape from the hideous treadmill of poverty, hunger and want, which has been their lot throughout the ages.

Fifth, we must show the country that we have something to say and something to offer on social as well as on economic issues. Here our theme should be the preservation and strengthening of the family. The maintenance, development and extension of child benefit provides the key to the future, and we must include within the parameters of our concern, the one-parent family, one of the fastest growing and most needy social groupings of our time. Let us speak out loudly and clearly on the preservation of moral and religious values in our schools. What has happened to all the work we did in this sphere while in opposition? Religious education is dying in our schools not through hostility but neglect. It needs to be treated professionally, it requires the support of tests and exams, but above all it requires dedicated and professionally trained teachers of which there is an increasing shortage. Let us continue and raise our support for the arts which provide us with returns out of all proportion to the public money invested in them, and let us avoid above all a return to that image of the Tory Party as a philistine party, an association which we have mercifully successfully shed. It is by their achievements in the arts that generations yet unborn looking back judge the societies of the past. Even Machiavelli knew, that power without glory is not worth possessing.

Sixthly, let us look to our institutions which it was Disraeli's counsel that we should preserve. We have already reformed the Commons by setting up a committee system which has done much to redress the balance between Westminster and Whitehall. Let us follow this up by entrenching and reforming the Upper House, now under a deadly challenge from the Left, and which this conference rightly made plain last year it wanted maintained and transformed. Let us reassert our historic support for the independence and autonomy of local government. It would be strange indeed if the Conservative Party were to espouse the socialist view that our county and borough councillors are mere agents of central government: it would never be forgiven if we destroyed their independence because we lacked the ingenuity and the will to abolish the unjust rating system and provide local government with a viable and autonomous means of financial support.

HOPE FOR THE FUTURE

Finally let me say this. No democratic government can survive without the trust, confidence and support of the people. We will not succeed in our task unless we offer the nation vision and ideals for the future and we will not do that unless we communicate a sense of hope: hope that the sacrifices that have been made have been made to some purpose, hope that from our present travails a better and more just society will emerge, hope that Britain in the future as in the past will contribute to the stability and peace of the world. In this task we have one incomparable ally—our native tongue. Let us use that to convince the country of the reasonableness and justice of our cause.

This speech was made in the House of Commons on 29 April 1982 and was my only one on the Falklands issue.

The Falklands

Despite some moments of rowdiness in the House, Members meet this afternoon in a sombre mood as the prospects of war loom before this country. There is no one in the House who is either a jingoist or a triumphalist, and I believe that we should congratulate my right hon. Friend the Prime Minister on having, in her opening remarks, so accurately caught the mood of the House. She was clear, analytical, constructive and moderate in her response to the remarks about the United Nations made by the right hon. Gentleman the Leader of the Opposition. Of course, she did not agree with him entirely—there are not many Members on this side of the House who would, but she did leave the door open—and I am sorry that he did not reply in kind to her.

In the rowdiness that ensued, for which the Leader of the Opposition must take prime responsibility, the House lost sight of the fact that my right hon. Friend the Prime Minister had rightly stressed throughout her speech that we were still looking for a political solution, that we would still prefer a diplomatic solution to the use of force.

We are right to take that attitude, for two reasons. The first is the gravity of the issue. Human lives are at risk—British and Argentine lives. No one has a right to be bellicose when other people's lives are at risk.

Secondly, we should support the political initiative, because it is vital that we should be seen to be doing so if we are to retain the support of world public opinion. That will be crucial in the coming weeks. The Leader of the Opposition has constantly stressed that important factor. There must be no suspicion in the minds of the leaders of other countries that we are not sincerely and committedly working for peace. Let us remember that even if the fighting escalates, in the end we shall have to come to diplomatic discussions; we shall have to come to consultations; we shall have to try once again to substitute the weapons of peace for those of war.

I agree with my hon. Friend the Member for Buckingham [Mr Benyon] that it would not be appropriate or useful for the House to attempt to discuss in detail the tactics of our naval task force. That must be a matter for those on the spot. We in this House must show that we have confidence in it. The South Georgia episode surely shows that that confidence is fully justified. It is vital that nothing that we say makes the task of our forces more difficult. We should heed the words of Admiral Woodward when he declared that our forces could well face a long and bloody campaign.

What is desirable is that, as far as possible, the House should speak with a clear and united voice. Of course the decisions are for the Government and the responsibility is for the Government, but they are immensely strengthened in decisions that they are taking on behalf of the nation if they can show that the House is more united than divided. What I have to say is intended as a contribution to that consensus and to set out certain principles that I believe are widely supported in the House and outside.

First, the entire House is agreed on the strength of our moral and legal case. And why not? Our sovereign territory has been invaded. Our citizens have been deprived of their rights, and there has been a brutal and flagrant violation of international law. If we look back over the whole history of international disputes, it is difficult to find a situation in which the moral issue has been as clear and unclouded as it is in the present case.

Secondly, of course, we continue to seek a political solution. Military force must be the arm of politics and diplomacy, and not the other way round. That has been fully accepted by Admiral Woodward. As the Leader of the Opposition made clear again today, the right hon. Gentleman and his colleagues in the Shadow Cabinet supported the dispatch of the task force, and continue to do so. But I must draw to the right hon. Gentleman's attention the point made by my right hon. Friend the Prime Minister, that if one dispatches a task force, whilst it is perfectly reasonable to suggest that it should be used in the last resort rather than the first or in the middle of events, it is inconsistent with that attitude to rule out its use altogether. Indeed, if one did that one would render its dispatch nugatory.

Thirdly, we must constantly have in mind that our task force is on the high seas and at risk. Of course the political aims are paramount, but we must face the fact that we could well reach a point where the safety and wellbeing of the forces must modify that. That is the point being made with increasing urgency by my right hon. Friend the Prime Minister. She is right to make it, because the nation would never forgive any Government who put our forces in jeopardy and then did not back them up and minimize the risks to them.

We should resolutely dismiss the anti-Americanism which has surfaced from time to time in our discussions and which we saw again at Prime Minister's Question Time today. There is no doubt about the massive support that this country is receiving from the American people. Like other hon. Members, I have recently been to the United States and I have seen that support for myself. In my view—other hon. Members may differ—it was wholly reasonable that at the first stage of the negotiations Mr Haig should take an impartial stance. We should be grateful to him for his indefatigable efforts to preserve peace.

But situations alter. It is now my opinion that the chances of preserving peace would be enhanced if the United States threw its weight openly and unreservedly behind Britain. There is nothing inconsistent between those two statements. It is merely recognition of the fact that the situation has developed and altered.

I have two further points that I wish to make only briefly, but I believe that they will become increasingly important. I make them as one who knows Latin America directly. We must never forget that our quarrel is not with the Argentine people. It is with the Argentine junta. It is crucial to distinguish between the two—to distinguish between an odious and corrupt regime which has denied human rights, which has sent people to their deaths, which is reigning by terror, and a people with whom this country has had long and historic ties. The junta is unworthy of the people whom it claims to represent. The attitudes to the Argentine people which have been taken, not in the House, but in some sections of our Press, are also unworthy. They are piling up trouble for the future.

British foreign policy in general, and Conservative foreign policy in particular, since the time of Castlereagh have been based not on the pursuit of abstract principles alone but on the protection of interests as well. What is the art of diplomacy but an attempt to decide possible conflicts between those two concepts?

Our first priority, of course, must be the wellbeing of the Falkland Islanders. They constitute a real community and they have rights of self-determination which are guaranteed by article 73 of the United Nations charter. I have my copy here as well. But there are other British interests in South America, and we must protect them. Countries such as Brazil, Mexico and Colombia have no sympathy with the Argentine, but if our views are expressed in a xenophobic fashion we shall drive them in that direction.

Let us always remember the context of the dispute. Latin America is the great continent of the future. It has immense resources and great potential, and its peoples are struggling endlessly for social justice and human rights. Let us not forget, either, that the Soviet Union is hovering, eager to get a foothold if it can for its programme of subversion and tyranny.

In resisting that threat Britain has a unique asset and that is our tradition of friendship with Latin American countries. I was delighted that the Prime Minister drew our attention to that in her opening remarks. After all, it was Canning, one of our greatest Prime Ministers, whose boast it was that he had called the new world into existence to redress the balance of the old.

I am not one of those who think that the House should not speak on these matters; that is what the House is for. I am not one of those who think that different views should not be expressed; it is right that they should. It would be absurd in a situation of this gravity, importance and complexity to suggest that there are not different views in the House, but I believe that underlying those differences of view there is basic unity and accord. I hope that the message that will go out from the debate is that once again the House of Commons is expressing the resolution and the will of a united nation.

In the summer of 1967 I went to Constantinople and visited the Patriarch Athenagoras. My impressions were recorded in the Catholic Herald *in June 1967. Pope Paul VI, who had first met the Patriarch in Jerusalem in 1964, also visited him in 1967, and this visit too was the subject of an article in the* Catholic Herald.

A Visit to the Patriarch

A few days ago, in the bright autumn sunshine, I found myself in the courtyard of the Phanar, the seat of the Orthodox patriarchate in Constantinople, on my way to see the Patriarch. From the simple eighteenth-century church of St George came the sound of chanting: it was the feast of St Euphemia, whose relics wrapped in blue silk and encased in a bronze casket are the church's most prized possession. They have followed the patriarchate faithfully throughout all its tribulations. Suddenly a tall, white-bearded, gaunt figure in flowing black, silver-topped cane in hand emerged from the shadows of the basilica and like some royal widow in mourning weeds moved with regal dignity into the enclosure. It was the Patriarch. A little old lady with wrinkled walnut face came running up to kiss his hand and overcome by emotion was seized with tears. Others followed and a tiny crowd surrounded His Holiness until suddenly he raised his hand and at once the people fell back. *Noli me tangere*—that's what it must have been like.

Patriarch Athenagoras received me upstairs in the study of his 'palace', a modestly furnished room decorated with portraits of Kemel Ataturk and Paul VI. I could not help contrasting this austerity with the pomp of the Vatican—the Roman baroque, the trappings, the sense of power. Somehow here in this Christian oasis set in a Muslim slum one felt nearer to the early Church. Here was the bride of Christ in poverty and adversity, a tiny faithful remnant, tolerated by the state because her weakness constituted no threat. One has to go to Constantinople to see the dimmed glories of Agia Sophia and the echoing emptiness of the great Byzantine church of St Irene, which once housed an ecumenical council, to realize how much the Eastern Church has suffered and to reflect that it was powerful and glorious centuries before the dome of St Peter's was raised against the sky of the Campagna. No wonder so many Orthodox feel bitter towards Rome, by whom they feel they were betrayed and abandoned. Rome has had the best of both worlds but Constantinople has been forced by history to look only towards the next.

I had met the Patriarch before both in England and in Turkey, and had been in Jerusalem for his historic meeting with the Pope, so that meeting him again was like being reunited with an old friend. He seemed to me to have grown thinner and frailer but within the gaunt frame (he is 6ft 4in tall) the spirit flamed as bright as ever. His eyes are dark and hypnotic and bright with life and fun. Evidently nothing has extinguished the boy within the prelate.

The Patriarch's devotion to the Pope is profound and real—'the second Paul' as he delights to call him. At the Pope's moment of greatest personal crisis—when *Humanae Vitae* had aroused dissension throughout the Church—a message of understanding and support from the Patriarch helped to sustain him. Patriarch Athenagoras looks forward to another meeting with the Pope in the not far distant future. We talked of course of ecumenism and the coming reconciliation between Catholicism and Orthodoxy. 'That day is coming,' said His Holiness in prophetic tones, 'I may not see it, but it will be. We love each other—there are no obstacles, no barriers.' I was reminded of Pope John, and that deep river of love he succeeded in releasing, carrying away the theological, jurisdictional and historical difficulties, like so much flotsam on the surface of the waters. It was Pope John again, when our audience was interrupted by the arrival of a young couple from the parish, who lifted up their newborn child to receive His Holiness's blessing.

Patriarch Athenagoras sees the end of dialogue not as the establishment of a corporate and juridical union—a merger between Rome and Constantinople— but rather the achievement of a full and reciprocal intercommunion between the two Churches. 'We share one chalice,' he said to me. 'When I went to Rome I was ready to celebrate with the Pope.' 'Why didn't you?' I cried, my imagination aflame at the thought of a gesture which would have reverberated throughout Christendom. 'Wasn't the Pope willing?' 'He was,' replied the Patriarch, and then with a twinkle in his eye, 'It was the theologians.' The Patriarch does not care for theologians and regards them with mischievous amusement. At our last meeting he commented: 'I often think it strange that the theologians in every Church seem to have had the same mother.' And, of course, in one sense, the Patriarch is right: at the level of love the divisions have gone, the obstacles are now cerebral. 'Why', he said 'do we not use the word "Christian" more often? It's the most beautiful word in the world.'

As to the infallibility of the pope, the Patriarch neither affirms nor denies it. 'Of course,' he said, 'the pope is infallible for you.' Here in a simple phrase was the essence of Cardinal Willebrands's celebrated Oxford sermon. You cannot abolish centuries of spiritual and theological apartheid 'at a stroke'. You have to live together in love, agreeing to differ on certain formulations, until time brings the fullest understanding and unity once more. His Holiness looks forward to the pan-Orthodox synod, which is likely to be held at Beirut, to inaugurate a new phase in the relations between East and West. . . .

Our conversation lasted nearly two hours—His Holiness speaks excellent English acquired in Corfu and the United States—and ended with an invitation to luncheon. I had an official engagement, but such an opportunity does not come every day, and fortunately I had the presence of mind to abandon it. The meal was simple but excellent—a family occasion shared with members of the Patriarch's household and the Metropolitan of Beirut, a distinguished theologian! At the conclusion of the meal the Patriarch said grace and I was fascinated by the

Orthodox form of the sign of the cross, made with three fingers as a symbol of the Trinity moving from right to left. The Patriarch must have caught my thought—holy antennae can pick up things unseen—as he passed from the head of the table, he bowed in front of me and with great deliberation he made the sign of the cross. It was in the Latin form.

In August 1978 I paid my first visit to China as the guest of the Chinese Government. On 17 August I visited the Catholic Cathedral in Peking. My impressions were recorded in articles published in the Catholic Herald *on 29 September, 17 November and 24 November 1978.*

Signs of Hope for the Future of China

To visit China is a great experience and one to cherish and reflect on for the rest of one's life. I was fortunate indeed that an invitation to go to Hong Kong last month opened the way for me to pay my first visit to the People's Republic, not as part of a delegation but *alone*, and as Queen Victoria found when she succeeded to the Throne (not to mention Miss Greta Garbo in a subsequent age) to be alone has a number of attractions.

I do not mean, of course, that I travelled from Canton to Peking and then on to Shanghai entirely unaccompanied—I had my fair share of guides and interpreters but I was able to go and see what I wanted rather than always having to accommodate myself to the wishes of fellow travellers, and was able to examine and discuss things in depth which would not have been possible had I been part of a group.

The first impression I want to record is the beauty of the southern Chinese landscape. China is an intensely agricultural country although much of its land is mountainous and barren; as a result the plains are intensely cultivated without a hectare of ground being wasted.

Visually the south of China still looks like an eighteenth-century print: in the background loom the blue hills providing a frame for the green rice and paddy fields with their great water buffalo and the immemorial peasants, straw-hatted and bent-backed, toiling as they have done for centuries to provide food for the millions of the Chinese nation.

Agriculture is the foundation of China's economy: the present Chinese leadership, following the example of Chairman Mao, puts agriculture first. Like him, they have an almost romantic veneration for the soil and the life which springs from it.

And there is a practical side to this outlook: famine has until recent years been an ever-present threat to the Chinese people. The leaders of the nation fear its recurrence, and they are determined to do all they can to keep the horror at bay.

My second impression is of the presence of huge numbers of people. No one knows for certain what the population of China now amounts to, but it is probably in the region of 900 million—a mind-paralysing figure.

In the towns there are people everywhere and the streets are filled with bicycles, which are the main means of transport. Cars are reserved for the official classes and for visitors: the Chinese factories put most of their automobile output into trucks and tractors.

The number of young people is striking, but there do not appear to be many children about. The Chinese Government has been conducting a vigorous campaign to reduce population growth and has had considerable success through a combination of policies: making contraceptives available free and insisting on a late marriage age.

Young men are not allowed to get married until they are 24 and women must be 18 or over. Great stress is laid on the desirability of small families, and to have more than two children is to risk condemnation as being anti-social.

My third impression is of the intense individualism of the Chinese. Despite the low standard of living, the drabness of their clothing, their concentration in urban masses, they somehow manage to convey an almost tangible sense of their own individuality.

Nothing is more absurd than to think that all Chinese look alike: they do not, and as soon as they get a chance I believe they will break out of both the baggy trousers and the restricting political parameters within which they are temporarily confined by economic necessity.

I never saw a people more unsuited to the over-simplifications and rigidities of Marxism than the Chinese. One of the ironies of the Far East situation is that the Chinese, who are individualist, should have turned to Communism while the Japanese, who are psychologically so much more collectivist, should have embraced capitalism.

The successes of the communist regime in China have been considerable: the standard of living is low but there is no starvation, and the degrading poverty of cities like Calcutta is mercifully absent. The plagues and the flies which used to be the scourges of old China have vanished.

The threat of a further population explosion has been averted and a moderate rate of population increase achieved. Industry is still primitive by Western standards and the factories tend to be shambolic, but there is movement forward.

Liberty in our sense of the word is unknown and everything has to be fitted into the ideological strait-jacket but, regrettable as this is, it has to be judged against the background of a history quite different from that of European liberal democracy. Even here there are signs of hope for the future.

China's Religious Traditions

During my visit to China in the summer, I was particularly anxious to discover what I could about the state of religion in the Chinese People's Republic.

China has one of the longest religious traditions in world history and the three traditional religions have been Confucianism, Taoism and Buddhism, all of which are more ethical and moral systems than religions in the Western worshipping sense.

All three lay stress on the interconnection of the spiritual and material orders rather than on the contrast between the Creator and the created, and on disharmony in nature rather than in the individual soul.

With the triumph of Marxism and dialectical materialism these philosophies have gone out of fashion or underground, and are afforded no official place in modern China.

China includes many millions of Muslims within its boundaries, and indeed they are so numerous as to make China the greatest Muslim power in the world—in the numbers sense. Christianity has always been a minority religion in China, but its roots go back many centuries.

It first reached China in Nestorian form from Persia under the Tang dynasty (618–917) and there is a record of a papal delegate—the Franciscan Giovanni de Carpine—having been sent to China by the Pope in 1425.

Christianity really took root in the sixteenth century with the arrival of the Jesuit Matteo Ricci (1552–1610) in Peking, who established considerable influence with the Emperor and high officials at court.

Fr Ricci had hopes at one time of an imperial conversion, and imagined that if this were achieved the Christianization of the rest of China would follow.

In fact, the Chinese leaders were much more interested by the Jesuits' scientific knowledge than their theological views. They provided the first contact between ancient Chinese civilization and Western science, but the prospects of a Christian China do not seem to have been very substantial.

Fr Ricci was a noted astronomer, and the Jesuit observatory instruments can still be seen in Peking as can no less than four cathedrals—huge churches which are found at the four points of the compass in Peking itself.

Three of these have been turned into factories or warehouses—as have the Catholic cathedral and the Anglican church which I visited in Canton—but the fourth or southern cathedral is still in use as a Catholic church.

There is also one Protestant church open in Peking, occupying the first floor of a private house. The non-Catholic Christian churches were reduced to four in 1958—Anglicans, Methodists, Presbyterians and Congregationalists—and finally amalgamated into one during the Cultural Revolution!

A Protestant service of Holy Communion is held every Sunday morning at 9.30, and I met two Protestant ministers at the house but they told me they had only a very small congregation, almost entirely from the embassies or visiting foreigners.

The Government provides the cash for maintenance and repairs and the Church has some funds of its own which help it to keep going.

I took the opportunity of one dinner with Chinese officials to raise the whole question of religion and religious liberty in China, and I was informed that there was full freedom of religion.

I am somewhat sceptical about this. There seems to be no means for religion to be made known to the people—no religious schools, no religious books or Press: and the opening of a handful of token churches and temples does not add up to religious freedom.

I also detected a strong strain of anti-papal feeling in official circles. At one point in our conversations I ventured to suggest that diplomatic relations might be opened up with the Vatican, but this was turned down out of hand.

The nub of the hostility lies in the fact that the Vatican maintains a papal mission in Taiwan—and that Taiwan has a representative at the Vatican. Until this diplomatic link is broken the prospects of a Vatican–Peking *rapprochement* do not look very bright.

One difficulty is that the Catholic Church in Taiwan is flourishing; there is a strong Catholic schools system, and even a Catholic university.

The establishment of diplomatic relations between the Vatican and Peking would have the same justification as the Ostpolitik of the Holy See in Europe. It would open up channels of information which are at present closed.

When I spoke to Bishop Wu of Hong Kong just before my entry into China it was plain that he knew very little of Catholics in China itself. The diplomatic difficulty could perhaps be met by changing the nunclature in Taiwan into an apostolic delegation accredited not to the Government but to the bishops.

A Catholic Interlude in Peking

The rain was pouring down out of a leaden sky as my car drew up in front of the Catholic cathedral in Peking. The cathedral is a huge gothic building dating back to 1900 and dedicated to the Immaculate Conception, but a Catholic church has occupied the site since the seventeenth century and through all subsequent vicissitudes.

The cathedral stands in a garden surrounded by a high wall which puts a barrier between it and the busy street outside.

As we approached, the door in the wall flew open and I was greeted by a youngish priest—he looked as though he might be in his early thirties, but Chinese faces are difficult for occidentals to date—in a beige Mao-type jacket with a Roman collar peering out over the top.

He led me into the cathedral, and it was like taking a step back in time into nineteenth-century France. The church was in a perfect state of preservation, spotlessly clean and with a splendid cluster of crystal chandeliers hanging from the ceiling. I calculated that it could seat six hundred on its highly polished wooden benches.

The high altar was where it should be, set against the eastern wall of the church and flanked by two altars in the side aisles—one dedicated to the Sacred Heart and the other to St Joseph. I noticed a confessional in the church which appeared to be functioning (although not with a penitent in it during the time of our visit).

I asked if I could go into the sacristy and we advanced into it with my eyes swivelling round, as though I were at Wimbledon, in order not to miss anything. The Mass vestments were laid out in the time-honoured style and the chalice and patten were ready waiting to be carried to the high altar. Hanging in the corner was one of the most splendid fur coats I have ever seen.

We had an animated talk in the sacristy and I was astonished when my priest friend informed me that there were one bishop and ten priests in residence at the cathedral. The 'old bishop', by which I presume was meant one validly consecrated before the break with Rome, had recently died and an 'acting bishop', consecrated ten years ago, was in charge.

I asked about the number of Catholics in Peking and was informed that they were between 50,000 and 60,000. The priest did not know about the situation elsewhere in China, but indicated that there were other Chinese bishops in existence. No students for the priesthood had come forward.

My visit was on a weekday, but Mass is celebrated every Sunday at 9.30. No sermon is allowed. The Mass is said in Latin except for the Epistle and the Gospel which are read in the vernacular. The congregation is almost entirely made up of foreigners, but one or two elderly Chinese attend.

I asked whether I could come to Mass on a weekday but was told it would be 'inconvenient' and difficult to indicate the precise time of celebration. Since ten priests were about, this did not make much sense unless the explanation in fact was that no permission is available for worshippers to come other than on Sundays.

The priest informed me that the Chinese turned out in larger numbers for the traditional festivals such as Christmas and Easter. I was also later informed by officials that it was possible for baptisms to be carried out, but of course I had no means of checking on the numbers or whether this was in fact so.

As we stood in the sacristy I raised the question of the relations with the Holy See, which were broken in 1958. How, I asked, could you have Catholicism without the pope?

The priest explained that it was not possible to have a 'foreign power' in China and that the Pope had committed the cardinal sin of recognizing the regime in Taiwan. Adding insult to injury, His Holiness was maintaining a diplomatic mission in Taiwan and was sending missionaries there.

The priest was friendly and affable enough and our conversation was quite open but of course there was an interpreter present throughout. As I walked down the aisle I was asking myself what would I have done had I been in a similar situation?

And I followed this up with another internal query. Would it be right to make an enforced break with Rome as the price of securing a Christian presence in Peking and some measure of freedom of worship?

If one asks the question historically the answer seems (especially in the light of the English experience) a straightforward negative, but somehow having to face up to the question in the setting of contemporary China made it more complicated. Should one compromise with wrong in order to secure some good?

Was Pius XII right to be circumspect in his public utterances about suffering Jews or should he have spoken out regardless of the conseqences? The question is a torturing one; but my conclusion at the end of my visit was that the religious gains for Chinese Catholics are marginal indeed but the advantage for the regime of having a showpiece cathedral considerable.

In January 1964 Pope Paul VI made the first papal visit to Jerusalem. It was also the first journey of a pope outside Italy since the reign of Pius VII in 1809. I was present at the event and sent this despatch to The Economist *in London. It was published on 11 January 1964.*

Pope Paul in Jerusalem

As the papal plane, emblazoned with Pope Paul's arms and the yellow and white Vatican colours, glided out of the cloudy sky to land at Amman on 4 January, a moment of history was born. Within minutes, eager to begin the pilgrimage, the slight white-clad figure of the Pope appeared at the plane's doorway, his arms extended in the embracing gesture, less dramatic than that of Pius XII, which he has made an intrinsic part of his style. In the piercing cold he hurried down the steps; King Hussein greeted him warmly. The band played the Vatican and Jordan anthems and a flock of white doves, symbolic of peace and friendship, fluttered into the air.

From Amman the papal cavalcade sped through the hills towards Jerusalem, making brief stops at the Jordan and at Bethany, where Lazarus was summoned back to life. As it approached the Damascus gate, the huge crowds of welcoming Muslims and Christians broke through the inadequate guard of police and Arab legionaries and engulfed the papal car. Protocol was scattered to the winds. Jostled and buffeted by the frenzied but friendly crowds, the Pope was carried along the Via Dolorosa towards the Church of the Holy Sepulchre, escaping injury only because of the squad of burly Vatican plain-clothes men who formed a protective phalanx about him. The Pope reached the Holy Sepulchre, serene but strained. The three elderly cardinals with him, Cardinal Cicognani, Secretary of State, Cardinal Tisserant, dean of the Sacred College, and Cardinal Testa, secretary of the Congregation for the Eastern Churches, prudently abandoned the struggle and sought refuge in a Muslim shop.

Beneath the crumbling, peeling dome of the Church of the Holy Sepulchre, wild confusion reigned. Cameramen and Italian television technicians, who had monopoly coverage, swarmed everywhere. Some clung to the scaffolding, others poked their cameras through the candlesticks on the tinselly altar set up by the Franciscans, some were even perched on the shrine of the Holy Sepulchre itself. Patriarchs, bishops, monsignori and high Vatican and Jerusalem officials were crammed together in an undignified gaggle at the side of the altar, fighting for every foothold. Friars, police and legionaries shouted, pushed and struggled. Above their heads the string of electric light bulbs suspended to supplement the cluster of smoky oil lamps fused and burst into flame. The tightly packed crowd mercifully failed to panic, and the leaping flames were beaten out with a Bedouin head-dress hoisted into position on a silver-topped patriarchal stave. Throughout it all, Pope Paul maintained an unshakeable dignity. Rapt and exalted, he celebrated Mass before the tomb.

Immediately afterwards he entered the sepulchre and laid a golden olive branch there. Then, in the tiny space in front of the tomb, he received Catholic, Orthodox and Protestant dignitaries. When the Lutheran leader removed his hat, the Pope, in a spontaneous ecumenical gesture, replaced it. Then he was borne out of the church, his white skull-cap bobbing through the crowd, his hands raised in blessing, his feet seeming to hover over, rather than touch, the ground, until he reached the shelter of his car and the safety of the apostolic delegation. One realized that the *sedia gestatoria* used in Rome is much more than a piece of ceremonial flummery. Responsibility for the chaos rests jointly on Jordanian insufficiency in face of the overwhelming enthusiasm, and Franciscan pettiness, which insisted on keeping control of the arrangements in the Basilica in the order's shaky hands; but the lesson was learnt. The papal holy hour that night in Gethsemane was liturgically excruciating but dignified and orderly. When Pope Paul visited Bethlehem on Monday to celebrate Mass in the grotto of the Nativity, troops lined the street, barbed wire and wooden barricades had been erected and photographers were kept under tight control. The Pope passed through the narrow door and down the precipitous steps to the manger in safety.

In Israel on his way to Nazareth and Mount Zion Pope Paul enjoyed a less hectic passage. The Israelis were determined to show their efficiency to the world and, fearing an assassination attempt by a Jewish extremist or a planted Arab agent, they insisted on strict security arrangements. The Israelis' reception of the Pope was undemonstrative and cool. They were glad of the visit for the prestige it conferred on the state and they hope it will facilitate the passing of the schema at the Vatican Council absolving the Jews from corporate responsibility for the death of Christ; but they saw nothing to cheer in the visit of the head of the Roman Catholic Church. Jews have long memories.

What is the significance of the pilgrimage? Politically, it has scarcely any. Both Jews and Arabs accept the religious character of the journey. The Vatican policy in favour of the internationalization of Jerusalem is equally unacceptable to both. From a religious point of view, the importance of the visit is profound. To assess the pilgrimage it must be seen in the context of the Vatican Council to which it was first dramatically announced by the Pope. The visit ranges him symbolically on the side of the forces working for change and renewal within the Catholic Church. The conservatives in the curia have taken the point. Already they are grumbling that the dignity and prestige of the papacy has been impaired. What they fail to see is that just as Pope John by his lovable character humanized the papacy, so Pope Paul by his imaginative and courageous initiative has commended it to the world. He has built up a foundation of good will from which he can address not only Christians but all men who value things of the spirit. The pilgrimage is intended to re-establish the papacy as a world spiritual authority. The Pope has moved himself and his office out of the baroque background of Rome into the setting of the Holy Land itself. This is a notable achievement.

The re-establishment of communication between the Latin and Orthodox worlds is just as epoch-making. Doctrinally, the Catholic and Orthodox Churches are much closer to each other than either is to Protestants and the Anglicans. The issues dividing them are virtually confined to papal infallibility and the part of the Holy Spirit in the Church. Mutual jealousy and suspicion are the stumbling blocks which keep religion's East and West apart. If these could be removed, the way for reunion could be rapidly opened. Every detail of the encounter between Pope Paul and the Patriarch Athenagoras, the primate of Orthodoxy, is thus significant: the marked friendliness of the meeting, the warmth of their joint communiqué, their exchange of the kiss of peace, their common prayer and the publication of photographs taken together. None was permitted when Pope John met Dr Fisher. Both have shifted from what were once thought immovable positions. Athenagoras has addressed Pope Paul as 'the first bishop of the Church', a revolutionary public recognition of the Roman primacy. Pope Paul, in his address at Bethlehem, used words unprecedented in a Roman pontiff: 'We shall put our trust in prayer which, even though it is not yet united prayer, rises up, nevertheless, simultaneously from ourselves and from Christians separated from us, like two parallel columns which meet on high to form an arch.' No less important was the Pope's declaration about the honour in which other Churches participating in the pilgrimage should be held—'for the measure of the authentic treasure of Christian tradition they possess.' The implications of these statements will be worked out in the theological dialogue which Pope Paul has welcomed and which was authorized by the Orthodox conference at Rhodes last September.

The meeting of Paul and Athenagoras has overshadowed the other exchange of visits between the Pope and Benedictos, the Orthodox Patriarch of Jerusalem, which is equally important in the reconciliation of Rome and Orthodoxy, quite apart from the extent to which it will soften rivalries over the control of the Holy Places in Jerusalem itself. This encounter should do much to overcome the resistance of the Greek Church to an ecumenical dialogue. The coolness of Greek Orthodox churchmen to Rome springs not only from innate anti-Romanism but also from distrust of Athenagoras, whom they do not wish to see transformed into an Orthodox pope. The Moscow patriarchate is also suspicious of Athenagoras because he spent eighteen years in the United States. The Greek Church considers that Athenagoras is no theologian, and it is afraid of where he will land them theologically. His proposal for a pan-Christian conference which was conveyed to the Pope just after Christmas by his special envoy, the Metropolitan Athenagoras of Thyateira, and of which more will be heard, is typical of his pragmatic approach. Cordial relations between Rome and Jerusalem will do much to calm these fears.

Pope Paul's pilgrimage is much more than an act of personal devotion or a colossally publicized religious sideshow. It is a major landmark in the history of the movement for Christian unity, which has been given a new impetus and direction. There seems little doubt that the religious historians of the future will set down Jerusalem 1964 as a major turning-point in the long story of the Christian Church.

In May 1982 Pope John Paul II made the first papal visit to Britain. I assess its impact in the following unpublished article.

Pope John Paul's Visit to Britain

The first visit of a reigning pope to Britain constituted a success which far surpassed even the most sanguine of expectations. Catholics and non-Catholics, those of every religion and of none were inspired by the charismatic presence of this extraordinary man. The thirteenth journey of John Paul II, since his election to the papacy on 16 October 1978, proved a lucky one for all concerned.

All the papal visits have had themes: in Poland it was the upholding of human rights and freedom; in Ireland it was the rejection of violence; in Brazil it was the championing of social justice; in the United States a sustained critique of materialism and the excesses of the consumer society; but in Britain it was the importance of the life of the spirit that informed the Pope's approach. In a very real sense the British visit turned out the most spiritual of all the journeys. Again and again the Pope returned to his theme of basic Christian values and the importance of the spiritual life. As an Anglican friend remarked to me the morning of his departure: 'Thanks to television it has been like a whole week spent in public retreat.'

The Pope turned out an evangelist of such simplicity and profundity that one has to go back in English history to the days of John Wesley to find a fitting parallel. The unfortunate Pastor Glass's Protestant banner brandished at Liverpool with its slogan 'Exalt Christ not the Pope' proved not a protest but a prophecy. At Cardiff when Pope John Paul addressed the youth of England and Wales on his final day his journey reached a charismatic climax. For thirty minutes he held the riveted attention of his youthful audience as he expounded to them the importance and the power of prayer, and how it brings the opportunity to know Christ and the power to communicate that knowledge to others. He was able to speak in such a moving and effective way because his words were coming out of a lifetime of following his own precept.

An equally important feature of his visit was the stress placed on achieving Christian unity and on the value of the ecumenical movement. It was notable that it was this theme which roused the most enthusiastic applause in the cathedrals of all denominations. The ecumenical highpoint was reached on the second day when the Holy Father and the Archbishop of Canterbury walked together to the high altar of Canterbury Cathedral with applause rippling all the way up the aisle until silence came when they knelt side by side in prayer. Then the Pope went forward to embrace in fraternal love virtually every member of the Anglican bench of bishops. At that moment the Anglican Communion with its beauty, its holiness and its learning was caught up into the Universal Church and recognized publicly in the words of Paul VI as a 'sister Church'.

At that moment Anglicans saw the Pope with new eyes and he them: Pope John Paul knew about Orthodoxy from his Polish pastoral experience but it was not until Canterbury that the closed book of Anglicanism was opened to him. The fruit of this meeting and that with the Moderator of the Church of Scotland was evident at Bellahouston Park in Glasgow on 1 June when in unforgettable and spontaneous words the Pope committed himself without reservation to the cause of Christian unity saying: 'We are only pilgrims on this earth, making our way towards that heavenly kingdom promised to us as God's children. Beloved brethren in Christ, for the future can we not make that pilgrimage together, hand in hand?'

The third theme of the visit was that of peace. From the moment he arrived at Gatwick to that when he left Cardiff for Rome, the Pope's appeal for justice and peace in international relations was reiterated. Pope John Paul has long been haunted by a nightmare vision of a nuclear catastrophe overtaking mankind and his prophetic warnings climaxed at Coventry when again in unforgettable words he dismissed the medieval scholastic theory of the just war and called on the nations to abandon war as a means of settling their differences. 'Today,' he declared, 'the scale and the horror of modern warfare—whether nuclear or not— makes it totally unacceptable as a means of settling differences between nations. War should belong to the tragic past, to history; it should find no place on humanity's agenda for the future.'

How can one account for the Pope's extraordinary impact on all those who saw or heard him? First because of his sincerity and authenticity—in the motto of the great Cardinal Newman, 'cor ad cor loquitur', heart speaks to heart. Second because of his feel for his listeners and an instinctive tact which amounts to a form of genius. Thus he referred to himself always not as Pope but as Bishop of Rome, thus anchoring himself not to the controversial quagmires of papal infallibility but to the firm historic ground of the Roman primacy, and turning what has been used as diminishing insult into an encomium. Again when processing through the close at Canterbury he imparted no blessings: pride of place was accorded to his host the Archbishop of Canterbury. Third because of his masterly choice of both words and gestures. He showed an actor's sense of timing, his cadenced delivery gave the right emphasis to every phrase, he spoke not only in words but in gestures, embracing babies and their mothers, welcoming little children, identifying himself with the sick and the terminally ill. At the beautiful service for the handicapped at Southwark Cathedral he exalted and protected their position not by an abstract disquisition on the wrongs of euthanasia but by declaring that if society moved the sick and the handicapped to the centre of care and concern it would not be diminished but enriched.

So this memorable visit, which can justly lay claim to be the most important religious event in Britain since the Reformation drew not to a triumphant but to a joyful conclusion. He expunged for ever that 'stain upon the imagination' which for four centuries has dominated the vision of the British people when they look towards Rome. He revealed and created a role for the papacy which goes back to the earliest Christian times and which is thus both old and new, showing it as an institution designed not to dominate but to serve the entire flock of Christ and indeed the whole human race.

On 7 April 1970, Dr Hugh Gray, the Member of Parliament for Yarmouth and a Doctor of Philosophy, sought leave to introduce a Bill legalizing euthanasia under the Ten Minute Rule procedure in the Commons. This allows two speeches to be made, one in favour and one against, and the House then votes on the issue. The Bill is printed but normally gets no further. On this occasion the Bill was actually 'shouted out'. The House was extremely hostile towards the Bill and there was no division. The following speech was my rebuttal of Dr Gray's arguments.

Euthanasia

The subject of this Bill is the question involving life and death. It is, therefore, a very grave and important issue. I would like first of all to congratulate the hon. Gentleman the Member for Yarmouth [Dr H. Gray] on the manner in which he has presented his case. I would like to congratulate him, too, on his courage, which always commends itself to the House. I believe that many hon. Members with majorities less exiguous than his might shrink from espousing such a controversial question in what is likely to be an election year. But it is doubtless because, like myself, he is a Doctor of Philosophy and so is able to adopt a disinterested attitude.

One great achievement of our age is that we have been enabled to conquer disease and illness and increase life expectancy in a way no other age has seen. I believe this to be a substantial blessing. Life is an uncovenanted gift, and if one can extend its scope and span, the possibilities for achievement and happiness are proportionately increased. But as one welcomes the advance of medical science one would be shallow indeed if one did not see the very real and complex problems with which we are faced by this prolonging of life. It is true that more people are exposed today to the chance of terminal illness than in the past. While more will survive, they may well find themselves surviving in a state where their powers and faculties have waned or wasted away.

The response of the supporters of euthanasia to this very real problem is to allow such people as painlessly as possible to be put, at their request, out of their misery. This is a response which I recognize is inspired by compassionate concern and by humanitarian motives. I do not doubt that, but equally I do not doubt that it is neither truly compassionate nor humane to facilitate euthanasia as proposed in the Bill.

My approach to the problem, first of all, as it must be, given my beliefs, is religious. In common with the majority, though not all, who find themselves heirs to the Judaeo-Christian tradition, I believe that it is ultimately God, not man, who has the disposal of human life. In the last analysis we are the created, not the Creator, and we are bound by the given of our condition.

Having said that, it is necessary to recognize that the hallmark of our humanity is freedom and that the glory of being human is precisely that we can transcend the limits of our nature. Between the two poles of our freedom and creaturehood there is inevitably a tension, never sharper than today when an advancing technology is putting greater and greater powers into the hands of man. It is on our resolution of that tension that the future of our humanity depends.

In helping us to resolve the particular tension which the Bill presents, there is one reasonably sure guide, namely, the moral values that are shared in our society that constitute both its inherited and its developing wisdom. It is now proposed to do away with part of that wisdom, namely, the fact that we deny to any individual the right to dispose of the life of another and that life can only be taken in extreme cases at the hands of the state. Many who do not share my theological presuppositions will, I think, subscribe to that view, because to do away with it would deprive our society of an essential protection and expose us to a whole variety of dangers.

The burden of proof that this is not so must lie upon those advocating this fundamental change. They must show that it will not undermine respect for the value of life. They must show that the safeguards they propose are adequate. I do not believe that this burden of proof has been discharged by the proposer today.

The central point of the case put forward by the hon. Member for Yarmouth was that the Bill presented a transfer of choice, that the Bill would take away a right from the doctor and confer it upon the patient. I think that that is a profoundly inadequate analysis of the situation. I believe that the Bill would not transfer a right, but would create an entirely new right of allowing one person to kill another, albeit at that person's request.

It is not true to imply that a doctor at present has a discretion to dispose of life. A doctor, whatever his views, is under a duty to preserve life. The knowledge that that is so is the basis of the patient–doctor relationship. That does not mean that there is a duty to prolong life at any cost. That would be neither good morality nor good medicine. Lord Horder, a very great doctor, once said that the good doctor will know how to distinguish between prolonging life and prolonging the act of dying.

There is surely a clear moral distinction between administering a pain-killing drug in the knowledge that it may or will shorten life and administering a drug with the direct intention to kill. The safeguard of that distinction is contained in the standards of the medical profession, supported by the law. Take away either of those safeguards and the patient and the doctor are exposed to equal danger.

Let us consider the case of old people in particular, whom the Bill sincerely intends to help. What kind of agonizing moral pressure could open up to a sick old person if the Bill were to pass into law? It is not only unscrupulous relatives who might create pressure—they would be a minority—but the mental processes of the old person that would do so. He would be asking himself, 'Should I cease to be a burden to those who are looking after me? Are they thinking that I am a burden? Should I take this step or should I not?' What then has become of the peaceful, easy death which is held out by the supporters of the Bill?

I believe these to be powerful arguments, but, strong as they are, my most rooted objection to the Bill is that it is a short-cut: it offers a simple solution to problems of the highest complexity. The problems that arise today in our society from the need and desire of those suffering from incurable disease to die in peace and in dignity are much more complicated than mere relief from physical pain.

There is an inner misery and loneliness which afflicts such people which needs to be assuaged. What causes more agony to dying people in these conditions than anything else is the sense of being written off when they are, in fact, alive; being treated as dead when they are still living. It is precisely this mentality that I fear the Bill will induce not only in the dying person, but also in relatives and medical attendants.

The final stage of an incurable illness can be a wasteland, but it need not be. It can be a vital period in a person's life reconciling him to life and to death and giving him an interior peace. *[Interruption.]* This is the experience of people who have looked after the dying. To achieve that needs intense loving and tactful care and co-operation between relations and medical attendants. This painstaking, conscientious, constructive approach to the dying is, I believe, more human and compassionate than the snuffing out proposed by those who are well intentioned, but who seem to understand little of the complexities of the needs of those they are attempting to help.

EPILOGUE

I am certain of nothing but the holiness of the heart's affections and the truth of imagination—what the imagination seizes as beauty must be truth—whether it existed before or not.

JOHN KEATS
Letter to Benjamin Bailey, 22 November 1817

Any day is a good day to be born and any day is a good day to die.

POPE JOHN XXIII

Index